THE *Naughty* LIST

USA Today Bestselling Author

JADE WEST

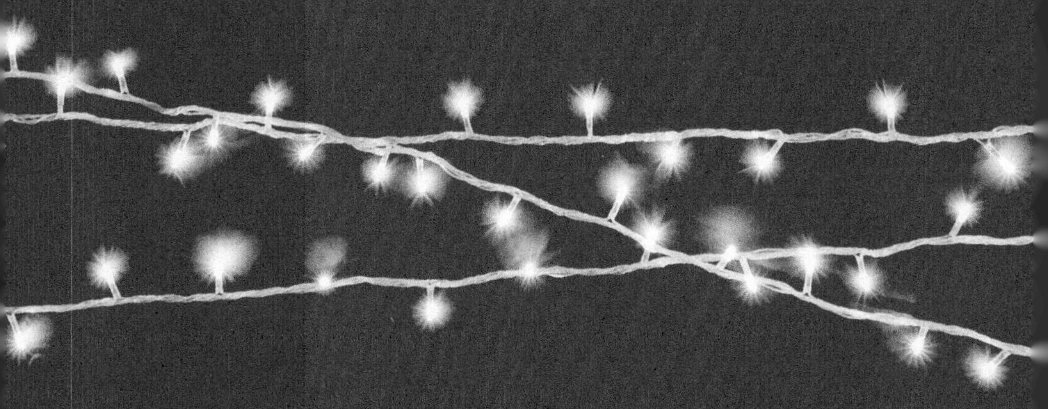

The Naughty List

JADE WEST

Cover design by Letitia Hasser of RBA Designs http://designs.romanticbookaffairs.com/
Edited by John Hudspith http://www.johnhudspith.co.uk
All enquiries to jadewestauthor@gmail.com
Formatting by Sammi Bee Designs

First published 2023

The Naughty List is dedicated to all of you dirty readers out there, and all of your amazingly filthy tastes.
They say variety is the spice of life – and you're not going to get much more spicy variety than in this one.
So, rest up in front of the Christmas Tree, legs spread, deep breaths, heart rate steady... and get ready for some entertainment with Holly.
Have you got what it takes to be a hardcorer?

one

"Hey, Ella! How are you doing, sweetheart?" Mum asks me.

My parents are glowing onscreen, with the warmth of the Australian sun behind them. Their beautiful house looks so inviting in the background, and Mum's tan really suits her. Sydney has always suited the pair of them, a dream come true. It's lovely to see, always, but tonight I get a pang in my chest, knowing they are so far away. No matter how hard I fight it, the truth is the truth.

I'm a heartbroken girl who wants her mum and dad.

I have to hide it. No tears, whatsoever. I don't want my eyeliner to run and give the game away.

"I'm good," I lie, knowing how much they worry about me. They have always been so protective.

I was an *unexpected surprise* when they were into their forties, having given up on ever having kids. They'd doted on me as the only child, and they'd fought back hard when they reached retirement age, saying I was too young to be left behind, but I'd insisted. Hard. I had my own life to lead, and it shouldn't stop them living theirs.

I was twenty-one when they emigrated. Old enough to be living my own life without them handholding me. Fine. No big deal. Video call is always just one click away, and it's cool. It's great. It's almost like being in the same room.

Or so I'd thought...

Now, here, at twenty-four, I want nothing more than to be right there beside them. I want to admit the truth and be a kid again in their arms.

My new 'life' in London isn't quite how I expected it to be when I packed up and moved down here with Connor last winter. I'm glad Mum and Dad's dreams have panned out better than mine. Except I don't have any. Not really. They weren't *my* dreams I'd been chasing when Connor and I upped and left for the bright lights of the city together. *My* dreams aren't the reason I'm living here, in a crappy house share with people I don't like.

It's taken a horrible, hard look at myself to realise that.

I fell in love with Connor Preston on sight when he appeared in the year above me at high school. He was the hot, punky weirdo who stole my heart, and I'd caught his eye since we first crossed paths in the maths hall. I was already dying my hair jet black by then, and wearing gothic rosary beads with my school blazer.

Call it destiny... or fate being an asshole.

I've been following *Connor's* dreams ever since then, because I believed in him. His dream of being a rock star, performing to crowds of thousands, with a huge record deal and massive hits around the globe. Fuck, how I'd supported him. Always. What a fucking idiot.

"How is the great musician?" Mum asks, as if on cue, and I can't bring myself to tell them the truth.

I fake my best smile. "Out at a gig at the moment. Should be finished soon."

"Is it a good one? Plenty of people there?"

"I hope so, yeah. Down in Camden."

I'm not lying on that front. He is down at a gig in Camden. I still remember his schedule by heart – the ever-loving girlfriend. Well, *ex*-girlfriend now. He'll be there, onstage with his guitar in his arms, singing about how hard life is when you really want to make it. So soulful. So fucking selfish.

I force the anger aside.

Dad's grinning at me on camera. My heart pangs again, I feel so far away from them. Video is never the same as real life, no matter how many times we make calls. It's got less and less in the three years since they've been gone, and I've grown used to it, kind of. Only now, without Connor, it feels so much harder.

I'd fly over there right this second if I could do, but there's no chance of that. Prices of flights are sky high in November, and as we get closer towards Christmas they'll only get worse. I push the hurt away as best I can.

Mum and Dad tell me about how they've been doing, and give me an update on their friends I've yet to meet, and I do the same, talking about my new friends at work and how everything is going. I play it upbeat, but the minutes tick by slowly in terrible torment, because I'm hoping, *praying*, they don't suspect that anything is wrong. The last thing I want is them worrying about me. The slam of the breakup is all but over now, anyway. The initial weeks feel like they've taken a lifetime, but they are coming to an end.

The remainder of Connor's belongings are in a crappy rucksack in the corner of my room. The shit he didn't want anymore. *Like me.* Tacky mementos from back home and some old boxer shorts with holes in them. I doubt his *groupie* lover, Carly, would want to see him in them.

I get a lump in my throat as the inevitable subject comes up.

"If only you could get here for Christmas," Dad says. He sighs. "Maybe next year, hey? Or maybe we could come to you, for your birthday."

Fuck no. Not here. I'd hate them to see this shithole.

"I'll be over to you," I tell them. "Definitely next year. Promise. As soon as I can."

I always make excuses why I can't get over there. Bleating on about Connor's gig schedule, and how hectic it is for me at work, but this year is more painful. This Christmas, I'll be on my own. I'd love to wake up on Christmas morning in Mum and Dad's place. I'd love more than anything to sit around together on their terrace by the pool and pull crackers with them. I'd love to say goodnight to my mum in person, going up to bed with a hot milk in my hand that she'd made for me, like she always used to.

If only I had the money to get there, but I *have* no money. Fifty-seven pounds in my bank account to last me until the end of the month. Three weeks of nothing but pasta. Amazing. At least I don't have to share it with my prick of an ex anymore.

I can't stand the call any longer. I'm welling up. I pretend I hear something at my door, turning around onscreen.

"Is that Connor?" Mum asks, hopeful she'll see him.

"No. A delivery, I think. I ordered a takeout."

"Go get it," Dad says. "We'll catch you soon. Love you."

"Love you, too."

I'm holding my breath as we wave our goodbyes and I hit the end call button. Takeout would be a luxury. I'd love a hot spicy pizza with a side of chicken wings. I look at Connor's fucking rucksack and want to throw it out of the window. Piece of shit.

My credit cards are maxed out from trying to support him. Years of investment for nothing. I'm working as many hours as I can in a job I hate, stacking shelves in a supermarket for minimum wage. I've been paying bills we should have both been paying between us, if he'd ever had enough money for them.

It's my own fault, though. We always make our own choices, and I chose him every step of the way. That's my own bad to have to live with. Seven years of life wasted on someone who cast me aside like a piece of nothing when something better came along. Carly isn't just a *groupie.* She has *connections,* or says she does. Whatever.

I close my laptop and put it on the bedside table. Moping will only lead to more tears, and I have to function. I go downstairs. So, what's dinner going to be? Pasta, or pasta, or pasta? Ben has left half of the pans over the worktop again in our grimy shared kitchen, spatulas filthy and unwashed. Jackass. I'm still in my work uniform as I clear up his mess, trying my best not to get any grime on my shirt. I can't be fucked to wash it again tonight. I can't really be fucked to do anything.

I've always found rage easier than tears, so I take it out on the kitchen mess with a scourer, scrubbing like a savage. FUCK YOU, CONNOR. JUST FUCK YOU.

I hate how I miss him. His cocky smile, his guitar strumming, his laughter when we were rolling around in hysterics at stupid YouTube videos. But now – three weeks in – more than anything, I miss sex.

I miss fucking him all night long. I miss the way he used to be a filthy freak of a sex god as we got twisted up in dirty games. How he'd make me come over and over with every session, like a woman possessed.

Toys will never, ever fill the void, and I'm really not up for a relationship yet. Not even dating. It's another bullshit angle of the breakup I'll have to live with for now. I'll add it to the list.

I eat my pasta on my bed, then fire my laptop back up. I check out flights to Sydney yet again, and then I check out my available credit. I'm over the limit practically everywhere, so not even the dubious credit agencies will give me a shot.

There is no doubt about it. I need more money.

I could work more shifts at the supermarket, but I already do seven days and two evenings on top. I was so caught up in being Connor's manager when he made it big that I didn't bother going to uni, so I have no career ladder to climb. So, what's left? What have I got going in my favour?

There's only one answer to that. I've been toying with it for nearly a week now, since the tears stopped flowing like a river.

I catch sight of myself in my wardrobe mirror, thanking my lucky stars that I was blessed with Mum's looks and not Dad's. I have her frame – long legs, tiny waist, huge tits, and the same big, blue eyes that she has. Mine look a lot more striking with my dyed jet-black hair than hers do with natural blonde.

I've been a goth since before I met Connor, so I'm a perfectionist with thick cat flicks and fake lashes, and I can pout like a dream in deep red lipstick.

So, how to put it to good use?

I log into one of my dirty online chat groups. I used to read out some of my conversations to Connor, but now they are all for me. I browse through the content, remembering some discussions about sex work and building up a paying fanbase, and then I notice one of the online member icons. *Ebony*. I've known Ebony through chat threads for years, and we've had some private conversations – enough that I know what she does for a living.

I call up a chat window.

Hey.

Such an idiot introduction out of nowhere, but she types right back.

Hey, how are you? How is the rockstar doing?

Jesus Christ. Did I really talk about him so much that everyone in the world asks about him? I guess I did.

For the first time since he left me, I'm honest about reality.

He left me for a pretty little redhead groupie called Carly.

There is no sad faced emoji in response, or any *there, there, you'll soon feel better*. Just one word...

Cunt.

It makes me laugh, because yes. He is one. For the past twelve months he's been nothing but a cunt, ego growing every five seconds.

You planning on meeting anyone else? she asks me. *Or still at the sobbing your heart out phase? It's a shitter. I know. I've been there.*

I let my fingers do the talking.

I don't want to meet anyone else right now. I can't be fucked to even think about it. I pause, weighing up my words before I hit send. *What I do want to do is* **get** *fucked, though. And I also want to earn enough money to spend Christmas in Australia with my parents...*

She knows what I mean.

She knows why I'm messaging.

I'm contemplating typing out another conversation angle, so I don't sound like such a blatant bitch, digging for info, but I don't need to. Her reply is another blunt one.

Want a video call? I'll tell you all about it.

two

My palms are sweaty as the *calling* icon flashes up on my screen.

I expect Ebony will look different on video call – due to the power of filters on most people's profile pictures, but no. She's smiling as she appears and sure, her profile pictures are taken from a flattering side angle, but it's no major distortion. She has beautiful brunette hair, mixed with blonde, perfectly shaped lips and great cheekbones. She has to be at least thirty, and she's so confident it shines through the screen.

I wish I was dressed for a night out, not sitting on my bed in a crumpled work uniform.

I notice her perfectly manicured fingernails as she waves. "Hey there! Wow, you actually look like your profile picture, you know that? Quite a surprise."

I laugh. "I was just thinking exactly the same thing about you. You look amazing."

"Thanks. You'd hope so, given how much budget I give to it. Work expenses and all that." Her smirk turns serious. "I'm really sorry the wank face you were with fucked you over. Screw the *rock idol.* He'll regret it, don't worry. He'll come running back."

I lean against my headboard, laptop propped on my thighs. I let out a sigh that comes right from the bottom of my soul.

"*Wank face* can regret it all he likes. I'm not taking him back. I've already given him seven years of my life, so he can fuck off. He can make it to the top of the rock industry for all I care, I'd still give him the middle finger. He's no rock idol to me. I'm done with it."

I'm surprised at how resolute I sound, but the rage is there, like molten magma, burning in the pit of me. I glance at his shitty bag in the corner. Yep. That thing is definitely going in the fucking dumpster.

Ebony gives me a thumbs up. "You've got real fire there. I love it."

"Fire *and* fury. Both, in magnitudes."

"Whatever works to get you through it."

"Yeah, some more softly focused therapy can come later, when I have the luxury of money and time. Right now, I'd rather just hate his guts."

"When you have the luxury of money and time, you can have therapy on the beach with your parents." Her grin is lovely. "That's what you want, isn't it? To go to theirs for Christmas? They're in Australia?"

Hearing it spoken out loud touches a nerve. The image of Mum and Dad flashes across my eyes, and that's what I want, at any cost. To be with them. I need to be with them this Christmas.

The fury and flames are still there, but a stab of pain jabs through the heat.

I nod at Ebony, and then I pluck up the courage. "Can you help? I mean... I know you do sex work for some kind of agency, and you said it pays really well. I'd love to try it. Honestly. I'd love to at least get the chance."

"It does pay well, yeah. And it can be great fun, if you're really up for it." She pauses. "Do you think you're ready to fuck other people, though? You wouldn't freak out when it came to it?"

I've got no reservations on that score. I need to do it, for my sex drive as well as my bank account. I may be nervous as fuck when it came to doing someone who is paying me, but I'll get used to it. I'm a resilient girl.

I have to let Ebony know that.

"I'm *definitely* ready to fuck other people. I love sex too much to stop. Messing around with toys every night just isn't going to cut it." I go for honesty. "If I'm not going to be fucking Connor, I'm going to be fucking random guys I pick up in bars or online. Whatever, really. Even in the cereal aisle at work, it doesn't matter. It's not going to mean anything. I don't want to settle down, or meet anyone *serious*, or get tied up in some new sappy relationship. I just want sex. Lots of sex."

She looks right at me. "And so you may as well get paid for it, right?"

I go for honesty again. "Connor left me with a shit ton of debt. On my crappy wages, it's impossible. I'm living on pasta, miserable as fuck, and really would love nothing more than to clear that shitty debt and visit my parents for Christmas. So yes, I'd *love* to get paid for it."

"You're living on pasta? Really?"

I sigh. "Mainly, yeah, but my daily bowl of pasta is the least of my worries."

"You really think your mind's in the right place to satisfy clients? No offence intended but I can feel your rage, babe. It might not be the best time to go for it, and fucking clients isn't quite the same as pulling people in bars. These guys aren't often Prince Charmings looking out for their soulmate."

"No, I get that, don't worry."

"So, you could do it? You really think so?"

I think of all the sex toys in my drawer, and how well I paste my smile on at work every day. I nod to Ebony. Confident.

"Believe me. Yes, I can do it. I'll make sure I leave clients very, very satisfied. Don't worry."

Ebony laughs. "Good for you. If you're really sure you're up for it, I can introduce you to the agency. And believe *me*, you'd have plenty of clients. They're crying out for hot goth girls. I've even considered dying my hair black, but my clients know me too well. I couldn't pull off being a goth chick."

"They want girls like me?! At your agency? Seriously?"

"Hell, yeah. You'd be so inundated with proposals, you'd be reading them all day long." I must look confused, and she twigs, shaking her head. "Sorry, I forget. You don't know how the agency works."

"No, I have no idea. You get proposals? You mean, it's a kind of dating app? People set up a profile and message asking if I want to fuck them? Swipe left or right?"

"No, no. It doesn't work like that," she says. "Not even close. It's all online and incognito. Our clients are vetted, confidentiality assured, of course. So are we. Would you be happy with that? Being checked out?

Think of it like an interview. They'll require a copy of your ID, and do checks in the background, and they'll need to be sure you're really suitable for this kind of role. We also have to undergo STI tests every month, and send the results over. So do the clients."

"Yeah. I get it. It makes sense. I'd be ok with that."

"If you're offered an account, you tailor it yourself. You put some pics up, an intro video, and you work through the list of kinks, selecting which ones you'd be open to."

"A list of kinks?"

"Yeah, we call it the naughty list. Especially relevant at this time of year."

"No shit."

Her giggle makes me smile. "I'm definitely a bad girl as far as Santa is concerned. He won't be climbing down my chimney." She laughs. "Still, a client who looks like Santa might be given the opportunity... he can give me a ho ho ho and unload his sack however he likes. I'm not picky, as long as the cash is right."

There's something about Ebony that draws me in and cracks me up. A lilt in her voice, so natural and so funny. No wonder clients go crazy over her.

"Sorry," she says when we stop giggling. "Right, yes. The naughty list. It's quite a detailed one. You've got your staples, of course – they don't give you an account if you don't tick the staples. BJs, being eaten out, pussy fucking. The rest is up to you. Most people have anal as standard, but the list goes on and on."

I'm fascinated by the idea of this list... I wonder what else could be on there.

"How dirty does it get?"

"Oh, baby, trust me. It gets filthy. As filthy as can be. And the money associated with that shit... holy crap. We call those *agents* the hardcorers. They are really something." She smirks. "Think you could be one?"

I shrug. "I dunno, I'm pretty filthy."

"There are plenty of shades of filthy."

I smirk back at her. "I'd say I'd be ticking quite a few naughty list boxes."

I look at her eyes, so alive. She's vivacious. Entertaining. Confident. Everything I was before I let Connor drag me down into the shit with him. I want that back. I want myself back, if I even *had* myself without Connor in the first place. It's been a long time.

I imagine the list there in front of me, and all of the things I've done. All of the things I've fantasised about. Everything from BDSM, to sex with another girl once, to outdoor play, to getting it on in public, to fucking a few of Connor's band friends in front of him when I was younger – *and drunk*. Connor and I jumped headfirst into everything, and I loved him for it.

Ebony carries on explaining things.

"Clients send you a message through your account profile, telling you what they want, and how much they're willing to pay for it. You click yes, or no, and if you give it a *yes*, you arrange a booking on the calendar app. The terms are filed and the *contract* is logged. The agency takes twenty percent, and you get the rest. The client pays the agency, not you. They never know who you are. Not in real life. And you never tell them. The same goes in reverse."

"And the agency just sends the cash through? Just like that? It appears in your bank account?"

"Yeah. Just like any other employment agency. We're in *entertainment,* professionally speaking. It's just the operational side that's a little more, um, underground."

I almost laugh to myself. I'd be an *entertainer*. A more successful one than Connor, as it stands. I imagine him there in Camden, with Carly cheering and listening to his 'heartfelt' lyrics. Bullshit, self-obsessed, wallowing. I'd rather make a load of cash having someone stretch my pussy with two dildos, than listen to him wail about the woes of emotional politics into a microphone.

"Do you want me to do it, then?" Ebony asks. "Shall I get the agency to contact you? The interview would be on video call, but they'd have their cameras off. It would just be you who'd be visible. They're great, I promise. You'd get to meet some of the other *entertainers* as well, if you're signed up. We have private chat where we talk about things. It's a good crew."

There's no doubt about it... I need that naughty list. I'll tick every damn box I can tick.

"Yes," I tell Ebony, with a grateful smile. "As soon as you can, please. I have a plane to catch, after all."

"On it," she replies and I see her typing, looking at a window off to the side. She asks for my email address, and wants me to send her some pictures of myself, which I do. I stare dumbfounded as she keeps on typing. I can't believe this is really happening.

"Done," she says. "Orla is going to be in touch with you. She's looking you up now."

"Thank you so much."

"My pleasure. I'm sure you'll get along just fine. I'd best be going. I've got to get a cab to Ealing. My client's already in his hotel room. My husband's putting our two little terrors to bed tonight while Mummy gets busy."

"Right," I say, my smile so bright. "Have fun."

A wave from Ebony and she's gone.

I don't have to wait long. A notification comes up at the side of my screen just a few minutes later. A meeting request with *Orla Brown* for tomorrow night.

My fucking God, I'm shaking with excitement when I click the *accept* button.

It's only later that night when the nerves kick in hardcore, filled with *what ifs* and a serious amount of stomach churning, but that's ok. I ease them off by sliding my hand down under the covers, and thinking about the *naughty list* instead...

I'm going to make sure I succeed at this. I have to.

three

I'm a blizzard of action with my supermarket duties right through the day, high with excitement and nerves. The thoughts keep coming. Fantasies, questions, fears, all tumbling together…

The possibility of being a sex *entertainer* still feels alien, but wildly thrilling. I always thought I'd be cheering Connor on from the sidelines, and sharing sexual kinks with him for the rest of my life, not fucking paying customers and fulfilling theirs.

I wave goodbye to my colleagues at the end of my shift, and I'm on the tube as fast as I can. I need time to get ready. There is no way I'm going to be taking a video interview with Orla in my work uniform with my hair tied up in a scrunchie. As soon as I'm through the door, I dash upstairs to my room and grab my towel. Luckily, the bathroom is empty. As usual the bath mat is a soggy mess and there are bottles strewn everywhere, but I don't give a shit tonight. I'm straight under the shower, lathering my hair, and shaving myself, every stroke filled with concentration.

Teeth done, hairdryer out, then a spritz of hair protector before I use my straighteners.

What shall I wear? This isn't exactly a regular interview.

Fishnet holdups, yes. One of my finest black satin bodices, which laces at the front, showing my cleavage off like a dream. A little tutu skirt, which barely covers my ass. So, jewellery… a collar, yes. Spikes? I look at my collection, and opt for the mid length. Not too hardcore, but enough to get attention. Then on to makeup. I move my laptop from my dressing table and set myself down, arranging my supplies neatly. I'm going to use a lot of them.

My contouring works well, and my cat flicks are extreme. I opt for decent length lashes and make sure my mascara shows them at their best. Lipstick... classic red, or deeper purple? Red. A staple.

I'm ready to go twenty minutes before my interview time. My hair comes down to my cleavage when it's straightened, but brushes away easily to give a decent view. I check myself out on webcam from a host of different angles and make sure I'm well positioned, my laptop ready on my dressing table, all set for the interview as I perch on my stool.

My foot taps, waiting for the meeting. I try the link, to make sure it's ready for when I need it, but it doesn't work. It just goes to a *page not recognised*, and I shit myself. What the fuck?! But then I remember the instruction in the invitation.

Browser must be in incognito mode.

I change the settings, making sure my breaths are as steady as they can be, but my heart is pounding, I'm so on edge.

I need to pass this interview and be accepted. I need to be an *entertainer.* I need to catch a plane and hug Mum and Dad so bad.

I jump as the notification pops up onscreen. *Meeting ready.* I click the link with a smile on my face, and it's not one blank camera window that greets me, it's three. There are three people on this call along with me. There are no names showing, just letters.

O – which I guess is Orla. *T* and *S.* All cameras off, but sound on.

"Hey," I say. "Nice to meet you."

It's *O* that speaks first, and I'm right. It's Orla. She introduces herself, and I'm relieved when her voice is warm and upbeat.

"Hi, Ella, great to meet you, too. We've heard from Ebony that you'd like to join our agency."

I nod. "I'd love to join your agency."

"Has she told you much about it?"

"A little." I laugh, just a touch. "She's told me about the naughty list. It sounds intriguing."

"Oh, it really is." She laughs back. "And it's quite a long one. Our clients are very diverse."

"I'd love to find out. I'll tick a lot of boxes, I promise."

I'm trying to sound so confident. So assured. *I really need this.*

"Glad to hear that you're open minded, but you always start at the beginning, if you're a newbie."

Another voice sounds out. *T.* He's a guy with a deep voice. He sounds hot, even though his chat window is blank.

"I'm Troy. I oversee the *naughty list*, as people like to call it. It's imperative to us that our entertainers only commit to what they are comfortable with. We don't want people in uncomfortable situations, neither entertainers or clients. We pride ourselves on our service."

"I understand. Sure." I pause. "I'm pretty open minded, though. Don't worry about that."

Orla's voice sounds out.

"Open minded, or experienced?"

I don't hesitate. "Experienced. I enjoy a lot of different things."

A new voice speaks. *S.* Stuart. "Please tell us about some of them."

Where to start? I go for the basics, listing them off on my fingers. "Oral, anal, bondage, full on ass play, I love rimming. I like BDSM, pretty hardcore. Mainly receiving, but I'm happy to give someone a decent slap, too." I pause. "Shall I carry on?"

"Yes, please do."

I wonder if they have the naughty list right there in front of them.

"Umm... degradation and praise. I love being told I'm both good and bad. I like the thrill of being naughty in public. I've done threesomes, and a foursome once, and I've got it on with another girl. I loved that."

"Anything else?"

Stuart is digging for more, so I don't hold back.

"Double penetration, mostly with toys. My ex liked stretching me. Fisting..." I laugh. "Or trying to. I do a lot of pelvic floor to compensate, but he never actually managed it."

"Excellent. And you've had practical experience with all of these things? You're telling the truth?"

"Yes. I'm telling the truth. I've always been very adventurous."

I don't mention that it's always been at the side of just one guy...

Orla speaks next.

"Have you ever offered sexual services before?"

"No. I haven't."

"Are you particular in your requirements for your clients? We aren't a dating service. We have quite a variety of members on our books."

I've thought about this already, and weirdly, I'd prefer people I'm not going to fall head over heels for on first sight. I don't want to *fall in love*.

"No. I don't. I really don't care."

"Would you be happy to offer services to older clients? We generally offer browse facilities up to a maximum of a thirty-year age gap. You're twenty-four, yes?"

"Yes."

"Would you be happy with a client selection up to fifty-four years old? Of course, you are always welcome to decline the proposals, but we don't want to waste anyone's time."

I wonder what that would be like, being with an older guy. I shrug. "Sure. I'm happy with that." I imagine a fifty-four-year-old silver fox fucking my ass and demanding I call him *Daddy*. It actually turns me on. I shuffle on my stool. Weird. It's not one of my usual fantasies.

"Excellent," Orla says.

I take a breath. It feels like I'm doing OK.

They ask me a few more questions regarding health issues, allergies and stuff before laying down the rules of client confidentially. They tell me how all of their clients are vetted, and how there is a rating and review section they use after their proposals are completed. This is important, as scores are used to influence the browsing position of entertainer profiles. I nod with enthusiasm and tell them I hope I'll top the charts with my service. I share some of my experiences in detail, and some of my fantasies, and I look straight at the screen, honest in my answers. I only hope I'll pass the interview.

"You're a beautiful girl," Stuart says. "We'd love to have you onboard, but we're going to have to put you through a final assessment stage first."

"An assessment stage?"

"Yes. We need to know you are truly comfortable and confident before we assign you a profile. We'll also need ID and personal information from you, to set you up on our agency accounts."

"Of course." I smile. "What do need me to do as an assessment?"

Troy speaks at this point. I love his voice.

"Do whatever you're instructed, please. From this point onwards. If you are uncomfortable at any stage, please be honest and tell us so."

"No problem."

My heart is thumping.

"Undo your bodice now. Show us your tits."

I didn't see that coming. And his tone is so demanding, it gives me flutters. *Shit.* I pull the ribbon free without hesitation, baring my tits for the camera. I display them instinctively, tugging at my nipples, trying to show them how good I can be. O, T and S are silent for a while, and I keep on going, mashing my tits together, and tipping my head back.

"Good," Troy says at that. "Suck on your fingers. Make it horny."

I start with two. Gentle sucks and moans. I feel so ridiculously on display in front of three strangers, but it's ok. I can do it. I pretend three of my fingers are a cock and show them how I give blowjobs. Connor always said I was great at that.

"Keep going..." Troy says, and I can tell he wants more.

Ok. Let's do it.

I go all in, four fingers straight in my mouth, right to the back, sucking like crazy and moaning as I use my tongue.

"Keep going," he says again, and I'm squirming, horny and nervous, both at once.

DO IT! I tell myself. Show them how good you are!

With that I let myself go. I finger fuck my own throat until I retch, showing them what I'm capable of. My spit is dribbling and dripping onto my tits, but I don't care, trying my absolute best to be a porn star – I only hope they're impressed.

"Can you move your laptop to your bed, please?" Troy says next.

I look to the side of me, reach over and chuck my work clothes on the floor, out of sight.

"Sure."

I position the laptop between my legs and sit myself down on the covers, angling the screen back up at me. I know things are about to get a lot more serious. My nerves are jangling.

"Do you have any toys?"

"Yes. Plenty."

"Get one, please."

I pull open my beside drawer and take out a decent sized dildo.

"Good. Now, lie back for us and hitch your legs up wide."

I do as I'm told, breaths shallow. I'm horny on instinct, even though I'm absolutely crapping myself.

Orla's voice comes in. "Now, it's up to you, Ella. Give us a taste of what you are comfortable with. What you're *capable* of."

Troy talks next, clearly testing me. "Cunt and ass, please. We want to see you use both."

I nod before I lie back for them, propped up on my elbows so they can still see my face onscreen, my tits still bare, nipples still hard. I start slowly, teasing my pussy with my fingers at first, through my sopping panties.

"I'm really wet," I tell them, the horniness taking over me.

"Show us," Troy says.

I slip off my panties then work my bare, wet slit, spreading myself so they can see me glistening. Then I moan as I slip two fingers inside myself, curling just right. Fuck, yes. It feels good. Two fingers turn to three, and I push them inside, circling then fucking myself slowly... slow but deep, over and over. I hitch myself higher, so they can see my ass as well as my pussy, and then – when my fingers are slicked up nicely – I move their position, teasing the first one over my asshole. I clench first. Tight and on purpose. I fight against the way I push it inside, and it's fucking bliss. I moan like a bitch in heat, I can't help myself.

There's no doubt about it now. Nerves be damned. I can do this.

I work myself up to taking all three fingers in my asshole, so they know I can handle it, spreading my pussy with the other hand so they can see how swollen my clit is... and how desperate I am for more.

I'm going to give them a show they'll remember.

I don't use lube on the thick dildo, just rub it up and down my slit, my ass still clenched around three fingers. *Fuck.* It's going to hurt, no matter how wet I am, but I don't care. I think of how many times I've taken this with Connor. I couldn't give a shit how hard I have to push to get it in my pussy while keeping my fingers in my ass. It's usually Connor using the dildo, or his cock inside me, but I can do it on my own. I know I can.

My moans and protests come hard and loud, but I don't stop. I won't stop. I force the thick toy in my pussy for the people onscreen, panting as I look right at the camera, and then I fuck myself, knowing they'll hear me squelch as well as moan. I'll impress them, and I'll make it real.

I close my eyes and work myself like I need to. I forget they are watching as best I can and focus on myself.

It doesn't take me all that long to come. I'm filled and stretched, and the head of the dildo is rubbing right against my G-spot as it slams back and forth, so I can't help myself. Faster and faster, deep and rough, and I'm crying out, genuine and real, lolling my head back as I peak for them.

I let out a coy little laugh as I pull the toy and my fingers free, still catching my breath as I smile for them in the aftermath.

They wait until I've come down from my high before Troy's voice cuts back in.

"Fantastic show," he says. "Very talented."

"Thank you."

I'm waiting for the verdict. Petrified at the silence. I know they are talking about me on mute.

Please. Please. Please.

Orla clears her throat before she speaks, and my pulse is going crazy.

"You're hired," she says, and I'm so happy I could skip around my bedroom as she sets up my account and talks me through the final practicalities. Fuck! Yes! I'm an *entertainer* now!

I'll owe Ebony one for the rest of my whole damn life.

four

I work at lightning speed over the next few days, providing everything the agency needs from me. I sign some official looking documentation, and dash to a clinic on my lunch break for an STI test on Tuesday – forwarding a copy of the results as soon as they come in. The job description I'm signing up to is nothing like my actual role, of course. The authorities wouldn't be happy to receive a copy of the 'naughty list' with my achievements ticked off to justify my wages. Officially, I'm in *PR.*

I tell Ebony I've been accepted as soon as I receive the message, and she gives me a video call, beaming as I thank her from the bottom of my heart.

"Amazing! When do you start?"

"I've got a meeting with Orla in just over an hour. She's going to talk me through setting up my profile, but as for actually starting? I don't know. As soon as I get a client who wants me, I guess."

"Don't worry about that, baby. Demand is off the scale right now, and you're one hell of a stunner."

This is such a contrast to how life was a few weeks ago. I'm no longer focused on Connor, ruminating on every memory we ever shared. Instead, my thoughts are filled with the ideas of clients, money, and the absolute drive to see Mum and Dad. The fire in my stomach isn't about my ex-boyfriend anymore, it's about ambition. It's about *me.*

"Good luck," Ebony says when my meeting is about to start, and I hang up with a thanks.

I log into the agency site via incognito mode, and Orla begins to talk me through my profile. I'm fascinated, scrolling through the *upload photos* and the *about me* section I have to fill in. A video intro section, too. Then, I see it. The naughty list. Whoa, I know the agency told me they had restrictions on new entertainers, but the limited version of the naughty list really is limited. Anal is the most extreme option I have on there, and even that is listed as *toy and cock only, singular. No stretch play.*

"It's for your safety, and our clients' satisfaction," Orla says. "Once we have your first review in and logged, we'll evaluate your options."

"Great, thanks. When will that be?"

Fuck, I hope I don't sound desperate. I'm glad Orla doesn't know my motivation is down to the cost of flights in December and getting across to my parents' place. I've only got a month to go, tops, so I need to make it count.

"Don't worry. We ask our clients to complete the feedback form as soon as possible," Orla says. "As long as it's a good review, we'll give you the control."

"Ok, great."

"So..." she says. "What's your profile name going to be?"

I've thought this through already. It's apt. This is my Christmas finance solution after all.

"Holly," I tell her.

"Holly?"

"Yeah, I went for festive and cute. I'm sure there are plenty of *Elviras* and *Jezebels* and *Lilliths* on here already."

She laughs. "There are a few, yes. I like Holly. It's... sweet."

"Hopefully your clients like it, too."

"They will. Right. Get to it, fill in your sections, and we'll get your profile live as soon as it's done."

I tick everything on my limited naughty list, and upload some dirty pictures Connor took of me when we were playing. I record at least five versions of my video intro before I'm happy, stumbling over my words until I get them right. Then I click submit, and I wait, tapping my fingers on my dressing table, heart thumping.

I get the notification and the link to my live profile about twenty minutes later. I look at myself onscreen, and I can't believe it, seeing myself advertised like this. I play my own video on loop, and scroll through my own pictures, wondering if they will be enough to attract clients. I've got Mum's good looks, and my pictures are filthy hot, but there must be so many entertainers, so many options for clients to choose from.

I jump as my first message icon shows at the top of the screen. My hands are shaking as I click to open it.

Proposal – User 1378. Male. 39.

Fuck. FUCK. I could cheer out loud. Someone wants me.

Several items from the naughty list are ticked off on their proposal. Oral. Vaginal. Two hours maximum.

Blowjob and different positions, his request says. *Doggy style is my favourite. Short goth dress. Fishnets.*

Duration – 2 hours.

And the fee he offers...

£400

Hardly enough to retire on, but it's my first go, and it's basic play. Like really basic. I'm sure I can suck someone's dick and offer them my pussy for that amount of cash to land in my bank account. I'd earn more in two hours than I make in three whole full shifts at work. I don't even think about it before I click accept. The calendar comes up once I've accepted. Three options.

The first is for tomorrow night. The address is a B&B in East London. I look it up and it seems ok. Nothing grotty. Should be fine to get to on the tube. Yeah, I can do it. It's another click from me.

I get the confirmation message through, and it's there, outlined. Set in stone.

At 9 p.m. tomorrow night, I'll be fucking a stranger for £400.

Ebony is still online, so I call her. I can't sit still, shuffling on my stool and fanning my face with my hands.

"I have my first client."

"FUCK YES! That is ridiculously fast, by the way. You're going to ace it. What do they want?"

"He wants basic. Blow job and pussy. He offered four hundred quid."

She nods. "Four hundred. That's alright. Easy enough."

"How much does the cash go up? You said the *hardcorers* are in a different league. How much do they get offered?"

She leans back in her seat. "The highest I've heard of is 150k."

I blink at her. "One hundred and fifty thousand pounds?!"

"Yep. She earnt it though, believe me. Don't ask." She does the zipper gesture over her mouth. "Confidential. You can ask them yourselves in group chat when you get added."

I wonder what the hell the entertainer did for one hundred and fifty thousand pounds. I wonder what *I* would do for one hundred and fifty thousand pounds right now. It's not a hard question. I'd do just about anything...

It only makes me more determined to get my *naughty list* extended. Quickly.

I barely sleep that night, tossing and turning – my entire body thrumming at the thought of being a whore. I imagine a hot, dirty guy as my client and get myself off, but it doesn't help me sleep. The nerves are just too strong. I look at my clock so many times I lose count, and then, when sleep finally does get me, I almost doze through my alarm.

I'm like a rabbit on speed dashing about the place to get ready for work, but I'm glad about it. Adrenaline is going to be a very, very good friend of mine this evening. I try to ignore the waves of panic at work, doing my best to keep my mind on tomato ketchup stocks and not on offering my pussy to a stranger, but it's hard. Understatement of the century.

I grab a sandwich as a token dinner as soon as my shift ends, and I'm out of the door, bounding down to the tube station. The trip back to my place is such a blur that I barely notice my tuna mayo as I munch it, my actions on autopilot as I get off at my stop, charge down the street, let myself into the house and head on upstairs. I already know the dress I'll be wearing. I lay it out on my bed before I shower and shave. I blow dry my hair and put my makeup on, being careful not to snag my fishnet holdups as I pull them up my legs. I choose decent stilettos, then I slip my dress on. Short and velvet, hugging me tight and barely covering my ass when I walk. I spin in front of the mirror. Yes. I live up to my profile video, and I've followed my client's requests. I hope he appreciates my efforts.

With that, I wrap myself in my long black coat and head to my destination.

I click *arrived* on the incognito app as I stand outside, and get a ping back straight away.

Head up to room 5.

A woman smiles as I arrive at the reception desk, and I point up the stairs behind her.

"I have a friend waiting for me. In room five."

"Sure," she says. "Next floor up. Furthest on the right."

"Thank you."

My legs are trembling as I make the climb, and I'm shitting myself, beyond any nerves I've ever known as I walk down the hall. I wish I'd downed a couple of shots of vodka first as I see the number 5 on the door.

My palms are sweating as I build up the courage to knock, but that's ok. I'm five minutes early. Plenty of time.

Breathe, Ella, just breathe.

Except I'm not Ella here. I'm Holly. I'm Holly the entertainer, and it's time to take on my role. I think of booking flights, and the £400 – minus the agency cut, that will be in my bank account very soon.

I smile as I knock, hoping *User 1378* doesn't realise how terrified I am. I do everything I can not to baulk and run as the door swings open, and there he is, my client. My *first* client.

User 1378 isn't some crazy, hot megastar, or a monster of a mountain man, or a sinister looking guy from the head of the mob somewhere. He's just a guy with brown hair and thin rimmed glasses. He's as tall as me in my stilettos, slim, but not muscular. Just a regular kind of passerby I'd barely notice in the street. He's not in a tux, or head to toe in leather, just a pale blue shirt and jeans. He steps aside to let me in, and it's a nice enough room with a decent double bed. It's bright, and warm, and he's drawn the curtains closed. There is nothing ominous here in the slightest.

"Hey, Holly," he says, and gestures to the dressing table. "Want a drink first, before we get down to it?"

He has a wine bottle there, already open. I recognise the brand from the store. It was on offer last week.

"Sure, thank you," I say, and he pours me a glass. It's not even chilled, but that's ok. It's welcome. I almost forget and go to ask him his name, but luckily, I remember in time. He's User 1378 and nothing more.

I slip off my coat, and he looks me up and down before he takes it from me and hangs it on the back of the door. I give him a cheeky smile as I take another sip of my wine, and I see the want in his eyes as he gazes at my cleavage. I like that. I find I'm wondering how big his cock is, shooting a look at the bulge of his jeans.

It feels a lifetime since I've taken one inside me.

"I absolutely love your tits," he says, and I give him a sweet laugh.

"Thanks. You haven't even seen them yet, though. Not in the flesh."

"How about we remedy that?"

I put my wine glass down and close the distance between us, beginning to pull down my dress zip. It becomes clearly obvious that User 1378 has done this before. He takes over from me without a moment's hesitation, loosening my dress until he can tug it down enough to free my tits.

"Yeah, even better in the flesh," he says.

"Thank you."

He strokes me, playing, flicking my nipples with his thumbs. Gentle.

I find myself wanting to say *harder,* but I can't. This is his show not mine. I remember Orla's instructions. *Play their game, not yours.*

"That feels good," I tell the man in front of me, and hold my tits up for him to play some more. *Inviting.* I wish he'd pinch and tug my nipples, and grip nice and tight, but he doesn't, just keeps stroking with a smile.

It's instinct that has me clenching my thighs, my body wanting sex, even with a stranger. I arch my back, hoping he'll drop his head and use his mouth on me, but he doesn't. He does the opposite. He pulls me in for a kiss.

I'm not expecting the way his tongue swirls around mine as he grunts like a teenager with a boner. I kiss him back, still clenching my thighs and clinging onto the forbidden. He's a stranger in a hotel room, and I'm being paid for it. I use that thought like a mantra.

His kiss gets more frantic as he walks me backwards towards the bed. It's me who shimmies my dress off and steps out of it, running my hands up and down his back as though I'm as desperate as he is. I find I'm moaning against his mouth as he keeps on teasing my nipples, hitching myself against him like I can't stop.

My fingers aren't nervous anymore as I unbutton his shirt, still kissing him. My eyes are on his as I sweep my hands down his chest to his belt and set it free.

"You're so fucking hot," I say between kisses, and being *Holly* is becoming much easier than I thought.

Holly thinks User 1378 is the hottest man alive. I look at him as though he is, murmuring about how much I want his cock in my mouth as I palm him through his jeans.

"Please," I say. "Please, let me see."

"You can show *me* first," he says, playfully, and I do as I'm told. I slide my panties down and push him away far enough that he can see me in my full glory, still in my stockings and stilettos, with my hands on my hips. I rock for him, then run my fingers from my tits to my pussy, squatting just a little so I can push two fingers inside myself. Yeah, he likes that. I can see it in his eyes.

"I'm so fucking horny," I tell him, and let my fingers work their own magic, while watching a stranger watching me. It's a performance, and I'm the one taking centre stage, moaning as I work my clit like the slut I'm being paid to be.

He pushes down his jeans as he watches me, and kicks them to the side, still keeping his socks on. His dick is ok, but not exactly a monster. I drop to my knees as he presents it, gazing up at him with fluttering lashes as I open my mouth in invitation.

He thrusts his hips a couple of times before he gives it to me, as though he's holding back a grand prize.

"Suck my dick, Holly," he says finally, and I do what I'm told, gripping his thighs as I take him right the way to the back of my throat. In and out, I work him, lips popping, and tongue lapping, murmuring like his is the hottest cock I've had in my life.

My clit is still tingling, and my nipples are still hard, sure, but this is a game of Holly and not me. In *my* game, he'd be wrapping my hair around his fist and fucking my face like I'm the slut he's paying me to be. He'd be talking filthy, and thrusting rough, and telling me how he's going to make me earn every fucking penny. But no. User 1378 is just someone with a hard dick who fancies a goth girl. A fair enough fantasy, and I must be fulfilling it. It's clear it won't take all that much talent on my part to get him to spurt for me. I feel his balls tense after no time, and he pushes me away with a *fuck, wait.*

Ok. It's obvious that there won't be a round two once he's unloaded. He's definitely a one load only kind of guy. I'll have to be careful if I'm going to give him the full two hours he's paying for...

I moan, reaching for his cock again, even though I know full well he'll hold it away. He grins down at my enthusiasm, believing me.

"Not yet," he says. "You're too hot. You'll make me come."

"Maybe I could come first?" I ask. "I'd love to come in front of you. I want to show you how wet my pussy is before you slam your cock inside me."

Slam might be an overstatement, but it's clear he likes the concept. He smirks, then takes a swig of wine, right from the bottle.

"Yeah. Show me."

I position myself on the bed, hitching my legs to show off my fishnets as well as my pussy. My eyes are on him as I splay my pussy lips with my fingers, demonstrating how wet I am, glistening.

"Please, help me," I say, and he nods before putting down the wine bottle. He sits next to me on the bed, and I let him take over my pussy play, wrapping my arms around his neck to pull him in for another long round of wet kisses. I could do this all night. It's easy.

He doesn't exactly find my clit and work the right spot, but he gives it some effort, at least. He pushes three fingers inside me, and that feels good, so I shift my angle until I like it even more, rocking myself against him. When he's working a good rhythm I guide him down by his shoulders, murmuring on purpose.

"You're so fucking good," I say. "This is so hot. It's so fucking hot. Please, kiss my tits like that."

For *Holly* it *is* hot. He plays with me and I tease his dick as he switches his kisses from my tits to my mouth, on a repeat cycle. I guide his hand, so his thumb is against my clit again, but he doesn't keep it there, just keeps thrusting the same three fingers inside me. It's nice. It's fine. It's just... boring.

Not for User 1378, though. He's so in the zone he's grunting as he fingers me harder, showering me with compliments between kisses, before he curses and pulls away from me, fisting his cock.

"You're fucking incredible," he says and I hitch my legs wide for him.

I don't need any prep in the slightest as he slides his cock inside me. It's a nice sensation, but nothing major. I wrap my legs around his hips and urge him on with frantic breaths, realising this could well be the first time I really fake an orgasm in my life. But I don't want to do that. I don't want to be a fraud. Holly is an entertainer, not a fraud.

User 1378 presses his weight down onto me, hips thrusting, and I gasp against his mouth, building my own jerking movements up underneath him like he's driving me insane, but it's *me* who drives me insane. I let my thoughts run riot, telling *myself* what a slut I am, fucking a stranger in this hotel room. I focus on his cock sliding inside me and revel in being this kinky, pleasing him like I should, because he deserves it. He deserves everything I have to give him.

"You're going to make me come," I say, deliberately pushing him up so I can see his cock sliding in and out of me, and then I use the advantage of the position to slide my own fingers down between my legs, working my clit as he fucks me.

"My God, this feels so fucking good," I tell him.

"Yeah," he says. "It fucking does."

He fucks me faster, and harder. I moan louder, fingers working like a dream as I focus on being a dirty whore who wants to come with a stranger's cock inside her. I urge him on, faster, FASTER, and when I do reach the peak, it's genuine, my gasps real as I clench around his cock and moan right up at him.

"Yes! That's it! That's it! Don't come yet, please! Don't come!"

He grits his teeth, and I'm glad he manages to hold it together, because we haven't reached his preference yet. We haven't ticked all the boxes of a five-star review.

I shift position as soon as I'm done coming, rolling straight onto my front and presenting my pussy for him, dripping wet.

"I need doggy style, please," I tell him. "It's my absolute favourite."

"Mine, too."

He rubs his cock up and down against me, and for a moment, I think he's going to bend the naughty list and fuck my ass. I'd love that. I really would. But he doesn't do it. He pushes back inside my pussy, slamming hard, but not hard enough to excite me. I bounce back against him, flesh slapping flesh, twisting so I can look at him over my shoulder, smiling with every thrust he makes.

It's good. Kind of.

I play with my clit again, still tingling from last time, and tell myself again that I'm a slut fucking a stranger, but it doesn't work so well. It would take me a long time to build to another orgasm, and it's time I don't have. User 1378 is bucking out of control in three minutes tops, gripping my hips and losing himself, eyes shut as he comes.

I'm not used to sex like this, so standard. I want hair pulling, and ass slapping, and anal as well as pussy – at least a little stretch – but User 1378 is done and finished in a few frantic thrusts. He collapses onto his back beside me with a huge grin on his face, like we've had the fuck of a lifetime.

"You're one hell of a girl, Holly."

"Thanks," I say. "You're one hell of a guy, too."

I give him an extra kiss, and offer him my tits for another play, but I was right. He's a one load only guy. His interest is already waning.

"Want another drink?" he asks as he gets up from the bed.

"Yeah, I'd love one, thank you."

We finish up the bottle of wine together, chatting about how crazy hot the sex was, and I play the final round of being Holly, with eye flutters as he puts his jeans back on.

"Time's nearly up." He sighs. "I've got to go soon. I'm really sorry."

"Shit, I'll get ready," I reply, and scurry to get dressed, but he holds up a hand.

"No, no. Stay as long as you like. I've just got to get across the city. I have things to do."

Work, I hope, but somehow I doubt it. I imagine User 1378 has a regular life out there somewhere to match his regular sex tastes, but that's none of my business. It's not my job to speculate. It's my job to give him what he's paying for.

"Thanks so much," I say as he waves goodbye. "That was incredible."

"Likewise. You are a star, Holly. An absolute star."

I love the sense of pride I feel at his grin as he leaves me there, in his B&B bedroom. I really have lived up to his proposal, and given him everything he asked for. I did it. I really did it. I was the *entertainer* he asked for, and more besides. I only hope he tells the agency the same thing on the feedback form.

I get dressed slowly, and finish up the final dregs of wine, set to make my own exit when a buzz comes through on my phone.

My review is in. Rating 5 stars. *Truly excellent. Perfect tits. Great smile. Kinky beauty.*

I check my bank account and the money's there already – £320.

Thank fuck for that, because it's obvious what I need as I leave the B&B, my clit already craving more kink, more challenge, more filthiness – and a load more cash. I need the naughty list available to me in all its dirty glory, every single option, ripe for my choosing.

There's no doubt about it whatsoever now. I'm flying so high that I grin at the stars.

I'm going to be a very, very bad girl for Christmas...

five

My extended *naughty list* is waiting when I log on at home, *be careful,* Ebony messages, *don't commit to too much, too early,* but I can't help diving straight in. I read through the new items, tingling at the thought that I may be doing these things for real, with paying clients.

Holly has so many options available to her. What a lucky girl.

I tick *anal*, that's a no brainer. *Roleplay*, sure, I love dressing up and acting. *Praise and degradation*, yes, please. *Other women*. Nice.

Bondage and BDSM have a big variety of tick boxes. I figure I'll go in easy at first and select just a few options, but why wimp out of my own dirty fantasies? The agency has a strict *safe word* policy in their terms and conditions.

So... BDSM submissive. Bondage. *Rope. Handcuffs. Spreader bars.* All fine. *Hand spanking, crop, paddle, dressage whip* – no problem whatsoever, but I leave out *cane* for now. That thing is like a beast on steroids. I've only had a go with it once.

Tit bondage – yes, please. *Clamps* – hell, yes. *Pussy punishment – hand slaps, clamps, spreading and crop.* I tick them all with a smile.

Next comes the BDSM dominant category. Could I be an authentic mistress? I'll likely be crap compared to the other entertainers with that skill on their resume, so I give that a miss for now. Wouldn't want to tarnish my five-star record.

Multiple partners. *Two, three, unlimited.* I tick unlimited. I can always turn down the proposals.

Stretch play. *Double penetration with toys.* Yes. *Double penetration with partners.* Yes. The thought of that gives me flutters.

Double vaginal. Fuck. Should I? Really? My finger hovers, then clicks. If I'm limping next day, then so be it. I'll happily limp with the flight booking app ready to roll on my phone.

Level up. It's onto *fisting*. Rough, pussy fisting – it makes it clear in the description.

I don't know about handling that for real with paying customers. I have the option to leave notes besides my *catalogue*, so I tick the box, but add some text along with it.

'Not very experienced, but I'll always do my best. Lots of lube, please. LOTS.'

Next. *Double anal with toys.* Ouch. My heart races.

I take a breath. I'm getting in deep here. Maybe I'm just overloading myself due to kinky fantasies and a terrible credit rating, so I get a grip of myself for now. I leave it unchecked, along with the others that follow.

Double anal, multiple partners.

Anal fisting.

I scroll down some more, and I begin to see where the hardcorers get their name from...

Bukkake. Unlimited men. I'm not quite there yet.

Double fisting. No way, I'd never manage that.

Breath play. I'd be thrashing around, terrified. I'd look like a fish, flapping about on the bed.

Watersports and extreme ass play. Jesus Christ... the options around that one. Could I do any of them? Honestly? I try to imagine a guy pissing in my face, and I could brace myself, but the even filthier stuff? If I wanted to be a millionaire on my flight to Australia, I'd be all over it, but right now, the flights themselves will do.

When I stare at my revised list, I feel a bit heady. Some of the options would get me off like a bitch in heat with guys I met in a bar and wanted to fuck, but walking up to a hotel room door, with the unknown waiting inside there, like it was with User 1378... I'd be quaking in my stilettos. I *will* be quaking in my stilettos.

I click submit on my new options.

My profile updates almost instantly, and my revised list makes me look so much sluttier, the filthy pictures of me so much more alive onscreen. It still seems so surreal. I was innocently stacking cereals and grieving over my ex just a few short days ago.

I'm still staring at my updated profile when I catch sight of the illuminated message icon on my account dashboard. I assume it's to do with Orla giving me new access and info about my new review, but, fuck, along with that I have five new proposals – FIVE. Five different users, with the same basic requirements. Pussy sex, with oral. One of them wants me to wear red lace for him. I could do that, but do I want to? Is my selection of new flavours already too appealing to opt for the vanilla?

I look at the proposal prices. One guy offers £600, saying he likes to play a long time. One seems cheap with £250, so I decline that one, no, thank you. Another one sets the service at £400, saying he likes rough throat fucking. Two more, virtually the same. I could take them all and earn a decent amount, but I'm too intrigued by what else is out there... how many other proposals might be brewing out there in the ether.

I don't have to wait all that long to find out. I'm still contemplating a few of the existing proposals when a new one pings into my inbox.

User 829 – Male. 46.

His proposal is a little more elaborate than the others.

I like to dominate cute goth girls like you. I like to treat entertainers like the sluts and whores I'm paying you to be. I want to make you gag on my cock and stretch you with toys until your pussy is used up and dripping, juicy. I want anal play, deep and hard, and I want to slap your ass while I'm doing it. Another thing, high on my list, is that I want to punish those lovely big tits of yours.

And all the while, I want you to be a good little girl and call me Sir.

Duration – 5 hours.

Proposal price – £1600.

Holy hell. That's quite a proposal. I read it through again and wonder what kind of 46-year-old man User 829 is. Does he look old for his age? Is he big? Strong? A suited, booted businessman? Will he intimidate me into a shivering little sub who promises to be a good girl, no matter what?

Only one way to find out... I click accept, and the calendar options come up. Three of them.

I could wait until the weekend, or give myself at least one night off to prepare myself, but what's the point? I have a flight to Australia to book and the proposal is hot enough to have me fascinated.

I click on the earliest available option, and my confirmation comes straight back through. Deal sealed.

£1600, for five hours with User 829, at 9 p.m. tomorrow night.

I look up the hotel online and it's more upmarket than the one I visited earlier. It's in Camden, and I know Camden pretty well.

I drop Ebony a message to let her know, but she isn't online, probably busy. So, it's just me, with my thoughts and fantasies, and an extra £320 in my bank account from earlier. Even though the agency took a decent chunk, my balance looks so much healthier already.

I get myself washed and in bed, playing with myself all over again, fresh from a paying man's cock inside me. Fuck, how I come as I think about what's going to happen tomorrow night.

Yes, Sir.

I've never played that game before with a stranger.

Connor did it sometimes and it was hot, but often more cheeky than dirty. Tomorrow night will be different. Very, very different. The idea of being with an older man – a stranger – with £1600 to go along with it is in a different league. A crazy one. Crazy hot, crazy dirty, crazy exciting and crazy absolutely terrifying, all mashed up together.

Even though I'm exhausted, sleep tries to be a bitch and evade me. Tiredness lets me sleep eventually, but I could throw my phone across the room next morning when it starts beeping at me.

I'm tempted to call in sick for my shift, but cash is cash, no matter where it comes from, and my job is still my job.

I drag myself out from under the covers and put on my uniform as usual. I do the same old duties in the shopping aisles, and make small talk with colleagues, but my mind isn't on this place in the slightest. I'm already imagining myself in Camden later, walking up to a hotel room door.

I grab another ready-made sandwich for my way home. This time it's chicken salad, and I can hardly eat it. I force myself to chew, trying to kick away the insane bout of nerves as the tube takes me home.

I'm a jittery mess as I get ready. It's going to be rough ass play, so I take one of mine and Connor's toys from the bedside drawer – an anal douche I've used plenty. I squat under the shower and clean myself out thoroughly, shaving again, even though I'm still nice and smooth. I want to earn my money by being a star performer, and I want another five-star review.

I choose a tutu skirt to wear for User 829. I put my hair in long straight pigtails tied with ribbon, and wear cute pink lipstick with my cat flick liner. A black bodice, lace top hold ups and platform Mary Jane shoes, and I'm in character. *Yes, Sir, I can be a slut tonight.*

I set off early enough that I have plenty of time in Camden when I get there. I know the pubs well enough that I settle down in the nearest and get myself a double vodka cocktail to take the edge off, watching the clock as it edges closer to 9 p.m. – it's going to be a late one tonight. So many people are oblivious as they laugh, drink and socialise. I watch the girls around the bar, and I wonder how many of them would do what I'm about to do for £1600.

The vodka takes the edge off my nerves and helps keep me steady as I head for the hotel, a way down the road, past the bridge. It's smaller than it looked online, just three storeys high. It's narrow, but posh, with a gravel path leading up to a grand black door. I look up at the glowing windows as I approach, and get a shudder as I see a silhouette in the one on the top floor.

It doesn't move as I stare.

I know the shadow is watching me, and I know the shadow knows I'm watching him back.

It's like there is something unspoken. Dirty anticipation sparking between us as I stand there, illuminated by the outdoor lamps in front of me.

The silhouette is User 829, I can feel it. He almost takes up the full window, and shit, it's a big window. Part of me is so scared that I want to cancel and run away, but another part of me – the deep, slutty part that Connor used to tease with ease – sees me walking towards the entrance, persuading me I want this experience as much as my bank balance does.

I'm possessed by enough of my dirty little demons to keep me going.

I click *arrived* on the app when I reach the hotel entrance and get a message straight back.

Come to the suite on the top floor.

Yes. I knew it. The shadow was him.

There's nobody at the reception desk, and I don't bother dinging the bell, just use the staircase to the side. I climb to the top, slowly, my breaths ragged with the thought of what's ahead. There is only one door waiting when I reach floor three. The *Master's Suite.* How apt.

I try to catch my breath, telling myself it's ok, but my knees are virtually knocking together now the assignment is right here in front of me. I shove my phone in my handbag and brace myself.

I'm going to do this.

I clench my fist, ready to tap my knuckles against the door, but it swings open wide before I get the chance, and there he is, User 829. Heavy grey beard. Heavy grey brows, and a heavy set of shoulders to go along with them – so heavy, he looks carved out of stone.

As I stare up at my client, I get a little more than a shiver between my legs. Lust and terror, both at once.

The silhouette in the window didn't do his size anywhere near enough justice.

User 829 is a mountain, not just a man, and now, for the next five hours, he's going to be my *Sir.*

six

User 829 – Male: 46.
I like to dominate cute goth girls like you. I like to treat entertainers like the sluts and whores I'm paying you to be. I want to make you gag on my cock and stretch you with toys until your pussy is used up and dripping, juicy. I want anal play, deep and hard, and I want to slap your ass while I'm doing it. Another thing, high on my list, is that I want to punish those lovely big tits of yours.
And all the while, I want you to be a good little girl and call me Sir.
Duration – 5 hours.
Proposal price – £1600.

User 829 isn't one for niceties, that much is obvious. He steps aside to let me pass, and eyes me up like I'm just a toy for his amusement. Nothing more.

He's right, I guess. I'm Holly here – the goth girl who's going to take his cock in her ass hard and rough, and call him Sir for five hours straight.

Time to get in the zone.

I shrug my coat off, draping it over the back of a chair so he can see me in my full glory. I give him a little curtsy, holding the ruffles of my tutu, and use the word of the night for the very first time.

"Hello, Sir. Pleased to meet you."

"You, too. Your safe word is *flag* according to the system. Is that right?"

"Yes, it is."

I left the red out of it when I set it up. No point going for overkill...

His voice is deep enough to give credit to his appearance. I try to hide my trembles as the mountain of a man walks over to the mini bar at the far side of the room. He has a bottle of whisky already open with a shot glass in use, but takes out a fresh bottle of champagne from the fridge and holds it up for me.

"Do you like champagne, Holly?"

Fuck, how I love champagne, I just rarely get the chance to afford it.

"Yes, Sir. I do."

He smirks. "If you promise to be a good girl, you can have some."

"I'd love that, Sir. I'll be a very good girl, I promise."

I have goosebumps up my arms, I'm so fucking anxious, but there is no doubt about it – User 829 is making me really damn horny. I've never come close to fucking a guy like him.

He's not in a designer suit, just a tight hugging t-shirt, and a pair of decent black jeans, but that makes no odds. He oozes confidence.

"Demonstrate how good a girl you are," he says, and clicks his fingers towards the floor as though I'm a puppy in training. "Get down and crawl to me."

The carpet is plush under my knees and palms as I crawl across the room like he wants me to. I look up at the bulky tower of a man when I reach him, and he pops the champagne cork, but he doesn't get a glass for me.

"Open your mouth," he says, and holds the bottle, tipped ever so gently. He feeds me, giving me just one tiny mouthful at a time.

It tastes delicious, and it feels fucking filthy to drink it like this.

"Want some more?" he asks, and I nod, mouth still open. "You'd better say please then, hadn't you? Mind your manners."

"Please, Sir. I'd love some more."

"Good girl. You're learning. Don't worry, I know your profile is new, *Holly*."

He gives me more champagne, just a trickle at a time, teasing, and I let my mouth fill right up before I swallow. I'm sure he can hear the fizz at the back of my throat.

"That's enough for now," he says. "I don't want a drunk little plaything. I want a sober one."

That's a shame, because I'd love to down the whole bottle.

He doesn't speak as he loosens his belt and drops his jeans. My eyes must be like saucers, because the size of his cock fits in with the rest of him. He's so tall he has to crouch to slap his dick against my tongue like a long, thick truncheon. I don't know if I'm going to be able to fit him in my mouth, but he answers that question for me. His hand is so huge it practically covers the back of my head, and he uses it as leverage – sliding his beast of a cock right to the back of my throat.

Fuck, I nearly throw up my champagne.

User 829 uses my throat like I'm a toy, and I take everything I'm given. I have no chance to moan or whimper, just gargle and retch as he tilts up my head and thrusts deeper. I feel so cheap as he wraps my pigtails around his fists, still pumping into me as he barks out some new instructions.

"Get your tits out, Holly. Now."

I struggle to loosen my bodice since I'm rocking so bad. Just as well he's supporting me by my own fucking hair to enable me to do it. I let my tits free and hold them up for him.

"That's a good girl. Fucking beautiful."

He pulls his cock from my throat, and a big stream of spit spews right down my cleavage.

"Rub it in," he says, and I do. I rub my spit into my tits, focusing on my nipples.

I'm still rubbing myself when User 829 gives me another dog click, gesturing over to the bed. I scrabble to my feet, dashing over there.

"On your back," he tells me.

I nod, still catching my breath from the face fucking, feeling tiny as he kneels up and over me. He mashes my tits in his hands, and I arch myself as best I can.

"You've been a naughty girl, you know that?"

I shake my head, wondering what the hell I've done wrong.

"No, Sir."

"You didn't thank me for letting you up here."

"Sorry, Sir. Thank you for letting me up here."

"It's too late for apologies now."

He doesn't take it easy with my tits as he punishes me. His slaps are brutal, with raw, hard strength. He pinches my nipples, and tugs and twists, and Jesus Christ – it's like he's been given lessons, doing it just the way I like it.

He slaps me until my tits are bright pink and my nipples are swollen, then he lowers his head to suck at me and I can't help myself. I take hold of his head and beg for more.

"Yes, please, Sir. Please!"

"Dirty bitch," he says, and I'm grinning.

Yes, I am a dirty bitch. How nice to be able to use the trait.

I move easily for him when he shifts his attention down my body. I spread my legs, fully willing and ready for him to tug my panties to the side, but he doesn't bother with that, just tears the lace and pulls them free. He runs his massive thumb right up my slit, and I'm dripping wet. Sopping. I don't need any extra fantasies in my head this time. It's all about him.

He slides two fingers in, and it's already tight for me. Another one in alongside them and I'm whimpering with a *fuck, fuck, fuck*. He won't need any toys to stretch my pussy. His fingers will do it on their own. Seems he doesn't share the sentiment, though.

"You can play with your clit," he says as he heads over to the bedside table. He has a big, fleshy dildo ready in the drawer. He slaps it against his palm as I watch him.

"Thank you, Sir," I say as I twirl my fingers around my sweet spot, panting as he holds the toy above me like a weapon.

"Are you ready for this? I wasn't joking in my proposal when I said I was going to use and stretch your pussy until you were all used up."

"Don't worry. I'm horny, Sir."

"I can see that, you dirty bitch. I meant are you ready to get your cunt stretched? I don't play easy."

I've been spoken to filthily before, but it's so fucking different when he does it. The money makes no difference anymore, my clit is already sparking, ready to come.

"I'm ready, Sir."

"Good girl."

I brace myself as he positions the toy, and he's right, he doesn't play easy. He shunts it straight in, using my own excitement as lube.

"Fuck!"

"Take it, Holly."

I suck in breaths as he works it – circling – and slowly, I relax into the stretch. My hips start to buck on instinct.

"That's it, show me how much of a whore you are," he says.

The beast of a man lowers himself so his face is between my legs, his big, grey beard tickling my open thighs as he sweeps his tongue against me. I use my fingers to spread myself, and his tongue finds my clit. He sucks until I cry out, and I buck harder, frantic. User 829 is going to make me come... and he knows it. He feels it. *Yes. I'm ready. I'm fucking ready.* But *he's* not. He laughs as he pulls his face away, beard glistening.

"You won't come until I let you, you understand?"

I groan at the ceiling, breaths rapid as I force a nod.

"Yes, Sir."

He pulls the toy out with a vicious slurp, and slips two fingers inside instead. I figure it's a switch out, pure and simple, but it's not. I raise myself up onto my elbows as he lines up the dildo in addition. Shit. The word stretch won't even come close...

"Relax and be a good girl," he says. "You can take it."

I grit my teeth as he twists the toy and eases it in, his fingers still buried deep. It hurts like fuck – that dildo along with two monster fingers – but I don't care. I like it. I'm panting, clenching my fists, but I don't want him to stop.

"You're so fucking full," he tells me with a low laugh. "You've got a gorgeous cunt, Holly. Tight but fucking needy."

"Thank you, Sir!"

"Ready?"

Am I? Fucking hell. I nod. "Yes, Sir."

His grin through his thick beard is almost manic. His blue eyes are piercing. But then I'm lost, screwing my eyes shut as he slowly pulls the dildo back out, inch by inch. It's another round of pain, but who gives a fuck? Not me.

And then he fucks me with it. With his fingers inside me, he fucks me. He fucks me so hard, I'm a wet, bucking mess – crying out without restraint.

I don't want toys anymore, I want his cock. I want User 829 inside me, pinning me down like a whore while he thrusts his hips like a monster.

"Please, Sir..." I whimper. "Please, fuck me for real. Please."

He rams the dildo into me and pauses with it buried deep.

I'm panting like crazy, sweat on my brow.

"You need to remember the proposal, Holly. I'm not going to fuck your cunt, you horny little bitch. I'm going to fuck your ass."

Oh fuck, yes, the proposal. It's already long gone from my mind. I'm tempted to say *have my pussy for free*, but it's obvious User 829 has his own agenda. He continues with the toy fucking, twisting his fingers as he goes.

"Good girl," he says. "You can come now."

He lowers his mouth back to my pussy, and I splay myself as wide as I can for his tongue. He grazes my clit with his teeth before he sucks, and it's the tip over the edge I've been desperate for. There's no faking it in the slightest when I lose control, my pussy squelching as I moan like Holly the whore.

I'm a wreck on the bed when I'm done coming and he pulls the dildo out of me. I could lie here in the aftermath all night long, but he wastes no time in going back to the mini bar and gesturing me over with a click of his fingers. *Fuck.* My whole body is wobbly as I drop to the floor and crawl to him. I'm sure my makeup must be a total mess as I grin up at User 829 like he's a king.

"More champagne, little whore?"

"Yes, please, Sir."

This time he graces me by giving me the bottle for myself. I take some decent glugs and hand it back with a *thank you, Sir.*

"How many times have you been an agency slut?" he asks, and I jolt in shock at the reality of his question. Should I tell him? Is he even allowed to ask? My mouth decides for me.

"Umm... twice."

"Twice before, you mean? This is only your third time?"

"No." It feels bizarre to admit it. "This is only the second."

He shakes his head, grinning at the ceiling in disbelief.

"Fucking hell, you're going to be a good one."

"Thank you, Sir." I laugh a little. "You could call me a natural, I guess."

"I could call you a lot of things. Cheeky being one of them."

The man mountain pushes his pants down and kicks them aside along with his socks before pulling his t-shirt off and over his head. He's a weird mix of flesh and muscle now he's naked, and his chest hair is as grey as his beard.

"I want you in just your stockings for the anal," he says.

"Yes, Sir."

I shimmy out of my skirt, still kneeling, my eyes fixed on his.

"I want you on the bed, doggy style, your face flat to the mattress. Legs spread wide, ass on offer."

"Yes, Sir. Of course."

My clit feels tender as hell, still tingling as I crawl back to the bed and climb up. I position myself exactly as he wants me, cheek flat to the duvet and knees spread wide. I wonder how wet and swollen my pussy looks from behind, after the fucking he's given me. I clench my ass over and over, trying to entice him.

He goes to the bedside table before he joins me. I count my blessings that I'm facing the same direction as I watch him. He shows me his cock, working it, clearly giving me a decent view before I take him inside me. Being fucked in the mouth isn't the same as seeing the full spectacle tall and proud. I've seen monster cocks in porn vids, but never in the flesh. I imagine how good it would be to be fucked in the pussy. I'm hoping he changes his mind about that option. I don't know if my ass can take it.

"I never use protection," he says. "Are you ok with that? I can assure you I'm clean. I send my test results to the agency regularly."

I know that's part of their criteria, so I nod.

"Yes, Sir. That's fine."

He takes out a big bottle of lube from the drawer.

"Don't look so worried," he says, "I know what I'm doing."

"Thank you, Sir."

I hope he fucking does.

"Ever had an anal orgasm?" he asks, fisting his monster.

I'm honest. "Yes, Sir. I love anal."

"I can assure you this is going to be better than you've ever had before."

I love his confidence.

He gets up on the bed behind me and the mattress dips and creaks.

I gasp as he squirts a massive stream of lube onto my ass, slathering it all the way between my butt cheeks. I jolt when he slaps me, one palm on each butt cheek – decent blows that have me prickling.

"I said on the proposal that I want to take your ass deep and hard, yes?"

"Yes, Sir, you did."

"I wasn't joking. I like it rough."

"I understand, Sir."

I clench my ass on instinct, and yeah, it's a relief to have so much lube, but right now, I have to admit that I'm as edgy as hell. His cock is so thick, it could tear me in two. My safe word comes to mind. But so does £1600 and I imagine myself on the plane, looking at the clouds through the window.

"Spread your ass cheeks for me."

"Yes, Sir."

I reach around and do as I'm told, exposing my ass like a dirty target. He takes aim, the meaty head of his dick all set to plough me, and I ready myself, shuffling as I hold in a breath.

"Keep your cheeks spread," he says, and then he pushes slowly into me.

I grit my teeth against the burn of the stretch and he doesn't stop pushing. Keeps on easing his cock into me.

"Good girl," he says. "Nearly there."

His big hands take hold of my hips and with one final push we're skin against skin and it feels like there's a fist up there.

He holds still, letting his cock pulse inside me, and the feeling is so weird. So weird it makes me moan.

"Your ass is beautiful, inside and out," he says.

"Thank you... Sir."

"How does it feel, you fresh little whore?"

It feels like I'm breaking at the seams, but I don't want to tell him that. He moves his cock again, just a little, and the sensation ripples through me. Jesus Christ.

"It feels so good, Sir."

"Couldn't agree more," he says.

I have to bite down a whimper as his cock pulls back a few inches.

And then he slams me. Once, twice, three times over until he's balls deep, and I'm crying out as my ass burns like sin. He leans over me, his solid bulk against my back. I feel tiny and pinned down.

"Tell me how fucking dirty you are," he whispers in my ear. "Tell me you're a slut."

"I'm a slut," I tell him. "I'm a dirty little bitch, Sir. I'm your whore. Nothing but a filthy fucking whore."

The words come so naturally. They roll off my tongue like I was born for this.

"Louder," he says, and I'm crying out again as he changes angle. Deeper.

"I'm a slut! And I love it, Sir. I want it. Fuck me. Use my ass, Sir. Give it to me. GIVE IT TO ME!"

His mouth is right against my ear. "You're a slut that's worth every fucking penny."

He lifts himself up, shunts my hands away from my butt cheeks and slaps my ass as he works up a rhythm. God, I can't help myself. My fingers are straight to my clit in a frenzy, working myself as he fucks me.

"No!" he says and yanks my hand away from me.

I could cry in frustration – the orgasm building inside me is as relentless as his cock.

"Take it, just like you're told," he says.

And I do. Like a ragdoll in his grip with his monster cock pounding me. I take it, floating in the pain and pleasure. I'm lost to it as he slams me, as his big balls hit my pussy with every thrust and I'm coming, no fingers needed. Coming like never before. Coming like a true slut as his slams become frantic and I know he's coming, too. Waves of pleasure ripple through me as he shoots his load, grunting expletives like a savage.

I cry out as he finally pulls his massive cock from my ass, lube and thick, hot cum dribbling from me like he's been plugging a drain.

I giggle in the aftermath, wincing as I shift to watch him move from the bed. I'm expecting more champagne, or maybe some casual chitchat now he's unloaded, but his mood shifts as he pulls his jeans back on.

"That was great," he says. "Excellent performance."

I feel taken aback a little, because it wasn't a performance by the end. Definitely not. I wanted it as much as he did.

"How was your orgasm? Did I deliver on my promise?" he asks.

"Incredible," I tell him, "really, it was incredible. Thank you, Sir. Yes, you, um, certainly delivered."

He shoots me a side eye with a smirk. "Don't worry. You don't need to say Sir now. Finish up the champagne if you want it. It's all yours."

The energy has changed, just like that, but I feel in limbo, still thrumming. He's buckling up his belt while I stare at him.

"I'll leave you a great review," he tells me.

"Thank you, S–" I start, then stop myself. "Thanks. That was amazing."

"Yes, it was."

He puts on his shoes, and takes his coat down from the back of the door. The leather suits him.

"Enjoy the rest of your night," he says, checking his pockets for his phone and wallet. I don't even remember where I put my handbag, still lost in subspace, but he's fully in control of himself, holding his hand up in farewell as he makes his exit.

And then he's gone.

Just like that, User 829 is gone.

It hurts like hell when I move to get up, and the duvet is a mess of lube underneath me. Shit. I took it hard. Thank fuck there's no blood. I give myself a token wash down in the shower before I get dressed, but I leave the rest of the champagne on the mini bar. It seems alien as it sits there. I can't believe that just a few hours ago he was offering me mouthfuls as I knelt for him.

It's almost 2.30 a.m. when I leave the room – hence, he'd timed the hours almost perfectly. I grip the handrail of the stairs, and there is still nobody at reception, so I let myself out and walk away. My fingers are still jittery when I order a cab at the hotel gates. I call up the app while I'm waiting, and there it is already. Another glowing five-star review.

Incredible slut. A sweet little fuck toy, who can handle it rough. Her tits look stunning when pinked up from punishment, and her ass is a fucking dream.

The pride feels distant somehow, fading behind the realisation that it meant nothing whatsoever. I was just a whore named Holly to him. *A sweet little fuck toy, who can handle it rough.*

I'm careful as I lower myself into the cab when it arrives, making sure I take my seat slowly. I'm silent on the drive back to my shitty house share, still thinking about User 829 and what he did to me.

Another notification comes through on the app. The cash is in my account, minus agency fees. Service signed off and completed.

But I don't want the service to be completed tonight. I'd do it all again, for free. I must be out of my head, but it's true.

seven

I have a message from Orla when I finish my shift next day, asking for a video chat update. My stomach churns all the way home as I think of telling her about my experience with User 829.

Her screen is still black with just an *O* as her name, but I'm in full colour, in at least a semi hot goth setup that I've thrown on straight out of my work uniform.

"So," she says. "How are you coping? How was your experience last night?"

"It was great," I tell her. "He was pretty awesome."

"Really? 829 is quite a notorious client."

I get tingles at the thought of his massive cock in my ass, spreading myself while he pounded me.

"He was hot," I say. "I could handle it."

She laughs. "Yeah, a lot of entertainers say that. User 829 shows up as a regular favourite in our surveys."

It still feels weird, how it's said so casually. Like User 829 is just a guy on the system. Not a man who feeds you champagne from the bottle and orders you around with finger clicks.

Orla brings me back to the conversation.

"I see you've been ticking quite a lot of fresh options on the naughty list. You're very ambitious."

And pretty desperate for flights.

I make sure I'm looking right at the camera. "I wasn't lying when I said I'm quite a dirty girl."

"Your reviews are backing that up. Very good. Well done."

"Thank you."

We talk through my experiences, and I keep my smile at full beam. I don't tell her that User 1378 was boring and vanilla, I say he was *lovely*, and as for User 829, I hold back, not wanting to sound like I'm attached to him. He was just a one-night fuck, after all. Or so he should be. My ass is still burning, and my pussy has been throbbing sore all day. But it hasn't made any difference. I'd still take him all over again.

"You can contact me at any time," Orla says. "Any questions, concerns, or to talk through specific proposals, I'm always just a message away."

"Thanks."

"Oh," she says. "Now you've completed some initial assignments, I'll add you to the entertainer chat group. It's quite active." She chuckles. "You'll find plenty of hot threads on User 829 if you type him in the search bar."

My smile drops a little when the call ends. I'm relieved to see Ebony's online icon next to her name.

Fancy a chat? I type.

She hits the call button straight away and there she is, looking gorgeous as ever.

"I'm fresh from the salon." She holds up her nails, so striking in neon green. "My next client has a thing for certain colours. Tonight, it's green. I swear he wants me to look like some kind of alien for him. He wants me in lime green latex, and scrunchies. The kids are going to wonder what the hell's up with me when I say goodnight later."

"Latex and scrunchies?" I can't hold back a laugh. "What the fuck?"

"You'll come to learn. Proposals can get very, very specific, and our clients can get very, very strange. I've seen this guy at least twenty times over the last few years. I've been every colour of the rainbow. He wanted me in purple dungarees once. I'm not lying."

"Jeez."

"How about you? How are you finding it?"

"I spent a few crazy hours with User 829 last night."

She raises her eyebrows. "Nice. Not too much for you?"

"No. It was great."

"People say that. I haven't had a night with him. He goes for the newbie goth girls with plenty on their naughty list."

I get a fresh lurch in my stomach.

"He's always seeking out the fresh prospects, then?"

"Yeah. Quite the opposite of some of the regulars. One entertainer has been seeing the same client every week for seven years straight. She must know him better by now than a member of her family. It's incredible really."

I try to imagine that. "Don't they want more?"

She shrugs. "I don't think so. She likes being an entertainer, and he keeps on paying. It works well for them. I'm sure you'll end up with regulars of your own." She pauses. "That's if you stay being an entertainer, of course. Think it's a phase for you, or are you in for the long haul?"

"*Until* the long-haul flight, at least." I lean back against my pillows, the laptop on my thighs. "I don't know. I haven't really thought about it."

"Entertainers come and go. Some stay long term. Some leave quick. Some come back and forth as relationships start and finish." She grins at me. "I dunno, though. I have a feeling you'll be a long-termer."

"Really?"

"Call it intuition. You may get hooked on some regulars for starters."

I wonder who the hell they'd be. Not User 829 from the sounds of it. I won't get the option.

"Who knows?" I say. "Maybe it'll be me getting specifically coloured nail extensions at some point."

She giggles. "Or purple dungarees."

"They'd have to be goth ones."

"Halloween print?"

"Something like that."

I love the easiness of our conversation. I know she must be a fantastic entertainer. Her energy is amazing through video call, like we're already lifelong friends. She must give that impression to her clients, as well as being a kinky bitch who plays out their fantasies.

"I checked out your new profile by the way," she tells me with a wink. "Sorry, I'm nosey, but I couldn't help myself. You've ticked one hell of a lot of options."

"Hardly a hardcorer. Double anal fisting? Just, wow."

"You might be a hardcorer someday. If you're ticking off that many options already, you might work your way up the ladder."

"Or down into the depths of pure, utter filth."

"The hardcorers love it there. You'll meet them when you get into the chatroom. Has Orla sent you the link yet?"

I check my notifications in another window, and sure enough, there's a link waiting for me. "Yeah, she has."

"Fab! Then get on in there." She looks down at the corner of her screen for the time. "Shit. I have to go. I've got to get myself into latex."

"Have fun in green scrunchies."

"I will. He's awesome at eating pussy."

I look at the link to the chatroom when she's gone. I wonder if I'm ready to head in right now, still exhausted from last night's pounding and my lack of sleep, but I can't resist. I click on it, and it opens up a new tab with a *set up user* screen. *Holly* I type in, but there is already a member called that. *Hollyella* I use, and it works. I choose a password and I'm in.

Jeez, there are more members in there that I'd have imagined. There are over fifty entertainers online. Group chat is flowing and there are so many threads it's insane. From types of fetishes, to people asking questions about clients, and another set I hadn't thought of. *Requests for associates.* I click on that, and it's where entertainers are sharing highlights of their proposals with requests attached. *Two more entertainers, needed. One guy, one girl.* Another post. *Who's up for a threesome tomorrow night? Needs to be blonde. £1300 up for grabs.*

I hadn't even considered that kind of thing.

Of course, the obvious search is eating away at me. I find the search option at the side of the threads and type in *User 829.* Orla wasn't lying. There are a lot of conversations about him.

Fucking hell. He has a monster!

Sure does, and he knows how to use it. Holy shit! Why does he only go for the newbies?! Urgh. Fuck, my poor ass.

On and on it goes, and I get a pang as so many other entertainers recount virtually identical experiences to mine. There is no doubt whatsoever, I was definitely a nobody to him. Just another notch on his filthy bedpost.

I need to get him out of my fucking mind.

I get a ping from the main chat thread. Good timing.

Hey, Hollyella! Welcome to the group!

So many people like and comment, and I thank them all, getting caught up in answering questions about who I am and what I'm into. People's interest is off the scale, and I feel great for it. There is no competition here. Entertainers are clearly from all over the UK, guys, girls, gay, straight, bisexual. None of it matters. It's all one happy, chatty crew.

I don't even notice the time whizz by, I'm so engaged by it. My exhaustion leaves me in the dust as I join in with people's conversations, and chat the evening away. That's when a new thread pops up.

NEW PROPOSALS! Who's got what coming in?

Shit. I haven't checked mine since I've been online.

Wow, ok. There are three fresh ones with higher proposal prices than my earlier ones, so I click *no* to the previous vanillas. These new three are much more interesting. Two want bondage, one of them with heavy use of a paddle. Pussy and ass, with some deepthroat. £1000 each. I could do those, but both of their proposals clearly want my services ASAP – like in the next twenty-four hours – and I can't right now. I need at least a few nights to recover. I owe it to my body.

It's the final new proposal that grabs me...

Users 1458 and 1459. Males. Both 25. Just a year older than me.

We want a hot girl to share. Ass and pussy at the same time – a fuck ton of hot DP for us. Call it a quest for a hot, kinky bitch for some party time. Big tits a must. Yours look fucking ace. Don't be surprised if we talk to you like you're a dirty little bitch by the way. Call it banter.

Duration – 4 hours.

Proposal price – £4000.

I have to blink twice. Have they made a typo?

Four grand for four hours with two guys?!

I look up the address and it's one hell of a hotel in Chelsea. Fuck, these guys must have some money. It's an easy click for me.

I look at their calendar options. Saturday night is on there, which is no problem. It'll give me a few days to recover from User 829. I select that one, and it's a goer. Deal confirmed.

Fucking hell, I can't stop staring at the screen. On Sunday morning, I'll have more money in my account than I've ever had in my life – another £3200 on my balance after agency fees. Insane.

My trip to Australia is looking a whole load more likely by the second. My parents are going to get a jingle bells in person from me this year.

I'm grinning as I settle down to sleep. On Saturday night it's going to be double penetration party and a little bit of *banter* in Chelsea.

Yes. Fucking. Please.

eight

Users 1458 and 1459. Males. Both 25.

We want a hot girl to share. Ass and pussy at the same time – a fuck ton of hot DP for us. Call it a quest for a hot, kinky bitch for some party time. Big tits a must. Yours look fucking ace. Don't be surprised if we talk to you like you're a dirty little bitch by the way. Call it banter.

Duration – 4 hours.

Proposal price – £4000.

Jesus Christ, this gig will be enough to set me up with my flights. Just four hours of hot action and kinky banter and I'll be able to book my travel. And then what? I smile as I take my cab to Chelsea, grinning in the back seat with pure relief.

I know what next. Money for presents, and spending during my trip, and so much more... If I keep doing this, I can clear my debt. I can get my own place. I can have a life again.

I tell myself not to get carried away. There only two things I should be thinking about right now. Users 1458 and 1459. I need another five-star review.

The hotel is a crazy rich one. The lights outside are huge domes lighting up the courtyard, and the black and gold doors are tall, guarded by two lion statues, one either side. This place is magnificent. The cab pulls up on the gravel, and I click *arrived* on the app before I pay the cab driver. I'm expecting a room number to ping through, but I don't get one.

In the bar is all the message says.

In the bar? How the hell am I supposed to recognise them?

I head straight through reception, knowing the staff are whispering about me in my long black coat and stilettos. My hair is loose and curled, and my lipstick is dark purple. I stand out in this place by a clear mile.

I've never been anywhere like this in my life.

I hear the bar easily before I arrive there – a hustle and bustle of a room off to the right. It's busy with posh guests, in suits and glamour dresses, and I've no idea who I'm looking for. *Two guys aged 25...* I'm scanning the place when I hear a wolf whistle, and there they are. A pair of guys sitting on barstools with one empty one between them. They wave me over with cheers, making a raucous spectacle, but they don't seem to give a shit about that.

I know the whole bar is watching me as I approach them. I feel tottery on my heels, shy and exposed and out of my comfort zone, but I force myself to hide it, pasting on confidence as one of them pats the stool between them. I tell myself that I'm Holly here. The entertainer. I'm going to live up to it, whatever it takes.

The guy on my left is blond, in a posh smoking jacket and bow tie, clearly born with a silver spoon in his mouth. The one on my right has hot ginger hair, slimmer, in a tight-fitting suit jacket with jeans. These two look like they own the place, clearly tipsy as they spin on their stools to check me out.

"I'll take your coat," blond guy says, and I hope he doesn't notice I'm trembling as I hand it over. I'm not dressed for this place, in my tiny PVC skirt and fishnets. My tits are on display in my tight matching crop top, my cleavage on show to the world. *Come on, Holly*, I tell myself. *Be an entertainer.*

I'm being examined by the Users. Their eyes rove all over me, and they give each other a nod and a high five, right in front of me.

"Good choice," the ginger haired guy says to his friend.

"Yeah, I knew she'd be a good one."

They don't even say hello. Mr Ginger hair points to the drinks displayed behind the bar.

"What do you want?" he asks me.

"I'll have a Coke, please."

"A Coke? Come on. That's hardly party fuel."

I lean forward, checking out the selection, and I sum up the confidence from the depths of me. They want a *party girl*, they can have one.

"Alright, then. I'll have a champagne, thank you. The finest."

"Good call," Blondie says. He taps on the bar for the bartender's attention. "A bottle of De Chante, please."

"Coming right up, Mr Leonard."

"Ooh, dear." *Mr Leonard* fake laughs at me as the bartender gets to work. "You aren't allowed to know our full names, are you?"

I've read that in the terms of service, yes – no asking for names.

"I'm now allowed to *ask* for names, no."

"Fuck the terms of service. We'll give them to you anyway. I'm Dean," the ginger guy says with a grin. "And that's Ryan."

"Pleased to meet you. I'm Holly."

"Yeah, right, sure you are." Dean checks his watch, clearly a Rolex. "You're nice and prompt, *Holly*. Just as well since we're paying you four grand for this filthy experience. You have a pair of cracking hot tits. Even better than your photos."

The bartender hears that, but pretends not to. He sets up three glasses on the counter and pops the cork.

Great. So now he knows I'm a prostitute, and so does everyone else in earshot.

I take a swig of my drink before I answer the lovely Dean. I shouldn't break the terms, but I do.

So this is banter? Fine. I'll take it. I flick my hair out of the way, propping an elbow on the bar as I answer him.

"Thanks. I hope you have a cracking hot cock when you fuck me with it later." I raise my voice. "I am being paid to use it, after all."

I'm sure the people around us must hate it. I can feel the crackle of disbelief in the air, but neither of these guys give a shit. It's clear they're loving it.

"My cock is bigger than Dean's," Ryan tells me. "His is puny compared to mine."

"You're talking shit and you know it." Dean slaps his hand on my thigh. "Don't worry. Ryan can say what he wants. He's full of tosh."

These guys are so arrogant and cocky, they're practically snorting with their own self-worth. Dean's hand stays on my thigh and climbs higher, slipping underneath my skirt, but it's not my job to give a shit about that. I spread my legs so he can do what he wants, and take another sip of my champagne. It's delicious.

"How long have you been a slut?" Ryan asks.

I keep up the cheeky banter, "Since the first time I rubbed myself off on the living room carpet while Mummy wasn't looking."

He laughs at that. "Ok, I'll rephrase it. How long have you been an entertainer?"

"About a week."

"A fucking week?!"

I look him right in the eyes. "Yes. About a week."

"Jesus. You'd better be a good one, then. Or we'll ask for a refund."

He gives another snort laugh, but my heart speeds up, in case he's serious. My flights are on the line here.

"Don't worry." I lean right into him and run a finger up his shirt. "I will be."

Dean's hand reaches my crotch on his climb, and I hold the inner quakes deep. Nobody else in this room matters. Not their opinions, not their tastes, not their whispers or looks of disgust. The 4k is coming from these two, not from them. I spread my legs so Dean's hand can hook inside the lace of my panties and graze my pussy.

"She's wet as all fuck," he announces to Ryan.

"I'm always wet," I say. "I'm a slut because I like getting fucked, not just for the money."

"We should have offered you a lot less for it then, shouldn't we? We'll know that for next time."

No, Holly is worth 4k. I'm going to make sure of it.

I lean back so they get full sight of my cleavage, my tits straining the fabric. I neck my champagne, and gesture for them to pour me another glass of high-end fizz, and Ryan does it for me. Fuck the pair of them and their dickhead chatter. I down that one as well.

I can handle these guys. Some of Connor's friends were full of *banter*, they just didn't have millions in their bank accounts to go along with it – most likely from their mummies and daddies. These two would be a lot easier to deal with in the privacy of a hotel room, though.

"Are you going to get another bottle or two to take upstairs?" I ask them. "I hope you're going to give me cock for the next four hours, not just parade me in the bar. Time is ticking, gentlemen."

They look at each other, and Ryan shrugs. Dean orders three bottles from the bartender, paying with an Am-ex card like he's a high roller. He holds two of the bottles up to me to show off.

"Fine, let's go," Ryan says, taking the other bottle as well as my coat as they lead me away. I don't realise how tense I've been until we're heading upstairs in an elevator, just the three of us. It's a relief to be out of public viewing.

"Time to fucking party," Dean says as he swipes their suite door open with a key card.

They don't close the curtains, just dump the champagne on one of the counters and get right on me, shoving me down onto the bed like a toy. I don't stop them as they drop down beside me on the huge mattress, just raise my hands above my head invitingly and give myself up to being theirs. The champagne has certainly taken the edge off my nerves.

Ryan pulls my top down and frees my tits, and Dean has my skirt off in seconds, rubbing my pussy through my panties.

"I hope you two are going to fuck me good," I say, thinking of the review I want from these rich pair of jokers. "You promised a fuck ton of DP in your proposal."

I'm still horny about the idea of taking two dicks at once, no matter who they belong to. It's been a long-term fantasy I've been dreaming of. Ryan's mouth is surprisingly good on my tits as he sucks at me, and Dean's managing to catch my clit really well as he slides his fingers up and down my slit.

Their arrogance does seem to have a solid foundation in here.

"Nice," I say, and move against the pair of them. "You've got some real talent there."

I know they're going to love me stoking their egos.

Dean pulls my panties off, and I help Ryan with my crop top. I'm still in stockings and stilettos, but I'm on full display now and I give myself up to it, offering my tits back to Ryan with a moan, and spreading my legs open wide for Dean. I let them know I want it.

"Do what you want," I say, making sure I laugh and remember *party time*. "You're paying a decent whack for me, aren't you? Take advantage of the goods, boys."

"Don't worry," Dean says. "We fucking will."

The banter is leaving the room now, I hear it in his voice. He pushes three fingers right the way inside my pussy, but I don't so much as flinch. Just whimper for him, letting my character take over.

"You're so fucking good," I tell them, and give myself up to the sensations. My body is thrumming on instinct. I always want cock as soon as my clit's sparked, and Dean's stoking the fire.

They don't play long before Ryan's stripping his suit off. He presents his cock like a trophy, and in fairness to him, he has a right to. He's pretty big. Impressive.

I take him in my mouth when it's offered, slurping as I stare up at him through my long, fake lashes. He bulges my cheek and I grin around his dick, my eyes switching to Dean who's stripping himself bare between my legs.

Dean arrives up at my head on the other side of me, both of them up on their knees. Ryan was talking millimetres, not inches, when he said he had the bigger dick. Taking both of them at once is going to be both a feat and a pleasure.

"My turn," Dean says, and twists my face away from Ryan's, my spit trailing.

He fucks my face harder than Ryan, more seriously, and I bob my head up at him like the kinky bitch they're paying me to be. It must be working, because they struggle to share, twisting my face from one to the other as they slam their cocks in my throat.

"Both at once," I gurgle around Dean's dick. "Do it. Fill me up."

"Dirty bitch," Dean says, and Ryan pushes his cock in as well, ballooning my cheeks. My eyes are watering as they mash their dicks together and fuck my face, but I encourage them, giggling and moaning, slurping for more.

I am a dirty bitch, and I can show it.

My hand slips between my legs, but these two are so busy fucking my face they don't even notice. I hook my fingers inside myself to get myself ready, and it spurs me on. My gasps are for real as I fuck myself, my palm rubbing my clit as I do it.

I picture the two cocks in my mouth pounding me in my ass and pussy at the same time, and I love the sense of the competition between them. I can already feel their rivalry fuelling their fires. Why not fucking fuel them some more?

"Which one of you is going to fuck me the hardest?" I ask them once I've gulped in some air. "I love it nice and rough."

They both shove their cocks back in my mouth as they eye each other up. Yeah, I am right. There's rivalry here. Maybe they've been schoolfriends, competing since they were young? Who knows? Who even cares?

Not Holly the whore.

I wait for another air break before I keep on going.

"Who's usually the best? You must know it by now. Who's going to get me off the hardest?"

"Me," Dean says, but Ryan gives him a sneer.

"Whatever, Dean. You know I always top the charts at everything."

"Fuck off, Ryan. We'll see."

Yes, we will...

I gurgle some more, still working my own pussy, knowing my face is covered in streams of spit. It's Dean who discovers I'm playing with myself, slapping my hand away when he realises.

"Cheeky little fucking bitch, using your cunt before we do."

"I can't help myself." I flutter my lashes. "I'm just too fucking horny."

It definitely pushes his buttons. His cock is away from my mouth in seconds, and he's storming down the bed, slamming himself balls deep in my pussy in one.

I cry out, and it's not fake.

"Mmm," I moan around Ryan's cock, still bulging my cheek out. "Yeah, like that, Dean. Fuck me."

"Your profile isn't lying, is it? You're a dirty bitch," Dean says, and I nod as best I can.

I think of the review. What it will mean for me. What the cash will look like in my bank account.

"Yes, I fucking am," I say. "I'm a dirty bitch who needs cock."

Banter is long forgotten now. This shit is getting serious. Ryan straddles my face to jam his cock right down my throat, and Dean fucks my pussy like he's on a mission. I grip Ryan's ass cheeks and urge him to pound my throat deeper, and I wrap my legs around Dean, coaxing him to slam me harder. *Yes*. I can do this. I *want* to do this. I want to be the best reviewed entertainer on the site...

I know Ryan is bracing himself to stop himself coming, my mouth working magic on his dick. I don't slow down. My hands keep gripping his ass, my moans still begging, and he curses, because he can't stop.

"I'm gonna fucking come already," he tells Dean. "The bitch is just too good."

"Yeah... her pussy is too fucking good, too. Fuck it."

Both guys come for me, both at once. Dean ploughs and grunts as he comes in my pussy as Ryan spurts his load right down my throat.

I'm so fucking proud of myself as they roll away from me, both of them gripping their balls as they recover.

I watch them, making sure my smile is teasing as I relax on my side.

"Please don't say that's all you've got for me. I need more. I want to get stretched by two dicks at once, remember? That's why I clicked on your proposal..."

Dean's eyes are fierce.

"Don't you worry your pretty little head. You'll get way fucking more than that, just give us a minute."

I point to the champagne bottles.

"Can I have some while I wait, please? I love being spoiled."

"Glug all you want," Dean says. "You'll need it to take us both. Your pussy is so fucking tight we'll tear you open with two at once."

I get up from the bed and grin at him.

"Now you're talking."

I look at myself in the mirror as I pop a cork and swig expensive champagne from the bottle. My makeup is a state, and I've got spit all over my chin, but I'm grinning. I never thought this would come so easily. Playing a role, being a servant – a slut for cash, but I'm changing.

I'm living in a horny drama school, playing to my strengths like I was born for it, and that's what I want it to be. A horny actress in a role where I get richer, and dirtier, and my reviews keep getting better, time after time.

Dean and Ryan are still catching their breath, *bantering* again about who of them is going to fuck me hardest as I stand in front of them and drink their expensive champagne. They join in and glug some champagne for themselves, and I learn a bit about them as they regale me with chatter. As I suspected, they were school buddies, who were on opposite teams in virtually every sports class they ever had. Friends *and* competitors. It seems to work for them. Their closeness is obvious, even when they are jibing each other like idiots.

They're clearly so well off, I doubt they'll even notice the 4k disappearing from their bank accounts.

Ryan gets another hard-on first. He fists it as he downs some more of bottle number two. Dean's not ready yet, so points to the bed.

"Why don't you bounce on his cock and jiggle those big fucking tits of yours? I'll be joining you in a minute."

Ryan clearly likes the idea of that. He's straight on over to the bed, relaxing on his back with his head on a pillow. After another glug of fizz, I place the bottle on the bedside table and climb onto the bed as sexily as I can muster. I straddle him reverse cowgirl, sinking down onto his cock with a moan that is partly real.

"Ride the fuck out of him!" Dean says. "I want to see those gorgeous tits bounce."

I go for it, riding Ryan like he's a bronco, up and down, tits bouncing hard and heavy for Dean. His cock is getting hard again now, his eyes are dirty.

He's definitely the filthy one out of the pair of them, and I like it. I prefer Dean over Ryan, grinning happily as I bounce on his friend.

"I want your ass," Dean tells me. "Spin the fuck around on him."

I groan as I twist myself over Ryan. It's his eyes that are on my jiggling tits now as I keep on riding him. I feel Dean behind me on the bed as he positions himself. He takes hold of my hair as he shoves me forward, flat straight onto Ryan.

"Keep bouncing, slut!" Dean says, and I brace myself on the mattress, hips still rolling as Dean spits on his fingers.

My ass is so fucking tight with Ryan's dick in my pussy that I cry out when Dean shoves two fingers inside, but this is pain I like... pain I'm used to.

"More, please," I say to him. "Yes! More!"

"I'll give you more, you filthy slut," Dean says and twists his fingers deep, and I keep on moving, eyes closed as I shift ever so slightly... so my clit is against Ryan's crotch. I'm so spread... so fucking spread...

"Filthy slut," Dean says again, and he forces a third finger right in.

He has me, then. Used by two, stretched by two, even though he hasn't even got his cock in me yet. This is going to hurt. A good hurt. It's going to feel so fucking good to be such a slut.

All I want is the pain of the stretch as his cock lines up against my ass. He uses my rhythm against Ryan to edge forward, making me take his dick, just a bit at a time. Fuck, it hurts. But I don't care... I'm high on champagne and dick, both at once. Holly and Ella blur into one, but I stop myself. No. I'm Holly.

Right here, I'm Holly.

My clit is frantic, and I'm panting like a desperate bitch, but the clients are what's important. I let Ryan kiss me deep when he pulls my head to his. It doesn't mean a thing.

He keeps on kissing me as Dean shoves his cock all the way in. The sharp stab makes me bite at Ryan's lip. He responds by biting mine and I groan like a true slut when Dean starts fucking my ass.

"My turn for mouth on mouth," Dean says, and uses my hair to twist my head right back, my lips puffy as he mashes his mouth on mine. He kisses me harder than Ryan. He fucks me harder than Ryan. He guides the game of double penetration as he owns my ass, slamming and slamming and slamming.

"Time to change position," he says, and it feels like my ass is tearing as he pulls out. "Ryan, move. You're taking her cunt from the front this time."

Dean gets on his back as Ryan gets off the bed.

"Holly, get your filthy ass on my cock," he barks, and I do as I'm told, straddling him in reverse – but rather than have me bouncing with his dick in my burning ass, he hooks his arms under mine, binding my back to his chest. I can't move and I don't want to.

"Fuck her cunt," Dean says to Ryan, and Ryan's eyes are fiercer now as he looks down at him.

"I don't need fucking instructions, jackass," he says as he climbs back onto the bed.

No. He doesn't. He shuffles up close between our spread legs and lines his cock up, shoving in hard in one long thrust. The stretch makes me hiss. Ryan likes that, grinning as he fucks me. Dean's breaths are in my ear, and Ryan is staring down as he fucks my pussy, and I'm gasping, lost in the headspace.

"You're a filthy fucking whore for real. Money well spent," Dean says, and I nod, agreeing.

"Yes, I am. I love being a filthy fucking whore for real."

"My cock is probably tearing your ass to pieces, you know that?"

I grin up at Ryan as I answer Dean.

"Yeah, I know that. I can feel it."

"And you don't fucking care?"

I close my eyes, revelling. I think of the cash, and the reviews, and all of the other men I'm likely to serve, but it's more than that. I'm loving it. Maybe Ebony is right. Maybe one day I'll be a hardcorer.

"No," I tell Dean. "I don't fucking care. Your cock can be tearing my ass all it likes. It feels like fucking heaven."

They both ramp it up, and I whimper. They pin me between them, slamming together in rhythm, before splitting apart, alternating back and forth, and it's a beautiful horny pain. I encourage them. I beg for more. I give them everything they want from me.

The pair of them fuck me like I'm nothing but two needy holes, eager to please. And I am eager to please.

"Harder!" I hear myself saying.

And then they come, blowing their loads with a stream of curses.

My clients come inside my stretched holes, grinning at each other like they've won the lottery.

I've done it. I've earned my money. Or so I think...

Ryan pulls free first, but Dean doesn't let me go.

"Play with yourself," he says. "You're going to get yourself off before

I take my dick out of you, and don't even think of faking it. Ryan's going to be watching. He'll be able to tell."

"You don't need to worry about that," I tell him.

It's an easy job. My clit is so desperate that I'm cursing myself as I play. I use three token fingers inside me, but Ryan shakes his head.

"Nah, we have another toy for you."

He takes the empty bottle of champagne, rips the foil clear from the top, and hands it over. Smooth glass. I don't hold back, practically snatching it from him as he offers it. It's thin but long, and I show him how I deep can go with it. It feels nice, so smooth...

I rub my clit at the same time, building the tension – feeling so filthy as I perform. There is no fakeness about it in the slightest as I come with the champagne bottle stretching me as well as Dean's cock, squirming against him with his cock up my ass. Ryan's drinking more champagne as he stares on, nodding with approval.

Dean only lets me go when I've finished coming, lolling back against him, panting. I roll away slowly, and my ass and pussy are both hurting like a bastard, but I'm laughing, high on champagne and post orgasmic bliss.

"Suck it clean," Dean says, and I use the bottle like a cock in my throat, sucking it clean with a pop of my lips.

"Yum."

Both of them are grinning at me. Satisfied. Just like I am.

"Thanks, guys. That was hot as all hell," I tell them, and I'm not lying.

Their *banter* is back as Dean gets up from the bed and joins Ryan for the next bottle of champagne.

I fucked her harder.

Yeah, right, like hell you did.

They offer me some more De Chante and I drink along, enjoying the *party* time as I laugh along with them, refusing to acknowledge who was the better fuck, even though it was obvious.

It was Dean.

"Time's up by the way," Dean tells me. "You fulfilled the proposal ten minutes ago."

I look up at the clock and he's right. My four hours are finished and

I'm a whole lot richer. I could be out of there like lightning, but I stay with Users 1458 and 1459 until the champagne is all finished up and their little party is over, both of them yawning, tired.

"Night, guys," I say as I leave, kissing them both on the cheek before I go. "Thanks for an incredible time."

"See you again," Dean says, and I give him a wink.

"I hope so."

I'm in a cab and on my way home when I get the ping through from the app. Even though both guys were ready to collapse in bed, I have my review there, glowing – and the cash is showing in my bank account.

Five stars isn't enough for this dirty beauty. Great mouth, great pussy, great ass, and as for her tits... find out for yourself. You'd be fucking mental not to. A+++.

I'm so happy I could cry when I get back home.

I search for flights to Australia, and I hit purchase, staring at the screen in shock.

And then I do cry. Pure, happy tears. I've done it.

I'll be on the beach this year for Christmas, sunbathing with my Mum and Dad.

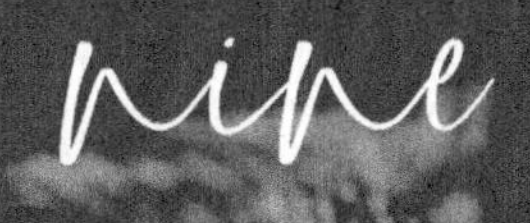

nine

"You did DP last night, right?" Ebony asks me on video chat. "Well done you! I saw it in the chat thread."

"Yeah, I did. It was hot as hell."

"Fake hot, or real hot?"

I think back to Dean and Ryan, both pounding me at once. I remember the sensation of Dean gripping me tight and Ryan's weight on the both of us, using me like a doll, and I grin at Ebony.

"Real hot. The guys were great."

"I've heard they're a right pair of dickheads."

"They're definitely dickheads when they're making a spectacle of themselves like loaded playboys, but they're hot in bed." I pause. "They were kind of cute, actually."

"Guess you'll be seeing them again?"

I sure hope so for the chance of another 3.2k in my account.

After paying for my flights, my bank balance isn't too healthy, and I'll need to be careful with it. I'll have a pause in action coming up in a few days' time as it is. Damn monthlies. I've considered skipping my pill break, just to keep them at bay.

I tell Ebony so, and she laughs.

"Really? You think you'll be out of action because you're on? Haven't you seen the option to click for your profile?"

No. I haven't. I tip my head to the side.

"What option?"

"There's a box you click on your dashboard. It highlights you have your period on your profile screen. Some guys go crazy for that. Your calendar will be rammed, if you're up for it."

It doesn't take me too long to consider – yeah, I guess I'm up for it.

I call up my entertainer login in another window, keeping Ebony on call, and she guides me to the option. I click without so much as blinking. The more money for Christmas the better. A red icon and date listing shows up on my profile almost immediately.

"There are plenty of filters the clients can use," she tells me. "Period play is on the list. You'll show up on it now. AND it pays well."

I really hope so.

I've been politely declining a lot of the regular requests that have been hitting my inbox, looking out for some of the filthier, better-paid ones, but I haven't had any through yet. Nothing serious, anyway. Ebony assures me it's because I'm new and people with the highest reviews come out at the top of the search lists. A day or two without anything high value means nothing, she says, but I'm still clinging so hard to my new lifestyle that I'm nervous. I'm not getting the visibility boost of a *newbie* anymore, after three sessions and reviews, so I don't have the advantage of that. I've been thinking of taking the average stuff to keep the cash coming in, but a decent fee for period play would be way more up my street. I'm becoming more of Holly the filthy slut every day.

"I give it twenty minutes before you get a proposal," Ebony says, much more confident than me.

"Do you do it?" I ask her.

"Period play? Sometimes. Depends how much I've got on my *want it now* list. I'm terrible for shoes. I must have nearly a hundred pairs. And it's hard, running the house. Costs an absolute fortune. Stephen's not on a massive salary, but he loves his job too much to quit, so."

It occurs to me then that I still know very little about her. I see her lovely cream living room in the background, and sometimes she rests her laptop on her thighs while sipping champagne, clearly making a very healthy amount of cash at her entertainer role. Her profile is quite a dirty one, but she's not a hardcorer. Not by any stretch.

"What's the dirtiest thing you've done?" I ask her.

"Depends on what you call dirty. I've done fetish a fair bit, but that's a bit different."

"Fetish? That's different from dirty?"

"Yeah. I'd say so. Or it can be. I like the odd proposals, like my guy who likes weird dress up sessions. There's another guy I like who's got this crazy medical room and treats you like a patient. Hardly a real-life doctor, though. He is fucked up, but it's cool."

"What does he do?"

"Puts you on his medical bed, hoists your legs up for a vaginal exam with a speculum. Examines you with latex gloves on, I mean *seriously* examines you. Takes some swabs. Gives you some *medication*. Some *cream* spread right the way inside your pussy. And ass sometimes. Depends how he's feeling."

Something feels weirdly horny about that. I shift on my chair.

"Oh," she says. "And he does your mouth, too. He's fascinated. All the while dressed up in a doctor's garb. Believe me, he pushes it, but it pays well. He binds your arms to the medical trolley with *straps*, for your *own safety*, but he's never been sinister."

My confidence is most definitely growing. The idea of me vanilla fucking for a few hundred quid a time is fast fading to nothing.

I get a proposal ping as she's telling me more about him.

"There you go!" she says. "I know what that one will be."

She's right.

User 319. Male. 43.

I want period play, so long as you're a heavy flower. Right in the middle of your period. I want a wet and bloody cock from fucking and playing. No condom. I like it messy. Very messy. No tampon on the way. I want you ready for it. I use waterproof sheets, and I like smearing. I play from home, and keep the sheets for later. Can you give me your wet, bloody pussy, please? I'd love to play with you.

Duration – 3 hours.

Proposal price – £2500.

Wow!

I read it out to Ebony.

"Not bad. You might well get some others through the week as well."

"I think I'd better try it out before I commit to a full week of it."

"Good point." She winks. "I think you'll be ok, though."

"You think I'll be ok at *everything*."

"Call it faith."

"Faith that I'll take double anal one day, and rim filthy assholes?" I laugh out loud, and she laughs along with me.

"It's true!" she says. "I think you'll be one of the hardest hardcorers of the hardcorers!"

"Hardly something I ever thought would be on my resume!"

We laugh again, and it's bliss. I've been so serious for so long it's like a release of something heavy. A pressure valve releasing. Connor issues, and money issues, and living in this shithole... none of it feels crippling anymore. I feel like I'm being set free.

"How hardcore do you think you can go?" she asks.

"I'm not doing scat play," I tell her, and she holds up her hands with a grimace.

"I'm not saying scat play, I'm just saying hardcorer."

"Is that what she does? The entertainer who earns 150k?"

"You'll have to ask her. She's called *Creamgirl* in the chatroom. Notorious. She does pretty much anything she's paid for. Part of a little gang. Her, Weston, Harlot and Bodica. But she's the main player. The hardest-corer of them all."

"Creamgirl. Right."

"Her real name is Tiffany. But *Creamgirl* is a lot of men's *dreamgirl*."

I roll my eyes at that, but I'm already calling up the entertainer search bar. "What's her profile name?"

"Same as her chat name. Creamgirl."

Sure enough, there she is. She's curvy, with gorgeous pouty lips and long pillar box red hair down to her waist. She's licking a chocolate finger, with her thick thighs open wide on her profile picture. Every option is ticked. Literally everything – with a note that says *don't hold back. Your fantasies are mine to deliver.*

Her reviews are off the fucking scale. 4.9 out of 5 with almost 400 listed.

Fucking hell, she's been busy. She doesn't look any older than me.

Hmm, maybe I'd consider double anal one day after all. I already added to my list with CNC – consensual non consent – earlier this morning.

Anyway, back to the task at hand. I click *yes* to User 319's proposal and the calendar comes up. I make sure I pick the day I'm going to be at peak flow. Fuck, this weird shit is becoming normal very, very quickly.

The proposal comes back as confirmed almost immediately. Four days' time. An address in South London.

"Have you done it before?" Ebony asks. "Period play, I mean."

"Not quite," I say, "Connor used to fuck my ass when I was on."

I realise then that I don't really know what real period play entails. Eb must clock my worried expression.

"You'll be fine," she says.

I shrug. "Suck it and see, I guess."

She laughs at that. "Ever sucked a bloody dick?"

I shake my head no. "Have you?"

She winks. "Yeah, just pretend it's strawberry jam, and make sure there's a drink on hand to wash it down."

I swallow at the thought. "Ok."

I flick through my other proposals again, but none of them really take my interest. I can't deny it, part of me is still hoping that User 829 pops up with another request, but I've checked through more and more chat threads about him and that never seems to be the case. I suppose it's one of those things. He was my first client – well, my first one that counted. Maybe that will mean something to me. Like the guy who takes your virginity.

God, what kind of weirdo crap am I telling myself? Sentimental over the first horny guy I enjoyed being a slut for?

"I'm off now," Ebony says. "Got someone to meet for the basics. Nice easy money for relaxing on a bed and moaning for a few hours."

"You do basics?" I ask, surprised to hear that.

"If you call basics being made to squirt in a guy's face every half hour, then yeah, I do basics."

"Wow," I say, "I like the sound of that. I've never squirted before."

"The guy's a pro, really knows how to empty a girl, and he says I'm the best he's ever tasted." She shrugs. "Who am I to argue?"

"What's it like? Squirting I mean, not the taste."

She considers for a moment. "Umm... it's kinda like coming while being poked with a cattle prod. After squirting three or four times in one session, you're knackered like you've just run a marathon. I always need to rehydrate with at least three glasses of wine. Don't worry," she adds, "the way you're going, I'm sure you'll experience it for yourself soon enough."

"I hope so," I tell her, and she waves goodbye.

"Ciao, hon!"

"Laters," I say, "enjoy your *basics.*"

She laughs and the screen goes blank.

I notice my reflection in the screen grinning back at me. What a change in fortunes in such a short time. And what a great friend I've made in Ebony.

Life is so fucking good right now.

I'm even looking forward to my period...

ten

User 319. Male. 43.

I want period play, so long as you're a heavy flower. Right in the middle of your period. I want a wet and bloody cock from fucking and playing. No condom. I like it messy. Very messy. No tampon on the way over. I want you ready for it. I use waterproof sheets, and I like smearing. I play from home, and keep the sheets for later. Can you give me your wet, bloody pussy, please? I'd love to play with you.

Duration – 3 hours.

Proposal price – £2500.

I'm sitting on my long PVC coat in the cab on my way over to User 319's place. I'm usually a tampon AND a pad girl, so this feels insane – knowing I'm bleeding through my panties by the second.

"Are we nearly there?" I ask the driver, as he indicates and turns down yet another street.

"Five minutes away."

The PVC coat will hold it, I assure myself. I've got a pad and some fresh underwear in my bag for later. So, it's just getting there I have to worry about. Only a few more minutes...

I don't even bother looking where we are when the driver pulls up, just pay him his cash through the gap in the seats, and jump out, checking for stains as I go. Phew, it's fine.

My thighs aren't fine, though. They're clammy and slick as I walk towards my destination, and I know full well I'm pooling in my lacy crotch. It must be a mess down there.

Here I am. House number 48.

I click on *arrived* and climb up the three narrow steps to his doorway. It's a nice house, tall and neat. Cost a fortune, no doubt, but regular. Nothing that stands out about it. Clearly, I *do* stand out, though.

I see a curtain twitch in a neighbour's window. Her face is quite something as her eyebrows raise sky high. I nearly blow a kiss to her, but the door to my client's house swings open.

User 319 matches his house. He's tall and neat. Short mousy brown hair and clean shaven, with a shirt and tie underneath a sweater. Just a regular guy.

"Come on in," he says, and I walk past with a thank you, afraid I'm going to be dripping blood all over the step outside, but that's the least of my worries.

A Labrador dog comes straight for me in the hallway, tail wagging like a propellor as his head barges straight for my crotch. Damn it. I try to push him away, but he's quite insistent. I must stink like a bitch in heat, literally.

"HARRY!" User 319 says, and points to the kitchen.

The dog takes one more long sniff at me before he does what he's told, tail still wagging.

"Don't worry," my client says. "He's a friendly guy, he can just get a little carried away." He laughs. "A bit like his owner."

I laugh back. "I'm sure he's a very friendly guy. It's not *his* face I want in my crotch tonight, though. It's yours."

The smile on the guy's face is priceless. "Indeed," he says.

It feels bizarrely more intimate walking into someone's home than it does walking into a hotel. User 319 has old looking family photos hung up in the hallway, and a portrait of his dog near the stairs.

He points to the kitchen as Harry walks on his way.

"Tea? Coffee? Juice? Anything I can get you?"

"I'm fine, thanks. I really am about to bleed down my legs, though, so you may want to get me to my destination, asap."

Fuck, how my client's face morphs at those words. His big brown eyes widen, and he drops a hand to his crotch.

"Show me," he says. "I want to see."

"Right here?"

"Yes, right here. Give me your coat and show me your thighs."

I hand him my coat, and he hangs it on the banister along with my bag, fumbling to make sure they're balanced. My heart is racing as I wait for his attention. I picked out a tiny black satin dress that barely covers my ass, and kept my legs bare on purpose. I don't need to look down at my thighs to know they're trailing blood. I gave him my heaviest flow day, just like he asked for.

As well as my short dress and bare thighs, there's something else I picked out for User 319. I hope it's an ace card that will lead to another five-star review...

"Want to see more?" I ask him, and he nods, with no concern for the cream carpet.

I hitch my dress up higher, slowly, inch my inch, to reveal the ace card. He groans out loud as my choice of lace panties come into view, pure and white. Only they aren't white anymore. I test my crotch with my fingers, and they come back soaked in blood.

"My fucking God," he says. "Get upstairs now, please. The bedroom door is open. First on the left."

I hurry up the stairs and on through the doorway, and whoa, he's prepared for me. Everything is covered in clear plastic sheeting. The bed, the floor, the bookcase. Even an old looking armchair he has by his wardrobe. He's put white bedding underneath the sheeting, and it feels so clean in here with his magnolia walls, and white furniture, everything so light and bright, lit up by a cluster of three spotlights on the ceiling.

It's going to look like a murder scene when he's finished with me.

"Take your dress off, please," he says, shutting the door behind us. "I want you bare apart from those beautiful panties."

"Sure, of course."

I pull my dress up and over my head, knowing the bleed through from the fabric is likely going to make me even more messy. I kick off my heels and throw my bra to the side, and it's just me in my stained white panties, standing in front of a guy who wants me so bad his hand is shaking as he points to the bed.

"Over to the mattress, please, on your back."

"My pleasure."

It feels so good when I take my position. I let out a deep breath of pure relief, relaxing as I open my thighs, with no more concern for bleeding in places I shouldn't. I'm User 319's plaything now. He can worry about the technicalities.

"Great choice of panties, Holly," he says, the first time he's used my name.

"Thanks, I was hoping you'd like them."

"Like them?! They're the hottest pair of panties I've ever seen."

"I chose them especially," I tell him, and his hand goes straight to his crotch again.

"Nice," he says.

"Tell you what," I say, with a wink. "You can keep them when we're done, if you like."

"I'd love to keep them when we're done. How generous. Thank you."

He looks like I've just offered him a cruise across the Atlantic, seriously. I should get a rush of the surreal, but those waves of WTF are leaving the old me in the dust. I'm becoming more of a filthy whore every minute, and it's more of a confidence boost than I ever figured it would be – to be wanted so much by people willing to pay for it.

User 319 looks at me like I'm a goddess on plastic sheeting when he sits down on the bottom of the bed. He eases my knees wider apart, staring up at my stained panties as he licks his lips. His animal instincts begin to show; his gaze is fixed on my crotch as he strips himself, tossing his sweater, shirt and tie to the side. His trousers and boxers slide off easily along with his socks.

A regular guy with a regular body and a regular dick. I'm relieved he hasn't got a monster, due to the tenderness of bleeding.

I wait for his move, watching him, watching me.

"Have you done this before?" he asks.

I shake my head. "No."

"Do you really mean that, or are you trying to make me feel special?"

I smile at him. "Honestly, I haven't done anything like this before. You'll have to give me instructions, since I'm a total newbie."

"I will. I just hope it's not too much for you."

"It won't be."

I sound so sure of myself, staring right back at him, because I *am* so sure of myself.

I feel more blood pooling as it leaks out of me, so I use the opportunity to rub my wet panties, spreading more wetness down my thighs.

My client drops into a crawl on the mattress and takes hold of my legs. His tongue feels divine as he laps his way up my inner thigh, and I can't believe this is hot, but it is. It really fucking is. I've always counted it as a curse that I get so horny on my period, not a blessing, but things are about to change this evening.

He licks one thigh clean, with long wet sweeps, moaning with every one of them. I'm tingling like crazy as he makes his way to my crotch, but he switches before he reaches my panties, turning his attention to my other thigh instead. He wasn't joking when he said he liked period play. He's licking his lips like he's in a five-star restaurant, savouring every taste.

The taste of blood from my sopping wet pussy.

His mouth gets more desperate as he climbs, his hands tight on my knees as he pins my legs flat. I know what's coming, and I urge him on, taking hold of the back of his head.

"Eat my pussy, please," I whimper. "I need it so bad, I could scream."

"We're on the same page on that."

He buries his face right in my crotch, slavering like a man gone insane. His whole face rubs against the dirty, wet lace, with his mouth open wide, and he's grunting like a fucking bear.

I tip my head back, eyes closed as I revel in the feeling. I can smell myself, dark and metallic, and it's beyond crazy to hear how much he's enjoying it. He tugs the crotch of my panties away from my pussy and grips the fabric in his teeth, sucking so hard that I can hear his breaths through his nose.

"Delicious," he says when he's sucked them clean.

I'm ready to beg for his mouth back on my pussy, but I don't need to. He tugs my panties off and teases my wide-open slit with the tip of his tongue, swirling just a little around my clit before pulling away.

"Tease," I say, with a dirty laugh.

Time to tempt him beyond restraint.

I push down through my pelvis with everything I have, and he groans loud, working his dick in his hand.

"You'd better be saving your cock for where I need it," I tell him. "You want it in my wet, streaming pussy, don't you?"

He smiles, but he doesn't look up at me. His eyes are fixed on the mess between my legs. I wonder if it's pooling on the plastic sheeting.

"Don't worry, my cock's going to be right the way inside you when I come," he says.

"Good. That's a relief."

"I want some other things inside you first, though."

"Be my guest. Your wish is my command."

His wish *is* my command. It's becoming so easy to say it now. It's becoming so easy to *feel* it.

User 319's fingers splay me open as I clench and push, clench and push to keep the river flowing. I'm pushing hard when he slips his fingers inside me, and it feels so good that I have to moan.

"Fuck, I'm so sensitive," I tell him and it spurs him on.

He squirms his fingers around and it sounds so dirty wet, it's incredible. He brushes his thumb against my clit, and I grip the sticky, hot sheets, aching for more.

"You really do like this, don't you?" he asks.

I can't hold back a grin. "I'm pretty sure you can tell I'm being serious."

"A load of girls aren't, you know. A lot of them just lie there for the money, pretending they're horny until I've had my fill."

"I'm not one of those girls."

"No," he says. "You're the best I've ever had."

I'm still grinning. "You haven't *had* me yet."

"Trust me," he says and looks so weird with my blood on his lips and chin, "I can always feel the vibe and it's usually a case of going through the necessary motions until the time is up and the job is done. But not with you, Holly. You're giving off horny vibes like you mean it. Like you're into this as much as me."

"Glad to hear it," I tell him. "But it's *you* that's making me horny."

"How so?" he asks, wanting to hear the words.

"I've never done this before, like I said, and didn't know what to expect, but I never in a million years thought it would turn me on like this. You turn me on when you moan against my filthy pussy. It's so hot, it's insane."

User 391 sighs and looks at me adoringly. I feel so at ease that I coax his head back towards my crotch, wanting it as much as he does. He lands his mouth on my pussy, and my shudders are all real. His tongue is on the right spot, just perfect.

"There!" I cry out. "Suck, please!" I beg, and he does.

Jesus Christ, the buzz of his moans as he sucks drives me wild. I'm going to come. I'm going to fucking come for him already, and I can't stop it. I can't. I flail, and gasp, gripping his head in a vice.

"Yes. Harder, harder!" I cry out, and his fingers pump inside me, so sloppy.

I come like a thrashing banshee for my client, with his mouth against my wet, bloody clit. I feel every detail. Every touch and tease, and every squelch of his fingers. Every nerve in my whole damn body is on fire. The room is spinning, and my chest is heaving, and I'm flying as high as a kite as the waves ripple through me.

Pure.

Fucking.

Bliss.

Whoa, I'm heady on the comedown, smiling up at the ceiling as my client keeps his face between my legs, still lapping at my slit as I bleed for him. He's spoiled me rotten, so now it's time for me to do the same in return. *He's* the one who is paying, after all.

Get with it, Holly.

I slide my fingers down to my crotch, curling them inside before pulling them out, nice and wet for him. I love the feeling of his flat, desperate tongue as he sucks my fingers clean over and over. It's only when I whisper *wait* that he pauses, still looking up at me like I'm a goddess.

Time to show him I am one.

I hitch myself up and use four fingers this time – two from each hand. What a lovely stretch as I spread my pussy open...

I cake all four fingers in blood and trail them up my body, teasing my nipples as he watches.

"You like that?" I ask him, and he gives me a smirk.

"You already know the answer."

I do it again. More wet fingers to smear my tits with blood.

"Come on," I coax. "I want you up here."

His tongue is already out as he hauls himself up and over me. The heat of his body feels so fucking good over mine. My fingers are messy when they tangle in his hair, guiding his mouth to one of my blood-smeared tits, my nipples hard as bullets.

I feel his hard cock against my thigh and fuck, how I want him inside me. My pussy is screaming, but I'm not giving in. Not yet. I can't... this is all about him.

His lips are puffy, and his cheeks are a mess with my blood. He's so up close as he feasts on my dirty tits that I can practically taste him. The scent in the air is primal.

I had no idea I'd like his fantasy this much.

Maybe Ebony is right. Maybe I'll be more of a hardcorer than I think I am.

Time to start acting like one...

My heart is pounding as I wriggle to get his attention. My thumb brushes his dirty cheek as I say words I never thought would be coming from my mouth.

"Kiss me."

He looks as shocked as I feel.

"What?"

"Kiss me," I say again. "I want to taste what you're tasting."

He smiles a lovely smile, so warm through the filth.

"Really? You want me to kiss you?"

"Really."

"I can't believe you want this. You're the real deal."

"Neither can I, and yes, I am. I'm the real deal."

"I should get you a drink," he says, "you've never done this before, the taste can be quite... heavy."

I remember what Eb said, a drink to wash it down. But fuck it, I don't want to spoil the moment. *His* moment.

I shake my head no. "Kiss me," I tell him again. And again he smiles adoringly.

He licks my lips before he kisses me, and I open my mouth wide. My tongue is already swirling with his before his lips land on mine. *Dirty.* The kiss tastes like iron and feels like sin. It seems the most natural thing in the world as we mutually position ourselves. He pushes his cock inside me, and in some surreal, alternate universe, this would be nothing more than making out while making love.

My pussy needs this. It's screaming, right from the depths. The thrusts are so slick, but so satisfying, and if he wasn't pumping his hips so quickly, I'd be ready to come again. But he does pump that fast. He pumps like a piston, out of control, cursing right into my mouth as he unloads into me.

"Fucking hell, just fuck–" he groans, and I'm smiling, my own orgasm irrelevant.

He collapses onto me when he's done, kissing my neck while I'm grinning at the ceiling.

"I have no words," he says, and I giggle.

"You don't need any. I just hope that's not game over."

"Well, that depends..." he says, voice trailing. His stare is full of dirty lust as he looks at me. "It depends on how dirty you can be."

"I'd say I've been pretty dirty already, wouldn't you?"

"You've been seriously fucking filthy, yeah. But there's more to come. We can play harder, and you can earn more. Just say the word."

It's like a crash of lightning on a summer's day. I get a twist in my stomach at the realisation this is still all about the cash, despite everything. I'm still Holly the whore, with a bank account waiting for a payout. Preferably a big one.

Being Holly the whore makes my answer a no brainer.

"I'll be as filthy as you want me to be."

With that, User 319 pulls his cock free and clambers up to the side of me. His cock is dripping with cum and blood, an absolute mess, already swelling fresh.

"Your turn to suck," he says, and my insides are twisting, even though my clit is still pulsing. "Do it," he tells me. "Suck me clean."

Can I do it? Can I? Suck it and see... I hear Ebony's giggle.

I open wide for his filthy dick and he's swollen hard again when he guides it into my mouth. I'm glad he's such a quick riser.

Ebony is right. I'm a hardcorer. I don't care what the fuck is on his cock as I work my head for him, sucking him like a hungry slut. My mind is clear of everything but making him feel good.

His fingers fuck me as I suck him, and I'm fully prepared when he switches. He alternates his dick and dirty fingers on loop, until I swear I must have swallowed the whole load of his cum from my pussy. What a perverse version of strawberries and cream.

"Nobody else could ever be this good," he says and I hope he's right. I'm giving it everything I've got and more. I keep on giving. Keep on going. Keep on doing my filthy best.

"I've got to stop," he says a few minutes later, and pulls away from me. "I'll never come again after another round."

I have no idea how long we've been playing, but he does.

"We've got less than an hour left," he tells me. "I want to make it count."

Fuck, we've been playing for two hours already. How time flies when you're having fun.

"Let's just take a minute," he says. "I need to calm myself down."

He doesn't move off the bed, just lies down beside me, his fingers still brushing my bleeding slit. Hardly calm down material, but I make sure to keep my legs open as I roll towards him, keen to face him.

"Has period play always made you horny?" I ask him, curious.

"Yes. It has."

"Do you know what started it? Where did it come from?"

He laughs. "Maybe I'm a reincarnated vampire."

I roll my eyes at him. "I should call you Dracula."

He brushes my hair from my cheek, eyes turning serious.

"It was a school swimming trip. A girl I fancied got out of the pool and there must have been something wrong with her tampon. She was bleeding all down her leg. She was so embarrassed that she ran off, all the way down the poolside, trying to push the tampon back inside her, but it made no difference. She was still streaming. Fuck, how I was fascinated. I thought about it for weeks, and those weeks turned into jerking off, and that jerking off turned into months, and years."

"Did you ever get to play with her?"

"No, no. She ended up with one of the rugby players. He'd have knocked my teeth out if I'd so much as looked at her."

I laugh along with him.

"Do you just play with entertainers? Or people in real life, too?"

"I've had some partners who didn't mind getting fucked on their period, but as for this," he gestures up and down my body, "not even close. It's entertainers all the way, and even then, the best of them by miles has been you. I wasn't joking."

I get a tingle of shyness.

"Thanks."

"That's one of the reasons I chose you, actually. The girl with the tampon accident, she had long black hair and lovely big tits. Just like you."

"I'm glad the choice worked out for you."

"Sure did." He kisses me again, just a peck on the lips this time. "Don't worry. I'm not a stalker or anything, but I'll be sending you plenty of proposals on a twenty-eight-day cycle."

"You'd be more than welcome to."

The figures click in my head. *That would be as much as my full-time salary.*

Holy crap. Three hours of hot work like this would add more to my bank account every month than my full-time salary. How fucking insane. And what a deal worth sealing...

I ask User 319 if he has any toys as well as his cock to use on me, and yes, he has a few dildos in a drawer. I hitch up and squelch as he fucks me with them, lapping up the mess between thrusts. He's good at it. I'm worked up again in no time, just like he is. We shift so I'm in doggy position on the soggy plastic sheeting, and he eats me out like a beast from that angle, dildos cast to the side. It's all about fingers now... fingers and tongue. A whole lot of fingers...

Shit. He's pushing deep and scooping me out.

"Too much?" he asks, but I shake my head.

"No."

He twists, and I know his thumb is pushing in along with his fingers. He's using my dripping menstrual blood to lube me up for fisting... but it's so tight and tender. Too tight.

"Ever taken a whole hand?" he asks, and I shake my head.

"No. Not yet."

"Want to?"

One particularly hard shove of his fingers gives me the answer. It will be too much. Too much for tonight.

"I'll pay you," he says, but I have to shake my head again, flashing him a genuine smile.

"Sorry, but I'm not ready for that."

"But you could be? One day?"

My eyes meet his, and I tell the truth.

"Yeah, I could be. Definitely one day."

"Great. I hope it's with me."

He rises up on his knees, and angles his dick towards my sore, dripping pussy, and I kind of wish I'd given a different answer when he pushes inside me so easily.

I want to be stretched open. I want to know what it feels like with someone's whole fist in my pussy... and if it's not User 319's, it's going to be someone's. Someone soon.

Someone who's paying a lot of money for it.

User 319 has a good enough angle with his cock that he hits my bruised G-spot like a pro. It sets me off on the road to a second orgasm, fisted or not, who gives a shit? I slam back against him as he ploughs me to the balls, and the wet slapping of skin to skin is so erotic it blows me away.

We've only got ten minutes left when my client comes inside me for the second time. He fetches my bag from downstairs and I use his bathroom to wash myself down, taking a huge glug of water to wash the taste away. I feel weirdly sad to be leaving here in fresh underwear and a sanitary towel. At least I'm leaving my dirty ones behind as a memento. He's already stored them away in his top drawer.

My client offers me a coffee as I grab my coat, ready to go. Part of me wants to stay, but for sensibility's sake, I have to say no.

"I have work tomorrow," I tell him. "Bedtime for me."

"Work? For real? You take clients in the mornings?!"

I shake my head.

"No, sorry. *Work* work. I have a day job, too. I'm not an entertainer all the time."

"Wow. What a busy girl."

Seems like I'm definitely becoming one.

I give his dog, Harry, a decent fuss before my cab turns up, and feel weirdly lonely as I say goodnight.

"See you next month," he says, and I kiss his cheek. Clean this time.

"We may need to skip a month, I'm sorry. I'm off to Australia for Christmas with my family. They emigrated a few years ago."

"Right," he says.

"Don't worry, I'm sure there are plenty of entertainers on the books before I get back."

The sparkle in his eyes is beautiful for a cute normal guy, living in cute normal suburbia with a dog called Harry.

"I'd rather wait for you," he says. "See you when you're back and flowing, and every other month you'll have me."

That will be every month, then.

The cab driver beeps like an idiot on the street outside, so I leave User 319 to it, and set off for home, less worried about the seat this time. We're still crossing London when a notification sounds out from my phone. User 319's review of me is even better than the others.

Five stars and more.

The best entertainer on the market, and believe me, I've tried a lot of them. No fakery, no grand ego, no playacting. Nothing but a beautiful, hot girl who loves filth, and makes you feel like a million dollars. She'd be worth that, seriously. If you have a million dollars going spare, then give it all to her. You won't regret a single bit of it. Period play was my happy place with her tonight, but I'm sure she'd turn her hand to anything – and likely come while she's doing it. Do yourself a favour and book Holly now.

Just not on the days I want her. I'll be a repeat customer every month, I can assure you.

The review sounds like him, and it almost chokes me up, it's such a compliment. Crazy really, being choked up with pride for swallowing cum and period blood for three hours straight.

I check my account and he's given me a full 1k bonus. I get another wave of pride as I see my balance totting up, and another wave of want between my legs – half tempted to get the driver to turn the cab around and go right back there.

There's only one conclusion to draw from that though, isn't there? My filth runs far, far deeper than I ever thought it did.

I call up a chat window to Ebony.

You're right. I think I might be a hardcorer. Creamgirl better watch out. I'm coming for her.

I end it with a line of laughing emojis, but I'm not all that sure I'm laughing.

I want to be the star at the top of the naughty list tree one day, and I just know I'll do whatever it takes.

eleven

I really don't want to get up for work this morning. I could launch the alarm across the room, I swear. I don't want to put my uniform on, and I don't want to eat my token bowl of cereal, and I definitely don't want to bustle my way through the crowds to get to the tube.

I used to have Connor to boot me out of bed with a *get the hell up, babe*, knowing full well he'd have the morning to snooze away without a care, but now it's only me. Self-regulation is becoming a lot harder. My shifts are getting busier by the minute, and the ever-coming festive jingles don't mask the angst. My tolerance for minimum wage is threatening to jump from the window and send me sailing – either onto a comfy mattress covered in money, or onto a disillusioned patch of concrete on the ground.

I'm not ready to make the jump yet. It's way too early. That's what I tell myself as I set off on my way. *Be sensible, Ella, be rational. Don't put all your eggs in one goddamn crazy basket.*

That doesn't hold back my irritation, though. I'm crampy and exhausted when I get to the store, running around our *special offer* Christmas aisles to keep them stocked up at the speed of light. Then, out of ALL the moments she could pick to be an asshole, my manager, Tracy, chooses right now.

She huffs before she speaks to me.

"Sandra says you left the shortbread delivery unfulfilled. It got hit by one of the forklifts. Three whole crates down."

Jesus fucking Christ. I can't leave people alone for two minutes.

I let out a groan. "Yes, I did leave the shortbread delivery unfulfilled, and I asked *Sandra* to finish it off while I got called in here to stock up the *two for ones.*"

I've had this before, plenty of times. Sandra vs me. Sandra always wins – useless cow. She's the niece of my manager's best friend and she's an idiot. The brand-new temp staff know how to work stock supplies better than she does.

I usually back down when I'm confronted, accept a guilty verdict and give my apologies, but today I don't say a word, I just stand there.

"What's with the attitude?" Tracy says, and I realise I've folded my arms across my chest.

"It's not an attitude, it's the truth. I asked Sandra to finish up for me. If she says I didn't, she's a liar."

You'd think I'd slapped Tracy across the face from her scowl.

"Sandra wouldn't lie!"

"Well, Sandra must be confused then. I asked her to finish up the delivery for me."

I'm not taking the blame for this. No chance. Sandra was probably flirting with Billy in the forklift bay, giving no attention whatsoever to her workload, and that's not my fault. It never is.

Tracy raises her voice over the Christmas jingles, loud enough that customers turn their heads.

"All you have to do is apologise and take more care next time, Ella! It's a verbal disciplinary, nothing more."

A verbal disciplinary! Is she having a laugh? I could earn a few k for taking a night of *verbal disciplinary* from a well-paying client.

Having a laugh or not, my work ethic still has my blood pumping with nerves, totally at odds with my rage. I'm all for keeping my head down, soldiering on, brushing off the criticism for the sake of holding things steady, but something is bubbling inside me, and it's not just the period demon.

I've been relying on my job at this store for over twelve months straight now. No sick time, no staff politics, nothing but pure, hard work. And what difference has it made to the people in the chain above me? The people who pay my wages?

None whatsoever. It never will.

I stare Tracy right in the eyes, still silent, and she looks puzzled.

"Are you going to apologise?" she asks.

"No."

"No?"

My arms are still folded across my chest. "No. I'm not. Give the *verbal disciplinary* to your best friend's niece, instead. She's the one who fucked up today."

Tracy looks so affronted.

"What the hell?! Sandra being Ashleigh's niece has got nothing whatsoever to do with this!"

"It's got *everything* to do with it. It always has."

My blood is pumping faster now I've drawn the sword of personal insults. My comments are close to the bone, and Tracy could take some fuel from them. So, what to do? Swing or yield. Put my head down and say sorry, or keep on pushing for an equality that will never arrive. The delightful Sandra will always have the top spot over me in this place, no matter how many *two for ones* I stack all day.

I brace myself for Tracy's onslaught, fight or flight mode engaged and ready, but there's no need. The sigh that comes out of her mouth is almost a let-down, it's so puny. It's her who puts her sword away, not me.

"Just take more care next time, will you? No need to get into a tizz about it." She pats my shoulder as she walks on by, and I'm in shock, open-mouthed at her response to me finally standing up to her.

A tizz?

I'd usually be shitting myself at her stock damage accusation, terrified that she'd use it against me to cut my shifts or log some crappy incident on my HR record. But the whole time I've been scared for nothing. Sweet fuck all.

I dared to accuse her of unprofessional favouritism in front of customers, and all she did was pat my shoulder and walk on by.

Yet again, my world is reeling. I feel almost sick as the aisles start closing in...

I've spent so long being afraid of losing money. Of not trying hard enough. Of not working hard enough, or being responsible enough, or earning every single penny I can in this place. And it's all been false. Fear for nothing. Tracy isn't going to do anything to me at all.

The store seems to stand still as I watch her pace away in her clacky shoes. The customers are still looking at me, and the tunes are still jangling overhead, but I feel distant. Empty. *Done.*

Yep. I'm done with this place.

My tolerance for both minimum wage AND Tracy is ready to take the leap.

"Hey," I call after my manager. "Wait a second. I need to tell you something."

She spins back, fake grinning like nothing's fucking happened.

"What's that?"

"I quit."

Her eyes turn to saucers as she clacks her way back to me.

"Sorry, what? You're handing in your notice? Surely not! It was only a misunderstanding."

"No. I'm not handing in my notice," I tell her. "I'm quitting. Right now."

She laughs like I'm having some crazy meltdown. "You can't just *quit*, Ella. We're struggling to cover shifts as it is! Why don't you take a tea break? Take five, chill out a bit, and forget it happened. A few crates of shortbreads aren't worth it."

Except they are. They're worth fucking everything right now.

Self-realisation is a portal that sucks me right up into itself, and there's a big mirror propped up in front of me. It shows me the girl I became on Connor's arm in vivid colours, run ragged as I tried to keep our world aligned. I'd been hiding it from everyone with smiles, corsets, and every shift at the store I could take. I've been fooling myself for years, just like I have with everyone else. I was nothing. I *became* nothing.

"Ella," Tracy says, interrupting my thoughts. "Calm down, will you? Sandra did probably get it wrong, ok?"

"No. *I* got it wrong by believing in this shit," I reply.

I'm out the back to the staffroom in seconds, grabbing my coat and bag as Tracy tries to catch up with me.

"ELLA!"

I take off my staff ID and toss it behind me at the doorway, focusing on the road that lies ahead, not the crappy job I'm leaving behind.

"ELLA!" I hear in the distance, but I don't care. I'm not going back there.

I'm on the tube when I message Ebony, hoping she's not with a client, because I need her. I need her right now.

Are you there?

A few seconds pass before she answers.

Yeah, I'm here. Jamie isn't back from playgroup yet. You ok? Aren't you at work today?

My fingers are shaking.

Not anymore, no. I just quit. I walked out of there without even handing in my notice. My manager was shouting my name, but I didn't go back.

I'm expecting some kind of dramatic reaction. Some OMG statement, with a load of emojis, or questions of *what the hell?!* But again, the universe is twisting on its axis. Ebony sends me a thumbs up and a smile.

Fuck, yes! You can concentrate on your real job now.

I rest my head back against the tube seat, trying to fathom the insanity of my new life. My *real* job. Being Holly the whore. I can't help but smile at the craziness of the prospect, because it's so damn appealing. Much better than an overworked, underpaid store assistant, taking any shift she can get.

Want a call? Ebony asks. *I've got a bit of time yet before I have to go on the pick-up run.*

Yes, please. When I get home, I reply, and with that my hands are on a mission, determined to quash my inner nerves before they get the chance to show their exploited, scared faces.

I go to the app. *Proposals.* What have I got coming in?

I flick through some standard new ones, but don't turn them down until I find a truly decent one. It landed in my inbox just an hour ago, and it makes me laugh out loud.

Fate is so ironic. What an apt time to get a proposal with a theme of *verbal disciplinary.*

This one won't be from a store boss, however. It'll be from a *daddy.*

User 762. Male. 51.

I want full roleplay, adlib and convincing. You'll be my daughter returning home after school, impudent after writing dirty stories in her notebook. You'll get found out by Daddy, and you'll get told off for it. You'll admit it's about a crush on a boy at school, and you'll let Daddy take your mind off him, and keep you as his sweet little girl.

Daddy will punish you for being naughty. A decent spanking, over the knee.

Daddy will show you what it feels like to be used and made to feel good in dirty ways, and he'll be much better at it than a silly little schoolboy.

You'll thank Daddy very much, and promise to be a well behaved daughter from now on, giving Daddy the love he needs from you. And then he'll give you bath time, put you to bed, and make you some breakfast before school in the morning. You'll kiss him goodbye when you leave.

Convincing actress, please. Schoolgirl outfit. Pigtails. White socks.

Oral, pussy, some anal play, bathing, spanking and being told off like a naughty bitch. An overnighter, sleeping in a girly bedroom.

Duration – 14 hours.

Proposal price – £5000.

Wow!

I read it through three times.

5k for an overnighter with *Daddy*. I force myself to think about it before I click accept on the proposal – I don't want a knee jerk reaction to walking out on my job.

Daddy play. Can I do it? Can I be that good an actress for 14 hours straight? Can I give a fifty-one-year-old *daddy* the love he wants from his naughty daughter?

I almost miss my tube stop, reading it through again. Overthinking might be my middle name with this one. I'm straight on a call to Ebony as soon as I get home. I tell her about Tracy and how much of a bitch she's been over Sandra ever since I've been there. It feels so good to vent to someone who isn't Connor, and who actually gives a shit for once.

I do an impression of Sandra twirling her hair for Billy in the forklift bay, and the stupid giggle she puts on when she's flirting. *Hell, yeah, Billy. Take command of that gear stick, baby.* Ebony is pissing herself laughing.

"Holy shit, Ella, you should be an actress. I can practically see her, the snarky little cow."

An actress.

Those words snap me right back to my proposal from earlier.

"Funny you should say that..."

I read out the proposal and she nods along, tipping her head this way and that. She doesn't freak out or think a 14-hour session is that weird or anything. In fact, she says sleepovers are pretty common.

"Sounds good to me," she says. "I'm sure you can handle it easy."

I wish I was as certain as she was. Her faith in me is astounding. I let out a breath, the reality of my job loss creeping up to bite at me.

"What if I fuck it up?"

"Fuck up Daddy play? Babe, you're smashing it. Every single review coming in is off the charts."

"But if I fuck it up now..."

"Ah, yeah," she says. "More pressure. I get it. So many entertainers spend ages trying to multitask when they're first getting started, scared their client list is going to dry up. That's totally normal. But you've got to have belief in yourself. You're soaring high for a reason."

"Thanks."

"But?" she asks, my expression clearly not convincing enough.

I sigh. "Taking a man mountain, or two cocks, or freaky period play, that shit came easy because I really was into it. Pretending to be a schoolgirl right the way overnight is a whole other ball game. I'm not so sure."

"Trust me," she says, waving a finger, "I can see you now, in pigtails and uniform, acting all coy for Daddy."

I stick my thumb in my mouth and pull a face.

Ebony laughs. "There you go, you're getting it already. Daddys gonna love you. I mean it. Don't look down, girl. Click accept on that proposal and find yourself a pair of cute white socks. The sooner the better. Go on," she says. "Do it now. Click yes, and get cracking."

I call up the proposal window.

Can I do this? 14 hours of roleplay?

Only one way to find out.

Self-doubt can stay back in the Christmas aisle – I'm not putting up with that shit anymore.

"Done," I tell Ebony. "Wednesday night, as soon as I'm off my period."

"Great stuff. The sooner the better."

She's right on that. Less time for the nerves to make a reappearance. I'll be a very good actress for User 762. Maybe I can even practice in the meantime. Say Daddy as sweetly as I can in the mirror. I smile as I imagine it. I'm sure I could come up with some cracking lines, all set for *adlib*, when I need them.

"It's great to see you coming to life, Ella," Ebony says. "Seriously. You're glowing brighter every single day."

She's right. I am. I just have to believe in myself.

Watch out, *Creamgirl*, I'm coming for you. And I'll be coming for *Daddy* in the meantime.

twelve

User 762. Male. 51.
I want full roleplay, adlib and convincing. You'll be my daughter returning home after school, impudent after writing dirty stories in her notebook. You'll get found out by Daddy, and you'll get told off for it. You'll admit it's about a crush on a boy at school, and you'll let Daddy take your mind off him, and keep you as his sweet little girl.
Daddy will punish you for being naughty. A decent spanking, over the knee.
Daddy will show you what it feels like to be used and made to feel good in dirty ways, and he'll be much better at it than a silly little schoolboy.
You'll thank Daddy very much, and promise to be a well behaved daughter from now on, giving Daddy the love he needs from you. And then he'll give you bath time, put you to bed, and make you some breakfast before school in the morning. You'll kiss him goodbye when you leave.
Convincing actress, please. Schoolgirl outfit. Pigtails. White socks.
Oral, pussy, some anal play, bathing, spanking and being told off like a naughty bitch. An overnighter, sleeping in a girly bedroom.
Duration – 14 hours.
Proposal price – £5000.

All my confidence-boosting mirror rehearsals over the past few days mean nothing whatsoever. I'm a nervous wreck as I get dressed up in my fake school uniform, shaking as I knot my tie.

One whole night playing *Daddy's girl* feels terrifying, like I'm going to goof up the very moment I step in through User 762's front door. I can't shake off the nerves. I haven't played a role since drama class at high school, let alone maintaining a character for 14 hours straight.

I've looked up User 762's address – outside the city in a posh village suburb. Daddy will be expecting the best from his pretend daughter, and can I deliver that? Really? I'm not so sure I can.

I send a message to Ebony.

I'm crapping myself.

I see the typing icon in return.

You'll smash it. Don't worry. It's your first all-nighter, so freaking out is usual. Plus, it's roleplay, so cut yourself some slack. The nerves will ease off once you get there. Believe in yourself!

I wish I had even an ounce of her faith.

I bought myself a genuine school blazer ready for this role, but feel like a fraud as I put it on. I put a long coat on over my *uniform*, but it doesn't hide my knee-high white socks and Mary Janes. Just as well I booked a cab. There's no way I'd be up for taking the tube. I'd feel every pair of eyes on me, every step of the way.

I tell myself I'm overthinking it. That people wouldn't even notice. Still, rationality means nothing when nerves are sparking through your entire body.

I'm already waiting outside when the cab shows up, with my backpack slung over my shoulder. I slip into the back seat with a forced smile as I give the address to the driver. I'm fidgeting and shifting in my seat as soon as he pulls away, and trying to distract myself with the view from the window doesn't help any. The bustle of streets are nothing but a blur.

My fingers are so jittery I have to twist them in my lap, or I'll bite my nails to shit.

It's about thirty minutes later that the bustle of London city truly eases. The calmness of the surroundings gives me a fresh bout of jitters.

It's been a fair while now since I've been out of central London. Being in the city with Connor has always felt alien, ever since we moved. The landscape of standard suburbia feels way more at home.

Home.

How ironic.

"Had a good day at school?" the driver asks, finally breaking the silence.

I look down and find my coat has fallen open, revealing my crested tie. Shit.

"Um, yeah, thanks."

He smiles in the rearview mirror.

"I used to be a goth at college."

I could laugh, honestly. He really believes I'm a goth student, fresh out of college. Thumbs up on the appearance front for me. I try to use it as ammunition to quell my nerves.

"You grew out of it, then?"

"Yeah. My parents used to kick off at me headbanging to Cradle of Filth every bloody day in my bedroom. Got older and kind of drifted out of it, you know?"

No, I don't know. I grin anyway, and use it as practice.

"It's hard when you play up for your parents, right?"

"Too right. They were always on my case."

I bet your dad didn't spank you over his knee, though.

We talk about goth and metal bands, and I focus in on him, trying to relieve the pressure. It works, kind of, until I see the signs for *Wrensham*.

"Almost home," the driver says, and fuck, the houses are even bigger than I thought. I see the sign for User 762's road, and tell the driver to stop here, at the end of the street.

"Can you wait a second, please?" I ask.

He must think I'm a total weirdo as I scrabble for two scrunchies from my backpack and put my hair up into pigtails. He doesn't say another word as I pay him in cash and give him a *thanks*, climbing out with my heart racing. He shoots me a weird glance through the window as he turns and drives away.

Shit. It's really happening.

I can see *Daddy's* house up in the corner of the cul-de-sac. I've scoped it out a billion times on street view.

My legs are wobbly, but I force myself to walk ahead. Every step feels like a mile, my feet feel so heavy. Reaching *Daddy's* driveway has me shaking like a leaf, so I keep my eyes focused on the doorway in front of me as I pass his Merc parked outside. I click on *arrived*, to tell him I'm here. The instructions come through in return.

Door is open. Welcome home, darling.

Darling... I'm his little darling. My God, part of me wants to walk away.

I remind myself that I can walk away at any time I want to. There's 5k up for grabs here. Least I can do is try.

My hand is shaking when I reach the door and clutch the handle. I count down from five and paste a smile on my face, swinging the door open and stepping inside.

I'm expecting posh, but whoa, User 762's house is like something from an interior design magazine, light and minimalistic. There's a huge gloss white kitchen at the end of the hallway. It has a huge kitchen island with a breakfast bar, and all the appliances are jet black. Daddy is definitely loaded, and he definitely has style.

I drop my backpack on the floor by the front door, and kick my shoes off on autopilot, then hang my coat up on the coat rack as my senses reel.

I jump as a voice sounds out from above, at the top of the stairs.

"Hey, sweetheart. How was your day?"

Somehow I manage to keep my voice steady as I answer him.

"Hi, Dad. It was good thanks." I revert to my practiced lines. "Mrs Evans was a bitch today, but that's normal."

I'm open mouthed when the User 762 appears on the landing. *Daddy* is fucking gorgeous, and I mean gorgeous. He makes his way down the stairs, eyes on me, a pleasant smile on his face. He may be in his early fifties, but it couldn't suit him any better. He's got salt and pepper hair, with a decent amount of mahogany brown shining through. His beard is trimmed, and his eyes are bright green, and he's tall, and muscular, wearing a tailored suit like it's the most regular thing in the world.

He comes to a stop at the bottom of the stairs and looks me up and down with a grin, and he's a great actor, but still, I see a flash of pure lust in his eyes. He swallows, and his gaze holds too long, meeting mine like he wants to devour me right here and now.

I'm in a crazy surreal dimension. A weirdo like me, being wanted so much by a guy like him.

Daddy smells incredible as he approaches and leans in for a kiss. I figure it'll be on the lips, but no, it's on the cheek, but he lingers... just a little. I feel his breath on my ear, and smell the cologne on his neck, deep and musky.

"What do you want to drink?" he asks me. "Cordial or juice?"

I follow him through to the kitchen like a lamb on unsteady legs.

"Juice, please." I almost forget I'm in role. "*Dad*," I add, but it's too late, and he flashes me a look, acknowledging my error.

He has fire in him. I can sense it.

"Sit," he says and I hitch my ass onto a stool at the island.

He pours me a juice from the fridge and sets it down in front of me.

"Thanks, Daddy," I say and he watches me as I take a sip. I feel so on display.

"Holly," he says. "We need to talk."

"Talk, Daddy? What do you mean?"

He places his hands on the kitchen island, towering tall. "I was in your room earlier, collecting your laundry, and I saw your gym bag. It was open."

I play along with raised eyebrows.

"It was open?"

"Yes. It was open. And you know what was in there, don't you?"

This must be the incident the proposal was talking about. I look down at my juice like I've had a secret uncovered, turning the glass on the counter.

He sighs at me. "Holly, look. I love you, you know that. I've supported you through everything, and always will, you know that, too. But, sweetheart. You've been a bad, bad girl." He pauses. "I saw your notebook."

I force myself to meet his eyes, and when I do, I'm transfixed. He's so in role, it's incredible, and it touches something in me. My heart is pounding to a different kind of tune, and I sink deeper into fake Holly's skin – the naughty daughter. It creeps up from my toes in a prickle of shivers. Looking at *Daddy* makes it so easy...

"You saw my notebook?"

He's well prepared, taking a book from the counter behind him and slamming it down in front of me, open on the first page. He flicks through the contents as I watch – dirty drawings, and poems of filth. Doodles of smutty content, and one name amongst it all...

Scott.

I take the notebook from him, fascinated.

"I thought you were over this?" Daddy says. "I thought we'd worked this through."

I let my instincts take over. My words come naturally.

"We had, Daddy, I just..."

"Just what, Holly?"

"I just... couldn't help myself."

He puts his hands on his hips. "Have you been touching yourself again?"

My cheeks are genuinely burning up. I nod, but that's not enough.

"Tell me, Holly," he says. "Have you been touching yourself?"

I take a breath. "Yes, Daddy. I have."

"And thinking about Scott while you're doing it?"

I look at my *daddy* and nod.

"Yes."

That enflames him. He shakes his head in fiery disappointment.

"You know Scott is a delinquent. You know you shouldn't be anywhere near him." His stare is so brutal. "I thought you'd learnt your lesson. I was hoping for better than this. I was hoping, *hoping,* I'd got it wrong when I saw this piece of filth in your bedroom. But I haven't, have I? You're still being a bad girl."

I feel his anger as though it's real. I feel guilt inside as though it's reality, and it makes it so easy... so easy to sink into the role.

"No, Daddy, you haven't got it wrong. I'm sorry. I've been being bad for months again. And I wanted to tell you. I did."

"But you DIDN'T. Why not? You know I'd have *helped* you."

My eyes flash up to his. *Helped.* I know what Daddy means. I get a flutter between my thighs and a twist of nerves in my stomach, but they aren't such bad nerves anymore. They're morphing into something else. Just a shiver...

"You know I'm scared when you help me," I tell him, my voice shaky, "It hurts so bad."

"Punishment always does, Holly, but it's needed. We always need to accept the consequences of our choices. You know this."

Time for a taste of the *impudence* he wanted. I summon it from the depths.

"Look. I won't do it again, ok? I know it's bad, but I'll stop it, alright?"

He sighs a heartfelt sigh. "You said that last time."

"Yeah, and I *mean* it this time."

His expression darkens. "So you were lying last time, is that what you're saying?"

"NO! I'm not saying that."

"You're contradicting yourself, you dirty girl, and you know what? That's only going to make your punishment more extreme."

"DADDY!"

He points a finger at me. "Stop it with the attitude, right fucking now."

I look at him as though it's a stand-off, but we both know who's going to win here, real or not. This space, this fantasy, this *game* – everything is growing blurry, and reality is coming to mean nothing. I'm becoming Holly the schoolgirl. I feel her guilt, and fear, and the want under the surface... and it's weird as fuck, but so good.

In fact, it's a filthy relief.

I relax. I breathe. I let my inner sensations guide me.

Impudence. I need to push him some more.

"Come on, Dad. I've said sorry! Don't make a big deal about it."

"A big fucking deal?" He smacks the island with his hand and it makes me jump. "Young lady, you disappoint me, you know that?"

I don't reply, just turn my attention to my glass of juice, pick it up and take a sip.

I nearly choke when he slaps the counter again.

"I asked you a fucking question, girl!"

His voice is so deep, so menacing, I can't even remember the fucking question.

I give him a sad face. "Sorry, Daddy."

"Tell me what you're sorry for."

Shit. "I'm sorry for... being dirty."

"You weren't even listening, were you?"

I shake my head in shame.

He sighs again. "I said, you *disappoint* me."

"I'm sorry," I tell him, "I don't mean to."

"Yes, well, you need to learn your lesson."

He points over to the dining table, a huge monster of glass and deep blue resin.

"Stand over there," he tells me. "Contemplate your punishment and how much you deserve it."

I'm trembling bad again as I get down from the barstool. I gaze up at him with wide eyes.

"If I take my punishment like a good girl, do you think you could make it nice, like you do sometimes? Please. It helps the pain."

He takes off his suit jacket, laying it neatly on the counter. He rolls up his crisp white shirt sleeves as I watch him. His forearms are lean and veiny. Muscular enough to pack one hell of a punch – or smack.

"You want me to touch you while I punish you?" The fire is still burning in his eyes. "I'm not sure you deserve that."

"Please, Daddy. You know it takes my mind off Scott when you do that. It'll help, I promise."

"I'm not sure I can believe your promises today."

I'm feeling young Holly's need churning in my stomach. I'm as desperate for it as she is. The man before me holds his stare, so firm. It gives me another flutter between my legs, and I'm sure the plain white panties I'm wearing must be soaking through. Nerves make no odds. My pussy is still wet for him.

"We'll see how well you behave during your punishment," he says. "If you're good enough, you'll get a reward."

"Thank you, Daddy."

I smile as meekly as I can, then I walk slowly to the position he wants me in, feeling his eyes on me with every step. I stand next to the head of the table in an instinctive position, head bowed and hands behind my back.

Daddy leaves me waiting there, horny tension like a cloud in the air between us. I'm shuffling, fear and want mixing and twisting as I imagine what's ahead for me. I don't dare look at him, holding my position like a good girl. My breaths hitch as I finally hear him approach. He pulls out the dining chair beside me, taking a seat.

"Come and take your punishment."

I lower myself gently across his thighs, and he hauls me into place. My ass is in prime position for a spanking, and my front half is dangling, pigtails hanging down around my face. I can only just reach the floor on tiptoes, balanced precariously. Every slap is going to jolt me like hell.

I know he can feel me trembling. I whimper as he lifts up my school skirt, remembering how hard he slapped the countertop. I close my eyes as he tugs my panties down around my thighs.

"You're wet," he says. "Dirty girl."

I feel like one. I feel so dirty over Daddy's knee that my clit is sparking like crazy.

"Sorry, Daddy."

"Oh, you will be," he says as he massages my ass cheeks. I'm so pleased when I feel the swell of him through his trousers, the bulge of his crotch pressing into my stomach.

It gives me confidence. A bloom of pride.

"I'm a dirty girl," I tell him. "I deserve to be punished."

His first hard blow makes me lurch forward so far, I'm scared of losing my balance, but he yanks me back into position and holds me steady, with an arm heavy against my back as he begins the assault in earnest.

I yelp with every smack, and fuck, my ass cheeks sting as he slaps me like I'm a criminal.

"Dirty girl," he says. "You deserve this."

My *owws* aren't fake in the slightest as I gasp and moan. His palm is a beast, with huge strikes, so fierce that he's grunting as he rains my punishment on me. My ass must be so pink and exposed. I feel weirdly shy at the thought.

My whimpers come so naturally. My words are nothing but the truth. *Daddy, ah! Ow! Daddy, it hurts!*

"Take it," he says, and hits me even harder.

My pigtails swish with every strike, my tie dangling and my tits bouncing. I can't stay still as he hurts me – squirming on his lap – and his bulge against my stomach gets harder with every strike. But then the inevitable happens... the sensation I know so well...

Slowly, *slowly*, the burn of my slapped ass turns to a beautiful, hot tingle, and my squeals of *ow* turn to shuddering moans.

I need more.

"Keep going, Daddy, please. Make me pay for being so naughty."

"Don't worry, sweetheart. I've only just started."

His words make me smile like my horny self, nerves fading away.

I relax over his lap, giving up control fully and completely as he tugs my panties down to my knees and switches his slaps to my thighs – fresh skin ready to burn and tingle. He spanks me like I deserve it. A deep rhythm of punishment that is enough to make me heady. Softly, I drift into the space between pleasure and pain. A place in my inner mind where all that matters is submission.

I'm giving myself over to a higher power, and that power is Daddy.

I take everything he has to give. So many slaps, my skin is on fire.

He's breathing so hard from the blows that he's almost panting when he speaks next. "Open your legs for me now, Holly. Let me make it feel good for you."

"Thank you, Daddy," I say as I spread my thighs as far as my stretched panties will allow.

I must be so fucking slick as he strokes his fingers over my pussy. He catches my clit like a pro, and I moan, wriggling against his touch as he plays.

"You'd better start saying thank you for this," he says. "Remember your manners, and ask nicely."

"Thank you, Daddy. Please don't stop. I love it when you put fingers inside me. Please do that. I'm going to be a very, very good girl."

He teases me by rubbing the tips of his fingers against my slit. "Are you going to show me how grateful you are after?"

"Of course, Daddy. I'll be grateful enough to do anything you want. Anything."

"Good girl."

He plunges three fingers straight inside me. It feels like pure fucking bliss as he pumps them deep, and I know I must be soaking his trousers.

I can hear my pussy squelching, my ass prickling raw from his slaps. A filthy combination. His arm is still heavy on my back, keeping me firmly in position, and I can't escape the building pleasure. I can't hold myself back – he's just too good.

"Daddy, you're going to make me come," I whimper.

"I know, sweetheart," he says. "And this is how it's always going to be, remember? Nobody else is allowed to touch you other than Daddy. Say it."

The words feel strange but beautifully perverse.

"You're going to be the only one to touch me, Daddy. I don't want anyone else. Not ever."

I tense up as he uses my pussy deeper, pushing back against his fingers. He has my whole body thrumming, alive. And yes, he has me. He has me... I'm dripping wet and moaning like a dirty little bitch as I buckle and come over Daddy's knees in my school uniform, and I don't care how filthy this game is anymore – God help me, I love it. I love his voice as he encourages me, telling me how much *Daddy loves me* as I crest and squirm.

"Good girl, Holly. That's it. I know Daddy's the one you want. Nobody else will ever touch you like this."

I'm rippling with shudders in the aftermath, and he massages my ass cheeks on my come down. I'm draped limp, floating high on endorphins when he gives me a token pat on the ass.

"I think it's time for you to show Daddy just how much you love him back, don't you?"

I'm still buzzing as he drops me from his lap, coaxing me onto my knees between his legs. I know what I need to do. My mouth is watering as he unbuckles his belt and frees himself from his suit trousers.

Daddy's cock is as gorgeous as the rest of him. Thick, long and veined. He's already dripping wet down the length of him.

I'm ravenous as he guides my mouth to him, licking up his dripping precum in one sweet lap of my tongue before slurping up him and down him like the good girl I promised to be. I want to please my daddy. I want to show him how much Holly loves him.

Daddy takes hold of my pigtails, tight to my head. "All the way in, like I taught you."

I take Daddy's cock so deep that I have to fight back the retches. I look up at him through watery eyes, smiling up at the filthy man staring down at me. I take him right to the back of my throat as he watches me, urging me on with soft dirty words.

"That's good, sweetheart... suck Daddy's cock as hard as you can."

I work my mouth up and down him, keeping my eyes wide on his.

"Harder, sweetheart. Suck harder for Daddy."

I do as I'm told, and suck as hard as I can until I feel the tension in him. I see it in his bright green eyes. I'm already moaning around his cock, wanting his cum, but he stops himself and pushes me away far enough to pat his knees.

"Panties off, Holly. Give Daddy your sweet little cunt now."

It should feel wrong, but it doesn't. It feels so right my soul is singing in the pits of me. I tug my panties down and I'm straight up onto Daddy's lap, still in my school uniform and truly feeling the part as I lower myself onto his wet cock.

"So tight," he says, grabbing my hips and forcing me all the way onto him. "Beautiful."

"Thank you, Daddy," I say, and I really mean it.

I can't help moving on his cock, it feels so good, but he stops me, forces me back down.

"Keep still," he says, and I feel the pulse of his cock inside me as he unbuttons my school blouse. His eyes light up and he runs his tongue across his lower lip when he sees my cute, plain white bra with pretty pink bows on the side. I chose the most innocent looking one I could find.

His small nod confirms how pleased he his. He takes his time, freeing up one tit first, and my breaths are coming heavy as he strokes my nipple.

"Look at the way your nipple gets hard for Daddy," he says, "Does it feel good, sweetheart?"

"Yes, Daddy. It does feel good." I almost add, *so does your thick cock buried deep inside me. Please fuck me, Daddy.* The urge to ride him is intense. But I say nothing and do nothing as he frees up my other tit. He plays with both nipples, pinching and rolling.

"You're such a gorgeous little girl, Holly."

"Thank you, Daddy," I tell him then moan and can't hold back as he twists my nipples hard.

This time he doesn't still me. He smiles lovingly at me.

"You may use Daddy's cock," he says.

With my hands on his shoulders and my tits bouncing in his face, I ride him – *Daddy*.

I ride my daddy and I really do feel like a horny schoolgirl.

Daddy laps at my tits, catches my nipples in his teeth and starts bucking back into me and it's fucking heaven.

"Fuck me, Daddy," I tell him and he does.

He's in the flow as deep as I am, bucking right back up at me. I'm bouncing like a doll on his lap as he gets ready to unload, and with panting breaths he gives me another instruction. One that has me reeling...

"Kiss Daddy, now. Kiss your dirty daddy and tell me how much you love me."

The words are obscene, but weirdly powerful.

"I love you so much, Daddy," I tell him, and then I press my lips to his.

His kiss is deep, his tongue is demanding, and I'm all into the motions as he slams up, up, up to come inside me. I could kiss my *daddy* for ever. Filthy as sin, but true. So fucking true.

I feel like a mess when he's finished coming – my head spinning with how roleplay like this can feel so real, and so disgustingly good.

"My gorgeous girl," he says, as he strokes my cheek.

I take a few seconds, smiling at him, both of us caught in the glow.

I don't want it to end yet.

I wrap my arms around him, pressing my bare tits to his shirt and tie as I snuggle into his neck like he's my world. He strokes my back like he's soothing me, his cock still inside me, and it's fucked up, but it's gorgeous.

"Time to get you some dinner, I think," he says after a few minutes, but I don't want dinner. I want more fun with him, more filth with him, more praise from him.

Yet again, I have to remind myself... this is about him, User 762, not about me. The thought is a flood of reality that stabs.

I pull away with a meek smile.

"Thanks, Daddy."

I rise from him and follow him over to the breakfast bar, my blouse still open as I take my seat.

"I'll make you your favourite, since you've been a good girl." He smiles. "Would you like that?"

"Yes, please," I say and wonder what my favourite is.

He heads over to the big fridge and brings out an oven dish, filled with something.

"Chicken casserole. I prepared it earlier, hoping you would behave well."

"Yummy," I say, and my word choice seems to please him.

There is so much I want to ask *Daddy* as the casserole cooks in the oven, but he keeps in character. I make up imaginary tales about my school day, and he keeps up the pretence, giving me fatherly advice about staying out of trouble. My adlib wants to fuck off and ask him who he really is outside of his fantasies. Who is User 762? What does he do? What does he like outside of schoolgirl play?

But it's none of my damn business.

We eat chicken casserole at the table together, and it's delicious, suited to the rest of him. He pours red wine for himself and juice for me.

"Thank you so much for making my favourite," I tell him, "it tastes so good."

He raises his glass to me. "Thank you, sweetheart. You deserve it for serving Daddy's cock so well."

Absurd, I know, but I'm blushing like crazy.

He brings me a chocolate mousse for dessert and watches me eat it with a sparkle in his eyes.

"It's almost bath time," he says.

His eyes are on mine, watching for my reaction, but I don't have to act. He must see the lust there.

"Bath time is my favourite time of all," I tell him, "I love it when you wash me."

I don't have to wait long. He's already rising from his seat as I lick the last of the chocolate mousse from my spoon.

Fuck, how my pussy is fluttering as I walk up those stairs behind him.

The bathroom is big and bright, and the tub itself is big enough for four people.

He pulls up a stool while the bath is running and I stand before him as he slowly undresses me, casting my clothes aside until I'm naked.

His eyes rove over me and my nipples are hard all over again.

"Such a beautiful girl," he says, gently tracing his fingers over my tits, my nipples, down over my hips. "I'm truly blessed."

My smile is genuine. I feel weirdly proud.

I gasp when he slides a finger between my legs and rubs it into my pussy lips, so wet with juices and cum.

"I love you, Daddy," I tell him, the words coming naturally.

He looks me in the eye, wipes his wet finger over my nipple. "And I love you, sweetheart."

He finishes seeing to the bath water, turns off the taps and picks up a sponge.

"In you get," he says.

With one hand on his shoulder, I step into the bath and settle down onto my knees. The tub is so huge, I feel really small as Daddy takes out my pigtails and shampoos and conditions my hair. He squirts bodywash onto the sponge and soaps my shoulders and down my arms, but I can't hold back. I'm arching my back in the water when he finally soaps my tits, offering them up to him in pure, filthy desire – and under the facade he must be as needy as I am.

The game play tumbles and falls into nothing but raw lust.

Daddy loses his composure, dropping himself forward into the bath with me – fuck his tie and shirt getting soaked. His mouth is on my tits, sucking, and we're a tangle, getting in position. I twist myself so my legs are over the edge of the bath, spreading my thighs as wide as they'll go, and my daddy gets me off all over again, rubbing my clit until I'm a moaning slut, desperate for play.

"Oh, Daddy, I need you inside me again, please! Please!"

I'm not lying. I do.

"Get out of the bath," he says, and hauls me out of there, dropping me onto my feet.

I reach for him again, dripping wet, not giving a shit about the towel he wraps around me. I want him. All of him. My arms wrap around his neck, hair hanging loose and dripping as I kiss him.

His big hands take hold of my ass cheeks and he lifts me up into his arms and I'm still kissing him as he carries me across the landing. He drops me down onto a bed in a room off to the side, and joins me on the pretty pink bedding, both of us still soaked and past caring. And there, on clinging wet sheets, my daddy fucks me again. Harder this time. More feral.

So much for sleep tonight. It's not going to happen.

I'm dribbling Daddy's cum when he gets between my legs and I open for him. He looks so damn proud, so loving as he stares at me, as he strokes me gently from my tender clit to my needy asshole, over and over and Christ almighty, I'm so in the dirty daughter zone it's unreal as he stares adoringly, stroking my clit, my pussy lips, my asshole. The tingles and sparks are off the scale, and I just know he's going to fuck me senseless.

"I'm so fortunate," he says, his finger circling my dirty hole, "so fortunate to have such a loving daughter."

I want to tell him to fuck my ass, but no, I play my part. "I'm the fortunate one," I tell him, "I've got the best daddy in the whole world."

With a heartfelt sigh, he slides that one finger into my ass and I moan for him.

"You like that, little one?" he asks and I nod.

"It feels so nice when you do that. I like it a lot."

"More?" he asks.

"Yes, please, Daddy."

He pushes two fingers in and twists them deep.

"More, Daddy," I tell him and he does. Three fingers and I whimper for him.

"Such a good girl," he says and I whimper again when he finger-fucks my ass.

That's enough to have him rising to his knees and pushing my legs back, his big cock hard once more. I'm desperate for it all over again, turned on like nothing I've known before.

"Fuck me, Daddy," I say.

He dips his head, drops a kiss on my clit, another on my pussy lips, and another on my asshole, and my God it takes everything not to jump up and ravish him.

"Please, Daddy. Please. I need you inside me."

"I love you so, so much," he says and sinks his cock into my sopping wet pussy.

"I love you so much, too, Daddy," I tell him and he fucks me hard. Pins me and fucks me and doesn't stop until he comes again.

And so it continues, we fuck on wet bedsheets for hours, through so many different flavours. From loving, gentle missionary, to rough doggy, to the filth of *Daddy* forcing his fingers into his naughty girl's asshole.

I love every single second of it.

He's holding me as the first hint of dawn lightens the room, and I'm smiling against his naked chest. I could be this version of Holly for ever.

He lets out a long sigh and strokes my hair.

"One last time before breakfast," he says and my heart leaps and so does my pussy.

But no.

"Pigtails in, please," he says and he's dangling my two scrunchies before my eyes.

I obey, pigtails in, and I realise what he wants when pulls the covers back and nudges me down there, opening his legs.

"Suck Daddy's cock like the good daughter you really are," he says, "and I want my cum all over your sweet face."

"Of course, Daddy."

My pussy is disappointed, but still. I'm more than happy to suck his cock. Happy to see my daddy moaning and groaning every time I retch.

"Now, little one," he says, "do it now!"

I pull away and jerk his cock fast, mouth wide, tongue out, and I take three spurts of cum across the face before the last spurts fill my mouth.

I lick him clean. I even scoop the cum from my face with my fingers and lick those clean, too.

"You're the best daughter a man could ever hope for," he says, stroking my hair.

"You're amazing too, Daddy. You're the best there could be," I tell him and I mean it.

"I'm proud of you, Holly," he says, "you've been such a good girl."

I actually feel proud. How about that!?

"Time for breakfast," he says, and my stomach lurches. I don't want cereals. I want him. "Come on, sweetheart," he coaxes. "Daddy can't be late for work and you can't be late for school."

Call in sick, I want to say. *Call in sick and fuck me again for free.* But I can't. It's against the rules.

"Shower first," he says, but he doesn't join me. He stands outside the shower, ready with a big towel, watching me as I soap myself up and rinse off. It could have been creepy, but it isn't. I step out, squeaky clean and smiling, and loving it when he wraps me in the towel and pats me dry.

"Good girl," he says and drops a kiss on my cheek, "get dressed and I'll go get the toast on."

I eat toast as well as frosted flakes, back in my role as he wishes me a good day at school, telling me once again to stay away from Scott.

"Yes, Daddy, I promise I will."

I drink juice while he drinks coffee, and I gather my things when he leaves for his pre-office shower.

Damn it. I call a cab when he's out of view, hating how fucking sad I sound when I give the operator the address.

It's strange how reality can take a total 180 in the blink of an eye.

I was quaking with nerves when the cab dropped me off at the bottom of User 762's road, and now it's the total opposite. I'm dreading the thought of being driven away.

I'm waiting with my backpack over my shoulder when he reappears, hair still damp, looking and smelling so damn good.

"I don't want to go to school today," I tell him, "I don't feel so good." I put a hand on my tummy.

He laughs at that. "Nice try," he says, "like I haven't heard that one before. Nice touch, in fact, Holly. You really have gone above and beyond. Thank you."

"Thank you, Daddy," I say, staying in character for him.

A toot of a horn tells me my taxi has arrived.

It's with a heavy heart that I step up to him and he leans down to accept my peck on the lips.

"Seriously," I say, "thank you."

He winks, pats my ass.

"Off you go, and work hard at school."

"I will," I tell him and head for the door, stepping outside into cold reality.

"You ok, love?" the cab driver asks me as I slide into the back seat. "You look a bit... dazed."

"Just woke up," I tell him. *And missing my daddy already.*

I tell myself it's just my job.

And what a crazy fucking job it's turning out to be.

thirteen

Ebony sees I'm online. A message pings through as my cab arrives back in London.

How was it? Did you like being naughty little Holly all night long?

She has no idea how much I liked it. My stomach is still churning with the want, *need,* to go back there right now, to *Daddy's* house. The thought of him is still so alive in my head it's making me dizzy.

User 762 was such a powerful figure. So caring, but so stern. So loving, but so commanding. The thought that it's over now – after just one single night – feels wrong. Again, oh the irony.

It's fucked up on so many levels, but my emotions are singing to a crazy, frazzled tune.

I loved it, it was weirdly amazing, I tell her, but what I really want to say is I loved *him*. I loved Holly's *daddy.*

And... her next message says.

I'm still trying to find the words to describe it, how to even begin. I type and delete, type and delete. How the hell do I say it? I'm crazy about a stranger I met last night.

She must see my stilted typing.

Are you struggling? Morning after syndrome?

I look at her message, puzzled.

What's morning after syndrome?

The cab pulls up at my place. It looks like more of a shithole than ever after the beauty of *Daddy's*. I don't even want to go in.

I'm stood looking at the wooden door, with its chipped black paint and loose handle when my phone buzzes with Ebony's next message.

Morning after syndrome. It's a term we use. Look it up in the chatroom, or I'll give you a call about it, if you like? I've just got in from an all-nighter with Mr Medic, and Stephen's done the school run.

Great, thanks, I say. *Give me five.*

At least it gives me the impetus to go inside.

I grab a glass of water from our gross excuse for a kitchen, stacked high with dirty plates, then head up to my room. I toss my backpack and coat aside and throw myself down on my bed.

Urgh.

I stare up at the ceiling, still in pigtails and my school uniform, already pining another round in Wrenshaw.

I want *Daddy* again.

I reach my laptop from the dressing table when Ebony's call starts pinging through. I'm virtually lying down when I click answer, and she does a double take. My pigtails must be sprawled across my pillows.

"Holy fuck, Ella. You make a convincing schoolgirl. I wondered if it was really you then."

My laugh is shallow. "Yeah, well, I wish it was convincing enough to be true right now. I'd love some more time as young Holly the naughty schoolgirl."

She sighs, her eyes scoping mine out through the screen.

"You missing him? Did you want to stay?"

"Want the honest answer?"

"Always, yeah."

I place a hand on my stomach. It's still churning. My brain is still trying to process things, like a spiral of a whirlwind, everything out of control.

"I swear to God, Eb, I didn't want to leave, and how I have, I feel sick. Like a pang, right here."

I point to my sternum, where the ball of aching want is.

"Yep," she says. "You've got morning after syndrome. It happens, don't worry. You're a newbie. Everything is intense. So many sessions will feel like they mean something. Totally normal."

I think of Daddy holding me in his arms last night and telling me what a good girl I am. It makes the aching ball in my ribs pang even harder.

"We were so up close," I tell her. "It felt so real. Not like in the proposal."

She looks confused by that. "It wasn't like the proposal? Did he tweak it, or offer additional terms or something? What happened?"

That's when it occurs to me. It didn't deviate at all from the proposal. It was exactly as he said it would be, it was just more heated… more real… more intimate. But that's *my* take, not his. To him it was probably just a game. He's probably played it a hundred times over. It likely meant fuck all. *I* meant fuck all.

The very thought of that hurts.

I sigh. "No, actually, it was exactly like the proposal. It's just weirded me out."

"Yeah," she says. "Morning after syndrome. It feels like it was real. It's ok, babe. It happens, all the time. You'll get used to it, and then it eases off again. Clients blur, roleplay becomes easier, less personal."

I look away from the screen. I'm not convinced.

"Ella," she says. "Listen to me. It's normal. Look it up in the chatroom. Morning after syndrome."

"Ok, I will."

"What was he like?" she asks. "He must have been quite a guy to get you this caught up in him."

I tell her about my night with Dadd–, no. No! He's User 762. I tell Ebony about my night with *User 762.* Because that's what he is. He's a client. He's not my daddy.

I have a daddy of my own in Australia, and I've never, ever, EVER in a million years contemplated getting off on fake daddy play, the proposal would have likely squicked me the hell out if it wasn't for the 5k on offer.

Wait… about the 5k…

I check the funds are in my account, and they are, minus the agency cut. Plus there's a bonus. An extra 1k. Fucking hell.

My eyebrows shoot up.

"What?" Ebony asks.

"He's given me a bonus."

"Great stuff! You might well be seeing him again, then. Another night with *Daddy* might well be on the horizon."

I'm still staring at my bank account balance. It's easily as surreal as the lovesick puppy feelings in my gut. I have money. Real money. The balance is healthy beyond healthy.

"Has your review come in yet?" Ebony asks. "If he's given you that much of a bonus, I guess it will be top marks."

I'm scared to look, in case it's not. Any criticism of last night would feel like a punch in the ribs.

Ebony's stare is quite something onscreen when I meet her eyes again. She looks as though she's worried I'm ill.

"I don't need hospital or anything." I laugh, trying to make light of it. "I'm sure I'll survive."

"Yeah, I know that, but this isn't like you. He's really had an impact."

"Sure. *Morning after syndrome*, like you said."

"Exactly. It can hit like a slammer."

"I'll look it up in the chatroom," I tell her, but she doesn't seem to believe me.

"People always say that, then they wallow for days."

I feel like a criminal caught in the act, because that's what I want to do. Wallow in memories of my fake daddy for days, still lying here in my pigtails. The realisation is so dumbass that my rationality switches back on, at least just a little.

Daddy was a client. For one night. I don't even know his name.

I now have thousands extra in my bank account and should be dancing around the room, not maudling in a fake school uniform, panicking that I didn't land an A++ in my review. *School report.* Ha.

"That's good," Ebony says, when she sees the glint of a smile on my face. "I thought you might be stalking out Wrenshaw from how you were acting."

"I'm not that bad!"

"Yeah, well, I wasn't so sure." She fake wipes her forehead with a *phew,* and I see the genuine care in her eyes. "Go on," she says. "Check out the review. The notification must be waiting there."

It is. I can see the icon at the top of my phone screen.

"Do it!" she says. "I'm as intrigued as you are."

"I doubt that, somehow."

"Ok, well, nearly as intrigued." She waves her hands at me. "Jeez, Ella, just open the review, will you? I want to see what he's had to say!"

"Fine, alright."

I still have an edge of the impudent schoolgirl Holly about me. That alone makes me smile as I finally click to read my feedback. My nerves are jangling as bad as they were in the cab yesterday. Damn, that feels so long ago.

Five stars.

Holly the schoolgirl was a pure treasure. Her acting was impeccable. Her roleplay was divine, and as for her bedroom skills – I'd be very surprised if anyone would be able to surpass this experience. I've enjoyed a lot of entertainers over the years, both naughty boys, and naughty girls, but this was a new dynamic. She almost blew me out of my role, and that speaks volumes in itself. I'm a very, very determined actor.

Her ass is perfect for a spanking, and her sweet voice is beautiful. She looks wonderful in pigtails, but she'd look wonderful in anything from lacy lingerie to a clown outfit, so take your pick.

Holly was the best entertainer I've ever shared the night with.

I don't say that lightly, so take heed.

Wow. Just wow. And oh my God. Daddy likes naughty boys, too. Fuck, that's hot. Insanely hot. Urgh. That's only made the pang of wanting him even worse.

I read the review out to Ebony, and she cheers for me.

"Five stars! Nailed it again! Go you!"

I'm glowing happy, but reading his words only makes the puppy dog lurch come back stronger. Maybe I will have to look up this *morning after syndrome*.

"How do you suggest I get over him?" I ask Ebony.

"It'll only take a few days. The trick is, stay busy, and remind yourself that he isn't real. He's a character, just like you were. It's easy to make characters into fantasy heroes when you've had a good night with them."

"Great timing, isn't it?" I roll my eyes. "The one time I need to keep busy is the one where I've just quit my day job."

"Tempted to go ask for your job back? You could beg and plead to be a good girl."

I laugh at that. "NO!"

"Exactly, so find some hobbies. Some actual hobbies, and I don't mean following Connor around like a groupie, cheering him on from the side of the stage."

Jesus. I haven't thought about Connor in ages. It's like he's been wiped from my head, erased into nothingness. I look over and his rucksack is still there, but I haven't even registered it. I haven't been giving a toss about him and Carly. I genuinely couldn't give a shit about him anymore.

He was the only *hobby* I really had.

How pathetic really. My life was all about him. Just WTF, seriously?

"Right, I'll get some hobbies," I say to Eb. "I might take up yoga. Pilates. Crochet." I laugh. "Drama classes. Sounds like with training, I could win an OSCAR... Will you walk down the red carpet with me?"

That sets us off in giggles, and I love it when that happens. We're laughing until she's holding her sides, and I roll over on the bed, pretty sure I'm snot-laughing into my pillow.

The comedown from that is special on its own.

"I have to go," she says, finally. "Got to shower and sleep before later. I've got a bondage booking at midnight."

"Jeez, do you ever stop?!"

"Nope. And if you have any sense, I suggest you get right on and at it again. One of the biggest ways to get over morning after syndrome is with another booking. Something totally different."

"Ok," I tell her.

"Catch you later." She blows me a kiss and I blow her one back.

Then I do as I'm told and fire up the chatroom.

Morning after syndrome.

She wasn't lying. There are loads of threads about it, mainly from newbies, with more experienced entertainers chipping in to help. One girl was so *in love* with a pair of masters that she was legit going to offer to live there with them for free. She would have split up with her boyfriend and everything. Luckily people talked her out of it, and she recovered. Plus, she searched their User IDs online, and they weren't anywhere close to being masters in real life. One of them was a traffic warden, who also made bookings for guys offering to give him blowjobs in exchange for fake parking offences. Hardly the aristocratic lord of bondage he portrayed himself to be in the session.

It's all fantasy. FANTASY. And being paid for it.

Reading through the thread makes me feel less alone, and considerably less crazy. The knot of loss in my stomach loosens, slowly, and Ebony was right. She usually is.

I should take the rest of her advice as well... and get another proposal booked in ASAP. Something with a totally different flavour.

I scout through my messages. Standard, standard, standard. Nope, nope, nope. There's a guy who wants me to pretend to be his dirty girlfriend at his work Christmas party, and hang out with his friends the next day, but I can't do that yet. That roleplay would be a whole other league. There's another guy who wants me to shoot ping pong balls from my pussy, for God's sake, but I haven't got the pelvic floor down nearly enough – I need to get on that again. And then, last on the list. Ooh. This one captures my interest...

User 1982. Female. 39.

I want you to fuck my husband while I watch you. I want you to fuck him like you're fucking crazy for him and he's the hottest guy you've ever had, begging for more of his dick while he pounds you. Anal and pussy.

I'm going to be a jealous bitch right the way through. I'm going to tell you you're a disgusting, cheap slut, and slap you around, and spit on you, but nothing is going to stop you fucking him. You'll be too crazy about him to stop, and you'll tell me so.

By the end, I'm going to be so frustrated that I'll make you take a 'dick' of my own at the same time. It'll be a big one. Call it punishment, but you'll be such a needy slut you'll want it anyway.

You'll be grateful enough to beg for it, and demonstrate that by eating my pussy like a hungry whore.

It'll be my husband's time to watch by then...

Duration – 6 hours.

Proposal price – £2400.

I read that one through a few times. Not something I'd have generally considered... fake adultery while a jealous woman tells me what a bitch I am and abuses me with spit and slaps. It sounds weirdly fun, though. Definitely one for the experience book. Plenty different from daddy play in Wrenshaw that the morning after syndrome can go take a hike. Or I hope so.

I consider the price and work it out – 2.4k minus the agency cut, divided by six, works out at just over 300 quid an hour. I work it out further – £5 a minute. Five pounds a minute for fucking a guy like I love him while his wife spits and slaps, ending with a meal of pussy and a good stretch.

I click accept – it's a great price – and I choose a date from the options.

Fuck it, why not?

I pick tonight.

Another address in suburbia. This one on the outskirts of West London. It looks an impressive abode on street view.

I'm about to log out of the app when the search bar catches my eye again, tempting me... I can't help myself. One more little nod to the morning after syndrome, and hopefully a bit of a reality check.

I type in User 762 and hit the search button.

My heart is pounding when the list of threads shows up. My stomach drops when I see just how many users have been with him.

The best daddy ever!

Seriously. His house is crazy. I'd move into his garage it's that flash.

King of spanking. His palms are SOLID.

Makes a great chicken casserole.

The last comment hits me pretty deep. The idea of other *sons* and *daughters* sitting at his dining table, eating chicken casserole with him makes me feel... jealous. But then again, on his review he did say I was the best of them...

I'm still scanning the threads when I find one that stands out to me. A lot. I click for more info.

Daddy is a lovely man, protective and fierce, like a good disciplinarian should be. He taught me my lesson for my naughty notebook, and I was the most convincing sorry daughter I could be. He loves big tits, and he loves bath time. I adored how he bathed my pussy clean and put me to bed like a good girl. If you get an offer of his, take it. You won't regret it.

All great, and true, and cool – but that's not what struck me about it. What struck me about it was the name of the entertainer who'd posted it...

Creamgirl.

The other hardcorers have given it a thumbs up. Weston, Harlot AND Bodica. Maybe they've played with him, too...

Suddenly my five-star review takes on a whole new significance. I read it through again with a flush of pride.

'*Holly was the best entertainer I've ever shared the night with.*

I don't say that lightly, so take heed.'

No, he doesn't say that lightly. He fucked Creamgirl. The top of the block – and maybe some other hardcorers, too. But even if not, Creamgirl is the most hardcore of the hardcorers, with the best reputation on the whole entire site.

Yet still, *Daddy* preferred me.

Proud doesn't even come close.

And now my heart's pounding to a whole new beat. I have a new role to play – an insatiable lover, so fucking cray-cray she won't even stop when being attacked by the jealous wife. Won't back down when she's forced to eat pussy. Won't complain at being stretched. No, this slutty character will beg for more – and take it. I want another five-star incredible review, and I'm going to do my utmost to get it.

fourteen

User 1982. Female. 39.

I want you to fuck my husband while I watch you. I want you to fuck him like you're fucking crazy for him and he's the hottest guy you've ever had, begging for more of his dick while he pounds you. Anal and pussy.

I'm going to be a jealous bitch right the way through. I'm going to tell you you're a disgusting, cheap slut, and slap you around, and spit on you, but nothing is going to stop you fucking him. You'll be too crazy about him to stop, and you'll tell me so.

By the end, I'm going to be so frustrated that I'll make you take a 'dick' of my own at the same time. It'll be a big one. Call it punishment, but you'll be such a needy slut you'll want it anyway.

You'll be grateful enough to beg for it, and demonstrate that by eating my pussy like a hungry whore.

It'll be my husband's time to watch by then...

Duration – 6 hours.

Proposal price – £2400.

I slip out of the cab at a stunning white house known as *Casa Boudique*. It's set back from the road, its imposing exterior hidden from view of the neighbours by mature trees and hedgerows. It's gorgeous.

I feel like an intruder as I pay the driver and swing my legs out of the back seat, which is good – since that's my job this evening, after all. To be an intruder in someone else's marriage.

And take punishment for it.

There's something I find very naturally kinky about this proposal. I played with myself this afternoon, morning after syndrome fast fading about my lovely fake daddy.

Ebony was right. The sooner the better to make the replacement, and the idea of this one turns me on.

A lot.

It's been years since I've eaten pussy, and the first time I'll have ever been sober and slapped around for it.

I wonder if User 1982 will make me call her Mistress?

Bizarrely, I hope so...

It doesn't matter how turned on I am. My nerves are still jangling at the forefront, and that only gets worse every second as fantasy slams into the cold, hard walls of reality. I still have my customary shaking fingers as I click on *arrived*, and my legs feel weak in my stilettos. I've gone for slutty red platforms, my hair loose and flowing free. I'm in a staple satin bodice from my wardrobe, and a tiny miniskirt with fishnet holdups. My bodice is laced with scarlet ribbon, to match both my stilettos and slutty red lipstick.

I should be confident. *Should be.* But it's already shrivelling away inside.

Press the doorbell, the instruction pings through, so I step up onto the front step and press the doorbell off to the side. I shuffle on my heels with a pounding heart as I wait for someone to answer it. Who is it going to be? Him or her? Or both of them?

I hold my breath as the door swings open.

It's him.

He's big, broad, clean shaven, and looking younger than I expected as he invites me past him. Thirty-five, tops. He's attractive, but nothing that would make my mouth water. Just a mid-range hot guy with short, dark hair. He's wearing a suit, but his tie is loose and the top few shirt buttons are undone, and he seems already on the road to tipsy as he smiles.

"Hey there, Holly."

I'm already feeling more confident as I look at him. I could fuck him happily for hours, no problem.

"Hey. Nice to meet you."

His hallway is gorgeous, modern and grey, with a bright row of ceiling spotlights, but he points to the stairs. No small talk.

"Upstairs, please. Last door on the right. Leave your shoes on."

"Ok, sure. Thank you."

I feel like such a slut as I make my ascent, trying to keep my eyes focused on the journey to the room, not flitting around looking for *her*. His jealous wife.

The room is already set up, with a ruffled bed – its luxurious white sheets discarded as though we've been fucking for hours. There are open wine bottles on the bedside cabinet, and both glasses have already been poured. Red.

User 1982's husband closes the door behind him and points over to one of the glasses.

"Have one, if you like."

Why not? I take a decent swig of one glass, and he smiles a decent smile in return.

"Have *both*, if you like," he says.

"Nah, thank you," I say. "One will do."

"You think that now." His laugh is low as he pulls his shoes off and casts them towards the door. He fluffs the pillows up, then loosens his belt, shrugging his jacket off and tossing it on the floor after his shoes. His keys and wallet go tumbling.

I get it.

This is a frantic setup of two people fucking. Two insatiable lovers, caught in the act.

I join in undressing, slipping off my own coat and kicking it to the side. I stand before him, showing off my outfit as he stares, and then I tug my bodice loose, spilling my tits free.

"How much time do we have, *lover*?" I ask him.

His eyes are fixed on my tits, my nipples hard and on display.

"Enough," he says, and pats the bed to his side.

I finish up my glass of wine before I join him, crawling up on all fours. I love the sensation of the wine hitting my belly. My nerves are fluttering to a different tune already. User 1982's husband is hotter now, up close. He's rough as he wraps a hand around the back of my neck, pulling my face close to his. He smells good, a hint of musk that I'm glad of. Musk and red wine, a potent mix for a pounding – or a slapping.

"You're quite a stunner, aren't you? My wife said I'd like you. She usually goes for girls she knows I won't like, but this time she said she'd make an exception. Happy Christmas to me."

"You like goth girls with big tits, do you?"

"How about I show you?"

I expected some intimacy while playacting an affair with someone's husband, but I jump slightly as he lands his lips on mine. I remember my role and kiss him back with fervour, making sure I smear red lipstick all over his mouth. He lets go of my neck when we're full on in the groove, and pushes me backwards, tugging my lacy thong to the side.

This guy doesn't warm me up. He doesn't work my clit, or tease my slit. He does nothing but force three thick fingers right the way inside me, ploughing them in like he's on a mission. It doesn't stop me bucking my hips and taking it, though. If anything... I want more. I want to be used like his filthy side bitch tonight.

"I like it rough," he says. "So does my wife. Only she likes to be the one watching it."

Weirdly, he's growing hotter by the second...

"You'd better show me how you like it before she gets here then, hadn't you?" I say. "I'm yours to play with, after all."

He uses his lipstick smeared mouth on my tits, and he's not gentle. His sucking is brutal, his teeth clamping and sucking into vicious love bites, but I don't give a fuck. I love this kind of play. I realise I'd been picturing the hen-pecked husband caught out – meek and apologetic to his wife – not a beast who wants to use me for his own filthy, rough pleasure.

That's always the risk of assumptions though, isn't it?

There's no warmup for his girthy cock once he drops his pants around his thighs. No. He slams straight inside me. He's deep enough that it hurts, sore, but I encourage him, getting into character. He doesn't give two fucks about me, that's clear, but I have to pretend to give a lot of fucks about him tonight. And I will...

"You're so fucking hot," I tell him, "I've been desperate for this. Desperate."

That spurs him on, still sucking at my tits as he fucks my pussy, and I imagine just how rough he's going to be with my ass. I know it's going to hurt.

I smile to myself as he swirls a tongue around my used tits and shoves his fat cock deep.

I want to mean nothing. I want filthy rough sex, and the pain of the forbidden. I want to be called a nasty, cheating bitch – not fed chicken casserole.

"Come on, *lover*," I say to mystery man. "Fuck me harder. Fuck me like you mean it."

"Yes!" he yells and thrusts in and out.

"More!" I tell him. "Harder!"

He pulls out, eyes hooded, dripping with lust.

"You're as dirty as the reviews say. Viv read them to me when she was booking you. She wouldn't let me see your pictures, though."

"Yeah, I'm as dirty as the reviews say. Dirtier, actually. Why don't you try me out?"

"Too fucking right I will," he says.

I want him as much in character as can be when his wife walks in. I want him genuinely caught up, ravenous, consumed when she walks through the door and sees him fucking a stranger.

He raises my legs, still in my stockings and stilettos, and pins them right back against the headboard. I take hold of my thighs, ensuring my tits are trapped between them. The guy is salivating, gripping his cock. He pulls my thong over to the side, and he can see my ass and pussy on full display, there for his taking.

"Gotta save this one for later before I slam my dick in," he tells me and forces two rough fingers into my asshole. "Viv will want to see that."

He keeps using his fingers as he positions himself like a fucking piledriver, ready to push his cock back inside my pussy.

"You want it?" he asks me, and I look up at him.

"Want it? That's an understatement. I can't do without it." I grit my teeth as he slams me. I keep my legs held right back, telling him he's so good, and it works like a dream as he sinks balls deep, his fingers still hurting my ass as he goes.

The glass of wine has helped take the nerves away. I feel like a true slut as the adulterous husband smirks down at me.

"Yeah, I can feel how much you want it. You're not playing."

"How much I want *you,* you mean."

His grin is so bright. "Viv's gonna go fucking berserk when she hears you talk like that."

"I hope so. I want her to punish me like I deserve it."

"Be careful what you wish for."

"Oh, I wish for it. Give me that big cock and fuck me like a guilty, dirty husband. Make her go fucking berserk!"

"Holy shit!" he says and moves position with brute force, pulling out and flipping me onto my front. He pulls my panties down and off as I fall flat on the bed, but he yanks me right back onto all fours in a heartbeat and slams into my pussy from behind. He grabs a load of my hair, and I'm his. I'm his. I'm fucking his. I drill it into my head so hard I'm panting, telling him so.

"My name's Mark," he tells me. "You'd better start using it."

"Mark," I repeat. "Fuck me, Mark. Don't stop. Please, don't fucking stop!"

I drop down so I can work my clit, well aware I'm leaving lipstick smears on the pillow as my face hits. The more the better. I want his wife to see them.

Fuck, how Mark pounds me. He's gripping my hips to slam deeper, on the road to fucking coming when he curses to himself and pulls out.

"I need to stop," he says. "It's only supposed to be a warmup until we're discovered. If I start shooting my load already, Viv is gonna be pissed as fuck."

I roll onto my side, watching him cupping his dick and balls.

"Have another drink if you want," he offers, and I reach across to the bedside cabinet to pour myself another glass. I stare at him while I sip it.

"This is the problem with Viv choosing someone so... so hot," he says. "You'll drive me fucking mental."

"That's what she wants, isn't it?"

"Yeah, but *after* she arrives, not before she even shows her face. She isn't home yet."

"How long do we have?"

He checks his watch.

"Ten minutes. She always gives me an hour first."

Shit... we've been playing for nearly an hour already? Time sure flies when you're having fun.

"How about this, then," I say, finishing up some more wine and relaxing back on the bed, legs hitched up. "I'll play for you until you hear her car pull up, and then, when you hear her arrive, you climb up on top and slam me like you fucking mean it?"

"Determined to give me every minute, are you? Most girls would just lie there and cream the cash."

"I'm not most girls," I say, and snake my hand down between my legs.

I play with myself while the *adulterous* Mark watches, spreading my slit wide open so that he can see my swollen clit. I spit on my fingers and use the opportunity to lube myself up some more, until I'm nice and wet, clit slick and needy. I look at the cock he's holding, and imagine taking another *cock* on top later tonight. I wonder how hard his wife's slaps are going to be, and if she's going to punish me even half as much as I want to be punished right now.

Mark looks over at the window a few minutes later.

"Her cab just arrived."

He starts to move towards me, but I shake my head.

"The longer you wait, the more feral you'll be when you fuck me."

"I'm fucking feral now," he says.

"Just one more minute," I tell him, "I'm close to coming," I work my clit fast, "I want to be real close when you slam into me. I want her to see me coming when you fuck me."

"Fucking hell," he says, gripping his cock tight.

I keep playing while he watches, and his eyes are so full of need. I spread my pussy and show him what he's missing... what he'll be getting... and he groans, gripping his balls.

I slap my clit once, twice, and I'm so fucking close, I daren't touch it again.

His wife calls out loudly, no doubt deliberately, from the stairs as she approaches the action.

"Mark! Are you up there? The party was boring, so I came home early."

Her voice is deep. Authoritative.

"Jesus Christ," Mark says and launches his body onto mine, pumping me like he's been doing it for hours, his mouth slavering as he kisses me. I wrap my legs around his waist and coax him on, urge him on, panting like a bitch against his mouth. We're still going strong as the bedroom door swings open wide, but it's a close call, since I can't hold back anymore.

"Mark!" I cry as he slams me and the orgasm is so intense, I'm seeing fucking stars as he pounds me.

"MARK!" his wife bellows and it's enough for him to pause, his cock buried deep.

I look over at the woman in the doorway as though it's a surprise to be busted, impressed by the fake disgust on her face as she steps on in and slams the door.

She's stunning. Her dark hair is twisted up in a bun, showing off her slender neck, and she's in a short red ballgown, as though she really has been out at a party. She's in tall, classy shoes, and has muscular legs that match her muscular torso. Her tits are high and impressive, just not nearly so big as mine.

"What the fuck is going on?" she asks him, as though I don't exist.

He stumbles over his words as she approaches, and she looks down at me, still impaled by her husband's dick.

"Get the fuck up," she snaps, and takes a fistful of my hair to pull me out from under him.

Shit, I fumble until I'm sitting upright on the edge of the bed.

She drops down to a crouch, right in front of me. "What's your fucking name, you little slut?"

"Holly," I tell her.

"And what the fuck are you doing with my husband, Holly?"

"Viv–" Mark begins, but she holds a hand up.

"You're the one who's been after him from the coffee shop, aren't you? He's told me about you, you big titted bitch."

I meet her eyes in shock, like she's caught me out.

"I, um, couldn't help myself... he's just so hot... and I–"

"Shut up!" she yells. "You knew he was married. He told you plenty of times."

"Yes, he did, but I know Mark likes goth girls! And I knew that if I dressed up and came to him..."

She wasn't expecting that. She flashes him a genuine glare.

"That's what you told her, is it? That you like goth girls?"

"She dragged it out of me!" he says. "She's been trying to fuck me for months, like a slutty little vixen." He looks at me with disdain, like I really am worth fuck all. "I couldn't help myself, just look at her, Viv. Look at her. How the fuck do you think I was going to turn that down?"

"Because you're married to me!" She straightens up and shoves him onto his back. "You're a married man who should know the fuck better, and as for *you*," she sneers at me. "You're an adulterous mantrap who deserves a beating. So get out of here before I give you one."

I remember the proposal. I shake my head.

"I can't," I say, and she double takes.

"Sorry, what did you say?"

"I can't!" I look at Mark, addressing him, not her. "What we have is too important to me, Mark. I can't stand to be without you, I never could. And now you've finally fucked me, it's going to be even worse, so I'm not going anywhere." I pause. "Tell your wife, Mark. Tell her how much you wanted me, too."

Viv looks at him. "Mark, is this true? Is this little bitch telling the truth?"

"Tell her what you said!" I insist to Mark, impressed by how natural my acting skills are becoming. "Tell her all the things you promised to do to me!"

Viv's eyes are blazing. "What *things*?" It's me she's looking at, not him.

I try to look guilty, dropping my gaze.

"He said he'd fuck me like I've never been fucked before. He promised he'd fuck my ass, even though I've never been fucked there before. He promised me that he'd fuck me like he meant it. He said he *would* mean it."

"Oh, right, I see." She looks at him. "Is that true?"

He doesn't speak. I turn to stare at him along with her.

"Mark!" she snaps. "Is that true?"

He blusters, shrugging. "I was saying whatever needed saying. I wanted a go on her, that's all."

I act like I could cry, and Viv laughs at me.

"Oh, don't play the victim here. You knew what you were doing." She pauses. "The question is, are you going to leave him the fuck alone now?"

I don't answer, don't look at her, don't do anything just twiddle my fingers.

"Answer me!"

I sigh as I shake my head, still refusing to meet her eyes. "No. I'm not. I can't."

"You're going to pursue my husband's cock regardless, that's what you're telling me?"

I summon a flare of fire. Of a girl driven insane. "I have no choice, ok! I want him so much, I wouldn't be able to stand it!"

Oh, the tension. It's palpable. It's real. It gives me tingles between my legs.

"I see," Viv says, and with that she paces around the room in her mega heels, looking at both of us as she scowls with folded arms.

Neither me or Mark move or speak. We just wait in silence, like too discovered thieves in the night. The seconds tick by. The *anger* in Viv mounts, and when she glares at me next, it's as though she's reached a filthy conclusion. The disgust in her eyes takes my breath.

"You can fuck my husband," she tells me. "But you'll pay for it. If you want to fuck him in *my* house, then it's *my* rules you'll be fucking him by." She smirks. "Don't worry, honey, by the time we're done tonight, you'll be pleased to leave him behind."

I shake my head. "I won't be. I'll take whatever, I don't care. Just don't make me leave him."

"And you," she says to Mark. "Do you still want to fuck this sad bitch?"

He stands up and takes hold of his hard-on.

"Show me a man who wouldn't, Viv. Come on."

She glares so well.

"Fine. You can fuck her, then, but I'll be watching, and I'll be doing whatever the fuck I want to her while you're doing it. Let's see if she really is just a cheap piece of trash to you, shall we? If she means nothing, you won't give a shit what I do to her, will you?"

"I won't give a shit, no," he says. "She means nothing to me. She's just a hot bitch who wants my cock."

"Mark!" I try, but he doesn't even look at me.

Viv downs the rest of a glass of red wine, and directs both me and her husband with a finger.

"Go on, then. Show me. Demonstrate just how fucking well you were getting it on while I was away."

I get back into position, with wide eyes, coaxing Mark up on top of me. His eyes are fierce, like he doesn't give two fucks about the piece of shit I am. He slams his cock back into my pussy like I'm a silly little bitch, but I work my hips. I roll them up and under him, like a challenge, gripping his cock with my pussy.

"You were sucking my tits, don't forget." I say to him, and offer them.

"Suck her tits, then!" Viv barks, and Mark does, but he's gentler now than before. His tongue feels so wet and fucking nice as he laps at me. I moan, and look over at Viv deliberately.

"He's just too good."

"Good enough to get them punished for?"

I nod. "You can punish them all you like... it'll be worth it for his hot mouth."

The challenge seems to be accepted.

She pulls him off and away from me and drags me right back up to sitting position. Yeah, she's made of muscle. Impressive. Too much to mess with, even if I wanted to. She grips my hair to hold my head back, and then she slaps my tender tits so hard I'm whimpering. They must be bouncing, turning pink before her eyes, but mine are closed tight as I gasp, soaking in every sensation.

It's been a long time since I've taken pure tit punishment. I curl my heel under myself so it presses against my pussy, craving pleasure. When Viv dips her head and bites at my sore nipples, she's better than he was, she can suck just right to aid the pain.

"You really will take some shit for him, won't you?" she says as she finishes, and I nod, tits on fire.

"Yes, I will. I'll take everything I need to."

"Vile slut." I start in shock as Viv spits in my face, still gripping my hair to keep my head in position. "Adulterous little mantrap," she says, and spits at me again, really hocking one up this time and rubbing it all over my face with her palm. My lipstick must be such a state, if I even have any left on me.

Viv twists me around by my hair so Mark can see my face.

"Not so pretty now I've spat all over her, is she?"

But she's talking bullshit. I can see how horny Mark is over it. His dick is so hard it's veiny. Dark, and ready to unload. She spits on me again as he watches, and this time I make sure I've got my mouth open to take some inside.

I moan, saying I'll take more, and she gives it. Another two rounds of spit, straight at me.

"You're going to ride my husband's cock now, bitch," she says. "You're going to show me how much you want him." She snaps her fingers to her husband. "Over here now, you cheating piece of shit."

He gets into position, shrugging nonchalantly, like he doesn't give a fuck whether I'm riding him or not. He lies beside me and holds his cock in his hand, offering it to me with a smirk. No respect whatsoever.

But I like that...

"RIDE HIM!" Viv shouts and shoves me towards him.

I take my position slowly, hitching myself reverse cowgirl onto her husband's cock as she watches. I work so softly, taking my time over every rise and moan, making sure he doesn't blow his load for as long as possible. I want to give them the most out of every moment.

I arch my back and murmur like Mark's is the horniest dick I've had in my life, telling his wife how lucky she is for having him. I whimper at Mark that *he's worth it, worth everything, just don't stop... please don't stop...* and a sick part of me believes it. My own eyes must be glazed and horny as I look over at his filthy, enraged wife.

I play with my own battered tits as she watches me.

"Dirty whore," she says, and I smile.

"Yeah, I am. It's your husband's fault, though."

I slide my fingers down to my clit as I ride him, still rolling my hips nice and slow. I work myself up as I take his cock, taking my time with little circles... and yes. It works. I come for real for a second time, crying out as my pussy clenches. *Yes, yes, yes,* Mark is cursing under me as I hitch and bounce, his dick being milked by my orgasm, and he loses it, grunting and bucking up against me like a man stripped of every ounce of cool he owns.

"See how much he wants me?" I ask Viv, when he's fully in the throes of his bucking. "Your husband is desperate for me. He'll be even more desperate for my ass, I promise."

"Cheeky bitch," Viv snaps, and she's right on me, pinning me flat against her husband in the aftermath and shoving her fingers up inside my pussy in tandem with his cock. FUCK.

Even though I'm slick from juice and cum, and his dick is shrinking, it still hurts like fucking hell.

I curse against her face, but she doesn't care, just smirks at me, up close.

"Oh come on, bitch, you can take it. Tell me to stop if it's so unbearable. Tell me you want to fuck off and leave him alone."

I shake my head. "Never."

"Yeah? That sounds like a challenge to me." She addresses her husband. "You'd better have your cock up again soon, Mark. I want you to fuck this bitch's ass in front of me." She grabs my arm and lifts me away from him. "And while we're waiting you can give me your fucking thanks."

Jesus, she's strong. She throws me from the bed onto my knees, and I look up in pure respect as she strips for me. She's absolutely stunning, and confident to go along with it. She unzips her dress and slips it down her body, stepping out of it in her gorgeous heels. She unclips her bra and throws it aside, and then she presents her pussy to me, legs spread, still clad in tiny black lace panties.

It's so natural to tease the lace to the side and brush my thumb up her wet slit. My mouth is watering as I dare to tease her with my tongue, lapping in long sweeps as I look up.

"Wow, you really do want my husband, don't you?" she asks, but I give her a different smile this time.

"Yeah. And I want you, too."

"I didn't have you down for a pussy eater, you dirty mantrap."

"Yours is delicious." I dig my tongue into her slit to demonstrate.

"Show me, then." She kicks her panties off and presses my face right into her crotch.

I eat Viv out as well as I can, hungry mouth ravenous as she spreads her legs wider. I splay her cunt like she's a beautiful butterfly, angled to be sure Mark can see us as he works his cock in his hand.

He's going to be ready to fuck my ass soon, no doubt about that.

But first, I want to make his wife come...

I start slowly, teasing... building with sweeps and twists of my tongue. She's dripping wet when I dare to slide two fingers in, and I know how to curl them as I clasp my mouth around her clit and suck, suck, suck.

It's obvious she's not that used to this – truly enjoying it. She takes hold of the back of my head, stumbling on her heels as we reverse backwards so she can brace herself against the dressing table. I really go for it now, determined.

I'm going to make her come for me.

"Fuck," she murmurs. "I didn't think you could..."

She can't finish her sentence before she starts bucking against me. My fingers turn frantic, and I suck, grip and tug her clit harder. She's beautiful as I stare up at her riding the waves, lost to everything but the thrill of her pussy against my mouth.

I'm so proud of myself that I'm smirking when she's done. I pull away from her pussy with a smack of my lips.

She's bracing herself on her thighs as she recovers – but it doesn't take long before she gets enough composure for the next round of playtime.

She addresses Mark, not me, still treating me like I'm a cheap little slut and nothing more.

"Take her ass. No fucking lube."

"Come here," he tells me and directs me up and onto the bed.

He does as he's told, right up behind me, and all of my pride dissipates behind the pain of him burying his way into my dry, raw ass. He pins me down with a hand on the back of my neck, and I'm a slutty servant as he pounds me, crying out against the pain, even as my clit tingles.

"Still like it now, bitch?" Viv asks, and I nod.

"Yes, I fucking love it."

"Want it harder?" she asks, and I force a grin, praying it's convincing.

"As hard as can be, please. Fuck me, Mark," I tell her husband.

I'm not surprised he's so horny after watching me eat his wife out. His dick is a weapon he uses as a perverted thank you, jabbing it into me like he wants to tear me apart.

"Roll over now," Viv says to him, and it's clear they know what the drill is between them.

Mark hooks his arms under my thighs and switches position so he's holding my back to his chest, still slamming up and into me. He sits up straight with me on his lap, and lowers my weight onto his thighs, perched on the edge of the bed. And then he spreads his legs between mine, until my pussy is exposed, open for entry. *Shit.* I'm gripped, held tight with nowhere to go as he slams my ass, making me bounce as I take him.

I whimper for real, nervous as fuck when Viv takes a huge rubber dildo from the bedside drawer. She slaps it against her palm, and I don't know if I'm going to be able to take DP like this... I really don't.

"Still want my husband's cock?" she asks, and I'm staring at that dildo, nerves rife as I consider my options – but there's only one answer to give.

I want five-stars, and I want all my money, and still, despite everything, my clit is a hungry little whore who wants the filth. Fuck the pain.

"Yes," I tell Viv. "Fuck me all you want. I still want your husband's cock in my ass."

I'm grateful she lubes it up before she approaches me and drops to her knees, rubbing the head of the toy against my pussy so it's nice and slick. I'm bouncing on her husband's cock in a steady rhythm, so she uses it to work the toy in an inch at a time, but I'm crying out, fighting back tears until she brushes a generous thumb against my clit. It's just a tease, but it helps.

"Still a long way to go," she tells me. "But I know a dirty slut like you can take it."

She's right, I can.

Crying out and tears mean nothing whatsoever as she forces that big toy into my pussy. I let them flow free and easy, relieved to fuck when it's all the way in.

"I'll show mercy and go slow," she says, but she doesn't need to after the first few thrusts.

The journey from that point is inevitable. It always follows the same solid path. Pain beyond belief through the world of *I can't, I can't,* to the meadows of *that feels good now*, and then onwards, until it's *me* begging for more. The words from my mouth sound so far away I can barely keep track of them, it's all about the beautiful fucking stretch between my legs.

Fuck me, Mistress, please! Fuck me, harder! Fuck me for wanting your husband. Yes, yes, fucking yes!

I come with her husband's dirty cock inside me, and her thick rubber toy in my cunt, stretched open wide. I come with slapped, pink tits, and spit all over my face, and the taste of Viv's pussy still in my mouth, and I love it. I love every single seedy second.

Mark comes inside me, and Viv comes again as she plays with herself, watching, and we're all buzzing, exhausted when showtime is over.

I can barely stand up from the bed, I'm battered so raw, and Viv helps me, now she's out of character.

"Are you alright, Holly? That was pretty rough."

I take hold of her arm, giggling in the aftermath. "Yeah, that was rough, but it was hot rough. Fuck, yes, I'll remember that tomorrow."

"Good. That was amazing."

We drink more wine together once I've cleaned up and used their bathroom. There is plenty of blood on the toilet roll this time, but hey ho. All par for the course.

They are a nice couple, actually. Really down to earth, and open and friendly. She's a high-end furniture designer and he's in some kind of IT engineering. Smart and professional.

No wonder they have a house like this.

Maybe one day, I'll have one myself...

They wave me off when my cab arrives, and I give them a genuine thank you for the evening. I'm sure they know I'm telling the truth when I say I've had a really good time.

I have. It's been incredible.

Within a few minutes, the cash is in my account, and another glowing five-star review hits my profile.

Holly eats pussy better than my husband does, no joke. Ha. She's brilliant. Takes a stretch even when it hurts like fuck, and works roleplay like a dream. I thought she might really have fallen for my husband at one point! Thank fuck it was a fantasy, or I might have found myself sharing him. Well done, and thanks, Holly. You're a star.

The cab driver has to help me out of the back seat and up onto my feet when we pull up outside mine, but I'm laughing as I tip him and say goodnight.

Wow, what an evening.

Chicken casserole and pigtails are a distant memory now. I'm too consumed by painful adventures and the quest for more, more, more.

Being with Mark and Viv has awakened an old fire in me – one that I want stoking, quick sharp.

Time to get looking through my proposals.

fifteen

"Are you deadly sure you're serious about this? That area can get sticky. I'm not saying that lightly, either."

"I'm positive," I tell Ebony onscreen. "It's always been a thing of mine. Always. Since Connor's gone, I just haven't really thought about it all that much. I've been kinda busy with other hot dreams."

I'm laughing, but she's not. Her piercing eyes are jabbing so hard, I feel like a kid on trial.

"Don't worry," I say. "I already had all these items ticked on my naughty list. It's no real shocker."

"It's one thing having some options ticked on your list amongst a load of others. It's another starring a load of hardcore ones on purpose to bring the punters in."

Maybe I shouldn't have said anything to Eb about my decision to flash my interests so brightly for the clients to see, but I was mega excited. It's a profile feature I only just found out about – starring naughty list options you're particularly keen on. The system keeps opening up further and further before my eyes…

"I can always back out, can't I? And I can always unstar them," I say to Eb, and she shrugs.

"Well, yeah, of course, but if you want the reviews you won't. And I know you. You'll want the reviews at any cost."

She's right. She is coming to know me very well, and yes, I do want the reviews at any cost.

"I won't baulk and flee from BDSM regardless," I tell her. "I know what I'm up for."

"Yeah, and you must be up for a damn lot if this list is serious. Your profile is showing an awful lot of starred options, there for the taking."

She's got a point. Maybe I did star a big list of items impulsively when I got back in from Viv and Mark's place, but the feelings are still there inside me – and every option I starred was on my original list anyway.

I want BDSM. I love BDSM. I love to feel out of control, and I love the thrill and the subspace of the pain. Of true submission. Why not get paid for it?

Eb holds her hands up. "It's none of my business really, I'm only looking out for you."

I smile at her. "I know that."

"Really though. How are you going to feel when you rock up to an anonymous client's house who has a dungeon, binds you up in it and beats you until you're a quaking, quivering mess?"

I laugh. "Brilliant. I'm sure I'll feel brilliant."

She points through the screen at me with a smirk. "Now *that* is false bravado, and you know it. You'll be shitting yourself."

I suck on some of my strawberry milkshake, fresh from my shopping trip earlier. I've stocked up on new shoes, and a couple of new bodices and... an O-ring collar. I want to be a sub crawling around on my knees.

Eb is right, of course. I'm not so much of an idiot that I don't know I'll be crapping myself as soon as a decent fantasy offering comes to life. I'm just high and happy. It's a feeling of lightness I haven't known in years. Optimistic about the future. No worries, just dreams...

"You do BDSM yourself, right?" I ask Eb.

"Yeah, to a degree. Not anything like this degree, though. The kids would notice."

"I haven't ticked the cane option. I'm playing it safe on that."

"Whoopty doo. How about the rest of it? Ready? Let's hear it in its full glory." She clears her throat. "*Bondage – extreme. Hands, feet, leg spreaders, tits, gag, dog on a lead, blindfold. Standing, doggy, flat. Tit torture – slapping, paddle, crop, clamps. Pussy torture – slapping, paddle, crop, clamps. General – hand, flogger, dressage whip, crop, paddle. Bruising – yes, acceptable. Tolerance – mid to high.*"

Ok, it does sound a lot when she says it like that, but nothing is too out of bounds. Ha. Another ironic word choice.

"I've done those before," I tell her. "Every single one of them."

"Not while someone is in total control and paying for it. Do you definitely know what mid to high even means?"

"Yes! I do! I checked out the chat threads before I starred the options."

"When you were horny?" she asks. I don't answer, and she laughs, rolling her eyes. "You did, didn't you? You checked them out when you were already horny, and you starred your profile then. Were you fingering yourself while you did it?"

I don't deny it, just shrug. "I still find it horny now, so who cares?"

She holds her hands up. "Fine, cool. I'll stop harping on about it."

It is brilliant to be cared for so much, by such a superstar as Ebony, but I'm not lying to her in the slightest. I *am* still horny for everything on the list. I went through every single item with purpose. Connor and I barely played genuine BDSM once we moved to London, and I miss it. Subspace was always one of my favourites, and people who want it enough to pay for it are going to be serious about it. They're going to know what they're doing.

If anything, they're going to be a lot safer than Connor when they're in command. They're going to know the setup they want, and how to reach it. And if there were any deviations... any complaints, they'd be right off the system.

"Better start checking your proposals, hadn't you?" Eb says, and she's back to her regular smile now, motherly speech over.

"Don't worry. I'm refreshing on loop."

In the meantime, I show her my new shoes and clothes, bragging about how I even treated myself to a burger meal. She shows me her new manicured nails, and some lovely new pearl drop earrings one of her clients bought her as an extra present last night. They must have cost a small fortune.

I'm distracted, but still clicking refresh every thirty seconds. I try not to panic, because it's still only mid-afternoon, but boy, I breathe a sigh of relief when my first starred proposal pings through.

"Here it comes!" I tell Eb, but my excitement is deflated as soon as I scan through the contents.

Basic flogging while bound, then being fucked from behind. £500.

"That's alright," Eb says. "A solid start."

"Don't get me wrong, that's fine," I reply. "But I want more..."

Another one comes in a few minutes later. Flogging and crop on the ass, over a flogging bench, with oral and anal. £700. Again, cool and fine, but I want something exciting, something extreme, something that will have me out of my mind with trepidation. *And excitement.*

Then it comes in.

User 109. Male. 40.

I read the rest of the proposal out to Eb.

"I like extreme BDSM, especially with newbies who are fresh to the scene. I have a dungeon set up at my home address, with a variety of equipment including a St Andrew's cross, a bench, rack, shackles and gym horse. I love variety, and love reading a scene.

You have tits built for bondage and pain, so that would be a must on my list. I love pussy torture, so that would also be a must. Stretching and clamps a necessity.

I will use crops, paddles and whips, and I'll leave extreme purple bruising on your ass, and both your outer and inner thighs. I'll leave light lashes on your back and ribs, and bruising on your tits.

You'll be gagged at points, bound at plenty of points, and I may push you hard enough for tears. However, I do use additional toys to keep pleasure levels high as well as pain.

My dungeon is soundproofed, so there is no need to worry about noise.

I like my submissives naked and ready to use from the moment they arrive in the dungeon.

Duration – 8 hours.

Proposal price – £10000.

10k????

I'm sure he must have put an extra nought on there by mistake, but Ebony shakes her head.

"Nope. Sounds about right. What's his User number? We should check him out."

My gut twists at that, because I don't want to. Knowing anything about User 109 before I turn up at his dungeon will only put presets in my mind. I want to be fresh, unprepared and scared shitless. I want to be the *newbie* he wants.

I shake my head. "I don't want to check him out first."

She widens her eyes. "Are you mental? He wants eight hours of BDSM with you."

"Yeah, and he's told me what he wants. I can handle that."

"At least see what his preferences really are from the threads," she says, but I'm grinning, shaking my head, summoning back the confidence I had from last night – getting punished for fucking a stranger's husband.

I'm gaining my confidence, and this proposal will be one at the top of the tree. If I can get through the nerves and come out battered and bruised with another five-star review under my belt, then that's a whole new world.

Ebony sighs. "There's no reasoning with you today. Whoever those clients were last night, they've definitely ramped up your horniness levels."

"They sure did. So has the idea of a 10k proposal in my inbox."

She shoots me a side eye at that. "You'd have done it for much less than five figures."

"May have done."

She tosses one of Jamie's cute little stuffed toys at the screen with a giggle. "God, Ella, you're so transparent. You'd have done it for a tenner, let alone ten grand, the mood you're in today."

"Probably." I giggle back, both of us shaking our heads, and I'm so glad I have her. So glad she's here for me through it all.

Chatrooms are chatrooms and threads are cool, but it's different in actual conversation. I don't know what I'd do without her on the other side of the screen. I can't wait to meet her one day, when she's not so busy with family life on top of work.

Maybe it'll be at the entertainer's Christmas Party – I've seen people talking about it plenty in the threads. I just hope the final date turns out to be before my flight, so I can make it. Eb says she'll be there.

"You going to accept that crazy proposal, then?" she asks me when the giggles stop.

I take another big suck of my strawberry milkshake, grinning around the straw.

"I clicked accept when it first came in," I tell her, and poke my tongue out. "I'm already signed up for Saturday night."

sixteen

User 109. Male, 40.

I like extreme BDSM, especially with newbies who are fresh to the scene. I have a dungeon set up at my home address, with a variety of equipment including a St Andrew's cross, a bench, rack, shackles and gym horse. I love variety, and love reading a scene.

You have tits built for bondage and pain, so that would be a must on my list. I love pussy torture, so that would also be a must. Stretching and clamps a necessity.

I will use crops, paddles and whips, and I'll leave extreme purple bruising on your ass, and both your outer and inner thighs. I'll leave light lashes on your back and ribs, and bruising on your tits.

You'll be gagged at points, bound at plenty of points, and I may push you hard enough for tears. However, I do use additional toys to keep pleasure levels high as well as pain.

My dungeon is soundproofed, so there is no need to worry about noise.

I like my submissives naked and ready to use from the moment they arrive in the dungeon.

Duration – 8 hours.

Proposal price – £10000.

I thought Viv and Mark had a house to dream of, *Daddy* too, but this place is a whole other league. It's out in the countryside, North East of London, and has a driveway at least half a mile long.

I sit in the back of the cab, staring in wonder at the lit-up building at the end of the lane. It has to be a mansion. It has to be.

It sends a fresh hit of adrenaline through me, a weird concoction of abject fear and excitement, blending into a thicket of nerves inside my stomach.

"Whoa," the cab driver comments as we reach the courtyard of the manor. "This is quite something."

"Sure is," I agree as I hand over the fare.

So much for running away from this place if I get freaked out. I wouldn't even make it back to the road.

I click on *arrived* once the cab is off, standing in the glow of the courtyard lighting. It's a cold night, and my bare legs are goosebumped. I'm wearing virtually nothing under my coat, just a short black dress that will pull off easily, and a lacy lingerie set. It won't take me long to get out of it – naked and ready to use from the moment I arrive in User 109's dungeon.

Use the door knocker, the message says, and I look at the huge arched doorway ahead. The twist of ivy looks magical in the warm glow of the lanterns on either side.

I'll be quivering with fear and nerves for the next eight hours straight, so there is no point delaying the inevitable or trying to calm myself down. Ebony's words play through my head – her concerns niggling like tickles at the back of my mind. Maybe she was right and this was too much for a newbie like me. I feel the urge to bolt, but keep walking until I reach the huge stone steps.

The door knocker looks fitting for a regal movie. A lion's head with a huge ring coming from its mouth. It takes real force to thump it against the wood.

And then I wait.

Shivering.

Edgy.

Crapping myself with the grandeur and gravity of what is lying ahead for me behind this door.

The door doesn't creak when it opens, just swings smoothly on huge hinges, showing a foyer lit up magnificently behind my client. He's hidden in the shadows as he gestures me in with a *welcome*, and I could laugh a little as he finally appears before me in full lighting. Part of me had been picturing him like Hannibal Lecter, but no. Of course not.

User 109 is lean and imposing, yes, but he looks like more of an intellectual than a monster. He has a chiselled jaw, and hazel brown eyes behind his glasses, dressed in a plush dressing robe over a shirt and tie.

He smiles and asks for my coat and bag, which I hand over with a *thank you*. Weirdly, I feel more exposed than usual in such a tiny, basic outfit. Less of a confident, dressed up slut, out to impress her clients. Here, standing before him, I'm just me, without the mask of fishnets and corset lacing.

"Take off your shoes, please," he tells me, and I nod before leaving them on the shoe rack. My bare feet are cold on his chequered floor tiles.

He makes no attempt at small talk, so I stay quiet, merely following. His energy deepens as he leads me through his house, through a corridor off to the right, and down a spiral stone staircase to another heavy wooden door.

Seems he wasn't joking when he said *dungeon*. My instincts shoot back in as I stand there on the steps, white knuckles gripping the railing in a vice as he turns the key in the lock. I could run. My legs are tense and ready to bolt, all fantasies of sinking straight into a heady subspace all drying up to nothing.

Standing here – ready to enter a real-life dungeon, in a manor house off grid from the rest of the world, feels like full on insanity. The crazy feeling doesn't ease off when the door swings open and I see the full scope of the wonder waiting inside. User 109 wasn't exaggerating in his proposal, this a BDSM dungeon worthy of a specialist club. He has everything laid out to perfection, spaced out with plenty of room, and a whole host of implements lining the walls, all lit up with spotlights. He even has a gas style mask for cyber play.

I repeat my safe word in my head on loop, *flag, flag, flag, flag, flag*, but he addresses that angle as he closes the door behind us.

"You are free to use your safe word at any time, Holly. I will loosen you from your bonds and call you a cab immediately with no problem whatsoever. I will simply deduct whatever fee is remaining from your earnings."

I nod at him. "Thank you."

"If you are gagged, or unable to use your safe word, there is a rhythm of beats you can use with any part of your body available. Hands, feet, fingers, whatever is free." He shows me by knocking the rhythm out on the wall beside us. *Three, pause, four, pause, five, pause.* "Any other noise or objections you make will be taken as part of the playtime. Please be as expressive as you need to be. Moans, begs, screams and protests are all perfectly acceptable, I will read them in line with the scene. I believe the proposal demonstrates what kind of experience is ahead for you, but do you have any questions?"

I'm still looking around in amazement. My eyes are fixated on the rack. I've never been on a rack before.

"No, thank you. No questions."

"It's Sir now, please."

His tone is so sharp, my eyes flit straight back to his.

"Of course, yes. No questions, thank you, Sir."

"Good girl. Now strip for me."

He steps away for a full view as I pull my dress up and off, casting it away to the side. I unhook my bra and toss it down, then step out of my panties. I've never felt so naked in my life as User 109 – *Sir* -- paces around for a full 360. His eyes rove all over me, and I bow my head, fingers hooked together as my legs tremble. I can't help it.

"You're certain you're ready for this experience?" he asks me, taking off his grand burgundy robe and hanging it on the back of the door. He's fully suited underneath, in posh brogues.

"Yes, Sir," I say, and feel a crazy need to defend myself, in case he deems me *unworthy* or something. "I love BDSM and pain play. I haven't done it like this, no, but I can do, I promise. I *want* to. It's why I starred the items on the naughty list, because it's what I want. I need it."

"It's ok," he says, with just the slightest hint of a smile. "You don't have to sell your suitability to me. A yes would suffice."

I take some breaths as the truth of my words sink in. I do want this. This is the stuff dreams are made of. It's exactly the kind of thing I've been fantasising over for years, and it's right here in front of me. I look at my *Sir* with stronger eyes.

"Yes, Sir. I'm certain I'm ready for this experience."

"Excellent," he says. "Then let's get started."

He directs me over to one of the large walls, where there are strong metal bars placed horizontally all the way up, like a ladder. He takes some leather cuffs from a side table, and I offer my wrists to him willingly. He buckles them tight, but professionally, checking their security before ordering me to stand with my back against the bars and raise my arms above my head, as far as they will go.

I do as I'm told with a *yes, Sir,* as I get in position. He fixes both cuffs to one of the bars, and I test them, tugging.

He's good. There will be no slipping out of these.

"You have gorgeous tits," he tells me, taking some bondage rope from the table. "Have you ever had them bound before?"

"Thank you, and yes, Sir."

But it turns out that my idea of tit bondage and his idea of tit bondage are two very different things. I thought Connor was rough with rope when he bound my tits together, but Sir uses the thin rope like ribbon, one breast at a time, wrapping the cord around and around until they are darkening in seconds. Fuck, this isn't like I've known it before. He uses a fresh piece of cord to bind them together, and I'm already moaning at that. I close my eyes as he wraps the rope around the back of my neck and uses it to hoist my bound tits higher.

My God, the blood is pumping through the rope. My tits are already pulsing.

It's the kind of stuff from my favourite porn movies, and through the fear my endorphins are already beginning to flow, breaths shallowing.

I love tit bondage.

I love the way the sensations become so intense that you can come from your nipples alone – a solid thread of electric that runs straight from your tits to your clit.

This guy – *Sir* – could get me off in seconds, I'm sure.

He brushes my swollen nipples with his thumbs, teasing me as I squirm. I'm already spreading my legs like a whore, and he looks down, but doesn't touch me.

"A true submissive," he says. "Excellent."

"I'm a good pain slut, Sir," I tell him, breaths rasping.

"I've no doubt of that, but still. I'm sure we'll find your limits tonight."

Fuck, it sounds scary, coming from his mouth, but I'm already losing my head to everything but the sensations. He gives my tits time to swell, staring, and I start to pant, squirming in my bonds as they prickle. God, I wish he'd touch me. I want him to hurt them. To tease them. To use them. But he's so calm, so stoic, so poised as he reaches slowly with both hands, his fingers gently gripping my nipples.

The sensation is incredible. I feel it all the way to my toes.

Sir is smirking as I moan, blinded by pain as he pinches my nipples sharp and hard. It makes me hiss. Makes me squirm and grunt as he stretches them before finally letting go.

"Good girl," he says, moving to the table and coming back with two clamps.

He tightens them on my nipples, slowly for maximum effect. I writhe against my bonds, letting out a whimper.

"Spread your legs," he says, and I do as I'm told, fighting the urge to beg him to touch me.

He's careful not to brush my clit as he applies clamps to my pussy lips, just tugs at them to make sure they are clipped solid. Ah, the blood pumps there, too. This is good. So good.

Sir takes a crop from the rack and taps it against his palm as he watches me squirming.

"Keep your legs spread wide," he tells me, and I nod for him.

"Yes, Sir."

He starts with gentle crop slaps on my thighs to warm them up, the speed of his slaps increasing into a barrage that spreads up and down, giving a blissful burn. He begins the sharper lashes amongst the taps, HARD, soft, soft, HARD, unpredictable. He uses the full length of my thighs, but stays just shy of my pussy, which has me reeling, because I want the tap of a crop on my clit so bad, I could scream.

I'm not at all prepared when he strikes my stomach and works his way up my rib cage. There are less taps now as he uses my flesh – just pure solid swipes with the crop. My hands are in tight fists as I try to enjoy the pain, but I'm struggling, crying out with every strike.

It's like he can read me as he looks into my eyes.

He nudges my nipple clamps with the end of the crop and I moan fresh, squirming. He presses the tip against one of my swollen tits for aim and then raises it high to strike me. Fuck, how I flinch, knowing it will hurt like hell – but he's only playing with me.

"Good," he says. "Always be ready to expect the unexpected."

He does slap my tits with the crop, but not with a belter. Each strike is carefully positioned, just hard enough to leave a stripe of white amidst the deep pink swelling. His taps are so much more intense on sensitive flesh, and I suck in deeper breaths, clenching my bruising thighs together.

I have no choice, because it's so tender, it's just too fucking good.

"NO!" he barks, and then rains punishment down on me. Heavy hard blows across my thighs until I'm crying out, shuffling them back apart for him. My heart is pounding right through my head.

"You will never take pleasure without my permission, is that understood?"

I nod. "Yes, Sir. I'm sorry, Sir."

"I don't give many chances. Next time your punishment will be significantly worse."

"I understand, Sir. I'm sorry."

"Time to get you moved," he says, and unclips the cuffs above my head. My wrists are aching, and time is already lost to me. I have no idea how long we've been playing, but I'm already dazed.

"Have a drink," he says, and offers me water direct from a glass. I take several sips with a *thank you, Sir.* It's a welcome relief.

"On your front, please," he says and pats the flogging bench.

I climb up gingerly, the clamps burning my nipples and pussy lips as he buckles my wrists and ankles to the frame. My tits fit perfectly over the front ledge, and every bounce will be magnificent in its wonder, setting me on fire with the pain.

Or so I think, until he lands the first heavy smack of a paddle against my ass cheeks with no warning whatsoever. I jolt forward, with a curse, but he doesn't hold back, keeping up a heavy stream of blows that have me gritting my teeth, trying to stay quiet.

I'm fighting it. The natural response.

My arms are tense in my bonds, and my legs are straining against the cuffs, but he doesn't slow down, or ease up, just smacks the same smarting flesh over and over, until my self-restraint loses its power.

My first whimper of pain sounds like a mewl, it's so pathetic, but it opens the floodgates for more. Tiny whimpers turn to yelps, but my squirming makes no difference, he pelts me right the way across my ass and down my thighs without mercy, so fucking steady I'm fearing every strike.

"Don't fight it," he says. "Accept your submission."

I nod amongst the yelps, but I can't accept it without struggling. My body just isn't there yet. My heart is thumping, and my bruising tits are bouncing back against the flogging bench and I'm sure I'm shaking all over, but he still keeps going. Keeps hitting me to the rhythm. And every time I think I'm coming to accept it, he changes position, or hits me harder, driving me closer and closer to an imaginary brink. The cliff keeps moving. The adrenaline keeps spiking.

"I'm not going to stop until you accept your submission," he tells me.

"Yes, Sir," I say, but it's brain over body, holding onto the fight, even though I don't want to. Giving up isn't easy. My body doesn't want to comply.

I flinch when he rubs his palm over my ass cheeks, and that simple touch makes me whimper.

"Your ass is so fucking red," he tells me, and I hear the lust in his voice. "You're quite a fighter, aren't you?"

"I wasn't lying, Sir. I'm a pain slut with high limits."

"Yes, I can see that. And we're going to break them."

He resumes with the paddle, and there is no mercy whatsoever, only pain. My burning flesh is too sore to tense against it anymore, and flailing against my bonds does nothing. I'm powerless, and beginning to feel it.

My yelps get louder, curses interspersed, and those curses become screams, but it doesn't hold him back. He uses me like an expert until I can feel the breakpoint coming. My screams are quietening, sucked in between hitched breaths as the tears start to come.

"Take it," my Sir says, and I nod.

"Yes, Sir."

He hits me harder, and the shakes start up – racking right through me – but they make me beautifully dizzy, the pain morphing as my adrenaline peaks and eases. The blows feel further away now... more distant... and my body starts reacting by rocking, not jerking.

I shift my weight from knee to knee and I take what I'm given. Without fight, without restraint, with nothing but silent tears.

The freedom in the release of control is pure, absolute bliss.

My Sir knows he's broken me. He approaches me from the front and tips my chin up towards him.

I smile through the tears. "*Thank you, Sir.*"

"You're welcome," he tells me, and he's smiling back. "And now, it's time we truly begin."

I'm in true subspace now, offering my arms and ankles willingly when he guides me over to the rack and stretches me tight. I'm smiling as he uses a dressage whip, stinging my front all over, then grinning as he flicks nasty strikes at my tits, leaving flashes of blood under the skin.

I cry and yelp and moan without care, staring up at him like he's God himself, controlling my destiny, and all the while I want more. More. More.

I want him to use my pussy...

I want him to torture me and stretch me, and drive me crazy...

He strokes my forehead when he's done with the dressage whip, and he reads the want in my eyes.

"Don't worry, Holly. Good sluts always get their rewards."

I'm staring as he walks away, wide-eyed when he returns with both a wand and a toy as thick as his wrist. For the first time in a while, I pull against my bonds.

His eyes are fierce, putting me right back in my place.

"Holly, who controls you in this space?"

"You, Sir."

"Who does your body belong to?"

"You, Sir."

"Who decides what pain and pleasure your cunt takes?"

I suck in a breath. "You, Sir."

He loosens my ankle shackles from the rack but only to fasten them higher, making sure my clamped pussy is on full display for him. There is no escape for me in this position. My cunt belongs to him.

"Be a good girl," he says, brushing his thumb across my clit, and it's tender enough that I moan like a whore. "This is going to hurt," he says when he pulls my pussy clamps apart, tugging to spread me open like a dirty butterfly.

I hear a jangle, and he binds my clamps to my thighs, pulled so tight that they sting and throb like a bastard, but I don't care. The subspace is already back and consuming me.

The buzz of the wand is electric, literally. Sparks and crackles against my clit alongside the tremors that have me writhing, toes curled, panting for him.

I hear a squelch of lube and I don't try to fight it, just let the pain slam hard as he shunts the beast of a dildo in my pussy, working it into my cunt as he zaps my clit to a rhythm.

He's got me.

With the throb of my bound tits, and my bruised, lashed skin all over, I'm nothing more than a sensitive canvas, his to own. When he makes me come it's from a subspace I haven't known in years, if ever, transcending the pain into the ultimate place of submission.

My pussy clenches, waves of pleasure like veins pulsing through my entire body, and I'm crying out like a bitch gone insane, bucking as best as I can against him while he abuses my pussy like the greatest man alive.

I can't believe this is happening to me.

I can't believe the fantasies are really real.

"Stay there, Holly, nice and still," he says in the aftermath, and I nod, sweat dripping from my forehead.

He raises my head and offers me more water from the glass, and I sip with gratitude. I'm so caught up in different sensations, I'm surprised I even know my own name. I have no concept of time, or how long he's been using me, or how the hell bad my bruises are going to be in the morning, but I don't care.

Nothing matters but being his plaything.

I squeal, but I'm smiling as he takes the clips from my nipples, tugging them first. I'm still swollen and tit bound, and Jesus Christ, it hurts. But his mouth doesn't when he lowers his face to my tits, and sucks at them so gently. Oh my fucking God… his mouth doesn't hurt at all.

The sensations building are intense in seconds, and he knows exactly what he's doing. He sucks my nipples just right, sending ripples to my clit, and I can't keep my mind.

I beg, in words that make no sense, just a long stream of bumbling whimpers that he intensifies by sliding a hand down and tugging the clamps on my pussy lips. My second orgasm is building on its own… but just one touch… one tiny touch of my clit would have me in hyperdrive. I'd be screaming from the rooftops.

If I could…

But my Sir pre-empts me.

He slaps a hand over my mouth, gagging me as he tickles my nipples with the end of his tongue, and finally he gives my clit the contact it craves, gentle little taps with his fingers that take my breath. A gentle tap, a nudge, a slow circle, and then… he rubs frantically and I'd scream, but I can't. His hand is just too solid, so I'm moaning, delirious as I come for him, trembling in bonds, clamps and chains, spent and dripping with sweat and tears.

And then it's his turn…

"Open your mouth for me, you good little slut," he says when he takes his palm away.

He takes his cock out of his suit trousers, and I twist my head towards him, legs still open wide and pussy still sore with clamps. My tits are swollen so bad now they're purple.

My Sir takes great pleasure, fisting his cock, its engorged head up close, so close my mouth waters at the pearl of precum that drips from it.

"Such a gorgeous little slut," he says and then he takes my mouth, bulging out my cheek before fucking my throat like it's just a hole for his service, and I'm grinning around his cock like a madwoman, wild with the thought of his cum.

I want to make my Sir come.

I want that more than anything.

He's standing up tall when he does unload his balls for me, splattering my face and swollen purple tits with long filthy streams. I have my tongue out, moaning and begging, and he gives me his cock when he's finished spurting, offering me the privilege of sucking him clean.

I'm so grateful, it's insane.

I'm dizzy as hell when he does finally uncuff me. My tits pulse so bad when he frees them that I cross my arms against my cum-smeared chest, teeth gritted as he does the same to my pussy.

My body has taken a hell of a lot of punishment tonight.

User 109 leaves me on the rack for a few minutes to recover, watching me from the flogging bench with a smile on his face, and I realise again how he's such a hot looking intellectual. I wonder who the hell he is.

It's such a bizarre thought to realise I may never know.

I look around the room at the collection of implements we haven't used yet. The gym horse, and the shackles from the ceiling and the St. Andrew's cross, and the idea I won't get to experience them feels horrific. I want to use everything, all with this one same man.

A man I don't even know the name of.

"I had no idea how much of a painslut you'd be when I sent you the proposal," he says, and I smile.

"Neither did I. I had my suspicions, but that was, um... quite an intense experience."

He looks around. "There is plenty more to play with. Such a shame we won't get the chance tonight."

"We won't?"

He shakes his head, and looks at his watch. "We have thirty-seven minutes left, and I want to make sure you are ok, in a clear headspace, fed, watered, and set for a cab home."

Fuck, we've been here ages... and I just can't...

I don't care about being in a clear headspace, or fed and watered.

"It's ok, Sir," I tell him. "I don't need that. You can keep playing."

He gestures to my tits. "I appreciate the offer, but you need to give yourself time for recovery there. I was a little irresponsible on my timings and should never have kept you bound that long, but I was too transfixed by them."

I couldn't give a shit about my tits...

"And your pussy," he tells me. "I think I may have torn you slightly."

He seeks out a tissue and hands it over so I can wipe myself, but again, I don't give a shit if he's torn me. I want him to do it all over again.

But I can't say that. I'm not allowed to discuss future dates, or more terms, or ask for any further information. So what the fuck *can* I say?

"That was incredible," I tell him, like an idiot. "*Beyond* incredible. That's the best BDSM experience I've ever had by miles."

He waves my compliment aside. "Thank you, but there is no need for compliments. It's most definitely *me* who should be thanking *you*."

Like fuck it is. He really has no idea how much it means to me.

He brings a pack of wipes, and is so gentle as he cleans the cum from my face and my tits. So gentle it feels surreal. So gentle I'd give anything for him to fuck me. But of course I can't ask for that.

He helps me up from the rack, and holds me secure as I get dressed. He gives me his robe as we go upstairs, and makes me a coffee and a club sandwich in his gorgeous, period style kitchen, insisting I down a big glass of juice for the sugar while he calls a cab for me.

But I don't want it.

I don't want to leave.

I hover at his doorway in my coat and heels when the cab arrives, but there is nothing I can do.

"Thank you, Holly, and goodnight," he says, then looks out at the faint hint of dawn on the horizon. "Well, good morning. However you want to term it."

"Goodnight, Sir," I reply, and fuck it. I go in for a kiss on the lips but he shakes his head at me.

"That wasn't in our proposal, and I never deviate. I'd love to, believe me, but I never do."

Damn it.

I feel so dejected when I step outside, until I hear his voice behind me.

"Maybe I'll change the proposal terms next time."

I spin to him with a massive grin on my face.

"Next time? But I thought you liked newbies?"

He smirks so beautifully before he closes the door.

"For you, I may well make an exception."

Holy shit, I'm a mashed-up ball of everything on the way back to London. I listen to the monotone chatter from the cab driver, nodding in the right places, but everything is whirring.

I check my account, and the huge amount of cash is already showing as a balance.

My review comes in just a few minutes later. It's succinct and to the point, like him.

A true painslut, and an excellent entertainer. She makes the most incredible squeals when she orgasms, and cries incredible tears when she's taking her punishment.

5 Stars.

I get a crazy glow, missing him already.

Damnit, is this how it's going to be from here until forever? Morning after syndrome on fucking loop?

I lean against the back seat and have to laugh at the pit of want already forming. Here we go again.

Next time I'm going to pick something with no chance of morning after syndrome – another Viv and Mark kind of playtime. A threesome at least, with no BDSM. Nothing but filthy fun on a plate with no chance of me falling for a stranger.

Maybe I'm being overly optimistic at that, given recent events. But at least I can try.

seventeen

"Fucking hell, he got you good."

"No shit."

I position myself right next to the webcam so Eb can get an up-close view of my purple bruised ass. The bruises run right down my thighs as well, and my front is lashed pretty raw. And as for my tits… wow. They are still mottled red under the skin, amongst the patches of bruising.

I sit down on my dressing table stool with a wince, and Ebony is wide-eyed, shaking her head as she grins at me.

"Ok, I misjudged you there, Miss Newbie. Seems you handled your night of hardcore pretty well."

"The review sure says so."

I'm glowing with pride, not embarrassed in the slightest at being nude on webcam in front of my new best friend. I must look ruffled to hell, my hair a mess along with the rest of me since I've had virtually no sleep since I got home at daybreak – too consumed by the memories of what User 109 did to me last night. I'd do it all again right now, if my body was up to it. Working my clit in bed in the aftermath was hard enough, though.

"You're going to be out of action for a fair few days, young lady," Eb laughs, and I roll my eyes.

"Shame. Hazard of the job, I guess."

"Yep. You'll have to hole up with Christmas movies until you recover."

I still remember the horrible sick feeling I used to get at the very mention of Christmas, just a few weeks ago. Back then the festivities were a terrible prospect, knowing I'd be alone in this crap hole of a room, with nobody to share the celebrations with. But not anymore. I've been playing Christmas songs, and ordering presents for my parents, completely enamoured by the thought that in just a few weeks, I'll be flying across the world to be with them.

I don't know how the fuck I've managed to avoid a webcam call with them all this time so far. I've cited everything from work shifts, to Connor's gigs, to having an upset stomach. I've even said I'm getting my hair done last minute, and the stylist can't possibly change it.

I don't want to ruin the surprise yet, and seeing them onscreen would foil my plans in a flash. Mum would read my expression a mile off, and I'd likely start blubbing like crazy the very second I tried to make the announcement.

I've been sending messages, of course, spinning the best bullshit I can about how great work is and how many chocolate biscuits I've been managing to stack on the store shelves, but it's not going to work for ever... I just want to leave it as long as I can.

Talking of presents, it must be delivery time. A buzz sounds out at my bedroom door, connected to the doorbell downstairs.

"Ooh, is that your mum's special cushion?" Eb asks as I grab my satin nightgown and wrap myself up as quick as I can. "I can't wait to see it."

It's one of the tackier presents I've ordered from online. A sofa cushion with a grinning picture of me, her and Dad on it from when I was younger – all of us in matching Santa Claus dressing gowns. Cringe. Should be cute, though. She'll love it.

"Call you right back," I say to Eb and close the call.

The doorbell buzzes again, and I mutter *Jesus Christ, patience,* as I make my way downstairs to answer it. I haven't even got my slippers on. There's another BUZZZZZ as I reach the hallway, and I'm going to curse the driver if he doesn't give me at least another damn minute to get there. I know they are busy and all that, and I know it must be a crazy time of year, so I'm fine, yeah, I'm ready to give them mercy with a grin, only when I swing the front door open it's not a cushion parcel waiting for me at all.

It's Connor, holding a bunch of budget garage flowers in his hand.

My grin dies in a heartbeat.

He looks like a sad puppy with his tail between his legs, shoulders hunched in his tatty leather jacket. I take three steps back, slapping a hand over my mouth in shock, because what the hell?!

"Can I come in?" he asks me. "Please, Ells. I need to see you."

I'm already shaking my head instinctively, looking at him like he's from another dimension. One I've left far, far behind.

"Ella," he says, looking at me with the expression I used to adore. What I would have referred to as a meaningful loving smirk, with his eyes locked onto mine. It used to drive me wild.

But not now. No fucking way.

It does fuck all for me this time, other than set a swirl of rage off, right in the bottom of my gut.

"No," I tell him, surprised by the strength in my voice. "You can't come in. I don't want to see you, so take your shitty flowers and get stuffed. I'll go grab your rucksack, and you can get the hell out of here, back to the lovely Carly."

"Me and Carly are over," he says.

I don't so much as flinch in surprise at the news.

"Great. Then go back to the lovely whoever else you've got lined up next. I'm sure you have a crowd of them."

He's still holding out the flowers, like they'll suddenly bloom into miracles.

"I don't want anyone else, Ells. I made a fuck up, ok? The only one I want is you."

I could laugh in his face, seriously, but I stare mute, surprised that Connor thinks he stands a single chance with me, crawling back after a *fuck up* that saw him ditching me for another girl.

"It was never about Carly," he says. "She sold herself to me with bullshit. She said she had contacts and could get me a record deal."

That only flames me.

"Right, I see. So it wasn't a *I've fallen for someone else, I'm sorry with all my heart* situation, after all? It was because you thought she could be a bigger cash cow than me?"

He has the audacity to look offended.

"No, of course not. I got confused!"

I want to push him off the doorstep and send him toppling, all the hurt bubbling deep under the surface. Memories of hating myself for not being good enough after everything we'd gone through. Sobbing here alone while he swanned around gigs with his new *princess* on his arm.

"Well, I'm not confused in the slightest," I tell him, deadpan. "I want you to fuck off, and I never want to see you again."

"ELLA! After everything?!"

"*Especially* after everything."

All the months and years I spent trying to support him with all I had. Slogging my guts out to provide us with food and a place to live while he coasted around like the next big thing waiting to happen. I could launch into a tirade, but what's the point? I could tell him how bad he hurt me, but why give him the ammunition?

So, I don't. I stand there, with my arms folded across my chest, in a slip of a satin gown with nothing underneath.

It used to be one of his favourites.

"I'll get your rucksack," I tell him, but I don't close the door quick enough behind me.

He follows me upstairs through the crap house we shared, bleating on about love, love, love and how we were going to grow old together and how we still can. I believed his bullshit once upon a time, but my ears are immune to him. My strength is resolute.

He stands in the room we used to share as I hold his rucksack up for him.

"Take it and fuck off."

"That's the last thing I want, babe."

"Babe?" I laugh at that. "Life can be a bitch sometimes, can't she? I'm sure you'll cope without me."

He looks at my new bedding, and my stash of new shoes all lined up neatly by my wardrobe. He scouts the room and sees the new makeup on my bedside table, and the beautiful fluffy rug I got for the floor, fuck the threadbare carpet.

"What's been going on?" he asks. "Did you get a promotion or something?"

"None of your business."

"If this is about money, I've learnt from my mistakes. I'll get a job around my gigs. I'll help out."

I look at the man I gave my life to, with the token bunch of flowers hanging at his side. He's still super attractive, with his flicked punkish hair, and his beautiful cheekbones, his lips highlighted with a lip ring. But I've seen so much better now. I've done so much better now.

"I don't need you to help out," I say, and toss the rucksack at him, since he isn't going to take hold of it. "Maybe you should have done it a few years ago, before you left me in the shit with debt up to my ears." I pause, looking him up and down, and the rage is dying off inside me now. All I feel is pity.

Poor Connor with his sad dreams, expecting them to fall in his lap rather than truly work for them. Leeching from everyone else to save putting in the graft for himself.

"I don't want you anymore," I say, meaning it with all my heart. "We're over."

He knows me well enough to know I'm not joking. There will be no changing my mind with a bunch of chrysanthemums and apologies. I've cried enough tears over him to last a lifetime.

My ex bites his lip, standing before me like a lost little soul.

"Have you met someone else?" he asks me, and I laugh. Really laugh.

It tickles me so much I laugh my head off. The truth so ironically brilliant that I end up clutching my sides.

"Have I met anyone?!" I ask him through the giggles. "Who cares?"

"I do!" he snaps. "I care a fucking lot!"

I stop laughing and kick his rucksack closer towards him. My eyes must be cold as ice.

"I've met plenty of them, actually," I say. "Now get the fuck out of my bedroom before I call the fucking police, and take your shitty flowers with you."

He still hovers.

"Please, Ella." His voice is so weak, he could be on his knees begging me, but I don't want to listen to it.

"GET OUT!" I shout, and he finally holds his hands up, grabbing his bag and backing away.

"If you change your mind–" he begins, but I'm shaking my head before he finishes.

"I won't ever change my mind, you cheating piece of crap."

"Ok," he says, and the sad little puppy dog I used to worship disappears from my life with his battered old rucksack on his back and his budget flowers in his hand.

The door closes behind him and I press my back to it, heart racing. I can't believe I just did that. I turned my back on Connor. The man I thought I'd share the rest of my life with. The one I loved with all my soul.

Surely it should hurt more than it does?

But of course it doesn't.

I'm not just the Ella who fell in love with him and moved on...

I'm a very, very happy girl called Holly now.

eighteen

User 3267. Male. 27.
A little birdy told me you might be a sore girl in need of some 'aftercare' post BDSM. I'd love to treat you like a princess as I worship you – kissing, tasting, massaging everywhere from the top of your head to the tips of your toes, and I mean EVERYwhere. As many places as you'll let me. Especially the tips of your toes, please. I adore feet.
I'd love to come over yours when we're done, but that's all. I expect nothing else in return. Just my cum over your toes when I've earnt it.
Please give me the chance to worship you.
Duration – 4 hours.
Price – £1000

What a thing to land in my proposal inbox.

I'd pretty much resigned myself to being *out of action* until my bruises healed, but I guess not. I grin my head off because it's obvious just who the 'little birdy' must be, and the 'little birdy' is right... I could do with some lovely 'aftercare' after the thrashing I took in his dungeon the other night, so why not take 3267 up on his proposal? I've never been treated to such a mega sounding spa day, let alone been offered £1000 to accept one.

I laugh as I share that with Ebony, but she shakes her head at me.

"Just be careful. Body worship isn't quite a spa day, Ells. I mean, it can be, but when he says he wants to worship you EVERYwhere, he probably has a lot of EVERYwhere places in mind."

I'm still smiling. "He can worship my EVERYwhere all day long. I can take it."

"What about your feet? Are you ticklish?"

"Nope. Connor sucked my toes a few times when we were drunk. I loved it. He didn't fancy it so much once we were sober, unfortunately. I used to wiggle my feet at him after a full-on day at the store, but he'd turn his nose up and push them away."

"Cheeky bastard. You should have got one last toe sucking demo out of him before you turfed him out on his ass the other day."

I hold my feet up to the camera, wiggling my toes. "User 3267 can have them instead."

"I'm sure he'll be mega grateful. Just take it seriously, ok? Worshippers can get pretty intense."

I can't wait to see how much more willingly my next client takes to the task than Connor ever did.

For all the laughing and joking, the nerves are still there like jingling fire sticks when the time comes around to get ready. Bravado shrivels up under the five-star reviews and my heartrate is as high as ever as I picture my task ahead with a stranger.

This stranger happens to want to worship my *everywhere* and jizz on my toes in the aftermath. Hardly another regular day at the office.

The idea of being body worshipped up close and personally is a way more intimidating task than I figured it would be. I've never been so careful with showering, and shaving, and moisturising than I am as I get ready for him. I make sure my feet are prepped as well as they can be – nails clipped and pumice stone used to the max, before I paint my toenails a cute shade of pink and set off. I make my way to User 3267's North London apartment in a short little wrap dress, hidden by my long leather coat. I chose stiletto-heeled sandals, and my feet feel the cold for it, but I want to take the tube today – not a cab. I love the atmosphere of Christmas brewing in the streets every step of the way. The lights are so festive, and the chill of the air is so alive.

I try to make the most of the trademark British chill.

Just a few more weeks to go and I'll be needing beach sandals – not stiletto ones.

I click on *arrived* when I get to User 3267's apartment block and get told to buzz the doorbell for number seven. The door clicks open as soon as I do, and I climb my way up the bright, open staircase. Even in the dullness of the late December afternoon, it's such a lovely, light place – tasteful but not extravagant. Just the kind of place I'd like to live, if I had the money.

But I do now, don't I? I do have the money to afford somewhere nice, like this.

I shove that thought aside for the moment. This afternoon is about body worship, and a guy who likes foot play. Not for pondering rental options.

The door swings open and User 3267 takes me aback with a sweet, broad grin on his face. He's a lovely floppy-haired blond guy, and he looks younger than 27, in a shirt and sweater with dark blue jeans.

He'd never be my type in the world outside, but here, now, he's a treasure.

He presents me with a gorgeous bouquet of roses and lilies that puts Connor's bullshit bunch to shame. I give him a *thank you*. They are absolutely beautiful.

"You're very welcome," he tells me.

He hangs my coat up with so much care, you'd think it was worth millions, and looks me up and down with such utter admiration I get prickles.

"Holly, I'm so grateful you're doing me the honour of letting me worship you today."

Standing with a glorious bunch of flowers in my hand, his sentiment feels kind of weird. He drops to his knees and stares up at me like I'm a queen, and I almost want to tug him to his feet and say *don't worry, it's cool, you're great, too,* but that isn't the point of this. I've got to get in the zone.

Holly needs to get in the zone.

He stares up at me and I stare down at him. What the hell am I supposed to say?

I clear my throat, give hm a little nod. "You may stand," I tell him and he smiles at that, rising to his feet and bowing his head in return.

"Please, this way," he says and leads me through to his living room.

I find a rich burgundy chaise longue waiting there ready for action, right in the middle of the room. It has gold cushions that I fluff up beside myself before I take a seat. It's quite a majesty.

"May I offer you a drink?" he asks.

"Yes, please. I'd love one."

"And what can I get for you? I have everything. Tea, coffee, juice, spring water." He pauses. "And the very best champagne..."

I know what he wants me to take from him.

"I'd love a champagne, please. Thank you very much."

His whole face lights up, like I've granted him a favour, and I want to giggle because it's so damn cute to watch him dash through the double doors into the kitchen. He uncorks the bottle in a flash, but only pours one glass.

"Are you not having one?" I ask when he arrives back, but he shakes his head.

"No, Miss Holly, this bottle is all for you." He hands the glass over, and takes the flowers from my side. "I'm sorry, I should put these in water, so they are fresh for you later."

"That's no problem." I raise my glass to him. "Cheers, and thank you."

We're both watching each other as he wanders back through to the kitchen and puts my flowers in a vase.

I get another set of prickles at the way he's so devout with his attention. He's staring at every move I make, from the way my fingers hold the stem of the champagne glass, to the way I take a sip and swallow. He heads over to me slowly once the flowers are safe, then drops to his knees on the floor by my legs. Very *up close and personal* indeed.

That movement of his changes everything. The atmosphere morphs and heavies, and the want in the room feels almost palpable, it's so thick. User 3267 reaches his hands up as though he wants to touch me, but they hover in mid-air, dithering.

"You can do it," I tell him. "You can touch as well as look. You have permission."

"Thank you."

He wasn't joking in his proposal when he said he likes feet. He peppers my toes with kisses through my leather sandal straps, almost delirious as he tells me how grateful he is. There is such fervour there already, my heart starts to race, thumping so fast I feel dizzy.

Eb was right.

I realise I've been an idiot to dismiss this kind of fantasy so easily – treating it like a spa visit, and not like a man who truly wants to worship a woman as a goddess in human form.

Time to get with it, and get myself in line.

I put down my champagne on the floor, and hitch my dress up, revealing my calves just an inch at a time.

His fingers are so gentle as he runs the tips up my skin. They give me goosebumps, and so does his mouth as he follows his tickles with kisses.

I'm already squirming when he reaches one of my knees.

"Want to see more?" I ask, and he nods.

"Please. Show me whatever you're willing to grant me."

That's easy, since I'm willing to grant him everything.

He gasps as I stand up from the chaise longue and pull my dress up and over my head. His gaze soaks in the mottled purple and green of my thighs

"Beautiful," he tells me, and I spread them, to give him a better view.

"I'd love you to kiss them better," I tell him. "They need some love right now."

He nods and carries on peppering kisses up my thigh, so meek that it gives me tingles on top of tingles, and he's got me squirming some more – feral instincts coming to the fore – already wanting that gentle mouth of his on my needy pussy.

I'm gaining so much confidence week after week now, it's unreal.

The nervous girl is definitely stepping into the confident woman, and this is a great environment to show it. I strip my bra and cast it aside, then tug my panties down and kick them free.

So, it's just me, naked and bruised. Exposed for his stare.

I sit before User 3267, upright and proud, feeling like the goddess he wants me to be.

His touches are like butterflies as they dance across the bruises on my thighs.

"I know Harvey told me that you are a stunning creature, but I had no idea you would be this perfect."

Harvey.

Harvey must be the guy who has a dungeon...

In the realms of normality, I could shake my head with a grin and tell User 3267 that I'm really not perfect, but even if I did, it wouldn't come close to bursting his bubble. It's a sensation that wraps me up in its glow and holds me tight. In his eyes, I'm the greatest woman in creation right now. It feels like he's Adam, first setting eyes on his Eve. It feels glorious to be wanted so much, in exchange for so little.

I'm going to be Eve today. I want to be a goddess in this man's deep blue eyes.

I feel an essence rising in me, from depths I didn't know. My confidence takes hold of me and rushes through my veins, because here, in this space, I *am* his Eve. His one and only. His princess of perfection to serve and please.

Only the Eve of creation unlikely had bruises like mine...

And she'd be unlikely to spread her thighs wide to offer him her pussy, there for the taking...

"You said you wanted to worship my body," I say. "So show me. Make me feel adored. Give me what you promised." I spread my pussy lips for him, wanting his mouth on me. "Show me how good I taste."

I don't know what he's experienced before from entertainers, but he stares mute, in shock as I hold myself open for him. All thoughts of this being a sweet spa day have gone from my shallow head. It's got nothing to do with bathing and massage. It's about adoration. Respect. Divinity.

"Are you certain? I may taste your... pussy?" he asks.

"I *want* you to taste my pussy. And if I really am your princess, you'll do it without the need for my bathing and cleansing first, won't you? You'll take my dirtiness and make me clean. It's been a long, dirty journey on the tube today."

My words work like magic. I see him tremble as he licks his lips, ready to heed my calling, and what the hell – User 3267 has quite an unusual feature. His tongue is so beautifully long and thick, it's going to be like a swirl of satin. He shows me again as he licks his way up my ankle.

"I'll clean you slowly, Miss Holly," he says. "I'll savour everything."

I'm transfixed as I watch him, lapping at me, and moaning at every taste. His tongue is magnificent, and my pussy clenches at the thought of what's coming, because this guy knows what he's doing with it. He uses it in places I never realised would be so sensitive – like the crease at the back of my knee – and sweeps it hard across tender, bruised flesh, like a massager. Twisting and twirling and it really is divine.

I could be his goddess Eve for days on end and never get bored.

I lean back on the chaise longue and tip my head back, eyes closed as I welcome him up and closer. I hold his head as he breathes into my ear, blessing me with shudders from tiny little kisses all the way down my neck. I always love those. They make me pant with want – and I have to stop myself urging him into me. It would be so fucking easy to take my want and have him use it. But no. NO. This is the proposal, and nothing more.

I play the dirty game he laid out to play, hitching myself and gasping as he worships my bruised tits with his tongue, flicking my nipples with the tip as he looks up at me.

"You're lucky, aren't you?" I say, trying to make sure I maintain my goddess position, and he nods, gratefully.

"I'm extremely lucky to be blessed with a queen like you."

The luck is all mine when he begins to suck. My tits are still so tender that they spark pleasure down between my legs, and it's going to be so much harder to keep my composure now… I won't manage it…

Not unless I summon the strength to make him begin all over again.

"You haven't earnt the honour of tasting my pussy yet," I tell him. "Start over. On the floor. Kiss my feet again."

I feel his hard-on against my thigh as he climbs straight down. No argument whatsoever.

"Yes, princess. Of course."

I don't know how I take another round of his tongue action. Even having my toes licked through my sandals gives me a fresh bout of shakes. My ankles are tickly, and my calves are tight as he kisses them all the way up to my knees. And then once again, slowly, he is on top of me, this time massaging my head through my hair, twisting strands in his fingers as I look to the side, so fucking sensitive on the back of my scalp.

"Fuck," I whimper. "that's so nice. More, please."

He gives me more. He works my scalp like an expert, pressing in incredible spots while bearing his weight right down on me.

I'm the one moaning when he starts kissing my neck for the second time around, my hands up and over my head, arching for him as his wonderful mouth and tongue seek out my tender nipples. This time I need him on my pussy. I won't be able to stop myself.

"You can clean me now," I tell him. "Clean my dirty pussy, and give me the honour I deserve."

"Thank you," he says. "I'll honour you with everything I have."

I let him free on my pussy, spreading my thighs and letting him knead my bruises before he reaches the juncture. He breathes on me in wonder, running his fingers up and down my slit like it's precious jewellery.

"Please, may I spread you?"

I remember my role.

"No. Not yet. You haven't earnt the privilege."

He groans at my words, teasing me with his fingertips some more. He tastes the creases between my thighs and pussy, then nudges his nose ever so slightly against my clit. But he can't see it. My slit is closed tight, even though I'm dripping for him.

"Kiss me," I tell him and he peppers my pussy with soft kisses, over and over and it's so intense I want to slam my needy cunt in his face, but no.

"Please, may I spread you now?" he asks, and I look down with a smirk.

"No," I tell him, "kiss my dirty hole."

My God, when he presses his lips to my asshole and drops kiss after kiss after kiss, I swear I could come if he kept it up.

He stops for a breath and looks up at me.

"I'm eager to clean you, Miss Holly. May I spread you now?"

"Are you going to give me the honour I truly deserve?"

"More than anything, I promise."

"Then yes, you may spread me now."

I try to stay still as he slowly splays my pussy open like it's a sacred flower, gasping at the sight of my clit swimming in pure, dripping want. His tongue is so thick it's like a long, wet swipe of brilliance as he tastes the length of me, sucking at my clit like a baby craving a nipple. That's the level of need I feel from him. He's trembling, shaking as he eats my pussy, coaxing me open with his fingers and sinking his tongue in deep.

I take hold of the back of his head, pressing against him.

"That's it. Honour my cunt, just like that."

He tenses up at my words, sucking and lapping harder, and I don't give a fuck about being a perfect goddess anymore, I'm a horny one.

"You're such a good servant," I say. "You're going to make me come. Would you like that? Would you like the honour of making me come for you?"

The way he nods against my fucking slit drives me wild.

"Keep nodding!" I say. "Keep telling me! Showing me!"

What a combination. Nods, moans, gasps, licks and sucks – but nothing inside me other than a probing tongue. No fingers, no cock to stretch me deep, just a guy's mouth all over me, sending me insane.

He's shuddering along with me when I come against his face. His tongue is lapping up and down me, his nose rubbing my clit as I burst and lose control.

Oh my fucking God, it's divine.

I'm sure I'm soaking the fabric underneath me as I dribble wet in the aftermath. I hitch myself up to show him and he breathes in the filthy wet patch with a smile.

"*Now* you've earnt my toes," I say, swimming in the sea of post orgasm bliss.

He unbuckles my heels slowly and slides them free, sitting cross-legged on the floor with his pants clearly bulging through his jeans as he begins the journey of foot worship.

Fuck.

If I'd have known how good it felt to have someone's tongue squirming between my toes with such purpose, I'd have waved my feet in front of Connor every night after work until he damn well relented.

The arches of my feet are more sensitive than I knew, and kisses on my ankles are pure windows to body shakes... but my little toes... the ones he sucks so gently on... *fuck.*

I can barely keep my breath as he switches from foot to foot... and my pussy can't resist the clenches that signal I need more.

"You're doing so well, I'm going to play with myself," I tell him. "Take it as praise."

"I take it as great praise, thank you."

I work my clit while he teases and tempts my toes, fucking myself with my fingers while he keeps working his magic on the floor.

"Your feet are beautiful," he tells me, and I grin at the ceiling.

"Thank you. Your tongue has a good way of demonstrating it."

He stares up at me with hooded eyes as I play, looking so fucking dirty with my big toe in his mouth.

"Have I earnt the honour of pleasuring you everywhere?" he asks me between sucks, and I watch him, trying to fathom quite what he means as my fingers strum to my rhythm.

"You want to honour my pussy again? Is that what you're asking?" I say, but he shakes his head, sucking my toe nice and deep again before he answers.

"No, Miss Holly. I'd like to honour your ass. I want to honour your ass as you play with yourself. Please, grant me the pleasure."

Even the thought has my clit buzzing harder, and I'm too far gone to give a fuck how exposed I am. I nod as I tug my legs up on the chaise longue and haul them up by my shoulders, because holy fuck, I want User 3267's long, wet tongue deep inside my dirty ass, and I'm going to come while he does it. We manoeuvre so easily, him helping me get my legs up even higher.

He pulls my ass cheeks apart, staring transfixed as I clench my hole for him, and he groans when he gently touches his lips to my asshole.

I sigh for him. "Clean me out," I order while rubbing at my clit.

"Of course, princess," he says and it's my turn to moan as he pushes his tongue in deep.

It feels so weird, his long tongue swirling inside me, but I love it.

"More," I tell him, sinking three fingers into my soaked pussy.

He pulls his tongue free and sucks on my asshole. Damn, it's fucking heaven as I pump my fingers.

"Suck harder," I tell him, and he does, he sucks so hard, it's a whole new experience for me. A whole new filthy experience that I want more of.

"Harder!" I say, "much harder!" and my servant complies, sucking my asshole so hard my hand's trembling as I finger myself.

"Now deeper!" I say and he stops sucking and slides his tongue all the way back in, lapping and swirling as the first sparks of orgasm burn me up.

"Don't stop," I order. "Don't you dare stop!"

I stretch myself with four fingers as I pinch my clit with my other hand and I'm done... squirming over my servant's face, his tongue still swirling in my ass as I come for a second time.

My whole body is racked with tremors on the comedown, every nerve on fire. I'm smiling, high as a kite as I stroke User 3267's dirty face, rewarding his efforts with a nod.

"You were fantastic. Thank you. That was amazing."

"Thank you, princess, but you talk as though we're finished. You still deserve more honour."

I don't know what he's talking about until he stands and helps me onto my unsteady legs. I'm still getting my balance when he scoops me up into his arms and carries me through his apartment to the bathroom. He's still holding me when he flicks on the shower and waits until it's hot. I feel so secure in his arms.

"I'd love to honour you by soaping you clean," he says, and I nod, ready for the flow as he puts me down under the shower head.

He puts even *Daddy* to shame with his bathing skills. His expertise with soapy massage is worthy of a damn salon. He's so attentive that I must be foamed up three times over, so softly scrubbed as he works his way between my legs. At one point I have to brace myself, the end of the sponge tickling my clit so hard it overpowers me for a third time running, and I can barely stand when he's finally washed me clean and helped me out of there. I'm exhausted with the thrill as he towels me dry.

"Have I pleased you?" he asks.

I almost say something clever about his incredible tongue, but remember my place – my role.

I place an appreciative hand on his shoulder. "More than I ever hoped for," I tell him.

His smile is so genuine, I actually feel happy for him.

"Then," he says, "if I may, can have my reward now?"

I give a solemn nod, wondering what his reward is going to be, then, ah, yes. I remember what the proposal said once he drops me back on the chaise longue.

He raises my feet up on the cushions, and then he drops his pants.

Oh fuck, I wish it was going to be plunging inside me, but his eyes are fixated on my bare feet as if they are gifts from Heaven above. He drops to his knees and holds my soles together, working his cock between them, like he's fucking a slit between the arches. He rubs the head of his dick against my toes, leaving them slick with precum as he goes, and soon he's a bucking wreck, slamming my feet like they're a pussy as he grunts and groans.

I urge him on by groping my tits and playing with my nipples. He's panting now, licking his lips as he thrusts and grunts.

"That feels so good," I tell him, and it pushes him off the cliff.

He spurts cum over my bare feet, then smiles down as he smears it in – massaging wet, sloppy jizz between my toes.

Damn, he looks so proud of himself.

"Thank you," I say, wiggling my sticky toes for him.

He grins at that. "May I buckle your shoes back up now, please?" he asks.

"Of course."

I'm going to be walking away from his apartment with drying cum all over my feet, but I couldn't give a shit. The thought makes me grin.

He puts my shoes on first, then helps dress me as I finish up my champagne, still treating me like a heroine from a romance story. He tells me over and again just how good I am to worship, and I take all of his praise with nods and smiles and thank yous.

It's a dirty thrill when I leave his apartment block, with a bunch of flowers in my hands and a client's jizz drying around my toes. So many people pass me by without a clue. Oblivious to the world of *entertainment* I'm involved with.

I'd take User 3267's jizz between my toes any day of the year – especially with the five-star review that comes after it, and the eight hundred pounds that land in my bank account.

Happy Christmas to me.

nineteen

User 2799. Male. 33.
My boyfriend and I have a fantastic relationship, but – being bi – sometimes we like a little extra playtime... especially him. He loves having the occasional session with a hot, dirty girl, so call this his Christmas present, and I want to make sure he is very, very satisfied. From your reviews, and your gorgeous profile, I'm certain you will be a great fit. We're in London on a pre-Christmas vacation, so I'm hoping to plan a festive surprise for him – a little gothic Christmas fairy, ready to play dirty games.
I would love it if you could join us, happy and comfortable with guy on guy anal and action. You'd need to take both of our cocks in a variety of combinations, and offer your pussy for very excited mouth play. Double penetration, most definitely – pussy and anal. Two in the mouth, a must.
Also, I have one extra requirement. Quite a major one...
I'd like both of our cocks in your pussy at the same time.
Trust me, we'll make it fun.
Duration – 6 hours.
Proposal price – £7000.

Thank fuck my bruises have healed by now, because I've been dreaming of seeing two guys getting hot and horny for years. I'm already turned on as I read the offer. Two cocks in the pussy at the same time? How could I ever turn that proposal down?

Eb claps her hands in glee. "That'll be quite a Christmas present for you as well, if they're even half decent at it."

It sure will, and what a precursor to my own greatest Christmas present? Just ten more days and I'll be on a flight to see my parents. Ten more days until the trip of my dreams. And ten more days to make as much money as I can before I go...

I accept User 2799's proposal and click on the earliest time possible. Tomorrow afternoon, I'll be a gothic Christmas Fairy for a guy and his boyfriend.

Weirdly, I'm not feeling the nerves at all this time around. Maybe it's something about the tone of the proposal, or maybe it's the new, confident me, knowing I'll come out of it feeling good, and a whole lot richer. Or maybe it's the festive vibe, looking forward to being some guy's Christmas fairy.

After chatting with Eb and hearing her stories of the many times she's taken two D's in the V, I spend the rest of the evening checking out porn clips with two dildos inside me, getting off to watching girls taking two cocks at once. I can't wait to try it for real.

The following afternoon, I opt for a tight little red velvet dress, which shows off my cleavage like a dream, paired with high top lace stockings, and some festive red heels. I choose scarlet lipstick and curl my hair, trying my best to look like a gothic Christmas present in human form before I set off on my journey. I hope I've done a good enough job. I want another five-star review with my name on it.

London is buzzing, with twinkling lights, carols and jingles, and people dashing around doing their Christmas shopping. I stroll along with my hands in my coat pockets, soaking up the atmosphere. It feels weird to think I won't be waking up to a frosty chill on Christmas morning this year. I'll have sun, sea and sangrias, most likely, and just thinking about it makes me feel warm all over. And warmer still as I approach the venue, tummy fluttering at what's to come. Their hotel is one of the huge towers right in the city centre. An exuberance of the wealthy at this time of year. I click *arrived* when I reach the revolving doors at the entrance, and step on inside.

Suite 23 the message says in return.

The hotel reception is a festive heaven, with fairy lights and tinsel all around. I stare up in wonder at the massive Christmas tree in the middle of the foyer before I head for the elevators. The angel at the top is quite something. A sparkly little queen with golden wings and a sweet, pretty smile on her face.

She can be my aspiration for this afternoon...

Suite 23 is on floor eight, and I get a little shiver of nerves on the ascent, but they're nerves of excitement, nothing more than that.

I reach suite 23 and find a *do not disturb* sign hanging over the doorhandle. There's a spyhole in the door, so I make sure I'm smiling bright before knocking.

The guy who opens the door is a beautiful specimen of a creature with light brown hair, flicked back with hints of blond. He has short stubble, and his eyes are the kind of blue you see in dreams. Jeez. Plus, on top of that, he's wearing a tux. A fucking tuxedo, in the middle of the afternoon.

Glory be to God. I do a start backwards as he does the same, both of us staring, transfixed.

"You, um, must be at the wrong door," he says, but a loud laugh sounds out from inside as he says it.

"No, she's not."

The door swings open wider and a taller guy steps up to his side, slipping an arm around his waist as he plants a kiss on his cheek.

"Happy Christmas, Jack."

Jack. So, the hot mousy blond is called Jack. It suits him.

Jack's partner is bulkier, and his hair is darker and longer, with a short, dark beard complementing it perfectly. He too is dressed in a magnificent tux, the two of them standing there like they belong in a movie. Absolutely fucking gorgeous.

Jack's dark-haired partner holds out a hand, and gives me one of those confident handshakes, with both of his hands clasping mine. Authoritative, but warm.

"Pleased to meet you, Holly. Please, come on inside. I'm Eric."

Jack is still looking on in shock as I step into their suite. He mouths a *WTF* at his boyfriend, but Eric grins his head off and slaps him on the back.

The term *suite* is an understatement. The place is massive, with a grand lounge area looking out over the city through full length windows. What an incredible view. Breathtaking. But the guys' eyes aren't looking at the London skyline when I turn around to face them. Both of them are looking at me.

"I knew something was up," Jack says, giving Eric a playful punch in the side. "As if we'd need bloody tuxedos for a *coffee* downstairs."

"What can I say?" Eric says. "I wanted to make a good impression for our cute little Christmas fairy."

They've certainly done that.

Jack is still looking shocked as he stares over, his eyes beautiful as he grins. I feel like I really am the angel from the tree downstairs, confidence growing every second. I slip my coat off as they watch me, placing it over the back of the chair at the dresser before doing a curtsy.

"Happy Christmas, guys. Lovely to meet you."

Their eyes rove over me, both of them scoping me out so intensely I could be onstage at a dirty beauty pageant. My pulse is racing as Jack gives Eric a high five.

"Great choice, baby. I'll owe you one."

"You'll be owing me more than one," Eric replies. "I browsed the whole fucking site for this beauty." He looks so pleased as he smirks at me. "I'm grateful you could join us, Holly."

The energy around these two has me churning up. Eric has a genuine gentlemanly confidence which makes my skin tingle, and Jack looks at him like he's the most incredible man on earth. It's a glorious dynamic of love that tugs at my heart.

Jack grabs Eric and plants a kiss on his lips, smiling as he lingers, and it gives me a rush to see them so intimate.

"Thank you. You're the brightest star in the whole fucking sky."

"Like I said, you can owe me one."

"Chalk it up on the board."

They laugh together before their attention turns back to me.

"Would you like a drink?" Eric asks, and I nod, requesting a *mineral water, thanks.*

The guys already have a bottle of red open, but I don't want to get tipsy this afternoon. I want to enjoy every single moment for what it is.

Eric places a hand on my lower back to guide me towards the

windows, pointing out the London Eye in the distance. It's then that I see the huge bed around the corner. Jeez, this must be a super, super, *super*king mattress from the size of it.

"Jack doesn't know the finer details of our proposal," Eric says, smirking at his boyfriend as he hands me my mineral water. "It would be lovely if you'd give him a rundown of what we have planned this Christmas playtime."

I nearly stumble over my words as I address Jack, but his smile has me smiling right back.

"Ok, so we have some lovely playtime planned. I'll be watching you guys up close and personal, which will be *amazing.*" I'm not joking. "We have my wet pussy on offer for your mouths." I take hold of my tits. "And whatever else of me you want, of course." I turn around and hitch my dress up, giving them a glimpse of my ass. "I can't wait to feel you guys fucking me, both at once. Ass and pussy." Then I pause before delivering the icing on the cake. "And another kind of DP, too. The pair of you in my pussy, both at once."

Jack's smile turns into a grin, looking between me and his partner.

"You for fucking real? Two in the pussy?"

"Like I said, I picked well," Eric says with another flash of adoration.

"You really sure about this?" Jack says to me. "Has Eric shown you a dick pic?"

I shake my head, and Eric swats his words away. "No, I haven't shown her a dick pic. It's hardly a big deal."

"Hardly a big deal?! An ironic choice of words. Maybe you should have, don't you think?"

Eric rolls his eyes. "I'm not a fucking donkey, Jack."

Jack laughs. "Not far off."

"Yeah, well, you're not so bad yourself."

"Thank you, *sweetie pie*. Such flattery. *I'm* not Donkey Kong though, am I? You are."

I have to hold back laughing along with them, they are so addictive. I find I'm holding up my hands to reassure them.

"I promise I'll handle it. Both of you. Donkey Kong with a Donkey Kong sidekick, no problem."

I find I actually believe it. Right now, it's true.

I'm surprisingly at ease as Eric grabs his partner by his jacket lapels and pulls him in for a deeper kiss. I'm transfixed as I watch the two of them make out, clit already pulsing at the glimpses of their tongues twisting together. I could put my hand between my legs right here and now, I'm already so horny.

Their kiss is feverish, Jack moaning against Eric's mouth as he palms his cock through his trousers, and their jackets come off, discarded. Bow ties are tugged free and thrown to the floor.

I could watch these two for ever.

Both guys' lips are already puffy when they turn their attention back to me. My actions come nearly as naturally as theirs as I pull down the side zip of my dress and shimmy the red velvet down to the floor. I hold my tits up invitingly in my red lace bra as I spread my legs, confident as I stand there in my matching heels.

"Merry Christmas, guys."

"You go first," Eric says to Jack. "Play with your pretty little Christmas present. Get over there and finish unwrapping her."

"Don't worry. I'm on it."

I'm ready for Jack's mouth on mine when he closes the distance, still hot at the way he was kissing his partner with such passion. His hands are straight on my tits once he's unclipped my bra, roving and playing – my nipples hard against his palms as he rolls them.

I'm already working on instinct, pressing up close with his thigh between mine. I could grind and use his thigh alone to come quite happily, all day long, every day of the year. I wrap my arms up around his shoulders and kiss him like a hungry little bitch, and Jack slips a hand down to rub my pussy through my panties.

"You're so fucking wet," he says with a smirk, and I moan for him again.

"How could I not be? You guys are hot as hell."

"Good job you are so wet, since you'll need it later." He turns to Eric, who's watching us. "Come on over here, baby. I'm missing you already."

I reach out for Eric as Jack does, both of us beckoning him over with happy giggles. *Dirty giggles.*

I'm going to enjoy this...

The three of us fall onto the bed together. I don't know who is stripping who, but within seconds the guys are shirtless – my fingers fumbling at buttons along with theirs, and someone has managed to slide my panties off. Jack urges Eric up and onto me first – despite Eric's protests – and *User 2799* grinds the swell of his crotch against my pussy, his tongue hot and hard against mine as we play.

Jack wasn't lying.

Eric is huge. This donkey really does have a kong in his pants.

"Come on," I say, intrigued as hell. "Please, fuck me. Show me how big you are."

He moves his mouth to my neck. "No, no, no. I want Jack to fuck you first. You're *his* present, after all."

Jack doesn't argue. He drops his pants, and kicks his shoes and socks off, leaving him totally naked. Eric wasn't lying when he said Jack wasn't hung all that bad either. His dick is a lovely length with quite a girth.

"It's been a while since I've fucked pussy," he says as he takes position on top, hoisting my legs up high. I watch him rub the big head of his dick against my pussy, teasing my slit. I'm whimpering like a slut, working my clit as he slides up and down, using my wetness. I won't be able to stand the tease much longer...

"Take her, Jack," Eric says. "Fuck her cunt like a good boy."

There's something in Eric's tone, in his words... something that hitches Jack's breath and spurs him on. He's watching Eric, not me, as he slams his cock inside me in one thrust, pistoning his hips like a fucking monster. The chemistry between them is electric. I lie there and take it, soaking in the gaze between the lovers as Jack's cock pounds me senseless. I can't move, and I wouldn't want to if I could. Jack's got my knees pinned so fucking high above my head, I'm stuck here, and he's leveraging my pussy for all its worth.

His eyes are hooded, fierce, when they meet back up with mine.

"You're so damn tight," he says. "You'll never take both of us at once. No way."

I feel a fire inside me. A craving. I nod my head to the contrary, determined.

"I will. I'm so greedy, I don't care if it hurts."

"It'll definitely hurt, believe me. Eric's cock hurts enough on its own. Time to show you."

He pulls out of my pussy without warning, and Eric climbs over to take his place, stripped bare himself and ready for action.

Jesus Christ, he really is hung like a donkey. He puts every other User I've had to shame, and that's saying something. He's so much thicker that I cry out as he fills up the needy hole Jack left behind, but that's ok. I want it. I *need* it.

"Harder, yes," I say, as he picks up pace. "Get me ready for two."

"We've got a long fucking way to go before you're ready for two," Eric says, but he slams his hips so hard that they thump against me, flesh to flesh. He grips me even tighter in position as Jack looks on, and there it is again – that electric charge between them. I'm insane, swimming in my own fantasies. I want to see these guys fucking each other. I want to see Jack's ass struggling to take this beast.

"Give me some," Jack says to me. "Give me your mouth while Eric takes your pussy."

Eric yanks me down the bed by my hips and Jack straddles my face, feeding his cock to me. I slurp like a hungry bitch, moaning against the stretch as Eric forces a finger inside me along with his cock.

"She sure is fucking tight," he says to Jack, and yeah, I am, but I don't care.

"Do it!" I spit out around Jack's dick. "Get me ready!"

I figure it'll be more of my pussy that Eric goes for, but it's my ass that he squirms two fingers inside this time. The strain has me choking around Jack's cock, retching with the burn of the stretch as well as the pleasure. But I don't give a shit. I'm pinned tight, and my clit is tingling, and I want to give these guys the service of their lives.

I choke and retch some more as Eric forces in a third finger.

"Let her up, Jack," Eric says. "Let her see what I'm doing to her."

Jack pulls his cock from my throat and lifts my head so that I can watch as Eric's thick cock plunges in and out of my pussy, but he pulls out after a few thrusts, and I see how far his fingers are buried inside my ass. He twists them as I watch, and then he lines his cock up against them, showing the difference in girth. His cock is at least three times as thick. My eyes must widen as I stare.

"Want to see what's lying ahead for you?" Eric asks. "Want to watch Jack take me in his ass before you do? He moans like a horny little slut himself when he's taking it deep."

"Sure do," Jack says, and I'm nodding like crazy.

"Hell, yeah. Yes, please."

The two of them manhandle me to the side so easily. I scrabble to get up close for viewing as Jack takes my place on the bed, flat on his back, raising his legs high.

I'm fascinated as I stare at Eric's monster cock, slick from my pussy as he lines it up against Jack's clenching asshole. Jack's looking up at the ceiling, teeth gritted, and I know this isn't going to be a gentle fucking.

"Take it, baby," Eric says, and Jack takes it like a pro, reaching down for his own ass cheeks and pulling them wide.

Eric buries his cock in Jack like a piledriver, so thick that the rim of Jack's ass gets tugged in and out with every thrust, like he's being pumped by a plunger. It's a beautiful sight. Pure, filthy magic.

"Suck Jack's cock while I do it," Eric tells me. "Give him a bonus treat."

Jack grins as Eric guides my mouth to his throbbing dick.

"As if it's not nice enough already..."

It's so up close and personal in this position. Eric's dirty cock grazes my cheek as I suck his boyfriend's balls and lick up and down the length of him, trying to tease before I please. I take Jack in my mouth, and smell the filthy musk of hot anal, my ears full of the grunts and groans of two men lost to the pleasure. My hand rubs at my wet pussy, fingers hooking inside me as I approach the edge myself, but I don't want to come yet. I want to come with them inside me. I want to come for *them*.

I force myself to stop touching myself, and it's almost in sync with them. Eric pulls out of Jack's ass, cupping his balls, and Jack scoots up and away, cursing as he pulls out of my mouth.

"Fucking hell," Eric says, with a dirty laugh. "That nearly got away from me there."

"Yeah, well, fucking ditto." Jack laughs back, grimacing as he grips his shaft, and I'm laughing with them, rolling onto my back on the bed.

"Well, that makes three of us," I tell them. "I was nearly there myself."

My clit is throbbing like a bastard, it really is. Both guys turn their heads to me, laughing some more as they realise just how worked up I am. I'm not just a playgirl out for the cash, lying back and *thinking of England*. I'm a slut who loves it.

"You were quite a find," Eric says, and I nod and lick my lips, scarlet lipstick no doubt long gone by now.

"Yeah. Well. The same goes in return. You two are magic. Absolute magic."

They share a look, almost telepathic. Jack raises his eyebrows, and Eric nods.

Jack's smirk is still on his face when he speaks.

"How about we drive you over the edge first? Call it an early reward for you, and a late lunch for us. I dunno about you, Eric, but I'm pretty hungry right now."

"Sorry, what?" I ask, still catching my breath. "You want to make me come first?"

"We'll show you *magic*," Eric says. "We may be out of practice, but you know what they say. A swimmer never forgets how to swim."

"Yeah," Jack says, and yanks me closer. "And a pussy eater never forgets how to eat cunt."

I stare at him as he lowers himself between my legs with an *mmm.* His eyes are feasting on my dripping wet slit like I'm the Christmas fairy of his dreams. I won't be able to take it for long... I won't... I'm a moaning wreck as soon as he lands his lips on my pussy, not helped in the slightest by Eric sucking at my nipple like a baby on a teat. I don't know how long I'm lying there as the two crazy hot studs use their mouths on me, holding my legs wide and spread as I come – only to shift the focus to my tits and mouth, kissing me hard before they do it again.

My God, my God, MY GOD. I'm practically delirious after a few rounds, sopping wet and so tender I have no words as they keep on slavering on my cunt like I'm the hottest dessert in the world.

"Stop, please!" I say after coming again. "I can't... I can't take much more... it's too good, my clit can't take it... I swear!"

Jack's mouth is next to my ear. "We're only just preparing you."

"Fuck," I say, but I'm already opening my legs back up.

This time they use fingers as well as their tongues, stretching me more and more as they use me. I don't know or care whose fingers are in my ass and whose are in my pussy, or how many they are using – the crazy spark of my clit is enough that I'll grip the sheets and happily take the whole of mankind right now.

"Time for Jack's cock to fill up that sweet cunt of yours," Eric says, and guides me up and onto his boyfriend, so I'm straddling him. My hands on his shoulders.

I ride Jack until he's balls deep, bouncing like I'm on a bronco, my tits so tender they hurt with every bounce. I'm fully in the groove when Eric lunges forward and pins me flat against Jack's chest.

Shit. Here it comes... two at once. I feel Eric's dick line up against my asshole, Jack's cock still buried to the balls inside in my cunt.

"Breathe deep," Eric tells me, and I do as I'm told. Long, slow breaths in and out as the huge fat head of his cock tries to force entry. Tight doesn't even come close. It hurts like hell the moment he starts.

I cry out, and wriggle until Eric gives me a gentle *shh*, before he tells me again.

"Breathe deep and slow, Holly. Deep and slow. It'll hurt, but it'll be worth it. Trust me."

I trust him enough that I nod my head, and take another deep breath, letting it out as slowly as I can as he eases his beast inside me. Jack cries out with a *fuck, yes* as he feels the pressure of Eric's cock against his – just the wall of my ass and pussy between them.

"Again, breathe deep and slow," Eric says, and I keep a rhythm of breaths, slow and deep as he edges just a little bit deeper each time. It hurts so much I grimace, sweat pooling all over me, sandwiched by two hot bodies, but Eric doesn't stop, just keeps his pressure steady as I begin to relax around him. "That's it, Holly. Almost in. Just a little bit more."

"Fucking hell," Jack says, and tenses underneath me. "I'm gonna shoot my load in a minute, Eric, so you'd better get those hips going."

"Don't you dare even think about coming," Eric says.

All three of us are grunting and moaning as Eric begins moving in and out, an inch at a time. I'm heady with the crazy pain as his thrusts get harder, and Jack's curses get louder, until he's bucking up underneath me in tandem. My last DP session was nothing like this. This is so feral that I feel I'm going to lose my fucking mind, wanting this with everything I have.

But I want MORE.

I want both of these guys in my pussy. I want them cock to cock. I want them cum to cum, squelching out of me in one filthy slopping mess.

I'm a writhing, squealing wreck as the guys thrust to their peak. Eric's girth is thrashing the stretch of my ass to breaking point, and Jack is pumping me like a bronco who keeps on bucking from underneath.

My clit is grinding against him, and every spot inside me is triggered to bursting, and I come right along with them, wailing like a banshee, moving as desperately as they do until there is nothing left. We're left as a pile of sweaty bodies, gasping for breath, gulping in air as the world spins.

Bliss.

I don't know who starts laughing first, giggling in the headiness, but we're all at it in seconds, revelling in the comedown. I wail out curses amidst the laughter as Eric pulls out of me, and Jack groans as I rise from his dick. I grip my pussy like I'm torn into pieces, afraid to look, but it's time to face the music...

I check my hand, and there is a bit of blood mixed with cum, yeah, but nothing catastrophic. Eric takes my hand for a look himself, then runs his fingers between my legs, checking for more.

"Fair play," he says. "You handled that well."

"Thank you." I glow at the bizarre compliment, so bright my eyes must be twinkling. "Hopefully my pussy is as up for the stretch as my ass was."

"We'll soon find out," Eric says, helping me from the bed before pulling Jack up along with us. "Let's shower off first, and get ready to get your cunt screaming."

I limp to the bathroom between them, one of my arms linked through each of theirs.

The shower is huge enough to dwarf all three of us under the cascade. Our hands wander happily, all of us soaping each other clean and sharing kisses between a stupid singsong of jingle bells that has me in stitches. Filth and fun. What a perfect combination. Something I'm coming to live by.

We share some red wine in the aftermath – screw mineral water – all of us wrapped in luxurious hotel towels as the London lights glow in the twilight outside. I don't want to know how much time we have left. I wish it was all night straight.

The guys are still sipping their wine when I put my glass down on the side and drop to my knees between them, pulling their towels down and free. They are hard in seconds, and I take them in my mouth one by one, sharing their cocks like the dirtiest little fairy I can be. Their wines don't last long before they take control, using my mouth like I'm a doll, back and forth before trying to ram in, both together. Good luck, but I do my best, cheeks bulging.

"Time to test that cunt before we have another explosion," Eric says, leaning down to take me under the arms.

He hauls me up and lifts me from my feet, delivering me to Jack and his hard cock, ready and waiting. My legs wrap around Jack's waist, his dick is straight into my sore cunt, where it should be. It feels so right. He leans back against the wall, and I use the support for extra leverage as I bounce up and down. I'm heavy into the groove when I feel Eric step up close behind me. His fingers trail down my ass crack before they align with Jack's cock.

"Do it," I say, and Eric does. He uses my own momentum to push two fingers inside my pussy along with Jack's dick, and it's sore as fuck, but yet again, I'm past caring. I'm going to take both of their cocks inside me, whatever it takes.

"Is she ready?" Jack gasps, his head tipped back against the wall.

"Not yet."

I grit my teeth, hissing like a cat as he spreads his fingers alongside Jack's dick to loosen me up. He's going to tear me. I can feel it. He adds another finger and keeps on going, and so do I. I keep on bouncing, focused on nothing but keeping my rhythm as I ride his boyfriend.

"Ok," Eric says, finally. "Let's do it. She's as ready as she'll ever be."

I'm tingling with nervous excitement as Jack carries me to the bed. He drops down so I'm straddling him, kissing me deep before he wraps me in his arms, taking me with him as he falls flat on his back. Here we go again… but this time it's not going to be my ass Eric is forcing his way into…

I don't know how he's going to do it, or manage it, but I don't care. I hear a squelch of lube, and I feel the cold wetness smeared right the way between my legs, coating Jack's dick as I ride him.

"Up and off for a minute," Eric says, and I hitch myself up so Jack's cock slides free. More squelches of lube, and my heart is pounding.

Eric positions himself above me, tight and parallel to Jack on the bed – another hot flesh sandwich of the three of us. Only Eric is lower this time. Heavier on my back.

"Now, slowly. SLOWLY," he tells me.

I feel how the guys are gripping their cocks together as one, and I get it. I'm going to impale myself on two at once. One huge pole of cock.

Slowly doesn't cut it. I'm barely able to move as I feel the two massive cockheads ready for my pussy. It's a mountain. A fucking monster.

"Come on, you can do it," Jack says. "Be a good little Christmas fairy."

The humour in his voice doesn't take away the flare in my stomach.

I am going to be *better* than a good little Christmas fairy. I'm going to be a five-star one, right at the top of the fucking tree.

I ease down onto the massive pole of man meat, determined to breach the hole, because once that's done… once they're in… they can fuck me. They can take control.

"Good girl, that's it," Eric says, and I grin with relief through the pain as my pussy lets them in.

Everything else is a gritted-teeth blur as the guys take over. Inching as one turns to thrusting as a pair, to thrusting in alternates – slam on slam on slam as they grunt and urge me on. I don't care about the pain, or the pressure. I couldn't give a shit whether I'm tearing, I just take their gorgeous cocks like the happiest girl on earth. It's a sloppy, stretched, slather of flesh as the lube squelches, and their balls bounce against me, cocks swollen deep… and then somewhere… deep… at some point, their huge double pole hits the right spot.

"THERE!" I shout without restraint. "There, please! There! Like that!"

Eric doesn't need any more encouragement from behind me. He uses his position to take hold of my waist and slams deeper, at the perfect fucking angle.

Jack kisses my neck as their two cocks fuck me senseless, and Eric keeps my momentum at the max, not letting up control as I work up to an orgasm.

"Faster, please!" I beg, but he gives me a simple, *no.*

He makes the right call, because the tension builds higher. Higher. Higher. My body wants faster, until it's desperate, and my orgasm is a tidal wave of an explosion. Me between two guys as they stretch my cunt with two cocks.

And then they fuck me, hard. No inhibitions. No concerns for anything but the power in their dicks as they work together as one. They come like animals, greedy and needy, ploughing me with brute strength as I lie pinned between their chests, at their mercy.

I'm glowing proud when they crest and fill me up with cum.

I'm heady when they collapse for the second time, gasping like they've run a marathon.

I'm grinning when they pull out and check my bleeding pussy.

I'm fixated as they celebrate with another deep kiss between them, both of them high on lust, and wholly and truly in love.

I'm grateful when they pull me in for a three-way kiss as a thank you, and I'm thankful for another glass of wine when they've helped me get cleaned up and dressed.

And then, I'm sad to be leaving when it's time to go.

Farewell, Jack and Eric.

I'm a mashup of emotions as I leave the lovers in their hotel suite and disappear from their world. Once again, I stare up at the Christmas tree in the foyer, and smile at the little angel at the top.

I hope I lived up to the aspirations I set myself in her name.

I hope I did a good enough job at being Holly, the gothic Christmas fairy for two of the hottest guys I've ever seen in my life.

I take a cab back to my place rather than the tube. I can barely walk once the adrenaline has worn off, flopping into the back seat, exhausted.

The notification comes through within moments.

Five stars.

The best Christmas present I could have ever shared with my boyfriend. She took it all like a gothic fairy dream. Came as she tore – two in one, which says a lot about the perfect kind of entertainer a girl like Holly really is.

What a threesome. My boyfriend will be owing me one for a long, long time after this Christmas surprise.

The funds are in my account, with a grand as a bonus.

The guys paid 8k for that experience. Nothing seems more insane as my heart pangs, wanting to stay in their hotel suite all night long.

I ping Ebony. Fuck knows what I'd do without her there, the greatest friend there could be. Just a few more days and I'll be meeting her in person, all set to make toasts to our careers at the entertainer's party, and thank God for that. But I need her now. I need her words more than ever as my soul throbs for the two gorgeous guys I'm leaving behind.

Got a case of morning after syndrome. Bad. I think I'm in love with two guys who just took my pussy at the same time. No joke.

She sends me a laughing emoji, but I don't send one back. My stomach is churning hardcore for Jack and Eric.

You're serious, aren't you? she sends when she realises. *Jesus, Ells. Double whammy of morning after and it's not even night time. Get in that inbox ASAP. NEXT PROPOSAL. DON'T HOLD BACK!*

I sigh.

She's right.

Time to move on.

I check my inbox before my cab's even pulled up at home, scouting through my options until I find one that takes my breath.

One thing's for sure – there will be no *morning after syndrome* from this next proposal.

I won't even get to see his face...

twenty

User 706. Male. 38.

I like to playact rough, in the middle of the night. I'll grab you while you're walking along a little park backroad. I'll tie your wrists while you struggle, and once you're bound, I'll bundle you into my truck. I'll drive you over bumpy lanes until we reach the backend of nowhere, and then I'll throw you to the ground, and let you struggle to get free. But you won't get very far. I'll make sure of it.

I'll treat you like you're a kidnapped victim, and you won't see who I am. You won't have a clue. I'll be masked and clothed in black. An anonymous monster who uses you like a slut.

A little backchat is welcome. Total submission is a must.

Pussy and ass. Tit fucking. Slapping. Choking on cock.

When we're done, I'll bundle you back into my truck, and dump you back where I found you.

This will be playacting. CNC. No violence, besides what's mentioned above.

Duration – 4 hours.

Proposal price – £8000.

"I'm not sure about this," Ebony pits her eyebrows onscreen. "I know I said don't hold back, but seriously. You might end up a traumatised wreck at the end."

"He's checked out though, right? So, it'll be safe."

"Course he is, but still. Girls normally take a long time to work up to this kind of shit. You're still a newbie."

Yeah, but I'm not a 'normal' girl. That's what I want to say.

I've checked out User 706 through every forum thread in chat, and they all say the same thing. This guy is true to his word, and the brief is always the brief, no unexpected surprises. They say he likes newbies in general, because the surprise and the fear is so much more genuine. There are a few girls who freaked out so bad they backed out of the proposal and screamed their safe word the very moment they got grabbed, but he didn't leave them a negative review, just let them go and went on his way.

I tell Ebony this, and she looks up a few of the threads for herself, but still doesn't seem convinced. She's still scrolling when she catches sight of something. She smirks when she sees it.

"Are you really going after Creamgirl? You're all out to be a hardcorer, aren't you?"

I play dumb, as though I haven't been checking out every comment Creamgirl has posted these past few days, fascinated. I've also seen her in 706's thread...

"Sure, I saw she played with him."

"*Played* with him? She's a regular from the looks of it. So are some of the other hardcorers, bar the newbies he goes for."

I've been busted. I've seen Harlot and Bodica have taken him, too. Weston isn't on there, but he's a guy, so maybe 706 is a girls only client. Anyway. Who cares? I've been looking, and I've been seeing, and Eb knows it. This guy plays with the hardcorers, and I want to be one of them.

She laughs. "Has anyone ever told you you're competitive as holy fuck, Ella?"

I'm honest with her. "No, they haven't actually. I've always been the weirdo on the sidelines, picked last for every team. And then, when I met Connor, he was the superstar, not me. I barely had a scrap of ambition of my own, you know? None. I'd have worked in the store for ever if it meant he could follow his dreams." I feel the passion flowing through me. "And now, for once, I have a calling of my own. Something I want to do for myself."

"And that's being a hardcorer? You want to top the agency charts?"

I get a bloom in my chest, and fire in my stomach. I've been reading my reviews on loop, along with some of Creamgirl's, wondering if I have what it takes to earn the seriously crazy money, and be a *dreamgirl* like her.

"I never thought these would be the kind of charts I'd be out to top, but yeah. I want to be a hardcorer. I want to be up there with Creamgirl."

Ebony gives me a round of applause, nothing fake about it.

"Good for you. The change in you is fucking awesome. You're on fire, babe." She pauses. "BUT, these kind of games can blow your world apart. Instincts are instincts, and yours will want to charge right on out of there and out of his sight."

I've already thought this through.

"And so what? If that happens, he'll leave me alone and let me go."

"He will, yeah. But you might be a shivering wreck, too scared to leave your room for months on end."

I look up at the ceiling, finally facing the truth of my demons. I'm not scared of them anymore.

"Once upon a time, I was afraid to leave my room every morning, full stop. I hated being in the city, and hated work, and dreaded going to the bitch fest of a store every morning, and dreaded hanging off Connor's arm every night, trying to convince everyone I was worthy. But I'm not that girl now. I've left her behind."

Eb is right, and so am I. I have been changing. Since Eric and Jack, I've been flying high – despite still getting a pang of wanting to be back in the suite with them. Screw the morning after syndrome. I'll forget about them when the next adrenaline spike hits, especially with one as powerful as User 706. These past few crazy weeks have given me a boost I never thought possible, and fuck any nerves. I can handle them.

Finally, for once in my life, I feel like I'm in control. Ironic, given the proposal I'm considering, but that hasn't knocked me. I'm ready to face life head on. And face User 706 for an extra chunk of cash in my bank account. I don't even bother considering the *vanillas* anymore.

"You don't need to convince me," Eb says. "If you feel up to handling it and you *want* to handle it, then go for it. Click on accept. Just be careful."

"I don't need to be careful of him," I repeat. "I've checked him out a zillion times."

"No, not careful of *him*, Ella. Careful of *you*."

"I do want it, actually." I smile. "I've been watching videos online of this kind of stuff since I saw the proposal in my inbox. You know, I once asked Connor to grab me while I wasn't expecting it, back when we were still dating as teens, keen for the crazy spike of endorphins at being snatched and used. It didn't go to plan, though. He raced up behind me and lifted me up from the ground, but he ended up saying *boo*, and that was it, game over, both of us in stitches."

Ebony bursts out laughing at that, shaking her head. "Jeez. *Boo.* What a passion killer."

We laugh again, back to us giggling so hard my sides hurt. I manage to take a breath and wipe the laughter tears from my eyes.

"User 706 won't be saying *boo*, will he? He'll be binding my wrists as I flail, then throwing me into his truck like he owns me."

"He definitely won't be saying *boo*, no."

"Win for me."

"Maybe."

I'm never going to convince her, but that's ok. I've surprised her before, and I'll do it again. It might just be quite a crazy adventure in the process. Four hours of pretending I don't want a stranger while he fucks me. But I can do it. I know I can.

I click accept. No morning after syndrome after this one.

I'm expecting he wants a night over the weekend, but no. His earliest option is Monday, and the location is a park, far on the eastern outskirts of London, amongst some housing estates. It looks rough around there. Getting snatched by User 706 will almost be a relief in that place.

The time? 1.30 a.m. – it'll be almost daybreak by the time we're done and finished.

I don't get too dressed up for the occasion. Not for an experience like this. A cami top with a lace bra underneath, and a short skirt, with tights. No stockings. I want this to be authentic.

I wear heels that aren't too high to dash in, and have my coat wrapped up tight around me as I get my cab to the park.

The driver does a double take when we reach the location. It really is the edge of a park on the side of a shithole.

"You sure this is where you want to be dropped?" She points to the nearest tower block. "Are you heading to friends or something?"

"I'm meeting someone for a walk," I say, and she raises her eyebrows, but she's smiling.

"Interesting time for a stroll."

I hand my fare over, then stop before I reach for the doorhandle.

"Don't suppose I could pre-book, could I? Can you be waiting here at just gone 5.30? Are you still on shift?"

"You want to be picked up here? At 5.30?"

"Yes, please. I'll pay you double your fare."

She seems to get a sense of what I'm doing here. I wonder if she's going to turf me out with judgement, but she doesn't.

"Fine, cool," she says. "I'll be waiting." She laughs. "With the doors locked, so rap on one of the windows."

"Will do."

I have a flash of fear that Eb was right after all as the lights of the cab disappear into the distance. It's cold, and I'm shivering on the edge of a park pathway, with a sense of fear that puts my usual jangle of nerves to shame.

My finger hovers over the *arrived* button, wondering if User 706 is already watching me from the shadows. Can I really do this? Have I been an idiot by jumping in the deep end so soon?

I remind myself of the dungeon, and being bound to a rack, to be hurt for real. I remind myself of Daddy play, and how terrified I was of pretending to be a daughter for 14 hours straight.

And I remind myself that User 706 is just a client, like any others. His fantasies are just... different.

Fuck it, I click *arrived*.

I'm shaking even worse when the reply comes through.

Walk. Don't look behind you.

Shit. I stare ahead. The park lighting is dim, and some of the street lights are bust. I'll barely be able to see the path in front of me, let alone look behind.

The reaction in my legs is weird. At first every step feels like I'm wrenching myself out of a bog. I have to force myself along like I'm walking into pure doom. But once I'm a little way in, the trees of the park rustle in the biting wind, and they give me a rush of terror that speeds me up – pacing along like I'm on a mission to get somewhere.

Anywhere.

Only there's nowhere to get to...

Even if I turned back now, the chances are that a masked man will be right there behind me, waiting to snatch me and run.

I repeat my safe word in my head. *Flag, flag, flag.*

He knows it. He's had to sign it off with the agency.

Flag, flag, flag, flag, flag, flag.

I hear something. A gentle crunch, off to the side, and it's enough to have me running like I've never run in my life, heels pounding the path as I force myself not to scream. My heels aren't cut out for this, and I stumble. Hard. I manage to grip hold of a streetlamp at the side of the path, but it's one of the broken ones. There's a crunch of glass under my feet from where some idiot has thrown a rock up and shattered the bulb.

I grip the metal pole, eyes frantic as I figure out which way to keep on running, but I get no chance. I don't hear the footsteps approach – my breaths are too loud in my ears. The first thing I know of User 706's presence is when his bulk slams against my back and a gloved hand clamps over my mouth, hard enough that I couldn't scream if I tried.

He pins me to the lamppost, and I feel the fabric of some kind of mask against my ear as he whispers.

"Stay the fuck still, and stay the fuck quiet. Do you get me?"

I don't answer him. I can't yet. I don't trust myself.

"DO YOU GET ME?" he barks. "You've asked for this, you little slut. Parading yourself around here in the middle of the night, like nobody is gonna fuck you. Stay still, don't even think about moving."

I do what I'm told. The chill of the cold metal post enough to focus on the sensation. *Get a grip, Holly. Get a grip.* But it's hard. So fucking hard when you have a man's hand clasped over your mouth, so fucking strong, he can do what he wants with you.

But that's the point... he can.

He can and he will.

"Let's see what you've got under here," he says, and pulls my coat loose. "Such a short slutty skirt for such a chilly night, don't you think?"

I try to nod.

"You know what *I* think? I think you're asking for this. I think you're a dirty bitch asking for cock. Now, I'm gonna tell you again. Stay the fuck still, and stay the fuck quiet. Do you get me?"

I suck in a breath through my nose as his free hand lifts up my skirt, and I do nod this time.

"You fucking sure?" he asks.

I nod again. My adrenaline is spiking like fucking crazy, and I'm trembling so bad he must be able to feel it against his chest, but I know what I'm doing here, in this pitch-black hellhole with a man out to kidnap me.

I gulp in air when he takes his gloved hand from my mouth and spins me around to face him. The lamppost is a rigid beast against my back, but nothing near as intimidating as the beast before me. He's got to be at least 6ft 5, and is built like a tank. His hoodie is black, with the hood pulled up, and he has a mask which covers everything bar his eyes and mouth. Eyes that are piercing and dripping with malice. I could scream, but I don't. I'm mute as he takes my arms and slams my wrists together.

"You're coming with me, slut."

He pulls some rope from inside his hoodie, and ties my wrists like a pro, knotted tight. Then he shunts me along the path ahead of him, his hand gripping the back of my neck.

"Keep fucking walking."

I nod, but don't say a word. My feet are heavy again, not flighty, so I have to force them with every step. We *are* going to an ominous destination now, not running away from one. I push back against him as I see a battered white truck off to the left through some trees, but it makes no odds to him. He practically throws me up a verge, and I skid down the other side before he catches me and shoves me onwards.

The double doors at the back of the truck swing open wide when he unlocks them, and the darkness inside is too much for me. I try to flee on instinct with bound hands, ready to let out a scream, but he's quick enough to catch me in the act, silencing me with another slam of his gloved hand over my open mouth.

He doesn't say anything, just picks me up like I weigh nothing and shoves me into the truck where I stumble in the darkness, falling to my knees on the hard metal floor.

The doors slam shut and I'm genuinely shitting myself, heart pounding like crazy.

I tell myself it's all an act as the driver's door opens and he climbs in – a brief moment when the interior light lights him up. He's wearing a ski mask, his eyes and mouth visible. He glances back at me and smirks before slamming the door shut and the light goes out.

He switches on the engine, and I manage to raise myself enough to hook my arms over the passenger headrest.

"Where are you taking me?" I manage to ask.

"Shut the fuck up," he says, putting his foot down on the accelerator.

I bounce around as he drives, hanging from the back of the seat, like I'm strung up for the abattoir, but it's ok. Through the terror I'm beginning to get intrigued, transfixed by watching the streets flashing past us on the way.

"What are you going to do to me?" I ask him.

"Told you to shut the fuck up," he says, easing off the accelerator as a police car passes us by.

I do shut up, my heart in my mouth, imagining what might happen if the cops decide to turn back and investigate what a battered old truck is doing out at this time in the morning. How the hell would he explain the bound girl in the back. *Just having fun, officer, nothing to see here.*

But the cop car disappears from sight and my heart is back to pounding.

"I'm going to treat you like the slutty whore you really are," he says.

I guess he's right – I am a slut, and a whore, truth be told.

"I'm going to take your cunt and ass," he says, "and punish those big tits like they've never been punished before. And you can beg me to stop all you like, it won't make any difference. You're mine now, until I'm done with you."

Until I'm done with you.

I picture him strangling me to death, snuffing me out once he's *done with me*. The emotions are weird, conflicting. I'm scared shitless but it's turning me on. He won't really hurt me, I remind myself. Just an act.

He smacks a gloved hand off the steering wheel and I start. "Fuck!" he barks and I don't know what the hell he's cursing at. "My cock is fucking raging," he says. "I'm going to plough you so bad you'll be begging me to stop." He laughs a crazed laugh. "Or begging for more. One of the two."

Jesus Christ.

The bumps in the road start as we hit a side track. My wrists hurt as I bounce, and I curse and whimper, but it doesn't stop him, he keeps on driving.

It feels like a lifetime until I see a looming building in the distance. It looks like a barn. I'm shaking like crazy as we reach the place. He pulls up in a cobbled yard, turns off the engine and gets out of the truck.

The doors open behind me and the smell hits me – cattle. It's a farm.

User 706 doesn't hesitate as he climbs up into the back and hauls my wrists up and over the headrest. I kick out on instinct, but he doesn't give a shit, just grabs me by my ankles and tugs me backwards so hard I drop out of the truck onto the cobbles with a yelp.

He puts a foot on me and shoves me onto my back, placing his boot on my stomach like I'm nothing but shit. He towers over me, his bulk lit up by the moonlight.

"Here, you're mine. Scream all you like. Fight all you like. Run all you like. It won't fucking matter. Nobody will hear you, nobody will save you, nobody will come running."

I look around, frantic. I can't stop the whimpers.

Flag. I could say it. It's in my throat. But I don't. I don't say it... because there's something else in the pit of me now... something familiar...

Something like being on a rack bench at someone else's mercy.

The beauty of pure submission.

He lifts his foot off me and I struggle to crawl away. He laughs as he watches, and I feel so cheap it's disgusting. But so fucking dirty that my pussy is wetting my thighs.

Submission, I tell myself.

I love submission.

I adore the sensation of giving up everything... my fate someone else's to control.

"Keep crawling all you like," he says, still laughing. "You're not going to get very far, and there's cow shit over there, so unless you want a face full of it, I'd think fucking twice."

My knees keep crawling regardless, my bound hands keep shuffling along. And it's not because I want a face full of cow shit, it's because I want him to come and take me. Come and grab me, and force me, and pin me to the ground with a big muddy boot, at his whim.

"I'm going to give you to the count of three," he shouts. "If you're not turning your pretty ass back towards me by then, you'll pay for it, you stupid bitch."

I want him to make me pay for it.

"Three!"

I keep crawling, like a warped, clumsy caterpillar in my bonds. I lose one of my heels, but stand no chance of getting it back, so keep on going.

"Two!"

I whimper as I squirm, scuffing my palms as I fall, and there goes my other heel.

"One!"

I'm still trying to get back onto all fours, frantic when he approaches. I scream and lash out and flail on the floor beneath him as he lands his boot back on me. Only this time he flips me onto my back with a thump of his toe, and his cold, muddy sole presses against my heaving chest, right on my tits.

"You're a feisty little fucking cow, aren't you?" he laughs again.

"Fuck you," I say, the words coming so naturally.

"No," he replies, his voice serious this time as he hauls me up to my feet, his masked face in mine. "Fuck *you*."

I'm trembling so bad I can barely stand as he unbinds my wrists. He takes a fistful of my hair and drags me back to the truck, slamming my back against the side. He tears my coat open, slapping the mud off my tits, rough enough that I cry out at the pain. Then, oh fuck, his eyes meet mine once he sees the points of my nipples.

"I knew it all along. You're a desperate horny slut," he says, and pulls my cami top and bra down so my tits are bare. My nipples are so hard in the cold, they're like freezing bullets – so much more sensitive when he slaps them.

"Harder," I say to him, with the backchat he wants from me. "If you think I'm such a cheap little slut, then at least slap me like you mean it. Take your gloves off."

"You're asking for fucking trouble," he says, but I raise my arms over my head, like I'm ready for it.

"Do it. Don't be a pussy."

"A pussy?" His voice is so low. "You really think I'm a fucking pussy?"

"I'll think whatever I think, until you show me otherwise."

His gloves are off and cast aside in seconds, and he slaps my tits like I deserve it. I stare him in the eyes with every slap, my whimpers turning to moans as the tingles turn to burns. The cold is burning me along with his palms. The contrast between ice and fire is a dream.

I'm still staring him in the eyes as he hitches my skirt up. I don't fight him as he does it. I don't make a sound as he tears my tights away and tugs my panties down my legs, just let him battle with each of my legs until he has them off me and my pussy is bare for him.

A bare wet treat, waiting to serve.

He plunges two fingers all the way in and I cry out for him.

"You have one soaking wet cunt, you know that?" he says, his breath fogging the air.

"I always do."

"Say it, then. Say you're a slut who wants dick, no matter where it comes from." I hesitate too long, and he pins me by my throat, his mask right up in my face. "SAY IT!"

The dynamic between us is serpentine, twisting. And weirdly addictive.

"I'm a slut who wants dick, no matter where it comes from," my voice is trembling just as much as my body is.

"And where do you fucking want it, huh?"

"Wherever you want to put it."

My pussy is squelching as he pumps me, and he's not hitting anything tender, just a slopping wet hole, ready to belong to him. He adds a finger, and that makes me whimper. He brushes a thumb against my clit, and the pleasure is enough that I moan.

"Dirty fucking whore."

He keeps playing, and my breaths quicken, my ice-cold tits heaving in the night. He pumps faster, and I shift my legs apart, squatting a little for the thrill.

"You're a dirty bitch with a dirty cunt," he says. "You're a lucky girl, since I'll make you come before I use it."

Another finger and I'm lost to him, still sore from the strain a few days ago. My G-spot is too tender to resist, and his thumb on my clit has a rhythm, and I'm done for. I'm a hostage in the middle of nowhere, with a masked man using me like a cheap little bitch, and I'm going to come for him.

It's so much easier to feel the wetness dripping down my thighs as I come in the cold December night. It's hot against prickling flesh, and makes it feel even more fucking filthy as he uses me. I pant without giving a fuck for the hitch of his masked breaths in my face, or the way he slams his weight against me to keep me still, or my bare feet, cold on the muddy cobbles.

I don't give a fuck as he pulls his fingers free of my pussy and forces them into my mouth, just suck like a whore and take what I'm given.

He unzips his jeans, and I'm ready for it.

He grabs my hand and pushes it against his hard cock. It's thick. Thick enough to make my pussy clench.

"Think you can take it, slut?" he asks, his masked face right in mine.

I almost say *yes, no fucking problem*. But no, I play the game.

"No," I tell him, "please don't, you're too big."

He likes that, I can see it in his eyes, piercing mine.

"Want me to stop, do you?" he says and I know he's giving me a chance to say the safe word.

The safe word I'm never going to use.

"Yes, please stop, please let me go. I want to go home." I'm trembling so much my shaky words sound so genuine. "Please," I repeat. "Don't do this."

"Fuck you," he says and lifts me up.

My legs automatically wrap around his bulky waist, and his long exhale as he shoves his cock deep has me whimpering.

He pins me there, his hot breath in my face. "Such a tight cunt," he says, "Know what I like more than anything?"

I shake my head no.

"A slut who cries when I fuck her," he says and starts pumping his thick, fat cock.

I don't object this time. I can't, it feels so good. I take it as he pounds me, whimpering with every thrust.

"That's it," he says, one hand squeezing a tit so hard I cry out. "Is that good?"

I don't reply, lost to the crazy moment.

"I asked you a fucking question," he says and licks his tongue up my face. "Is that good, bitch?"

No saying *no* this time. I switch to backchat, knowing it'll rile him.

"Could be better," I tell him.

"Oh yeah?"

He pulls out of me, drops my bare feet to the ground, grabs me by the throat and drags me along the side of the truck. *Yes.* He shoves me, so I'm bent over the front, the cold metal icy on my tits. He takes me from behind, slamming all the way, and it's much, much dirtier like this. The angle is deep and his thrusts are vicious, just the way I like them.

"That's better," I tell him.

"Cheeky bitch!" He slaps my bare ass so hard it stings like a bastard and I cry out into the night.

"Fucking whore!" He slams into me again and again and I could come like this, all over again. He feels me tense up, flying high, and keeps on slamming, bringing me closer and closer... but then he stops.

"You really think I'm going to let you come again? This is about my fucking pleasure, not yours, you dirty slut."

Once again, he wrestles me, and I'm done with the fight as I land on my knees in the mud. My mouth is already open for his cock. He fists my hair and bulges my cheeks out one by one, making me retch and bringing tears to my eyes as he laughs at me.

"Pretty when you cry," he says.

He has to crouch to fuck my throat, because he's so damn tall, and that only drives his dick deeper. I choke, dribbling all down my chin, but I keep sucking, keep giving, staring up at him as he treats me like his servant.

"You're good at sucking cock," he says, "which is just as well since your spit is going to be lubing me up for your dirty little asshole. Make it easier for yourself and get me wet."

I do get him wet. Hacks of spit and drool that have his whole shaft dripping when he finally pulls me to my feet.

I'm ready for it when he shoves me against the truck, my face pressed flat against the metal.

I reach behind and spread my ass cheeks for him, but he slaps my hands away.

I cry out again when fingers push into my ass.

"Fuck," he says, pumping me like he's on steroids. I'm a trembling mess by the time he yanks them free. It's a moment of relief, until he plunges his nasty big cock in instead.

My cry sings out into the night and he can't hold back. He fucks my ass like it's the last fuck he's ever going to have, and my head is spinning so bad, I love it, already bucking back against him, desperate for more.

"Yes," I tell him. "Like that, but harder. Harder. Fuck me, harder!"

He slams all the way in, using all his weight as solid, brute force, and I take it like I want it right back, grinning as I hear him cursing.

"Put your fingers in my dripping wet cunt as you come," I tell him.

"Dirty fucking bitch," he hisses, but he does it, wrapping his arm around to fill my pussy with his fingers, mashing them against the right spot – just like I knew he would from this position.

He's a relentless monster on the brink, picking up the pace and fucking my sorry ass with a vengeance, grunting and slamming.

I know he's coming, and so am I. I'm coming in sync with a masked man fucking my ass against a battered truck, by a derelict barn in the middle of the night, and I'm smiling. It's pure fucking insanity.

Beyond words. Beyond reason. Beyond anything I could have ever imagined.

Jesus Christ, I'm shivering, coming down from my orgasm. My teeth are chattering loud when User 706 pulls out of me and zips his jeans up.

"Don't you dare think we're done yet," he says, sucking in breaths through his mask. "I want to see the full filthy state of you. Get in the truck. Passenger side."

I do as I'm told with nothing more than a nod, tugging my skirt down as I go. Damn, my bare feet are like ice blocks. My toes must be fucking blue. He switches the engine on as he climbs into the driver's seat, and flicks on the light overhead. I blink against the glow, almost breaking role and thanking him as he puts the heater on. The blowers feel like heaven as they warm up.

It's the first time I truly get sight of him, in his hoodie, looking absolutely terrifying with his black mask over his face.

There's something instinctive about a thick, woollen face mask with eye holes. Almost criminal. His eyes are still dark and thirsty, and even through the cold, I'm grateful our time isn't up yet.

"Show me how filthy you are," he says, and I turn towards him, baring my muddy tits.

I look down at myself as he does, and I really am a state –my skin smeared with dirt and my cami top a scrunch of mud around my waist. I don't even look at my bare legs, just show him the goods of my top half, my nipples still hard, even though the blowers are beginning to blast out heat.

The warmth is like heaven.

"I want to see the wet wreck of your pussy and ass," he says. "Spread for me. Heel up on the dash."

The size of his truck makes it easy to give a good display. I rest my head against the passenger window and hook one leg between our seats, raising my other foot up onto the dash. I'm watching him as he soaks in the sight, and it's my own horniness, not his instruction, that has my hands roving down between my legs.

I spread my pussy lips to give him a better view, and he leans over me, offering his fingers to my mouth.

"Spit on them."

I hack up a decent amount, and he uses it to twist three fingers straight back into my asshole.

"I know how much you fucking like it," he says, and I nod for him.

"Yeah, I'm an anal loving slut."

I'm sore from taking his cock, but it doesn't hold me back from moving against his thrusts, silently urging him on. I tip my head back and curse with a *fuck* when he slides in another finger, but I don't protest, just keep on leveraging myself against the stretch.

I work against my masked attacker's thrusting hand, happy at the burn of the four-finger stretch. I'm looking straight at his hooded face as I slide a hand down and play with my clit as he fingers my wet ass.

I smile. "You were right, you know? I did want to be fucked earlier. I was desperate for cock when you grabbed me."

"Some sluts are always gagging for it, even when they kick and scream."

"I'm one of them."

"Show me, then. Play with your needy cunt until you come."

"I'll come easily, as long as you keep pumping those thick fingers."

"Fucking dirty whore," he says.

"Says the man who's fingering my cum-filled ass," I reply and he grins at me, twisting those fingers until I'm gritting my teeth.

He's rougher now. Stretching me with a fresh bout of force as I circle my clit. I focus on his eyes as I lick my lips with a slutty grin, hoping I get snatched by a guy like him in the future.

Maybe he'll be kind enough to offer a repeat performance.

I know my next orgasm is going to be a big one. Hy heel is braced on the dashboard as I press down, wanting extra strain as he stretches me. My fingers work faster, and my breaths get quicker, building up to a filthy crescendo.

I push two fingers into my pussy before I explode, working them like crazy as my ass and my clit send me wild.

"Fuck," he says, and that one simple word speaks volumes as he stares at me, such a kinky bitch in his passenger seat. He's impressed. I can see it. It gives me a glow of heat that's got nothing to do with his heater fans.

The masked beast's eyes are on my heaving tits as I come down from the orgasm. I grimace, but I'm still smiling as he pulls his fingers out of me, and then I push my dirty tits together, mashing them tight.

"Are you going to use these? I'd love to feel your jerking cock between them. Why don't you get some filthy slick cum on me as well as the mud?"

He slides his seat back to the max, and there's plenty of room for me to clamber over him. I kneel in the footwell between the monster's legs, looking up at the brute strength of him.

He's not the only one who enjoys having the light on.

His dick is still dirty from my ass – a perfect blend of filth along with the caked-on mud. He takes hold of my tits, crushing them together so tight that it hurts. My God, he has to work to slam his cock up between them.

"Fucking gorgeous," he says and spits on my tits as his cock thrusts.

I know my tits were built for tit fucking. I know how to bounce up and down until he starts to pulse between them, frantic as he uses my tits like a pussy, warm and tight.

His breaths are ragged, full of grunts as he jerks and shoots – one spurt impressive enough to smack off the underside of my chin.

He keeps grinding in the sopping aftermath, staring in wonder at the filth he's been fucking. His cock must be as muddy as my chest, but he doesn't give a fuck, slapping his wet dick against my dirty nipples.

I don't stop there, take hold of his filthy cock and suck him into my mouth, cleaning him and licking up every last drop of cum. Fuck. My filthiness just reached a new peak and sent me to hell.

"Jesus fucking Christ," he says before shoving it back in his pants with a groan.

I feel like a winner as I take over, smearing my tits with his cum.

"Back in your own seat now," he says.

He gets out of the truck and grabs my things from outside, tossing them over in a bundle – coat, torn tights, panties and heels.

"Thank you," I say as he climbs back beside me.

He turns off the overhead light as we set off back to London, so I brush my coat down as best I can, and slide my heels back on in the footwell. I don't even bother with my tights and panties. They are done and finished.

"Leave those behind, if you like," he says, "I'll enjoy them later."

"Sure," I say, and shove them in the glove box.

The journey is considerably easier now I'm not bouncing around the headrest, and a hell of a lot more pleasant with the heater on.

There is no conversation to be had on the way back to the city, and the silence is heady in its dirty brilliance. I only hope I served him well. From the way he keeps shooting glances in my direction, I'd say the chances of that are pretty high.

"We're ten minutes early," he says when we turn the corner to the park entrance. "Have you got someone coming to pick you up? Do you want me to wait with you?"

"Nah, don't worry, they're already here," I say, and point to the cab up ahead, parked up with the lights on.

"Thanks for the fun time," User 706 says. "Sorry about the mud. You're caked in it."

"No problem." I laugh. "I can have a shower easily enough, cow shit or not. Will just be a shame to wash your cum down the plughole."

"Dirty bitch," he says with a laugh.

I pull my coat closed around me before I get out, hoping the taxi driver doesn't see what a state I'm in as I rap my knuckles on the car window, but it doesn't work. The interior light shows up the mud on my front as soon as I open the door. I hope I don't stink too bad.

"Sorry," I say to her, trying my best to keep the muck off the seats, "I fell over."

Her eyes meet mine in the rearview.

"Sure, right. The park is slippy, but not that slippy." There's humour in her voice, no chiding in the slightest as she laughs. "Was it worth it? Getting caked in mud for?"

I grin up at the festive lights as the city comes into view, so bright in the darkness.

"Hell, yeah," I tell her. "It most definitely was."

twenty-one

User 2155. Male. 34.
Work party to celebrate our end of year. There are eight guys in our team. Yeah, you read that right. Eight of us, all planning on having a great time in our office, with whisky, music, and a girl's hot, horny holes ready for some fun. We've even got disco lights.
I hope you can be a filthy, gothic playgirl for us, Holly, and get right on into the action.
Strip show. Oral. Pussy. Anal. Tit play. DP. Lots of cum and getting down and dirty. We're quite a team.
Duration – 5 hours.
Proposal price – £5000.

"A grand an hour isn't that bad," I say to Eb, then have to check myself.

Seriously?! A grand an HOUR isn't that bad? My standards have changed to high hell in a few short weeks. I was working for £11.87 per hour at the store.

"Nah, I guess not," she replies. "Plus, it should be fun. A good foray into getting it on with a load at once, *and* they'll probably be so hammered and horny, you'll get off easily."

"Get *myself* off easily, I hope," I say with a smirk. "If recent events are any indication, I'd say that's a certainty."

She shakes her head onscreen, still taken aback by my encounter last night.

"I can't believe you enjoyed getting covered in dirt and cow shit."

"It wasn't the dirt and cow shit I enjoyed. It was the guy who threw me into them."

"Yeah, still. The stench must have been horrific."

I tipped the cab driver £300 when she dropped me back at home this morning. She'd earnt it. And as for my filthy bathroom? For once I was glad I don't live in a show home. I was an absolute state when I climbed in the shower.

"I've never done a strip show," I say to Ebony. "I might look like an idiot."

Eb laughs. "Eight guys want a gangbang and you're worried about stripping? Practice makes perfect, hon. You've got a full-length mirror, it's really not that difficult."

"How about you? Do you do many of them? Your practice must be pretty damn perfect by now."

She flicks her hair and flutters her lashes. "I try my best. You might get to see at the entertainer's party, hey? Depends how hammered we get."

The thought of the looming entertainer's party still gives me nerves, which is crazy, given that I've taken to filth like a duck to water. That makes no difference, though. A party with the other entertainers feels like a whole other affair. A more personal one.

It won't be about ass-fucking fantasies, or taking two at once. It'll be about meeting people. People I want to get to know.

Making friends.

I'm still haunted by my school days, worried that nobody will like me. Nobody except Eb, that is.

"You going to accept the proposal, then?" she asks.

"Yeah, why not? I've got one whole week left to get as much in as I can."

"You sound like you're on a dash for cash mission. You've done more than enough work this year to deserve your break, Ells. I'm scaling down to one appointment a week after New Year, and that's going to be knackering enough."

She's right, I *am* on a dash for cash mission. Even now, with my bank balance looking like a gift from the stars, I'm still holding onto my work ethic – no matter what extremities that work ethic might entail.

"I'm not too knackered for a hot party with a load of guys," I say. "Not yet, anyway."

"When is it?"

I check out the calendar onscreen. "Friday."

"Friday. Cool. Getting fucked by eight guys. Nice. Then it's our party on Saturday. And that's going to be it, right? You're set for your holiday. Don't run yourself into the ground, babe. You'll have a hangover for three days straight after our celebrations."

I hold my hands up. "Yeah. This will be it, for sure. Last gig before my holiday."

I only hope it's another five-star review to add to my perfect record. I need to get practicing to make sure my ratings are top notch, and I do. I choose my outfit from my wardrobe. Multi layers of hot gothic chic, with stockings and suspenders on underneath. A lingerie set worthy of a strip show. A tight bodice that pulls loose from the back. A short flared skirt that'll shimmy down nicely, and a new set of platform shoes from my growing collection.

My sexy outfit doesn't stop me feeling like a goofy idiot as I put on some Christmas tunes and practice a strip show in front of my mirror. I have myself in stitches a few times as my skirt gets caught around my knees as I bend over, trying to be alluring as I bob my ass up and down. Nope, I'm definitely not made for twerking. I keep it simple instead, take it slow as I reveal all. That looks much better. By the end of the evening, I've got it down.

As down as I'm likely going to get it, anyway...

I head out next morning to buy a new coat – since my old, trusted favourite got trashed by cow shit. It feels insane to be looking in high-end shop windows, knowing I can afford the luxury of whichever coat I choose. I opt for another leather one, long and belted, but this one feels so much better as I try it on in the changing room. So heavy and thick. It smells glorious. And it should be, given the cost of it. It's over £400.

No matter how prepared I am, I flinch as I see the price come up on the card reader, the memory of eating pasta on loop still lurking in the depths. I still feel almost guilty about buying it, having to remind myself that this is a coat for work, as well as for me. I'll be wearing this bad boy for my strip show on Friday night. Just two more days to go.

I put in a load more hours of *practice* before then, viewing online tutorials to help me shake my butt like a pro. I manage a catwalk style totter, looking authentic in my heels, and even manage to twirl like a sexy ballerina, shooting a glance full of want in the mirror as I spin.

I'm buzzing when the cab arrives at mine on Friday evening. I'm ready to go, dressed up to the max in my gorgeous outfit, my hair slick and long, and my makeup fit for a showgirl. My beauty and skin products have definitely been worth the investment, and so has my growing wardrobe. I feel on top of the world as I step up to the doors of CR Corporate once the cab's dropped me off. I look up at the office building, and it's dark, besides one floor where the windows are flashing green, red and blue. Ok, so I guess I'm at the right location. I click *arrived* as I stand outside.

The instruction pings through in an instant.

Third floor, head on up.

There's a solitary guy minding the reception desk. He'd be quite a beef of a boy in his dark uniform, if he wasn't wearing a silly Christmas hat with a goofy smile.

"Party's up there," he says, and points to the stairs. "Half of them are probably passed out by now."

I hope that's not the case as I make my ascent. The more eyes on me the better, after all the work I've been putting into rehearsals. *The more cocks ready to fuck me, bonus on top.* I'm becoming such a horny cow I want to be on it 24/7. No joke.

I push through the double doors to their office with a shout of *HEY, GUYS!* and everyone in the place turns to face me. Some of them are wearing tinsel around their necks as ties, some of them in pom pom Christmas hats. One of them has Rudolph antlers on his head and his shirt already off, grooving to the beat of *Merry Christmas, Everyone.*

The office desks and chairs have been pushed away from the centre to allow for a makeshift dancefloor, but the sales score boards are still up on the walls. There we have it, in a nutshell.

This is a sales team's office. And these guys are the team members.

The whole room thumps with their demeanour. *And natural competition.*

It makes no odds who User 2155 is amongst the crowd right now. They all let out a cheer as I step up to the 'dancefloor' to join them, clearing out of the way to give me some space as I twirl.

There's a Christmas tree in the corner. I head on over there and the guys gather before me, eight pairs of eyes giving me their full attention.

I feel like the hottest girl on the planet as I shrug my coat off and let it slip to the floor. I'll be their gothic, Christmas disco queen tonight, no problem at all.

"Santa, baby!" one of the guys shouts, and dashes on over to change the track.

I cheer along with the guys as the song starts up, the tune drowning out the remnants of nerves in my stomach. Here we go... time for the grand strip performance. I'm ready, and it's time to show it.

I strut from guy to guy like I'm on a catwalk, giving each of them a hot pout and a needy flutter of my lashes. The first in line is an average kind of hot guy in a suit, mid brown hair. Nice, but not memorable. Guy number two is the shirtless one, dancing to the tune in his Rudolph antlers as he pumps his fists in the air. Guy number three is hot. Like really hot. Brooding dark eyes and a smirk on his face that gives me flutters. My gaze lingers on him for too long, which is unfair, so I give his tie a flick and force myself on by. I take the tinsel from the neck of the fourth guy, and wrap it around my own like a scarf, making sure I give him a decent flash of my cleavage as a thank you. Guy five is short, but cute, and has to be late fifties. He's grey and balding, but that doesn't stop him taking hold of my ass and giving it a squeeze. Guys six and seven have to be brothers. They're virtually identical. Tall and slim, with the same light blond hair, catching the colours of the disco lights like a dream. And guy number eight... he has to be User 2155. He looks so pleased with himself as he stands there with his arms folded, nodding his head like I'm another achievement on their target board.

I like User 2155. Stocky and confident. Serious and firm.

I step up close, drop to a crouch and work my hands up his body as I rise, grinding against his thigh as the other guys cheer for him – but he doesn't get me for long. I spin, then step along to the brothers at his side, jiggling my cleavage as a tempter. The older team member next to them grabs my ass all over again. I use his hold to squirm against his crotch, and he's hard. I can feel him.

It's turning me on already.

I hand the next guy along his tinsel back with a kiss on the cheek and another shimmy, and then it's on to mega hot guy. I'm ready with a flutter of my lashes as I run my fingers down his chest to his belt. I tease by hovering, and the other guys let out a fresh cheer.

Yeah, I'm performing well.

Rudolph acts like a playboy when I reach him. He buries his face in my cleavage and blows a raspberry like a fucking idiot, pretending to ram his cock against me as I laugh. Jackass. Kinda cute, though.

Then it's average guy. He barely gets a look in before the crowd start chanting with a STRIP, STRIP, STRIP!

"Yeah! Dance for us, baby!" Rudolph shouts, and I hope he shuts up soon. He's going to be a pain in the ass when we start playing around later. I only hope it's literally.

STRIP, STRIP, STRIP! the chants continue.

The sexy confident face of Holly devours any reservations as I take my place by the Christmas tree and begin my strip routine. I'm driven by excitement as I pull my bodice loose and dance before the crowd in my bra, holding my tits up as a teaser for playtime. My skirt shimmy is faultless, and so is my spin as I drop and take hold of my ankles, giving the guys a full-on view of my ass in my lacy black thong.

More cheers. More tension. More sexy electric in the air as I unclip my stocking tops and cast the suspender belt away, kicking off my heels along with it.

I dance some more in bra and panties before I finally let my tits free. I clasp an arm tight across my chest as I twirl my bra above my head, and then launch it over to the crowd like a trophy. It's Rudolph that catches it. He hangs it from one of his fake antlers like an idiot, but I ignore him. I ignore everything but the vibrant sense of want in the room, and the newfound confidence zipping right through me.

Fuck, how I let the rhythm free once I've unveiled my tits. I see the want in their eyes, burning me alive through the festivities. I soak up the pure, uninhibited horniness in the room as I drop my panties, roving my hands over my tits, my hips, my ass as I shimmy.

I imagine myself being taken by all the men in this room.

Eight guys who want to fuck me. EIGHT. It's bizarre, but I don't give a fuck who is who, or what they want to do to me. I'll take it all like a hungry little bitch, and beg for more.

That's who Holly is. Who *I* am now. A hungry little bitch, desperate for as much as she can handle.

I know my strip show has been one hell of a success as I finish up, blowing kisses. The guys give me a full-on round of applause before Rudolph takes hold of my hand and leads me over to their makeshift bar, set up on one of the desks.

"Happy Christmas, Holly!"

I down a whisky and Coke along with them, and another on top for good measure, pouting like a good girl as they eye up my slutty naked body.

Why hold off any longer? I want it as much as they do.

"Come on," I say, as I put my empty glass down. "Take whatever you want, guys. I'm here to serve."

The mood changes in a flash of disco lights. This party is no longer about fun and Christmas tunes, and swigging back whisky. It's about me – their filthy plaything.

"Do it, guys," I say, and lean back against the desk. "Use me like your party whore. The clock is ticking, and your cocks are rocking."

My humour dries up when I'm shoved down onto my knees, with cocks appearing all around me. Fuck, they were quick...

I take two cocks in my hands, working them as well as I can while Rudolph shoves his dick in my mouth, jamming deep. I'm so glad I've got five whole hours of this... I want to take them all. A five-star service for every single one of them...

The carpet is thin and rough against my skin when they lower me onto my back, their cocks straight back on offer to my hands and mouth as the guys drop to their knees around me. I'm busy looking up at Rudolph, choking around his cock when the first round of fingers slide inside me. I don't have a clue who they belong to, and I don't care. I spread my legs wide and rock my hips for more.

They can fill me up. Every single one of them. I fucking want it.

Someone slaps my tits, and a wet mouth feasts on my nipple. The fingers in my pussy switch out to fresh ones, and the cocks in my hands swap over as the guys shuffle.

I love every minute of it. Right here, I'm nothing but a plaything. An entertainer. A fucking slut.

"Fuck me, someone, please!" I shout as Rudolph pulls out of my mouth and grabs his balls, dangerously close to coming.

Oh, yes... I'm happy when I see who is ready to accept the invitation. I grin as one of the two brothers gets up close and ready to slide into my pussy. He's long enough to bury deep... and God yes, so is his twin – kneeling over me to take Rudolph's place in my mouth.

I can't believe I'm having it so lucky – getting two brothers at once. Fantasies sometimes do come to life.

I'm being such a good girl on the naughty list as I roll over and get spit roasted by two dirty twins, begging them for more every chance that I get. They have me gagging, gasping, desperate... but unfortunately, they pull out before I manage to get them off, with other guys taking their places. Fuck, I'm getting needy. I want cum. Rounds and rounds of it.

I'm given another whisky right down the throat before another dick plugs me, and I revel in the whole lot of it. Everything. I'm nothing but a pretty piece of flesh as the guys get more confident in their filthiness. Soon, I'm up on all fours, taking two cocks in my mouth like I was born to be face fucked, my pussy pounded by different dicks, one after the other, like my cunt is a trophy to be claimed.

"Yes, more, please. MORE!"

I'm hauled up onto the old guy's cock, riding him like a showgirl until another guy shoves me forward. Hell yes. Here begins the true action. I cry out in lust, not protest, as someone jams their cock in my ass to work with his friend in tandem.

"Fuck me!" I shout over the music. "That's it! Fuck me!"

They happily oblige...

My mouth is filled up and pummelled along with my cunt and ass, and I'm passed around the men like a cheap, horny bitch, so wildly that I lose track of the faces. Everyone is a blur now. All that matters is cock.

Eight cocks... all for me. I'm groaning and grinning, sucking like a good girl on meat lollipops as my ass and pussy clench as hard as I can clench. I want to milk these cocks clean. I want to be filled up. Dripping with thick, creamy cum from every hole, slicked up like a needy whore. A five-star entertainer. *A hardcorer.*

I gargle another whisky, open mouthed for the fun of it as I bounce on both brothers at the same time, one in each hole. I swallow and show the circle of clients my empty mouth, inviting them all up to fill me.

It's Rudolph who comes first, spurting all over my face with his fist in my hair – three hot streams, right on the diagonal. I'm licking my lips clean when Mr Mega Hot steps into his place, plunging my throat like I'm a gulley of filth. Just like the rest of me.

The brother in my ass curses as he shoots his load, and that sets off his twin, bucking up as he christens my pussy with its first round of cum. I'm so fucking slick that I'm dripping. I get up and bend over the desk, spreading my ass cheeks so the guys can see just how wet and used I am.

"Who's next?" I ask, looking at the crowd of faces behind me. "Who's going to make my hot, wet cunt even wetter?"

With that, they're all clamouring to step forward at once, and I'm like a kid in a sweet shop, whimpering like a slut as they take their turns. I'm hauled around, passed between dicks while guys groan as they pump me. I don't know whose body is whose anymore, it's all just flesh on flesh. My cheeks are sticky with cum, and my tits are soaked from spit, and I'm working my clit every chance I get.

It's Rudolph who slaps my hand away from my pussy when he fucks me from behind. He uses his own fingers instead to work at me, and he's much, much better than his goofy antlers would suggest. He has me gasping and wriggling, desperate to ride him, but he gives me no control whatsoever. Instead, I'm pinned to the carpet, its rough thread grazing my cheek as he makes me come with wails and groans. My first orgasm of the night.

It only makes me hornier...

I push guys' cum out of me between every round I'm given, until my thighs are a dripping mess. My ass is fucked so hard, I must be gaping – and I'm choking up with cum so bad I snort a load through my nose to rapturous cheers, but that doesn't matter. I'm still smiling. Still begging for it. Still screaming for more, like a whore.

I guess that's what sends me crazy...

It's *me* who offers two at once in my pussy – a freebie on my part – and the guys are all up for it, battling to get up close, but they don't get the chance. User 2155 is shaking his head as he shoves the other guys away from me. He argues that it's not in the brief, but he doesn't need to. I meet his eyes and tell him it's a *freebie*. A Christmas present from me for being such good clients.

I expect he'll let people get on with it, but no. He gets down on the floor beside me and puts his face right up to mine.

"If anyone's going to get a *freebie* here, it's going to be me, you horny bitch, since I'm the one paying for it."

I realise then that User 2155 is stone cold sober – not a hint of whisky headiness in sight. His voice is steady, and his stare is filthy, and out of nowhere he breathes into my ear, with a counter offer.

"I want you to take my fist in your cunt."

My breaths hitch. Shocked. I've taken two in one before... yeah, but the idea of a fist is different somehow... it makes my stomach lurch.

"You want me to take your whole hand inside me?"

"Yes. I'll give you another grand if you'll take my fist in your cunt, legs spread wide so everyone gets to see," he says. "So how about it? A grand for my fist? You're wet and used enough to take it."

He doesn't give me much time to consider before he turns back to the guys, the whole host of them with their dicks still in their hands, hard and ready.

"Who wants to see me fist this little slut until she comes?"

Their cheers turn me on even more. My dripping pussy is clenching and thrumming, telling me I want it... even if my head has reservations.

Reservations are pointless, though. It'll be coming at some point soon enough. There's no denying it. I'm going to be a hardcorer. Fisting is just one more step on my journey, so why not let it be now, for an extra grand, with User 2155 displaying me wide and proud for the watchers?

"Are you up for it?" he asks me, and holds up his fist before my eyes.

I feel used enough already, holes gaping and dripping, head spinning from the whisky and the Christmas tunes and flashing lights. I find myself grinning and nodding.

"Yeah, I'm up for it. On one condition."

"And what's that?"

"I want to play with myself while you fist me. I want to come with your hand in my pussy."

He grins a filthy grin. "My fucking pleasure, deal accepted."

He lifts me up from the floor and drops me flat onto my back onto a desk, sweeping off a load of paperwork to the side of me. He guides my legs up to my chest, and tells me to keep them open wide.

I do as I'm told, sucking in breaths as he pushes four of his fingers straight in, wriggling them inside me as a tester.

"I can take it," I assure him, even though my thighs are trembling with nerves through the whisky.

"I know you can, you dirty bitch," he says, and lines his thumb up. "Play with your cunt and show us all how fucking filthy you are."

"I'll be the best you've ever had," I reply, smiling brightly for the gathering onlookers.

I must be a dripping, drooling state as I rub my clit, but they're all working their dicks, eating me up with their stares as User 2155 tries to work his fist inside me. His thumb is catching, my pussy fighting, and it hurts. It really fucking hurts. I tip my head back and curse, still fingering my clit against the pain.

"Want me to stop?" he asks, but I shake my head. I'm adoring pleasing the crowd too much to stop, even if I wanted to. So many dicks hard, all for me.

"No. Don't stop. Just do it. Get your thumb inside me and fuck me like a slut."

"Merry fucking Christmas," he says, and forces it. He forces it so fucking hard, I feel like I'm being torn open, burning up as cum slurps out around his fist. He has so much power it's beautiful, and so much restraint, it's insane. "Keep playing," he tells me, and I realise I've stopped using my fingers. "Relax your cunt and accept it. Before you know it I'll be up to the wrist."

Fuck, his words do something to me.

Up to the wrist.

He'll have his whole damn hand inside my pussy, while people watch.

I think of the reviews, of the threads, of the hardcorers. I think of Creamgirl and all the filth she must do for fun.

It works. I relax my cunt and accept it. Every single dirty inch of his big, strong hand.

The music has stopped and the room is silent bar my cries as User 2155 stretches my pussy open. The guys are working their dicks, but there is no whooping or cheering, just pure filthy fascination as my pussy gives up the fight and lets a whole chunky fist inside me.

User 2155 smiles like a dirty lord as he moves his fingers in my pussy. He's so deep, it's like he's in my stomach, and it hurts like hell, even though my clit is tingling like a bitch.

"I'm up to the wrist now," he tells me. "My whole fucking hand is inside you. Can you see that?"

I raise my head as best I can, groaning at how dirty it looks to have a wrist jutting out from your pussy.

"Time to play now, slowly," he says, and I rub my clit faster as he starts to work his hand in and out.

He's so steady. So sure. My grunts don't put him off in the slightest, my curses don't make him stop. He's done this before... he's definitely, definitely done this before.

And who was it with? Has he been with Creamgirl? Has she been pumped with his fist like this, while his office pals look on with their dicks in their hands?

I hope so...

I want to be just as talented as she is...

My pussy takes it like a good girl, just like I am. Cum – and whisky – really does make an excellent lube.

My fingers work like magic as my client fist fucks me, and I scream in pure, dirty bliss as he hooks his fingers against the spot.

Fuck, yes. FUCK. I can feel the peak beginning, the room spinning, breaths quickening. And so can he...

"Get up here if you want to shoot your load, guys," he tells his friends. "Cover this horny little bitch with a fresh round of jizz while she comes."

His invitation is welcome. I close my eyes as a group of them drag the desk away from the wall and out into the open, holding me steady on top. I'm circled by a crowd of men jerking their cocks, while the ringleader pumps his hand in my pussy. And I come for them. A dirty whore in a raining cascade of jizz, spurting all over me.

I grip User 2155's wrist with an OWWW as he tries to pull it free in the aftermath, but he tells me to relax. To trust him.

"Ok," I say, "Do it."

I'm whimpering as his thumb pulls free, but that's the hard part – the rest of his hand slips out like I've given birth once his knuckles are out.

Shit. I'm done for the night. I really am. Which happens to be pretty good timing...

"Time's up," he says, and points to the clock on the wall. "Well done, Holly. Good fucking show."

The memories of my strip performance are all but faded now. They feel like a lifetime ago. I'm a mess on unsteady legs as I thank them all for their time.

Praise be to Rudolph, who goes and grabs my clothes for me. Praise be as well to the mass of hands helping me get dressed as I teeter.

I use their office bathroom to clean the jizz away – wiping round after round of squelch from my pussy and ass until I'm at least vaguely sure I'm not going to seep jizz all over a cab seat. *Or bleed all over one.*

There's hardly any sign of blood, actually. Just a pale smear of red amongst the white streams.

The guys all have their dicks back in their pants for the final goodbye. They wave me off with a round of *thank yous*, but the thanks are all mine. Despite feeling like my sanity has upped and run, leaving me in the pits of madness, I've had a great time tonight. The more dicks the better. I'll be booking up a whole load more.

And maybe there will be a few more fists to come as well...

The security guy is still sitting at the reception desk when I reappear downstairs. He gives me a look up and down with a laugh.

"Need a cab? I guess the party's over."

"Yes, please."

"Dialling one now."

Thank fuck the cab seat is soft when I slip into the back seat, but not soft enough to avoid burning me sore every inch of the way. Luckily, I have a distraction.

The five-star review from 2155 is a glower. The words give me a solid, heartfelt grin as they show up on my phone screen.

One of the greatest nights of entertainment we've ever had. Eight of us, all milked dry and in gratitude. Every part of her gorgeous body is begging for cum... just like her mouth is. Expect the unexpected, since we had a surprise fisting negotiation at the height of the action, and she took it well – bringing herself off through the squealing.

Happy Christmas to us. Holly is a superstar, up there at the top of the charts. And we've had Creamgirl, so that's saying something.

Holy shit.

User 2155 mentioned Creamgirl, by name, and compared me to her. HE COMPARED ME TO HER. And he *still* thinks I'm worthy to top the charts.

Despite my throbbing pussy, I grin all the way back home like a crazy cow, humming jingle bells, so happy I could scream.

twenty-two

I wake up late in the afternoon with a groggy head and one hell of an ache down below. Hardly a surprise, really. There are only a few hours to go until the entertainer's party, and my nerves start up as I stare at the ceiling. No doubt, I'm going to be feeling it. Hopefully I won't be limping all night long.

Tonight won't be anything like a proposal. The party is at a posh hotel in Chelsea, courtesy of the agency, and it's a *formal* occasion – no matter how eccentric that *formal* might be. People are going to be making an effort and so will I.

The forum has been bustling with confirmations. There are going to be a load of us there, rocking it with Christmas celebrations. A fair few are based in London, an easy commute, while some entertainers are travelling down from up north, and a few are coming over from Birmingham. Although I've scoped out a load of their profiles during my searches, I won't know who most of these people are. There are just too many to keep track of. Unfortunately, most of the hardcorers won't be making it. I almost cried when Creamgirl posted that she was going to be busy tonight, but there will be plenty of other people there for me to meet and chat with. More than enough to keep me busy. Not least Ebony.

I'm so thankful she's offered to meet me outside the venue. It will be like a dream come true, finally getting to meet her in person.

She's going to be wearing a beautiful full-length gown in blue, stunning, with a dainty gold heart necklace, and delicate drop pearl earrings.

I've gone for a black velvet number, tight and fitted, with silver sparkles over the neckline. It's a heavy drape, and drops all the way down to the floor, contrasted with a split right up the thigh. Chic but festive. Certainly not one to be limping around in.

Ok, time to face the music. I need to move and get to the toilet.

I hold my stomach as I roll over and wrench myself up to my feet. Yowch. It's sore.

The shower last night hasn't made any difference to the fact that leftover cum has drenched my panties through. I wipe it all away with a *damnit.*

After some painkillers and a glass of water, I stay in the shower for an age to sooth my aching bones. This one should have me clean and fresh, ready to roll.

I blow dry and curl my hair, making sure the spirals frame my face just right. I use contouring, and line my lips before applying deep red lipstick. My super dramatic catflicks are accentuated with long, fake lashes, and my push up bra works wonders with my dress, showing off my cleavage without being too excessive.

I wear a silver bracelet, with onyx black stones, and long sparkling earrings. And then for the crown on top, literally – I've got a tiara, with gemstones that catch the light from every angle.

I slip on my high black heels and do a twirl in the mirror.

I can't believe this is really me now. A *me* with the ability to be exactly who I want to be. The clothes I want, and accessories that sum me up. But not just that. It's the heart *within* me. The soul within me. The life within me.

I can't wait for my parents to meet my new confident self. I can't wait to see their surprise at the woman their daughter has become. I'm desperate to see them. And, in the meantime, I'm desperate to see my new best friend, Ebony, too.

My heart is thumping like mad as the cab drives me to Chelsea. I catch sight of her before the cab pulls to a stop in the drop off area. She's standing in the hotel doorway, looking like a Christmas goddess in her gorgeous blue gown. Her eyes shoot straight over to the cab, with a tentative smile on her face, trying to check out whether it's really me inside as I pay the driver.

She lets out a huge squeal and comes running as soon as I'm out, slamming against me like I'm a long lost relative, and slinging her arms around my neck.

"ELLA!"

I get a lump in my throat, welling up at finally having my friend in my arms.

"Eb! Oh my God, it's really you."

She pulls away enough to look me in the eyes, and hers are filling up with tears, just like mine.

"Fuck." She lets out the laugh I know so well. "I'll be ruining my mascara already."

"Yeah, well at least you won't end up with eyeliner down your whole face. I'll look like I've been throat fucked for three hours solid if I don't watch it."

"Better get in there before that happens. At least get through the door first."

We walk through the magnificent chandelier-heavy reception, pressed close, side to side, and I rest my head on her shoulder in the elevator. She's the best friend I've ever had in my life.

"I'm scared shitless," I tell her as the elevator dings on the right floor.

"You've got nothing to be scared shitless of," she says. "You're a high performing stunner, who everyone is going to love. Just like I do."

Love.

What a beautiful word.

"I love you, too," I tell her, and she takes my hand again, giving me a reassuring squeeze as we step into the hall.

This place is crazy. Truly. There are as many chandeliers on this floor as there are in the foyer, with strings of lights and decorations between every single one of them. There's a sign on the double doors in front of us. *The Agency.*

"Here we are," Eb says and walks right on in as I teeter beside her.

Fuck, the tree by the dancefloor is the biggest I've ever seen, decked out in flashing lights and a zillion golden stars. I can barely even see the angel at the top, she's so far away. The tree is flanked by two metallic reindeer swathed in multi coloured flashing lights and this place is already busy, with little crowds of people dotted around the room, chatting against the backdrop of Christmas songs. A couple of girls come racing right over to Eb, hugging her so hard they lift her from her feet.

They are Chantel and Sarah. *Missy More* and *Daisy Chain.* Two of the girls from Birmingham. I love the lilt of their accents as they introduce themselves. And, oh my God, they know who I am! They know I'm Hollyella from the forum!

"Great to meet you," Chantel says, and the four of us are straight up to the bar – no cards or cash needed, since the agency are funding the whole thing. There's champagne on tap, and we take four glasses, holding up a toast with a *cheers.*

Cheers, indeed.

Cheers to fun, friendship, Christmas, filthy encounters, and all the opportunities the agency has given me. Damn, I'm welling up again at the realisation of just how lucky I am.

A guy joins us after our toast. A brooding, broad shouldered beauty in a tux. *Devon.*

"Hey, Holly. Sorry, *Ella,*" he says after saying hi to Eb, and I can't believe it. Jesus Christ, he knows me, too.

The small groups get bigger as more and more guests arrive. It's a sea of eclectic wonder, thrumming with a huge variety of styles and tastes, just like the industry we work in. There are princesses in dresses so big they are practically pantomime costumes, and hot guys in suits who look like they've come straight from a casino. So many faces and names as they introduce themselves. Some I recognise, some I don't. Some profiles I've seen before, some I've never caught sight of – but every single one of them is lovely. Warm, and fun, and full of festive spirit as the champagne flows.

It's beyond my comprehension to think I belong in this place, with so many incredible people. I scan the room in awe and disbelief, checking out the dancefloor where people are hitting the groove. I choke with laughter when I see someone in Rudolph antlers, and Ebony laughs along with me when I tell her about last night's proposal.

"He hung your bra on his fucking antlers?!"

But then my laughter stops dead in my throat, my eyes widening as I catch sight of the doors swinging open. Because, no. NO WAY.

A couple walk in together holding hands, raising them above their heads like superstars as the room lets out a cheer.

"Fuck!" Eb says. "I didn't think they were coming! I thought she was away at a proposal."

But no. She's here. Creamgirl is here with us... in a figure-hugging black velvet dress, her pillar box red hair in curls down her back, with a sparkling silver tiara displayed proudly on her head.

Eb elbows me in the side, laughing all over again.

"There you go, see? You're so fucking similar. She's even in a bloody tiara."

Creamgirl sure dresses exactly the way I love, but no. She's on another level to me. She has sparkles of silver above her cat flicks, and her tiara is bigger, bolder, and so is she. She's a plus size dream, the incredible curve of her ass tapering into her waist, only to explode again into one hell of a fucking cleavage. She's absolutely beautiful, and so is her boyfriend – which is hardly a surprise, given how stunning she is.

He's tall and muscular, in a jet-black suit, with a thin black tie over a crisp white shirt. His jaw is to die for, and his nose is strong and straight. He reeks of cheeky charisma, a huge grin on his face as he leans in to whisper something to her. She lets out a roar of a laugh, and it's clear she has a cracking sense of humour from the way she tips her head back and slaps his arm.

They are a couple to die for. His brows are shaped as well as hers, and his hair is messy, and punkish – the look I love – just not as unkempt as Connor's. He has a streak of deep, dark purple at the front, giving him an edge of indie, and the pair of them are so hot they burn their way straight into my eyeballs. I must be gawping like an idiot. I jump as Eb leans in to me.

"And there you have the hardcorers of the hardcorers. What utter beauties. I really didn't think they were coming."

"I didn't know Creamgirl has a hardcorer boyfriend," I say. "Fuck, what a couple they must be."

"Eh?" Ebony says. "Oh, no. No. Josh is a hardcorer, yeah, but he isn't her boyfriend. They're just friends. He used to be with an entertainer called Magpie, but they split back in the summer. In fairness, she did look quite a lot like Cream, but those two have known each other since they were kids. I think they dated for like three weeks when they were teenagers. Platonic ever since."

I'm still staring at them as they head through the gathering throng like celebrities.

"*Josh*," I repeat. "Which hardcorer is he?"

"Weston."

Oh my fucking God! I've checked out Weston's profile, but it doesn't show him like this. Not in such crystal clarity. I've mainly seen his massive, pierced cock, and filthy pictures of him using it – in gritty, shadowy images to make it look even dirtier. His intro video shows him working his hard-on, and saying how he'll use it for anything, but his full face isn't on it. I didn't see his hair... and he wasn't grinning with such a perfect smile...

"His reviews are off the scale," Eb says. "You won't see him on chat much, as he keeps himself to himself. He's bi, and his clients are mainly guys." She giggles. "Very happy guys, no doubt. And jeez, his cock. He's pierced, right the way up."

"Bi, with all the boxes ticked, yeah, I've seen that. Just like Cream, Harlot and Bodica." I pause, staring at him. "I've Weston's profile. I just didn't realise he was so..."

"Hot?" she finishes for me. "I'm surprised you haven't figured that out, since you're such a hardcore stalker. Literally." She nudges me. "You'd better get your tongue back in your mouth before you dribble all over the floor."

"Stop it." I laugh. "I'm not *that* bad."

"Whatever. You're crushing on him, and idolising her like a fangirl. I know you, Ells."

Yes. She does.

Cream and Weston step up to the bar, standing right beside us when they've finished with the first round of hellos. I'm transfixed as they take their glasses and raise their champagne to each other. You can see how close they are from the look in their eyes. I must be still gawping at them like a dickhead, because Cream catches my eye. I feel sick, like a crappy emulation of the queen herself, but she lets out a squeal and closes the distance, grabbing me straight into a hug.

"Hollyella! I was wondering if you'd be here!"

What the fuck–

I can't believe she's even heard of me, let alone wondered if I'd be here tonight. She steps back and gestures to our outfits, so similar it's almost embarrassing. My cheeks bloom, like I've been caught out trying to copy her, but her smile is so bright that it's plain she doesn't think that at all.

"Congratulations, Holly," she says. "What an impression you're making. I was up to my knees in cow shit the other night, and on the way back Mr Mask wouldn't shut the fuck up about you. I had to promise to swing from the bloody headrest next time he chases me, so thanks for that."

People clamour around as she compliments me.

"Well done," she says again, then tugs Josh – *Weston* – over. "This is Holly," she tells him. "The stunner who is going to have me bouncing from the headrest."

Josh looks me up and down with gorgeous bright green eyes, and my legs feel like they're going to buckle right under me. I feel like I did when I first saw Connor up close, butterflies on butterflies... but I'm twenty-four now, not a teenager. This shouldn't be happening, but it is. I can't stop the sensations. I feel lightheaded, a smile still bright on my face as I struggle to handle myself.

Morning after syndrome has nothing on this.

"Hey, Holly," he says and offers his hand for a handshake. "Tiff's been talking about you. Says you'll be in our hardcorer gang pretty soon at this rate."

Eb claps her hands.

"She will be! I've been saying that from the start. You know she took eight last night. EIGHT. One of them hung her bra off some Rudolph antlers."

Both Creamgirl – *Tiff* – and Josh laugh.

"Was that at, what's it called... CR Corporate?" Tiff asks, and I nod.

"Yeah."

She rolls her eyes. "Yeah. I did their party the year before last. He did the same to me. I bet they're the same fucking antlers." She laughs. "Only he hung my panties from the other side, and then danced in my goddamn stilettos like some kind of joker."

"I got off easy, then."

She raises her eyebrows with a dirty sparkle in her eyes, her natural kinkiness twinkling brighter than her tiara.

"Did you, though? I mean did you get off, for real? Taking eight is quite a tall order."

My cheeks are scorching as Eb, Tiff and Josh all wait for my answer. There are other people around, too. So many entertainers waiting on what I have to say, so fuck it. I take a breath and tell the truth.

"Yeah, I did get off. A lot. I took my first ever fist and got off on that, too. I can't believe it, honestly. It still hurts like a bitch but it was so crazy hot, it's unreal."

My idol, Creamgirl Tiff, gives me a high five.

She turns to Josh. "Ebony is right. We have us a hardcorer right here already." She pulls me in for another hug. "Welcome to the club."

It's most definitely a club I want to be a part of.

I feel almost honoured as Tiff and Josh take a table with me and Eb, and the butterflies are at an all-time high as he sits down opposite me. I try to play it down, breathing steady, and the surroundings make it easier. I'm full on engaged in chat with Tiff about hardcoring, having a million questions that she answers without so much as a flinch. Eb is fascinated too, chipping in with questions of her own. But Josh keeps looking at me. I can feel it. His eyes burn, even when I'm staring over at Tiff's sparkling eyes and awesome cleavage.

Surely not. A guy like Josh can't be interested in a girl like me...

The conversation flows, so natural it's like I've known them all my life, but the butterflies don't stop, and the flutters only get worse. Josh's grin drives me insane, and his laughter gives me tingles.

"I'll get us some more champagne," he says when we're done with our third round.

Tiff wastes no time. She gestures an elbow in his direction as he walks away to the bar.

"Do you fancy him?" she asks me across the table.

I suck in air. "Sorry, what?"

"Josh," she says. "Do you fancy him? It's pretty obvious he fancies you."

"I, um..." My cheeks are scorching now, probably glowing pink under my makeup.

"Of course she fancies him." Eb laughs. "Who wouldn't?"

"Me!" Tiff laughs back. "It would squick me out now. He's like my brother." She turns her attention right back to me. "So, do you fancy him?"

"Like Eb said, who wouldn't, besides you? He's absolutely gorgeous."

"And you're single, right?"

"Yeah, I'm single."

The tension is so palpable, I can hardly look at him as he returns with our champagnes, but Tiff has no restraint in the slightest. She pats Josh's knee as he sits down.

"Ella is single, and she thinks you're hot," she tells him, just like that. "So, there you go. Foot in the door. You're welcome."

He raises his eyebrows at her as he hands over her glass.

"And you're the fastest matchmaker in creation. At least give me five fucking seconds, will you?" He's laughing as he meets my eyes. "Sorry, Ella. I do have a spine of my own. I don't usually rely on Miss Big Mouth to set up my dates."

"You don't usually *have* dates, Josh. I haven't seen you slaver over anyone this bad since Magpie first walked into the Star Bar." Tiff takes her glass, kissing him on the cheek before she stands up. "And, yeah, I am Miss Big Mouth, it's part of the reason I get paid so well."

He sticks his tongue out at her, and I notice his piercing. Josh's tongue is pierced as well as his cock. Damn, that's hot. Could he even get any hotter? I doubt it...

"Fancy a dance, Eb?" Tiff asks.

Eb gives me a grin and a side-eye before she gets up.

"Sure, catch you guys in a bit."

Josh groans. "Sorry, Ella," he says as they leave us to it. "Honestly. Tiff's been going on and on about me meeting you. She's shown me your profile at least eight hundred times."

The scorch of my cheeks notches up a level.

"She has?"

"Yeah, constantly. Your reviews really are amazing, by the way. Well done."

I try to summon all my strength. I remember I'm Holly as well as Ella now. The entertainer. The girl so confident, she can walk into a room full of strangers and take everything they've got, without even a hint of a freakout.

"Did you like what you saw?" I ask him, with a smile. "Did you like my profile?"

He nearly chokes on his champagne. "How could I not?" His eyes lock onto mine. "You're absolutely stunning."

What a crazy fucking universe.

The gorgeous guy sitting opposite me has seen my slutty introduction video for potential clients. He's seen pictures of me spreading my pussy for the camera, of me sucking cock, of my bare tits crushed together as I play with my nipples... and he's saying I'm stunning, like it's no big deal. Like I'm a girl he's met right here, right now, at this *formal* ball in the middle of Chelsea.

He's heard about me taking a fist for the first time last night, and bouncing around on a headrest, bound in rope, and read reviews of me taking rough, hard cock in the ass... and it doesn't faze him in the slightest.

But then again, why would it? He's a hardcorer, too. I've seen his hard, pierced cock, just as he's seen my pussy.

My mind runs wild. I wonder what he's done and who he's done it with. What he likes, and what he doesn't like. What kind of filth he performs for fun. And I wonder what that tongue piercing will feel like when he sucks on my clit.

Holy, fuck. I want to find out.

"So, how about it?" he says with a smirk. "Would you be so kind as to consider a date with me sometime? Even if just to shut Tiff the hell up." He laughs. "No. I'm being deadly serious. Do you want to meet up? For a meal that is, not an eight-way fucking session, of course. Unless that's your bag every day of the week."

I'm nodding before he's finished speaking. Giggling like a damn schoolgirl.

"Yes, please. I'd love to meet up for a date with you. And I'm more than happy with one cock at once, in the main. Especially when it's attached to someone truly awesome. I think you might well fit the bill."

We swap numbers, and my hands are shaking so bad, he notices. He takes hold of my fingers, and squeezes them tight, his gorgeous eyes locking straight back onto mine.

"No need to be nervous. Hardcorers can play it a little bit gentle some of the time." His face lights up. "I'm a kisser, not a biter. At first, anyway."

My God, I'd die to kiss him right here and now. He takes my phone and keys in the rest of his number, saving it to my contacts.

Eb and Tiff must have been watching from afar this whole time. They jump up and down, whooping and cheering as they beckon us over.

"Shall we grant them the honour of success?" Josh asks. "Fancy a dance?"

He holds out his hand, and my fingers are steadier this time when I take it.

"I'd love a dance, just as long as my sore, bruised pussy can handle it."

He leans down to laugh into my ear. "We'll go for slow, don't worry. I've coped with the after effects of stretch play many, many times. I know the drill. Just wait until you take a fist in the ass. I was in bed for two days straight. My client took it right back in return, though. Tit for tat."

I stare up at him in shock. His dirty talk is so natural, it's insane. It suits him as well as his suit does.

The girls are so pleased when we join them on the dancefloor. We dance around to Christmas tunes as champagne flows, and Eb steals the Rudolph antlers from a guy by the tree. We twirl and spin, and Tiff does the best twerk I've ever seen. Christmas magic at its best.

"Go on! Give them the performance, Josh," Tiff says after a while, pointing to a crowd of girls checking him out. "Give everyone a freebie Christmas present. Just a teaser."

"Fuck off, Tiff." He laughs.

"I mean it! Give them the performance!"

She's looking at me as she says *them.* Her naughty grin says it all.

"Only if you give them yours."

"Tits for chest? Halfway only?"

"Deal," he says, and I stare on, amazed by their humour and confidence in equal measure.

A load of the crowd chants their names, Eb included.

Cream and Weston! Cream and Weston! Cream and Weston!

Jesus Christ, when these two get to it, it's plain to see... I've got a *long*, long way to go before I match Creamgirl at the top of the league. And my pussy doesn't give a fuck about the pain of fisting anymore when *Weston* strips his shirt and tie off. The heat has my clit on fire.

What a pair of fucking stars.

Screw the crowd, Josh's eyes are all on me.

He tugs the string of coloured lights from one of the metallic reindeer and wraps them around himself, lighting up his beautiful form up as he dances. My God, he's got some moves. Some seriously hot, topless fucking moves.

He's breathing heavily when he walks up to me with the same trail of Christmas lights in his hands. He snares me with them to pull me up close, and points out the garland of festive fun hanging over our heads... a hotel decoration so apt for the moment.

"How about starting our date right here and now, *Holly*? Fancy using the mistletoe to break the ice?" Josh says, and I wrap my arms around his neck with a grin, not giving a fuck who is watching us. Those days are long gone.

My lips are ready when he lands a kiss on my mouth. My tongue is craving his, like it's meant to be. The other entertainers are cheering for us as we grind together in tangled Christmas lights, all set to dance right through until the dawn.

I've completed eleven five-star proposals since becoming an entertainer. Eleven days of filthy festive fun that have given me the best Christmas of all time. But here, tonight – kissing Josh under the mistletoe, with my new friends dancing all around – is the icing on the Christmas cake. Another gorgeous gift from Santa, landing right in my lap.

The very best twelfth day of Christmas there could be.

twenty-three

It's almost 7 a.m. when I walk in through my bedroom door, still flying high after the cab ride. I haven't even shrugged off my coat when I feel a buzz from my pocket. I'm glad I've been dancing too much to get completely wrecked on champagne. I can still see my phone screen happily enough when I pull it from my pocket.

I get a storming mass of tingles when I see it's a message from Josh. I still can't believe I've made such an impression on him.

I flop down on my bed as I read it. Butterfly city in my stomach. They are swirling like a tornado.

Had a great time, Ells. Let me know when you're back from Australia, and I'll book a table for the date.

Funny, how one of the biggest hardcorers of the hardcorers is the most gentlemanly man I've ever met. No groping, no fucking in a toilet cubicle, no diving into a cab and heading to his or mine together. Just a kiss under the mistletoe. An amazing one at that.

Ok, that's a lie.

At least three... but still. Just kisses. Hardly throat fucking me with a Christmas lolly, or fisting my pussy under the tree.

I'm about to reply when I catch sight of the missed calls from Mum and Dad. Shit, what the hell? There are seven of them... seven, all in a row. I've just been partying too hard to notice. I feel beyond guilty as I click play on their latest voicemail. It's Mum on the line, and she sounds petrified.

Ella, will you call us, please? What the hell is going on? We're seriously worried now. We messaged Connor, and he said you've left him.

Left him? What a joke.

There is no getting around this anymore. My guise is over. No more *I'm fine, just busy* messages from me.

I grab my laptop and fire it up. I only take a few seconds to calm myself before I hit the call button, taking deep breaths with my finger hovering. I know this is going to be emotional. I'm quaking at the brilliance of breaking the news of my trip, I only wish they weren't going to be so upset about my split with Connor. Wanker. I wish he hadn't replied to them, the idiot. What a way to piss on my parade.

The butterflies swarm off and I get one hell of a lurch in my stomach as my parents appear onscreen in front of me, both of them looking horrifically nervous. No surprise there, though. Thanks, Connor, you absolute prick.

"Ella!" Mum says, with her hand on her chest. "What's been going on? Why haven't you been talking to us!?"

I don't have the chance to answer before Dad jumps in.

"Don't even think about brushing us off with the *work is busy* bullshit this time. No bullshit, please. NONE."

The tears are already prickling my eyes. I can't help but grin, as my eyes start flooding, and they look so confused. Dad's got his WTF expression on his face, eyebrows raised.

"I've been keeping a few secrets," I admit through my tears.

"No shit," Dad says, and folds his arms, clearly confused as hell.

"Ella, you could have called us at any time, ANY," Mum says. "We'd have been there for you! You only had to say."

I nod. "Yeah, I know that."

"So why didn't you tell us about Connor? Seriously, Ella. Why keep us in the dark like that? Why?"

"Because there is a bigger secret," I tell her. "One I've been trying to avoid on purpose. Seriously. It's been so hard. I knew you'd see through the crap I've been spewing eventually."

Mum and Dad look at each other before they address me again. They must think I've gone mad.

"A bigger secret than the break up?" Mum asks. "What? Have you met someone else or something? Is that why you've left him? Did you leave Connor for someone else?"

I laugh at that. "This has nothing to do with Connor, I swear.

And I didn't leave him actually, he went off with a stupid cow called Carly a while ago. He turned up with a crappy bunch of flowers the other day and expected me to take him back. *That's* what he means by *I left him*. He's full of shit. But it's ok now. I'm over it. Honestly. I couldn't give a toss about Connor. My big secret has nothing to do with him."

They try to digest it. I know it's got to be hard. They've known Connor as long as I have. They love him, like I did.

Or so I think...

"Thank fuck for that," Dad says, with a sigh. "He's been an arrogant fucking idiot since the day you met him. Good riddance to bad rubbish. Stupid asshole."

Mum's smiling. She's actually smiling. I can't believe it.

"I'll send this Carly a thank you card. She deserves it. Just so long as you're ok, sweetheart. Please tell us you're ok." She scopes out my twinkling tiara, and the sparkles on the neckline of my dress. And at the party worthy makeup still on my face, and the wave of curls still in my hair. "You look ok, actually. You look great." She pauses. "Ella, what's been happening over there? You look... different."

"Thanks," I say, and then I can't hold it back anymore. I blink and the tears coming flowing now. Hard. The weeks and weeks of avoiding my parents finally burst the dam and storm free. But they aren't sad tears, I'm grinning at them both the whole way through, trying to find the words.

"What?" Dad asks. "Ella, what is it? Talk to us."

I'm choking on the joy when I answer him. I'm blubbing so hard I'm not sure I'll be understandable.

"I'm flying over to see you, in three days' time. I'm spending Christmas with you. I'm coming to Australia! I've been trying to keep it a surprise, but I can't anymore. I mean it. I'm coming to Australia!"

"You're coming to–" Mum's words trail off as she clasps her hands over her face. "You're flying over? To us? Are you serious?"

"Yes! In three days. I'm getting the flight from Gatwick on Tuesday. I was going to tell you tomorrow, I promise. I wanted to keep it as close to Christmas as I could. To make it a surprise."

They stare at me in silence, open mouthed as I blub away. I wipe the tears from my eyes as I giggle. The relief flows through me like liquid gold.

I figured they'd be ecstatic, but I didn't think my mum would start crying along with me. She starts blubbing as hard as I am, and Dad wraps his arm around her shoulder. He's never been very emotional, all stiff upper lip and all that, but this time his stiff upper lip falls short. His bottom lip shakes, and then *he* breaks, all three of us buckling with emotion as the truth finally comes out.

"We've missed you so much," Mum says. "We were trying to save up to come to you. Dad's got a part-time job, so we could get the money together."

I shake my head. "You don't need to. I'm coming to you. And I've got a great job now, I can come whenever I want. Dad doesn't need to work to save up." I know I'm rambling, but I can't stop. "Dad can quit his job right now. I'll be able to fly you over, and after Christmas I'm going to get a bigger place, my own place. A place with a guestroom."

"But how?" she asks. "What job have you got?"

Oh boy. I hope this description works...

"I work in PR, in the entertainment industry. I get assigned clients and work through proposals with them. It's great. Fantastic money."

"You're in PR? In London?"

"Yeah. I got referred to an agency, through a friend of mine, and they took me on. I got the job! And I'm doing well. I'm one of their top performers already, after just a few weeks."

"I just can't believe this," she says, still wiping her tears away. "I've been waking up in the night, I've been missing you so much. We've even talked about moving back home, just to be with you again. We've been so worried."

"Moving back here and giving up your life in the sun?" I shake my head, so proud of myself. "You don't need to now. I promise. I'll be able to visit you loads. So much you'll probably be sick of me."

They both laugh at that.

"No chance," Dad says. "You can be a little pain in the ass all you like, we won't get sick of you. You can stay here for ever if you like."

But I can't do that... I can't stay in Australia for ever. I realise that from the flood of pure energy that swallows me up. I have a life here now. I life of my own. Plans of my own. Dreams of my own. And none of them involve the dickhead with garage flowers and half-assed apologies. It's all for me.

"You're flying on Tuesday?" Mum asks, and I send her over the flight details.

"Don't worry. I've got a cab booked straight over to yours."

"No need for that," Dad says. "We'll be waiting at arrivals, don't you worry. *Dad's cab* will always be ready for you, Ells."

I'm so overwhelmed that I touch the screen. I'll be so happy to see them that a fresh pang sets the tears off again.

"I love you both so much." My voice is practically a sob.

"And we love you, too," Dad says, Mum too choked up to speak.

Fuck the fact it's gone seven in the morning. We talk about Christmas plans, and what we'll have for dinner, and how they're going to show me the sights, and take me to the beach with them. I'm crying happy through all of it, the joy churning me up. And then Mum says the inevitable words... *tell us about your new job in PR...*

Um, well. I'll need to think on that one. That's a job description that will take some working out...

"PR, for clients," I repeat. "It'll be another surprise for you. I'll tell you all about it when I get there."

"Alright," she replies. "We'll let you off one more secret, just this time."

"Well done, Ella," Dad says. "We're really proud of you."

"Thanks. So am I," I say, and I mean it. I am. I'm very, very proud of myself indeed.

There are another round of tears as we say goodbye, and I'm still sobbing my happy little heart out at the *call ended* screen when I notice a notification flag up in the agency app window.

Hmm, I should get to bed... but I'll just take a look. Just to see.

User 5639. Male. 47.

Help me, please. I've got a Christmas party with people at work today, and nobody to take with me. I've got nobody here, in London. No friends, no family, no anything, and I can't face turning up there alone.

I've got practically no money, and I'm sorry about that. I really am.

I just need some help if you can give it to me. Just a little bit of time to help me out. Nothing more than a few hours at a party. Call it charity. Please.

Proposal price – £30.

Duration – 3 hours.

I have to read it through three times over.

It hits me in the guts, his pain in just a few words – almost pure desperation. I've felt like that myself, all alone here in London. No friends, no family, no anything, having to force myself out to face the people at work every day. Let alone at a social. I also know how it feels to have no money. I know that sense of doom very, very well.

But it's this afternoon. I'll be exhausted.

Crazily, the green icon is next to Eb's chat profile.

Are you there? I type.

Yeah. Ryan's up already, rushing around the place, excited. He thinks he saw Rudolph outside the window last night.

I've seen plenty of pictures of her kids. Ryan's her five-year-old. He must be going crazy over Santa Claus. Cute little guy.

I've got a proposal in, I tell her. *For later on this afternoon.*

This afternoon? Are you crazy? You haven't even been to bed yet. I hope it's worth mega bucks.

I can only imagine the surprise on her face when I send it over to her.

£30???? she says. *The agency have seriously goofed up there. He must be a new user. They check them out thoroughly, though. They never take on anyone who's skint. I can't believe it. You should get right onto them.*

I look at the threads. Yeah, 5639 is a new user. There is no mention of him anywhere in the forum.

He sounds desperate, I say.

Yeah, but £30?? That's less than minimum wage for 3 hours. After the agency take their fees you'll barely even cover your cab fare.

I must be quiet for too long.

You're thinking about it, aren't you? she types. *You're seriously considering a party this afternoon for £30? Come on, Ells. Click no, and get some sleep.*

But I can't. The situation feels too close to home. Too real. I can picture having nothing but a few bank notes in my purse, worried about getting to work and back and hating the idea of seeming so broke in front of my colleagues. If I turned up for this guy, I could buy some drinks for him and his colleagues as well. At least make him feel comfortable. He must be so alone to reach out like this.

The sympathy churns inside me. It's not sympathy though, is it? It's empathy. I've been in this guy's shoes. Sure, I've never reached out to anyone via an agency website, but I met Eb in a dirty chatroom, and she was there when I needed her. She changed my life. Surely I can do it. Just to help someone.

Fuck it. I click on accept. The party is at 5 p.m. – time enough to get a bit of sleep and get over there, to *Central Parade shopping centre* in the middle of the city. Maybe he even has a job like I had, in a store at the shopping centre.

You've done it, haven't you?? Eb asks. *Ells, you're mad. You could take on another last-minute client for another few k in your bank account, AT LEAST.*

I'm going, I say. *It's only a few hours, and it's hardly 14 hours of Daddy play, is it?*

Just as well, since he can't afford it.

She's been in this game so long now that the thousands must rack up to seem like usual wages. But I'm not there yet. Not even close.

Fine, she says. *Let me know how you get on later. If he tries anything on say NO.*

Will do. Love you.

Yeah. Love you, too. Even if you're being suckered in by a twat.

I laugh at her tongue out emoji.

I've been suckered in by a twat since I was a teenager, on the arm of a wannabe rockstar. At least this will be a guy who appreciates it.

twenty-four

User 5639. Male. 47.
Help me, please. I've got a Christmas party with people at work today, and nobody to take with me. I've got nobody here, in London. No friends, no family, no anything, and I can't face turning up there alone.
I've got practically no money, and I'm sorry about that. I really am.
I just need some help if you can give it to me. Just a little bit of time to help me out. Nothing more than a few hours at a party. Call it charity. Please.
Proposal price – £30.
Duration – 3 hours.

I almost wish I'd said no when the bleep of the alarm starts ringing out. My eyes will barely open, I'm so bloody tired, but I drag myself out of bed and into the shower, putting as much effort into User 5639 as any other proposal, the payout irrelevant.

I wear a posh black satin number which comes just shy of my knees, and a dainty little garnet pendant around my neck – the same colour as my lipstick. I re-curl my hair, and choose some mid heel shoes to make a good *work party* impression. Yeah, that should do it. One final twirl in the mirror, and I'm off.

I get a cab to Central Parade shopping centre, and whoa, the street outside is heaving with shoppers, bustling like mad. But amidst the Christmas chaos, almost everyone ignores the people sitting in the entrance, begging for cash in sleeping bags. I watch as the security guards start to move them on, and I wish I could get involved. It breaks my heart to see. But I have a charity engagement of my own to get to, and the clock is ticking fast. I'll help these people on the way out, I promise myself. I'll withdraw more cash if I use all mine at the proposal event.

Arrived, I click when I'm in through the main entrance.

Santa's grotto, the reply comes. *Wait there. Don't worry. I'll recognise you.*

Santa's grotto... I look for the signs, and there is one up ahead. A snowman with a twig arm as a pointer. Cute. I look at him with a smile, with his carrot nose and his coal eyes. I used to love snowmen when I was a kid. I'm looking at his bright blue buttons when I see the placard underneath. A charity logo. The grotto is a charity event, offering free presents in exchange for donations, all given to homeless families. I get a prickle of tears, thinking back to the helpless people outside, and try to banish the pain in my stomach. I have to get myself together. I have a date to attend to, and Holly needs to be at her best.

I'm glad when I see an ATM between a few shops. I take out a decent wedge of cash for a Santa's grotto donation of my own, as well as some money for the people outside. It's the least I can do.

Santa's little home has a cute path leading up to it with artificial grass and snow. I have to let out a laugh as I see a big plastic Rudolph standing proudly outside, wrapped up in twinkling Christmas lights. I beam as I think of Josh snaring me in a similar set last night and kissing me under the mistletoe. I can't wait to see him again when I get back from Australia. He's a dream come true.

But for now, it's time for User 5639...

I look around the place, trying to find him. Santa's little house is just closing – the last few kids coming out and racing up to their parents, proudly showing off their new reindeer toys. I hand my donation to the woman dressed as an elf as she's closing the fake gates, and she starts as she sees how much I'm giving her.

"There's two hundred here! Are you sure?" she asks, and I nod, most definitely sure. I wish I'd have taken out a whole lot more when I see how her eyes light up. "Thank you. This kind of generosity makes so much difference to so many families."

"I'm just glad I can help."

She squeezes my arm. "So will the families that receive it be, I promise you that."

Now for my next charity event of the day. I scan around the place as she carries on working, but there is no sign of anyone looking for me. I do a loop of the grotto and catch sight of Santa getting ready to leave, setting up his fake cabin room ready for a new round of activity tomorrow.

How amazing, and how generous. He really is a *ho ho ho* figure. His costume is awesome.

But, where the hell is User 5639?

I look up at the escalator, and back at the main shopping corridor, but nobody comes up to introduce themselves. I'm getting concerned I've got the venue wrong, all set to call up the app when a voice sounds out.

"Holly. Lovely to see you!"

I do a one-eighty, and no way. I have to blink. I stand open mouthed as the guy before me offers me a red and white gloved hand.

User 5639 is Santa. For real. He's the guy in the grotto. I look him up and down, and his outfit is mega convincing. The white fur around his red coat looks so realistic, and his huge black belt is classic. Not to mention his beard. It covers half his face and trails all the way down to his chest.

He points to the toilet sign opposite.

"Give me a few minutes, will you, please? I'd better take my beard off, at least."

I can barely see his face, but his eyes are rich, warm and dark, and his voice is deep and friendly. He's sure in the mode of Santa Claus.

"Sure," I say. "I'll be waiting right here."

"Great, thank you."

I don't say anything to the woman still closing up the grotto, of course, but I do ask her if I can help as she switches the lights off on Rudolph. I help her re-align the blankets in Santa's cabin, wondering what the hell is going on here.

I'm going out on a work date with Santa...

Except when Santa comes back, he's definitely not Santa. He puts his outfit under the chair, out of sight, along with the pillows he must have stuffed under his jacket. His dark eyes are owned by a guy in a suit, clean shaven with dark grey side-parted hair, and he looks like he owns the whole damn shopping centre, rather than dressing up as Santa in it.

"Please to meet you, Holly. I can't thank you enough for coming."

"You're welcome," I say, and shake his extended hand again, no gloves this time.

"Come along with me, please. There is a very good restaurant upstairs."

"Is that where your work party is?" I ask him, and he looks down at me with a smile as we reach the escalator.

"Something like that." He stands at my side as we ascend. "Do you know how many people I reached out to this morning?"

"No, I have no idea."

His eyes are so bold on mine. "One hundred and fifty-seven."

"One hundred and fifty-seven entertainers? Really?"

"Yes. And you're the only one who accepted my proposal. Some people sent vulgar messages in response, in fact, and said they would report me to the agency."

I don't know what to say, so just stumble over an apology.

"I, um... I'm sorry about that. People are... busy sometimes."

"No need to be sorry," he says. "And people are *selfish* sometimes, not just busy. I was very keen to see who would accept such a last-minute cry for help."

I look up at him. "I knew what you'd be going through. I've been there myself. Broke, with nobody to help. It's a horrible feeling."

"Humility and empathy are both beautiful qualities, Holly. Please don't lose them, no matter how much you earn from your job role."

"I won't. Don't worry."

He smiles as we step off the escalator on the next floor. "I saw you gave my little helper a very generous donation."

"Not generous enough. I just didn't have any more cash from the ATM. I need to grab another round, actually. There were people outside who need help."

"Yes, there are. I told the security guards explicitly to leave them alone, but something must have gone wrong down the chain. They won't be shoving people in need out of the way again."

This is crazy. My eyes fix on his. My stupid observation must have been right – call it intuition, I guess.

"Yes, I own the shopping centre," he says, clocking my expression. "The work party here is always my work party, so to speak. I own the restaurant I'm taking you to."

I'm trying to make sense of things.

"So you don't need help?"

"No, I don't. But plenty of people do. Plenty of people are crying out for people with good souls, willing to help at short notice, no matter what the circumstances."

I stay quiet, still unsure what the hell is going on as he directs me through to the restaurant *Firenzo* – it looks very grand. He directs me to a table, and I take a seat on one of the Chesterfield style stools, still mute as he hands me a menu.

"Time to be upfront. I'm going to do something for you, Holly," he says, then laughs. "Call me kind of eccentric, but I like to channel my charity through many different outlets. Some outlets are like Santa's grotto, some direct charity donations, some more time based. And some of my charity situations are completely off the wall. Which is why I sent so many of you a proposal this morning."

"Ok," I say. "And I responded. But I didn't expect this, genuinely. I really thought you were a guy who needed my help."

"Exactly, which is why I trust you'll stay humble, and think carefully about what you do with the outcome."

"The outcome?"

"I saw you are a new member of the agency."

"Quite new, yes."

"So, you're still a fledgling. You said you know how it feels to need help."

"Yeah, I do. Very much so. I was in a horrible situation when I came to London. Working long hours, with barely enough to live on. At least I had a room in a house, though. No matter how crappy it is. A lot of people in need don't have that luxury."

The waiter comes over, and User 5639 gestures me to order a drink. I go for an orange juice with a *thank you.* He chooses mineral water.

He leans towards me across the table.

"I'd like you to do me another favour," he says, once the waiter is out of earshot. "I'll be giving the agency plenty of money in fees over the coming months, but I'd rather you didn't lose the twenty percent on this particular one."

"On thirty pounds?" I say, and wave it aside. "Don't worry, I don't need payment for this at all, we can put it down as cancelled."

"No, no. The agency are welcome to the fee on the thirty pounds. *That's* not the money I'm talking about."

I'm so confused now, it's crazy.

"I'm not just giving you thirty pounds," he answers. "I'm giving you thirty thousand."

I drop my menu in shock.

"Sorry, what?!"

"Thirty thousand pounds," he says casually. "That's the reward I'll be giving you for your generosity today. Please, choose to do with it as you will, but take it with my warm thanks."

"But I don't–"

"Need it?" he says, and smiles. "No, I'm sure you don't. I'm sure the clients are flooding in, but from me to you, please, call it a thank you. For your help." He gives me back my menu from the tabletop. "But as I requested, please don't tell the agency of this. They will be having plenty in fees from me. We all have our personal tastes and hobbies, don't we? I do allow myself some little privileges."

"Ok," I tell him, in a bluster. "Um, I don't know quite what to say."

"It must be a lot to process, maybe focus on the menu for the time being."

How can I focus on the menu? I look him right in the eyes.

"You're giving me thirty thousand pounds? Just for turning up here today?"

"Straight in your bank account, if you'll let me."

"But I don't deserve that. I only came to help."

"And that says a lot."

"Not enough for thirty grand!"

He looks over at the waiting staff, and I curse myself. I need to keep my volume down.

"Plenty enough for thirty grand," he says. "But please, do keep this between us. This has nothing to do with the agency. I'm a newbie myself. I only joined last week."

I stumble through giving him my bank details once we've ordered dinner, but my stomach is churning so bad, I feel sick. He's going to give me thirty grand, just like that. And I don't know what to do. I don't know what to say, but he helps with that. He asks about me and my life, and my journey here, and how I made the transition to being an entertainer. He tells me about himself, and his own journey through life in London, and how he was in the same situation as I'd been, many years ago, struggling until he found his route into commercial retail.

User 5639 is quite something. He's one hell of a man.

We finish up our meal at the allotted time, once we've finished talking. I've been with him three hours and I've barely even noticed the hours flash by.

He stands up and kisses my cheek as we say our farewell.

"Please do keep being yourself, Holly," he says. "Who knows? Maybe we will meet again under different circumstances."

I stumble away, with a stream of thank yous – checking my account on the escalator down, and sure enough, my balance has changed. Thirty grand extra, right there.

I just can't...

I go to the nearest ATM, and withdraw everything I can, hundreds after hundreds after hundreds in different transactions until I reach my *take out* limit, and then I race outside, up and down the street, handing out wedges of cash to the people who need it. I see a woman collecting for charity across the road, and I stuff a load of notes in her collection tin, and I look for more people struggling, handing money out to everyone I can. Women, men, people standing in crappy coats, some on the floor wrapped up in sleeping bags, it doesn't matter – I give some to everyone, and it hits me in the heart to see the joy on people's faces. I hand out the cash until it's all gone. And I'll do it again. I know I will. I'll keep being generous, keep being kind, keep doing my best to help other people, just like User 5639 does. Maybe it'll be me helping him in the grotto next year. It would be an honour to be his little helper.

When I'm done with giving out the cash, I stand with my back to the wall beside a general store with tears in my eyes and such in joy my heart that I've never felt before.

When I look up, I see that the store offers cashback on purchases, and I'm grinning like crazy, realising that I'm not done just yet. So, in I go. I load up on purchases. Sandwiches, chocolates, pastries, anything that will fit in my shopping basket.

Then fuck it, I walk down more streets, dishing out sandwiches, chocolates, pastries and cash to the people who need help.

Thank you, *Santa*, and thank heaven for my good fortune.

Merry Christmas, everyone!

epilogue

"Fancy another sausage, sweetheart?"

I hold back a laugh as I look over at Dad, standing proudly at the barbeque. I'm messaging Josh about sausages right now. Not the kind you have with onions and ketchup in a roll, though...

"Yes, please, Dad. I'd love one."

The summer sun beats down as I lie happily on the lounger with Mum beside me, thinking how weird it is to be having barbecued sausages for Christmas lunch. And how weird to be basking in the sun in my bikini, with surfers out on the water. So much better than the chilly London streets.

"Come on, then. Who is he, this new guy?" Mum asks, and I turn my head to her.

"What do you mean?"

She nods towards my phone. "You can't fool me, Ells. You're grinning like you did over Connor whenever he used to show up at the door."

God, that was years ago.

Mum is smiling at me. Happy. Just like I am. We haven't shut up for days, none of us – but so far, Josh has been kept under the radar. Still, it was only time.

I take a deep breath and soak in some more of the sunshine. It's bliss being here with my parents, in their gorgeous home, overlooking the sea. I sobbed like a baby, wrapped tight their arms when I charged over to them in the arrivals lounge. I didn't stop crying all the way back to theirs.

"He works at the same agency as I do," I tell Mum. "His name is Josh."

"Josh, right." Her eyes are probing, I can tell, even through her sunglasses. "And he's a good guy, is he? Not a sack of shit who'll ditch you for a groupie?"

I shrug. "Too early to say, but the signs are good."

"Can't wait to meet him. Maybe you'll be bringing him next time." She gestures over to Dad, who's making lunch as he whistles. "He'll get grilled hotter than that barbie by your father, you know. He'll give you the verdict, thumbs up or down. He gave Connor the thumbs down from the moment he first showed up. But you wouldn't have listened."

"I'll take more notice this time. I'm a bit older and wiser now."

"Maybe," she says, leaning over to pull me in for a kiss. "But you'll always be our little girl."

I feel like it. A little girl back at home, even though *home* is now on the other side of the world. Nothing will ever change that. But home is truly where the heart is, and my heart is with my parents, here on Christmas Day.

As if reading my mind, Mum takes hold of the necklace I bought her. *World's best mummy* it says, with a cute little bear on the front. Eb said it was cringe, but I knew Mum would love it. Same as the cushion I bought them, with the picture of the three of us dressed up in Santa robes. It has pride of place on their sofa.

Dad is proudly wearing the high tech watch I bought him, too. It was lovely to see his face when he opened it.

"Maybe I'll ask Josh if he wants to come along for a trip," I say.

"We might see him in a few months, then."

"A few months might be a bit premature." I laugh. "Don't you think?"

She gives me the side eye.

"We'll see."

My next flights here are already booked for May. Another three weeks in the sun with Mum and Dad. Who knows? Maybe Josh will be at my side, too. Our messages have been getting more and more spicy, and intense, and deep, to the core. He's a guy who wears his heart on his sleeve, as well as bares his ass for his clients, so Tiff tells me. She sings his praises all day long, saying she's already got ideas for bridesmaid dresses for her and Eb. Both of them are rooting for us.

Dad brings over our next round of Christmas hotdogs and takes his place on the lounger next to Mum. He looks at her with utter adoration, like he always has, but it's more obvious to me now than when I was younger. Not just the love, but the respect. It's hard to see it in other people, when you're not getting it for yourself.

But I am now. I respect myself enough to hold the bar high, and Josh is doing the high jump right from the off. He's already booked the restaurant for our first official date. One of the very finest in Kensington. I suspect he'll turn up with something a little more tasteful than garage flowers.

"Ells has met someone," Mum tells Dad, and he sits upright so he can see my expression, chomping down some hotdog before he speaks.

"Is he half decent, or some other punkish prick who thinks he's a legend?"

Ouch. Dad hasn't gone easy on Connor since I told them the full story about Carly.

"How about a punkish legend?" I laugh. "A hybrid? Will that do?"

Dad rolls his eyes, but Mum taps his leg playfully.

"Don't get judgy until you meet him, Ted!"

"I'll get judgy as soon as he steps off the plane. If he's as much of a jackass as Connor, he can turn straight back round again. I'll kick his butt right through departures."

"That's enough, Ted," Mum says.

"No, it isn't. Not where our daughter is concerned. Connor's a bloody snake, and a fool. I'll not have Ella walked all over. End bloody of!"

The heartrate monitor on his new watch bleeps at the increase and Mum tells him to calm down. I laugh out loud. I love how protective he is of me. I type out a message to Josh between mouthfuls of hotdog.

My parents are asking when they'll get to meet you. I've been busted messaging.

I see the typing icon.

Well, ditto. Mine have been asking me since I helped chop the veg this morning.

You told them about me??

I grin my head off at the thought.

Sure did. They said they'll welcome you with open arms, as long as you aren't a bitch like Amy.

Amy – Magpie.

Turns out she treated Josh pretty bad. We're in the same boat on that score.

That's another ditto, then, I type. *Dad says he'll send you straight back to the departure lounge if you're anything like Connor.*

I'm still grinning to myself as I wait for his reply.

Maybe I should take the purple out of my hair, forget about my piercings, and wear a suit on the plane. He sends a laughing emoji.

Don't even think about it!

"He's from the same agency as Ella," Mum tells Dad. "Josh."

"Josh... right. And what does he do at the agency?"

"Same job as me," I say. "PR."

"Good."

"Yeah," I say. "It is."

One day it would be very, very *good* to work directly with him... I'd love to see *Weston* in full-on action mode.

It's been so hard navigating the work questions from my parents – Mum especially. I've told her I meet clients to discuss their requirements for corporate socials, and I can blag it all I like, but she knows something more's going on. Maybe one day I'll tell her the truth, but for now it'll be hotdogs by the pool and hugs at bedtime.

She might not be all that happy I'm an *entertainer* if she knew what it entails, but she'd definitely be happy with how I've handled the opportunity I got from Santa. I've got just a few thousand left after his Christmas gift – the rest I've donated to charity. Something I've only shared with Eb, on a strictly 'secrets for ever' basis. She couldn't believe it when I told her. She said she felt like Scrooge for dismissing the desperate proposal so easily, but we all live and learn. Every day is a chance to learn something, and I'm learning a lot right now. It seems every single day has a new lesson for me. Some more philosophical than others...

Dad says again how he's doing to teach me a bomb dive in the pool this afternoon. No excuses. We're going in, just as soon as we're done with our hotdogs!

"Fine. I'll do a bomb dive, no problem," I say.

I think he means a cannonball… but they never allowed them at our local pool. It'll be a new experience for me.

I take my place at the poolside next to him when it's time, and wave over at Mum, who has her phone in her hand, camera at the ready. But before we take the jump, I put an arm around Dad's waist and lean my head against his shoulder.

"Thanks," I say to him, and he chuckles.

"For what? Hotdogs and bomb dives?"

"Nah," I reply. "For being you, and helping Mum be Mum. Oh, and for *Dad's cab* at the airport. This is the best Christmas ever."

"The first of a load more to come now you're a PR pro," he says, and squeezes me tight. "Now, let's get on with the bloody bomb dive. We've got Christmas pudding coming up."

He launches himself from the poolside like he's trying out for the Olympics, his arms wrapped tight around his knees as he plunges. Yeah, it's a cannonball. My dad's doing a cannonball.

"COME ON, ELLA!!!" he yells, but I can't jump in straight after him. I'm laughing way too hard, and so is Mum at the other side of the pool. My dad's a champion, an absolute superstar, just like Mum is.

I can't wait for Josh to get to meet them…

THE END

The Naughty List Tropes – Jade's other novels

If you enjoyed some of Holly's proposals, and fancy reading more in their style, I have a whole catalogue for you to choose from.

Here are the books of mine you might want to check out.

Are you ready?

Anal – Most of them. Probably all, actually!

DP – Dirty Bad Strangers, Sugar Daddies, Dirty Daddies, Strangers in my Bed.

DVP – Sugar Daddies.

MMF / MFM – Sugar Daddies, Dirty Daddies, One Too Many, Buy Me, Sir.

MFF – Dirty Bad Wrong, Dirty Bad Secrets.

Mfmmmmmmm – Dirty Bad Strangers, Strangers in my Bed, Bang Gang.

Daddy – Call Me Daddy, Dirty Daddies.

Spanking – A lot of them. Especially the Dirty Bad Series.

Degradation – A lot of them. Strangers in my Bed is hardcore on that. I'd suggest Poison, too.

Praise – A lot of them. Dirty Bad Series. The Man Upstairs. Most of mine contain a fair amount!

BDSM (hardcore) – Dirty Bad Series.

CNC – Bait!

Stretch play – Dirty Bad Wrong, Dirty Bad Secrets, Sugar Daddies, Strangers in my Bed, The Man Upstairs.

Goddess worship – Dirty Bad Secrets.

Foot fetish – Actually, you know. I'm stumped on this one. Possibly none! Horror.

Period play – Dirty Bad Savage.

Roleplay – Call Me Daddy.

Age gap – The Man Upstairs. Teach Me Dirty. Hello Stranger. Dirty Daddies. Daddy's Dirty Boss. Buy Me, Sir. Strangers in my Bed.

Acknowledgments

As always, John Hudspith, my editor who has been with me from the start. Thank you. You are a wizard, and a superstar, and a master at keeping my words on track. Don't know where I'd be without you!

Leticia Hasser, what a cover! Need I say more? Thank you so much, as always.

Timmy – for your organisation and help in my career, as well as outside of it. You are Mr A, always. I love you for it.

Keyanna, Gel and Sam – thank you all for your work in promo, PA duties, graphics, and PB formatting. You are all fab.

To my author friends, and reader friends, thank you. I appreciate every single one of you.

To my friends – Isabella, Lisa, Lauren, Sue, Sara, Hanni, Maria, Dave and TT.

To my family – Mum, Dad and little Siddy. Nan, Mish and Emily, Marie-Boo-Boo, Brad and Stevie. And of course, Tim and the girls.

Also, to Little Jonny Wilson – the lovely tribute chameleon.

About Jade West

I'm as filthy as my books suggest, and the characters become my world.

I am a fantasist, living in the English countryside, with a great family and some amazing friends around me – mainly already mentioned in the acknowledgements.

I have a chameleon named after my late partner, Jon, who passed away in 2018.

He'd have been very impressed by the tribute.

I'm also epileptic, which has been quite a journey – still ongoing. Learning to live with disability when you're used to being independent is... hard. My support network is incredible.

So, what else... I haven't grown out of being a goth since I was seventeen. Black velvet is my friend. So is glitter. Strawberry and cream flavour Huel, long hair extensions, and Carl Jung.

Oh, and books. Writing them, reading them, losing myself in imaginary realities. I'm always right there.

I'm best known for my novels Sugar Daddies, Bait, Call Me Daddy, and the Dirty Bad series.

Join Jade on Social Media

www.facebook.com/jadewestauthor
www.facebook.com/groups/dirtyreaders
www.instagram.com/jadewestauthor
Tiktok - @jadewestauthor
Sign up to my newsletter at www.jadewestauthor.co.uk/newsletter.html
www.jadewestauthor.co.uk

Made in the USA
Las Vegas, NV
28 December 2024